Southbourne Library
Seabourne Road
Southbourne BH5
Tel: 01202 428784
KT-144-684
BOURNEMOUTH
410092806

Published by Harvill Secker 2014

10 9 8 7 6 5 4 3 2 1

Copyright © Tim Parks 2014

Tim Parks has asserted his right under the Copyright, Designs and Patents Act 1988 to be identified as the author of this work

This book is sold subject to the condition that it shall not, by way of trade or otherwise, be lent, resold, hired out, or otherwise circulated without the publisher's prior consent in any form of binding or cover other than that in which it is published and without a similar condition including this condition being imposed on the subsequent purchaser

First published in Great Britain in 2014 by
HARVILL SECKER
Random House
20 Vauxhall Bridge Road
London SW1V 2SA

www.randomhouse.co.uk

Addresses for companies within The Random House Group Limited can be found at: www.randomhouse.co.uk/offices.htm

The Random House Group Limited Reg. No. 954009

A CIP catalogue record for this book is available from the British Library

ISBN 9781846557170 (hardback)
ISBN 9781846557187 (trade paperback)

The Random House Group Limited supports the Forest Stewardship Council® (FSC®), the leading international forest-certification organisation. Our books carrying the FSC label are printed on FSC®-certified paper. FSC is the only forest-certification scheme supported by the leading environmental organisations, including Greenpeace. Our paper procurement policy can be found at www.randomhouse.co.uk/environment

Typeset in 11/14pt Iowan Old Style BT by
Palimpsest Book Production Ltd, Falkirk, Stirlingshire

Printed and bound in Great Britain by Clays Ltd, St Ives plc

Tim Parks

PAINTING DEATH

Harvill *Secker*
LONDON

PAINTING DEATH

ALSO BY TIM PARKS

Fiction

Tongues of Flame
Loving Roger
Home Thoughts
Family Planning
Goodness
Cara Massimina
Mimi's Ghost
Shear
Europa
Destiny
Judge Savage
Rapids
Cleaver
Dreams of Rivers and Seas
Sex is Forbidden (first published as The Server)

Non-fiction

Italian Neighbours
An Italian Education
Adultery & Other Diversions
Translating Style
Hell and Back
A Season with Verona
The Fighter
Teach Us to Sit Still
Italian Ways

For the Veronese,
who put up with this Englishman for thirty years

PART ONE

CHAPTER ONE

MORRIS WOULD ARRIVE LATE for the ceremony. That was appropriate for someone of his importance. It was in his honour after all. But not so late as to be disrespectful; if one disrespects those doing the honouring, one diminishes the recognition. He watched in the mirror as steady hands pushed a Tonbridge School tie tight into the still-firm skin of his strong neck. He would look smart, without being obsequious; neither formal, nor casual. These were fine lines to tread and that he could do so with ease was one of the rewards of maturity. Ease: that was the word. Morris would appear at ease with the world, at ease with himself, his scarred face, his thinning hair; at ease with his wealth, his wife, his fine family, fabulous palazzo and now, at long last, this distinction conceded *in extremis*. All's well that ends well. You're a happy man, Morris Duckworth, he told himself out loud, and he smiled a winning smile. No, a *winner's* smile; not a single niggle that nagged, not a prick of the old resentment. Thank you, Mimi, he mouthed to the mirror, admiring the brightness in blue British eyes. Thank you so much!

'*Cinque minuti*,' sang a voice from below. It might have been the dear dead girl herself!

'*Con calma!*' Morris called cheerfully. After all, they lived only a stone's throw from the centre of civic power. If he had one regret, it was that this was only Verona, *la misera provincia*; Piazza Bra, not Piazza di Spagna. But then think how dirty Rome was.

How chaotic. And how grey, grim and gauche Milan. This prim little town is your destiny, Morris. Be happy.

As he left the bathroom, the flick of a Ferragamo cuff revealed a Rolex telling him it was indeed time. *Le massime autorità* would be waiting.

The maximum authorities! For Morris!

'Papà!' came the voice again. His daughter's wonderful huskiness, so like dear Mimi of old. She was impatient. All the same, Morris couldn't resist and stepped into The Art Room for a moment of intimacy with his most recent acquisition.

The heavy old frame rested on a chair. Morris hadn't quite decided where to hang it yet. He ran a finger down its mouldings. How austere they were! The gilt had gone gloomily dark, from candle smoke, no doubt. It was a pleasure to think of sombre old interiors made somehow darker by their flickering candles. But in the painting itself the two women were walking down a bright street. It was the Holy Land, millennia ago: two bulky figures, seen from behind, in voluminous dresses. Between them, trapped by hand against hip, the woman on the right held a broad basket. It was partially covered, but the white cloth had slipped a little to reveal, to the viewer, unbeknown to the two ladies as they sauntered away, not a loaf of bread, not a heap of washing, not a pile of freshly picked grapes but, grimacing and astonished, a bearded male face: General Holofernes! His Assyrian head severed.

'Papà, for Christ's sake!'

Now there came a deeper voice, 'Morrees! You mustn't keep the mayor waiting.'

Morris frowned, why did he feel so drawn to this painting? Two women carrying a severed head. But the scene was so calm and their gait so relaxed it might as well have been the morning's shopping.

'Dad!'

In her impatience, Massimina switched to English. Morris turned abruptly on a patent-leather heel and strode to the broad staircase. As he skipped down stone steps, running a freshly washed hand along the polished curve of the marble banister, his two women presented themselves in all their finery: Antonella magnificently matronly in something softly maroon; Massimina willowy in off-white, and both generously bosomed in the best Trevisan tradition. Morris smiled first into one face, then the other, pecking powdered cheeks and catching himself mirrored in the bright windows of four hazel eyes. Only his son had inherited the grey Duckworth blue.

'Where's Mauro?' Morris asked, pulling back from his wife. Her gold crucifixes still galled, but he had learned not to criticise. He was not a control freak.

Antonella was already making for the door where the ancient Maddalena stooped with her mistress's mink at the ready. Antonella pushed her arms into sumptuous sleeves. 'The cardinal will be there,' she was saying, 'and Don Lorenzo. We're late.'

'But where's Mauro? We can't go without Mauro.'

Morris couldn't understand why his wife wasn't taking the problem more seriously. Or why the decrepit maid wasn't wearing a starched white apron over her black dress, as specifically instructed. This was an occasion for family pride.

'I don't think Mousie came home last night,' Massimina said.

'Don't *think*?' Morris stopped on the threshold. 'Home from where? Haven't you phoned him?' He was not happy with the thought that a son of his could be nicknamed Mousie.

'I'm sure he'll meet us there,' Antonella said complacently. She was standing in the courtyard now where threads of water splashed across the stony buttocks of a young Mercury apparently leaping into flight from a broad bowl of frothy travertine. All around, vines climbed the ochre stucco between green-shuttered windows while just below the roof a sundial took advantage of the crisp winter weather to alert anyone still capable of reading such things that Morris was now seriously late for the ceremony that would grant him honorary citizenship and the keys to the city of Verona.

'He went to the game.'

'What?'

'Brescia away. I called him, but his phone is off.'

'He knows when the ceremony is, *caro*.' Antonella hurried back and took her husband's arm. 'We were chatting about it yesterday.' Her manner, if only Morris had had the leisure to contemplate it, was a charming mix of anxiety and indulgence. She treated her husband as a troublesome boy, which rather let their obstreperous son off the hook. 'I'm sure we'll find him there before us. But we mustn't keep the mayor waiting. In the end, the only person who really counts today is you, Morrees.'

This was such a pleasant thought that Morris allowed himself to be pulled along, outside the great arched gate and into the designer-dressed bustle of Via Oberdan. All the same, he hadn't begged his boy two days' truancy from one of old England's most expensive schools, and paid a BA flight to boot, to have the lout abscond at this moment of his father's glory. For some reason the word 'coronation' came to mind: Morris was to be crowned King of Verona. He frowned to chase the thought away; one mustn't lose one's head.

'By the way, who won?' Antonella asked. Morris's wife had a magnanimous air; it was the mink's first outing this season.

Massimina took her father's arm on the other side. 'Alas, Brescia,' she sighed. 'Own goal in injury time.'

Comfortable between them, though it was disconcerting that his daughter was so tall, Morris marvelled that his lady-folk should be aware of such trivial things. What was injury time in the end? He had never really understood. Dad had not wanted company when he set off to Loftus Road and anyway his son would not have been seen dead with a man wearing a green and white bobble cap.

'But if he didn't come home,' he protested, 'where did he spend the night? And why wasn't I told?'

There was no time to hear an answer, for on emerging from Via Oberdan into the wide open space of one of Italy's largest squares, it was to discover that Piazza Bra was not, right now, wide open at all. They had chosen this of all mornings to erect the stalls for the *mercatino di Santa Lucia*. Damn. From the majestic Roman arena, right along the broad Liston, past Victor Emmanuel on bronze horseback and as far as the Austrian clock, palely illuminated above the arch of Porta Nuova, the whole cobbled *campo* was chock-a-block with gypsies, *extra-comunitari* and assorted exempla of Veneto pond life scrambling together prefabricated stalls for the overpriced sale of *torroni*, candy floss and other vulgar, sugar-based venoms. It was a dentist's Promised Land, which fleetingly reminded Morris that this was another area in which his son was proving an expensive investment.

Through clouds of diesel from trucks unloading trifles and baubles of every bastard variety, not to mention the construction of a merry-go-round, Palazzo Barbieri on the far side of the square, solemn seat of the Veronese *comune*, suddenly seemed impossibly distant. Morris almost panicked. What if they called the event off? What if they mistook his belated arrival for a deliberate snub? One could hardly blame the traffic, living only 300 yards away. Morris began to hurry, at first dragging his women with him, then freeing his arms to dive between a wall of *panettoni* and their leering vendor, the kind of squat, swarthy figure one associates with black markets the world over. It was a disgrace! He would say something to the mayor.

'Da-ad!' his daughter protested. 'Why do you always have to be in such a rush?' Only now did Morris realise the girl had put on four-inch heels, to cross a sea of cobbles. The original Massimina, who had been half her height, would have known better. And he had thought his first love dumb!

Antonella laughed. 'This way, Mr Nonchalant,' she said and pulled her husband to the left, out of the throng and down the small street that ran behind the arena. Here, almost immediately, the way was clear and though the change of route had added a hundred yards or so to their walk, Morris understood at once there would be no problem. Thank God he had married such a practical soul! So much more sensible than her dear departed sisters. Nevertheless, he kept up a brisk pace, past beggars and chestnut vendors, just in case something else should come between him and his overdue due. The complacency of ten minutes before now seemed a fool's paradise and Morris knew from bitter experience that there was nothing to be gained from seeking to retrieve it. It took carefree weeks and important art acquisitions to consolidate a mood as positive as that; or at least an afternoon's revelling with Samira. For a moment, then, passing on one side a café advertising hot chocolate with whipped cream and on the other the arena ticket office promising the world's largest display of Nativity scenes – from the Philippines to the Faroe Islands! – Morris found himself struggling to relate two apparently remote but peremptory thoughts: first the memory of how he had ignominiously scuttled through these same streets thirty years ago, a wretched language teacher hurrying head down from one private lesson to another, always at the tight-fisted beck and call of people richer and stupider than himself (dear Massimina among them, it had to be said); and second, the reflection that his son was hardly likely to have taken his Tonbridge School uniform to a winter evening football game; so that even if the boy did make it to this morning's ceremony after a night slumming with thugs in foggy suburbs, he was not going to be sporting a burgundy and black striped tie that matched his own. Only now, still striding along in the shadow of the Roman amphitheatre with Antonella panting to keep pace in her furs, did Morris realise how much he had been looking forward to that little touch of father–son complicity; it was the kind of quietly significant detail he liked to think a fashion-conscious Veronese public would register with a twinge of envy: style the Italians might have in abundance, but never the sober solidity of a great British educational institution. In which case, come to think of it, the ungrateful boy might just as well not turn up for the ceremony at all. Perhaps I should pull him out of Tonbridge, Morris wondered, save myself thirty grand a year, and have the boy eke out a living teaching English, as I once had to. There! Realising that the two apparently separate thoughts had after all found a very evident and purposeful link – his spoiled son needed reminding what was what – Morris suddenly felt pleased again: whatever happened this particular morning, or any other morning for that matter, he would always have his wits, his wit. Hadn't he, in the end, Morris Duckworth, got himself to Cambridge University from Shepherd's Bush Comprehensive, the first and very likely the last pupil ever to do so? Let Mauro 'Mother's Boy' Duckworth do the same!

'I asked, have you prepared a speech?' Antonella was saying. 'Morrees! *Eih, pronto?* Aren't you listening?'

They had arrived at the bottom of the grand steps. The columned facade was above them.

'Of course,' Morris said, realising as he spoke that he had left the thing at home: three sheets of A4 on the windowsill beside the loo. He had allowed himself to be distracted by Judith and Holofernes.

His wife reached up to straighten the lapels of his jacket. Very quietly, she said: 'Just be careful not to say anything stupid.'

Morris was taken aback.

'Like the time at the Rotary.'

The English husband felt a dangerous heat flood his loins. 'It will be fine,' he said abruptly.

'Only trying to help,' she explained, brushing something off his shoulder. But he knew she was laughing.

'I was drunk,' he insisted.

'I know,' she smiled.

'The punch was too strong. They should have been gaoled for poisoning.'

'We're late, Morrees,' she said calmly. 'Come on.'

Right. But now where was his daughter? Son or no son, at least the three of them could ascend the town hall steps together. Morris turned but couldn't find her. The ridiculous Verona *trenino* was passing, a fake electric steam locomotive, bright red, with an open carriage behind and piped Christmas music deafening the dumb tourists on board. 'Hark the Herald'. How anybody could have imagined introducing such an atrocious eye-and-ear sore into the centuries-long sobriety of the city's ancient piazzas was beyond Morris. Had anyone ever sung 'Hark the Herald' in Italy? 'Late in time behold Him come!' Indeed. Just as Morris fought off a fleeting memory of his carol-singing mother (he himself had solo-ed 'Once in Royal David's' at St Bartholomew's, Acton) the train lurched forward with the clanging of a bell and Massimina emerged from behind, swaying impressively as she stepped out to cross the road, closely watched, Morris noticed, by three motorcycle louts smoking outside the wine bar at the corner. The girl was too attractive by half, too present and alive for her own good. Those heels would have to come down an inch or three. Confident nevertheless that his daughter was still a virgin, otherwise he would surely have known, Morris held out his hand as if to draw his child toward him. They would cut a fine figure entering the corridors of power side by side. Except that now an ancient gypsy woman reached up from the pavement – *Grazie, grazie* she wheedled – she must have imagined the wealthy man's outstretched arm held an offering of change. Irritated, Morris was about to shoo the crone away when he caught his wife's quick intake of breath. They were in full view of a dozen dignitaries and newspaper photographers standing under the portico at the top of the steps. Morris reached into his pocket and found the fifty-cent coin one had to keep ready for such occasions, because to open your wallet was always a mistake.

For the next fifteen minutes, it would have been hard to imagine a more gratifying occasion. On the door they were greeted by the faithful Don Lorenzo, for many years the family's spiritual adviser, who took them into the first reception room to meet Cardinal Rusconi, gorgeous in stiff scarlet. Morris kissed a puffy hand and agreed that, for all the commercial exploitation, Christmas never quite lost its magic, while Antonella spoke of the importance of sponsoring Nativity scenes in the poorer suburbs where the camels and shepherds created a much needed sense of festive spirit. Glasses of bubbly in hand, nobody seemed to have noticed how late they had arrived and Morris couldn't decide whether this was wonderful or irritating. He might just as well have been on time, which certainly came more naturally, in which case he could have enjoyed feeling superior to the latecomers. A radio journalist wanted him to explain yet again the circumstances that had led to this honour, but under the prelate's approving if somewhat haughty gaze, and nodding to a fellow Rotarian across the room, Morris demurely told the sycophant that it would hardly be appropriate for him to sing his own praises: the mayor, he said, would no doubt put forward the *motivazione* during his presentation. Massimina, he noticed from the corner of an ever observant eye, was chatting to Beppe Bagutta, son of the man who ran the Verona Trade Fair and quite a few other things beside; decent results at art college were all very well, but a little more would be required if the girl was to make her Duckworth mark on the world. Nearer at hand, there was a pleasant buzz of mutual congratulation with the ascetic Don Lorenzo telling the corpulent cardinal how much he had appreciated his article 'A Eucharist for Our Times' – he and Antonella had studied it together, he said – and the cardinal actually deigning to ask Morris how he thought Italy might come out of the present financial crisis; a subtle way of fishing for some kind of donation perhaps. Why else would such a powerful man have bothered to turn up for a ceremony of no religious significance? Old acquaintances and business partners, gallery owners and building contractors waved their hellos but Morris decided he would be best served standing beside the ecclesiastical red, so similar, it suddenly crossed his mind now, to the Father Christmas outfit Dad had donned to hand out half-bottles of Teacher's to shop-floor friends on Christmas Eve. Was Samira here, perhaps? That was an exciting thought. He hadn't invited her, but you never knew. The girl was clearly infatuated. Or even inspectors Marangoni and Fendsteig, from the old days? That too would be oddly exciting. But the meddling policemen must have retired long ago, Morris reflected. Just as well, with all this DNA wizardry they'd recently come up with. He smiled at the cardinal who smiled back as though they had been friends for ages, and Morris was just rummaging through the clutter of his mind to see if there was some favour he could ask of the prelate before the prelate asked whatever it was he planned to ask of him, when, at the blast of a trumpet, four extravagantly befeathered Bersaglieri raised four ceremonial flags to form an arch of honour at the door to his right: there were Europe's circle of quarrelling stars, Italy's bureaucratic tricolour, the razzmatazz of the dear old Union Jack and finally, white on red, the ladder of Cangrande della Scala, erstwhile Duke of Verona. Morris bowed his head as he stepped beneath these proud symbols into the great Sala degli Arazzi and that world of honoured tradition he had always, after his rather particular Duckworth fashion, aspired to.

So it was mildly irritating, having reached the inner sanctum, to find that the mayor hadn't bothered with a tie. 'I'm afraid we'll have to get moving,' the younger man said, hurrying between elegant chairs to give Morris his hand and then immediately withdraw it. He wore a white shirt, open at the neck, black blazer and denim jeans, so that if it weren't for the red and green mayoral sash across his chest it would have been hard to imagine why he was in such solemn surroundings at all. A delegation of Arab businessmen was expected for eleven o'clock, he explained. One couldn't be late for the Arabs. 'Our new masters, alas!'

Morris had always despised the Northern League and chided himself for having expected anything better of Verona's local hero, first separatist mayor of this exquisitely Italian town.

'We were waiting for my son,' Morris said frostily. 'I'm afraid his flight's been delayed.'

They took seats behind a polished table while a crowd of seventy or so settled in rows beneath Paolo Farinati's huge *Victory of the Veronese over Barbarossa* covering half the wall to the left, a great oil-brushed tumble of bodies, blood and heraldry with some fine fabrics and polished armour tossed in for good measure among neighing horses and silken banners. Oh to have a palazzo big enough to house such splendour, Morris thought. A whole war in your front room! But with undue haste the mayor was already jumping to his feet and plucking one of the microphones from its stand.

'*Buon giorno a tutti!*' he began, even before people had had time to take their seats. 'We are here as you know to honour a man who has been among us for many years, indeed who arrived in this town *the very season our beloved Hellas Verona won the Scudetto*. You brought good luck, Meester Dackvert!' the mayor smiled down on his guest. 'We are extremely grateful.'

This shameless crowd-pleaser of an opening, which immediately raised a shout of applause – even Antonella and Massimina clapped enthusiastically – wasn't actually true, since Morris had arrived in Verona in 1983, not '85. But the Northern League people, he remembered, were invariably Hellas fans, theatrically rough and tough, the town's would-be bad boys. Mauro surely wasn't messing with the league, Morris hoped. Even the Communists dressed better.

'Not, alas, a success we are likely to see repeated in the near future,' the mayor added with pantomime gloom, 'or not if last night's abject performance is anything to go by.'

The public sighed.

'Though the disturbances after Brescia's late goal, if I may say so in parenthesis, and I know because I was there, were certainly *not* initiated by Hellas fans.'

'*Verissimo!*' a voice called from the back.

What on earth, Morris wondered, did all this have to do with honouring Cittadino Duckworth?

'Actually,' the young mayor laughed, 'for a while the terraces looked rather like our old painting here.' He gestured to the raised swords, rearing horses and trampled corpses in Farinati's *Victory*. 'Though I personally was unarmed of course.'

Another laugh. This was infuriating. But Morris had learned over the years to keep calm, if not exactly cool, especially when in full public view. Sitting tight, his body steaming with angry heat, he consoled himself with the reflection that he was very likely the only one in this room who had ever had the courage to raise a weapon in anger and kill a man, or woman for that matter (on the very weekend Verona had won the championship if he was not mistaken), hence the only one here who could really understand the heat, horror and wild elation experienced in Farinati's magnificent painting. What was a scuffle at a vulgar football match compared to real killing? His knowledge went deeper than theirs, Morris told himself, inches of steel deeper, though come to think of it he'd never used a knife. Reaching to pour himself a glass of water, Morris noticed his wife in the front row trying to catch his eye and shaking her head slightly. Was he doing something wrong? He hadn't opened his mouth yet. And who was the man on her right who looked so oddly familiar?

'Aside from that magnificent achievement,' the mayor paused – he had a thrusting jaw and close-set, merry eyes in pasty skin – 'Verona having been, as I shall never tire of repeating, *the last provincial team ever to be CHAMPIONS OF ITALY*' – again he waited for the obedient applause to die down – 'aside, as I said, from that alas unrepeatable *exploit*' – he pronounced the word *à la française* and turned to grin complacently at his guest – 'Meester Dackvert's first years in Verona were not entirely happy, peripherally involved as he so sadly was in the murderous tragedies that beset two of the town's finest old families, the Trevisans of Quinzano, and the Posenatos of San Felice.'

Again there was applause, but subdued this time, as many present would remember the violent deaths of three prominent citizens, unaware of course that these were precisely the occasions when Morris had been obliged to learn the lethal skills celebrated by Paolo Farinati on the magnificent canvas beside them. Sipping his glass of water, the Englishman began to wonder whether it had really been wise to accept this invitation and, glancing towards Antonella, saw that she had lowered her face, perhaps to shed a tear over her dead sisters, or even, however misguidedly, her first husband, while the man sitting to her right patted her shoulder with surprising familiarity. Suddenly Morris found himself alert. It couldn't be Stan Albertini, could it? Stan had left Verona decades back.

'There was also, as friends of the family will recall, an unfortunate incident with a German shepherd, which, er, rearranged, as they say, our English guest's rosy-cheeked physiognomy, obliging him to rely henceforth on brain rather than beauty!'

How inexcusably clumsy and insensitive these remarks were! But since Morris's old scars had at that very moment begun to sing and burn in cheeks and temples, the English guest (*guest*, after thirty years!) was grateful for any supposed embarrassment that offered cover. If there was one person who possessed the facts to bury him, if only it ever occurred to the halfwit to string them all together, it was Stan.

'But the English are a resilient race,' the mayor continued, 'as we Italians know to our cost.' Speaking without notes, he raised and lowered the microphone, swinging his shoulders from side to side with the panache of a stand-up comedian. Clearly his audience loved him, for they never failed to titter. 'In short there are many reasons for our decision to honour Meester Dackvert today.' Again he looked indulgently down on his guest as if the fifty-five-year-old multiple murderer had just been born in a stable under a sparkling comet. 'Having married the beautiful Antonella Trevisan, surely an indication of the best possible taste' – the tasteless remark raised a storm of cheers; if there was one quality Antonella did not have, Morris thought, and had never remotely claimed to have, it was beauty; unless of course you considered a sort of exemplary piety beautiful – 'Meester Dackvert single-handedly turned the family's traditional old wine company into one of the dominant economic forces in our town, offering employment to scores of Veronese and even larger numbers of African and Slav immigrants, who, it has to be said, without the precious resource of paid work, might well have become a danger to our community.'

The mayor paused, apparently unaware of anything offensive in this reflection. This time there was no applause. 'He very astutely developed the older vineyards to build a fine new luxury housing estate on the hills above Parona – Villaggio Casa Mia – offering a chance to many of our youngsters to buy their first properties. And, together with his splendid and most Veronese wife, he has been over many years a generous sponsor of the university, the arts and the Church, always ready to help out when some worthy project runs into rough financial waters.'

Again the mayor paused, again there was no response from the crowd. But now the man seemed to relish the silence, as if it was exactly what he intended. He hadn't mentioned, Morris noted, that Fratelli Trevisan SRL also made regular contributions to all political parties that polled more than five per cent in local elections, not to mention a wide range of minor and indeed major officials in the customs and tax offices. Only now, however, did it occur to Morris that what he really should have sponsored was Hellas Verona Football Club.

'But the immediate reason for our decision to extend this honour to Meester Dackvert' – suddenly the mayor's voice slowed to something pondered and solemn, as if all the preamble about championships, murder mysteries and Morris's astonishing entrepreneurial skills were the merest patter to settle the public's mood – 'is his generous and completely unsolicited response to the vicious media attack that has been launched on our town and on this administration in particular.'

There was much muttering and scraping of chairs. Nothing, as Morris well understood, was taken more seriously in Verona than the town's national and international reputation. Far more important than any concrete reality, was the business of what people thought of you.

'As you know the attempt to paint our fair city as a den of

backwardness and brutal authoritarianism has been going on since the time of the Second War and the Republic of Salò. Entirely unfounded, it forms part of a squalid game of political conditioning by which our envious rivals – and I need not tell you who they are – seek to cut us off from what very little funding is available for urban development in these hard times.'

The murmurs of assent now began again.

'But if this propaganda war was bad before, it has become even more aggressive since the Northern League took over the governance of the town and brought some order to the chaos and cronyism that had been going on for far too long. It is clear that even our supposed political allies in Rome, not to mention the hopeless band of ex-Communists who occupied and abused these same public offices not so long ago, have been running a smear campaign that now extends beyond the national to the international press, culminating in the libellous article that appeared in a British newspaper a few months ago. I shall not repeat the gross accusations that were made there. They shall never sully my lips.'

At this point there was such a roar of applause that the mayor, who was checking his watch with embarrassing frequency, had to raise his arms to quieten the crowd and hurry on. 'What I intend to do instead, as sole and sufficient motivation for our conferring on Morrees Dackvert THE FREEDOM OF OUR CITY' – and here the mayor picked up from the tabletop, and quickly put down again, a parchment scroll and open, navy blue gift box containing a large silver key – 'is to read out the letter that our excellent friend wrote in reply to those accusations in the same newspaper. And I shall read it, *amici miei,*' he raised his solid jaw and grinned, 'in Eengleesh, yes, to remind our envious neighbours – their names shall never be mentioned – of the level that education has reached in this proud province.'

Morris was startled. The man was going to read his letter to the *Telegraph*. In English! When he couldn't even pronounce

Duckworth properly! Morris wanted to grab the mike from his hand and read the thing himself, if read it had to be, though at this point he began to wonder whether the double-barrelled snob who had carried out his hack's hatchet job on the ancient town – the offensive article that Morris had responded to – didn't perhaps have a point after all. For at last it dawned on him that this whole ceremony had been organised, not to reward Morris Duckworth for being a fine citizen at all, but as the merest PR for the Northern League. The separatists had a British intellectual on their side!

'Unlaiykk,' the mayor waved a scrap of newsprint, 'yor mendaayshuuus correespondent who publeeshed VERONA: CAAPEETAL OF KIIITSCH . . .'

It had all begun some months ago at Samira's place. She and Morris had made love in the usual lavish fashion on the mattress under the ochre tapestry, then, while she was preparing one of her excellent herb teas – and there was still frankincense smoking in the corner – her brother had come out of his room and started talking about wanting to do a Masters in economics in London. Tarik was a very respectful young man and showed none of the disapproval one might have feared from a jealous brother raised in a backward Moslem community, though that might have been, of course, because Morris was paying the siblings' not insignificant rent. But what was to be gained from being cynical? There was nothing bunga-bunga-ish about what went on between Morris and Samira, it was genuine affection, and of course now that he had found the girl a six-month work-experience in the local council's Heritage Department she would be more than worth the price of her two-bedroom flat in San Zeno. If nothing else she had access to the files of all paintings possessed by churches in the province.

Always ready to help, and save a friend a costly mistake, Morris had pulled his MacBook Air from his Armani attaché case and sat down at the glass table with the two young Libyans each side of him. They had browsed a few university sites, compared curriculums and requirements, and considered whether it would be wiser to apply now, before Tarik had finished at Verona, or wait till he had the Italian degree in the bag, at the expense of having to take a gap year. 'I could find something for you to do,' Morris had smiled, 'if it's a question of filling the time. I can always use a smart young man.' It seemed important to have Tarik understand that Morris's affection for Samira extended, overflowed rather, to her nearest and dearest. Tarik frowned, asking his sister's benefactor to explain again – his Italian was excellent but his English still shaky – the mysterious workings of UCAS, and as Morris clicked back and forth, enjoying his expertise these days with all things bureaucratic, he suddenly became intensely aware of their three pairs of legs side by side under the stylish glass tabletop: Samira's, to his left, wonderfully young and vulnerable as she distractedly opened and closed honey thighs in a black bathrobe; his own solid and steady in sober grey flannel, and, to his right, in tattered jeans, casually crossed at the bare brown ankles, this fine young Arab's. 'I love them both.' Morris suddenly found himself saying these words inside his head. 'I love sister and brother both!' and he felt a surge of energy and excitement such as he had not experienced these twenty years and more.

Then, intending to show Tarik where to read the economic news in the English press, Morris opened the *Telegraph*'s home page, and there it was. 'Verona: Capital of Kitsch', by Boris Anderton-Dodds. Who the hell was he? So extraordinary did it seem to open an English national newspaper and find an article on the small Italian town they lived in, that the threesome read it at once. Nicolas Sarkozy was planning to take his pregnant Carla on holiday to the town of Romeo and Juliet. It was typical of the French president's abysmal taste. Over recent years the once elegant Veneto town had seen no better way to solve its self-inflicted economic problems than to become Italy's dumb Disneyland of romantic slush and sleaze. Tourists were met at airport and railway station by pesky guides pressuring them into Love Tours of Romeo's house and Juliet's balcony where cohorts of Korean businessmen had themselves photographed with hands cupping the bare breast of a bronze nymphet before being hauled off to karaoke evenings where they learned 'O sole mio' and 'Santa Lucia', hardly Veronese tunes. The Renaissance palazzo housing Juliet's tomb – though of course no one knew whether it had really been Juliet's tomb, as no one knew whether it had really been Juliet's balcony – had become an upmarket registrar's office luring sentimental suckers from five continents to empty their wallets for overpriced ceremonies and third-rate costume jewellery. It was the globalisation of vulgarity; everywhere you looked the city was choked with cheesy cliché, the hotels advertising 'consummation' suites (and sheets!) for honeymooning couples and the mayor himself offering his services as registrar at a special price to milk the cash cow to the last drop. This was the same xenophobic Northern League mayor who pursued a racist policy against kebab outlets, denied Moslems a place to build a mosque and introduced fascist regulations that prevented people from sleeping on park benches or eating sandwiches on the steps of public monuments, and all in a town where the church pretended to be charitable but in fact kept hundreds of apartments empty (without paying any property tax) rather than rent them to poor Africans. Every year, towards Valentine's Day, lovers all over the world were invited to write a Letter to Juliet, alias the town council, with a prize for those who managed the best homage to love. A prize judged by whom? Boris Anderton-Dodds demanded. What did the city's administrators know about love? If they had any respect at all for the myth of romantic love they would return the town to its ancient dignity and remember that the quality most alien to romance was greed, the quality most akin, charity. A modern *Romeo and Juliet* would not be about the Montagues and

Capulets, let alone the Sarkozys and Brunis; it would be the thwarted love between the son of a Northern League official and the chadored daughter of a dusky kebab vendor.

What pious nonsense! Morris was aghast that a reputable British newspaper, one, he would never forget, that had turned down at least three job applications from a certain Morris Arthur Duckworth thirty and more years ago, should stoop to such disgraceful misrepresentation. 'But Verona is a fantastic town!' he shouted; the thought that his UKIP father might very easily end up reading this nonsense and enjoy a chuckle at Morris's expense was immensely irritating. Then he noticed that his young friends were smiling.

'What's there to smirk about?' he demanded.

'It's true the city's racist,' Samira said.

'You bet,' Tarik agreed.

'What's that got to do with it? Just because a place is racist you can't say it's the capital of kitsch. Verona must be one of the most beautiful cities on earth. The English haven't got anything to hold a candle to it.'

'I wouldn't know,' Tarik said. 'I just think the racist accusation is the one that matters. Who cares if we call it kitsch or not?'

'*I* care!' Morris fumed. 'Everywhere's racist. You think Milan isn't racist? And Rome? You think London isn't racist? Why are they rioting? Blacks are always rioting in London. They have their good reasons. Calling a place racist is like calling a spade a spade, or telling me grass is green. But calling it *tasteless* when it's one of the most beautiful places on earth is sheer envy. It's vandalism! Imagine the number of people who'd lose their jobs if the Brits stopped coming to Verona because of a criminal article like this. Think of the museums they'd have to close. The restaurants and hotels giving work to people without papers or permits. Albanians and Pakistanis and Moroccans.'

'Come on Mo, darling,' Samira laughed and leaned a head on

his shoulder. 'Don't take it so seriously.' Morris caught the wink she sent to her brother under his nose. Literally.

'How are you two discriminated against?' he demanded. 'Tell me. Is there any problem finding a kebab? No. I'd eat them myself if I wasn't a vegetarian. Do you need a bench to sleep on?'

'There is no mosque to worship in,' Samira said.

'For heaven's sake, you're in a Christian country.'

'We have trouble getting a *permesso di soggiorno*,' Tarik said, 'finding a landlord who will rent to Moslems.'

'But *I* sorted out your *permessi*! And I found you the apartment!'

Morris remembered in the past certain young immigrants who had been more grateful when he helped them.

'But if they didn't have these immigration laws, we wouldn't need . . .' Tarik stopped himself and put his face in his hands.

'I'm going to reply to this,' Morris announced importantly. 'Talk about getting away with murder!'

He opened Word and began to type. He was furious with the kids, but also aware that, at least partly, he was writing to impress them, to show them that Morris Duckworth was the kind of man who could see the wood for the trees, and get his name into print in the process. In the end, they were young; like Mauro, they needed to be taught a thing or two.

'Dear Sirs,' he typed, 'Unlike your mendacious correspondent who published "Verona: Capital of Kitsch", I actually—'

'What does mendacious mean?' Samira asked.

'Someone who lies all the time. *Mendace*.'

'Ah.'

Tarik said a few words in Arabic and they both burst out laughing.

'Now what are you sniggering about?' Morris was incensed. He liked them. Liked them both. He loved their fine young features, black eyes, and snake-smooth skin. But not if they were planning to gang up and treat him like an old fogey.

'Don't be so sensitive, Mo.'

'But what did you say?'

'Tarik said you should come to Tripoli if you want to see what beauty is.'

Morris didn't believe for one moment this was what had been said; how could Tripoli possibly surpass an Italian town in beauty and why would the remark have created so much amusement, at his expense? But he let it go. Or rather, he let the anger flow from his fingertips:

> Unlike your mendacious correspondent who published 'Verona: Capital of Kitsch', I actually live in this town and have done so for almost three decades; well, I can assure your readers that Verona remains one of the finest and most elegant city centres the world over, a forward-looking and vigorous community where the rumour of Romeo and Juliet exists only as a pleasant background murmur of antique romance, its few scattered and very beautiful shrines, apocryphal or otherwise, attracting the same tourists who flock to see the London Dungeons or the execution place of Anne Boleyn; frankly amour, however clichéd, seems preferable to the bloody glamour of Anglo-Saxon vulgarity.
>
> Pork scratchings, lager louts, race riots, football hooliganism, vomit on street corners and stinking public urinals, such are the English charms the judicious traveller is spared in the shaded piazzas and stuccoed sobriety of this Renaissance gem. No wonder romance seems credible here. Your article, the journalistic equivalent, if I may be so bold, of a contract killing (since clearly Mr Anderton-Dodds had viewed no more than a blurred photograph of his victim prior to pulling the trigger), simply aligns your newspaper with those enemies of sentiment who once brought the lives of two young lovers to tragedy. Shame on you! Shame on you too for putting at risk the jobs of those whose honest endeavours on behalf of Verona's tourist industry gives work to thousands, many of them refugees from the Third World, people who can barely

believe their luck to find themselves in this Italian paradise. All power to President Sarkozy and his splendid Italian signora for choosing the perfect place to renew their love before the long, hard slog of parenthood.

Morris Arthur Duckworth
The Duckworth Foundation
Via Oberdan
Verona

Just like that! It had come out just like that: The Duckworth Foundation! Without a thought, without forewarning of any kind. This was what it meant, Morris thought, to be creative. Suddenly, from nowhere, an idea came into being. Most definitely he should have been a writer, an artist. He copied the passage and pasted it into the comment box below the offending article. Then not satisfied, because it really was such a well-written letter, he emailed it to the editors as well. Damn them. Let them see who was the better polemicist, Mr Anderton-Dodds (Boris!) or Morris Arthur Duckworth. It was years since he'd signed off with his second name; it had always worried him that people would spot the obvious acronym. But this time it felt right. If the *Telegraph* needed a man in Verona, MAD was definitely better than BAD.

'Morrees!' Samira breathed.

Entranced by the eloquence of his indignation, Morris had not registered the growing incredulity of the two young people beside him.

'I never knew you could be so romantic!'

The Englishman smiled and turned to kiss his girl on her dark lips.

'What is the Duckworth Foundation?' Tarik asked cautiously, and with new respect, Morris hoped. Speaking off the top of his head, the rich lover launched into a very promising explanation, and only four days later received a call from the town hall. The city council wished to express its gratitude.

* * *

'. . . the long, ard zlog ov paarent-hhud,' the mayor concluded with a flourish. 'Morrees Artoor Dackvert! The Dackvert Fowndayshoon!'

There was a moment's bewildered silence from a public who understood only that they were supposed to approve. Nobody seemed sure whether the reading was over or not, until, with a whooped Californian cry of 'Way to go, Morris, man!' the balding figure beside Antonella began to pound his hands in enthusiastic applause. It *was* Stan. From top to toe Morris thrilled with shivery sweat. Christ! Why? As the Italians politely clapped their ignorant ovation, while his wife and daughter, he noticed, seemed to be studying him with the rapt apprehension of one who has found a brightly coloured mould on a bidet towel, the Freeman of Verona jumped to his feet and, invited or no, snatched the microphone from the mayor's unsuspecting grasp.

'Grazie, grazie!'

He felt a little unsteady on his feet in front of so many people. The Tonbridge tie seemed to tighten round his neck. Undecided whether to sit or not, the mayor quite brazenly tapped on his watch. Morris was having none of it. Seize the day. There is a tide in the affairs of men. He hesitated, looking out across the well-groomed scalps of the city's applauding elite to where, in the piazza beyond, he could just glimpse the balcony from which 150 years before Garibaldi had exhorted *'Roma o morte!'* In his cheeks and above his eye, the scars that had robbed him of his youthful beauty had stepped up their song to a fierce descant. Or perhaps it was a battle cry. His face was throbbing. Once again, in the most adverse circumstances, Morris must launch himself into the fray.

'Signore e signori.'

The clapping abruptly stopped and a fascinated silence fell on the crowd; most of them knew Morris as a respectable and quietly obsequious businessman, almost more Italian than the Italians themselves in his understanding of what must be said and what left unsaid, what paid, whether under or over the table, and what, with grace and aplomb, evaded; a man who in twenty years had turned a second-string family vintner's into a major business concern, becoming a key figure in the local consortium of industrialists and, of course, the Rotary Club. But now, rather disconcertingly, there was a flash of fear in this sedate man's face, something wild and perhaps even dangerous had surfaced from beneath the dark scars and pale shining eyes, while his posture, oddly contracted and unsteady, betrayed the kind of hunted, animal-at-bay anxiety that would have reminded some present that this man had once stood trial for murder.

But Morris had been acquitted of course and the moment passed. He straightened up, filled his lungs and squared his shoulders. His face relaxed in a broad smile. Get a grip. Speak your best Italian. Stan was just an old friend visiting the haunts of his youth. Not the man who could put him in gaol.

'*Signori, grazie*. I had prepared, I should tell you, a long and generous speech in praise of the city of Verona, a city that has given me, to be blunt, all that I have. But I shall leave it aside. You have already heard my little letter, so movingly read by our excellent mayor. My feelings will be clear enough, even to those very few who don't know me either as a business partner or a member of the many organisations in which we are all involved. I am told that we are running late and that the mayor must meet a delegation of Arab businessmen; the last thing I would wish is to compromise a chance to bring fresh investment to our town.'

There were murmurs of approval. Seeing Antonella's relieved smile, Morris enjoyed the awareness that when it really counted he always got it dead right. And in perfect Italian.

'So I shall just say thanks to you all for coming here today. It's a great pleasure, in particular, to see a face I haven't seen for twenty years and more. Welcome back to Verona, Stan Albertini!'

Apparently there were no limits to Morris's magnanimity. Stan, of course, stood up and bowed to laughter and applause.

It was the man's baldness and the absence of the old goatee, Morris realised now, that had delayed his recognition.

'But I will, if I may, take this opportunity to explain just one thing. At the end of my letter, the mayor read the signature, Morris Duckworth, the Duckworth Foundation.'

The mayor, who had sat down, reassured that his guest would be brief, now gripped the arms of his chair and half stood again. Morris motored on:

'It was precisely on reading that cowardly attack in the British press, and with a profound awareness of all that Verona means to me, that I decided I must give something back. That something, far more than any letter, is the Duckworth Foundation. Its capital will be made up, in part, of the considerable art collection I have had the good fortune to build up over the years, some eighty canvases, which, on my death I shall gratefully bequeath to the city's museums.'

As the crowd burst into applause, a door to the right opened and an elderly official hurried in, scuttling along the wall and behind the polished table to whisper in the mayor's ear.

'To celebrate,' Morris continued, determined to score all the points he could in the very brief time at his disposal, 'I have proposed a major exhibition of these paintings together with other old masters from all over the world at a grand summer show in Castelvecchio, on the theme, I am pleased to announce . . .'

Here Morris stopped a moment; for he wondered if he really had the courage to pronounce the idea that had come into his head *literally this instant*. He hesitated. This was seriously mad. What an idea! The audience waited. The mayor fidgeted. Do it? Don't do it? The truth was that however much Morris schemed and planned, it was only his moments of pure extemporary genius that had ever really got him anywhere or reconciled him, for that matter, to the unhappy destiny of being his father's son – God loves those who love themselves, he thought and raised his voice – '. . . a show entitled, I was saying: *Painting Death: The Art of Assassination from Caravaggio to Damien Hirst*. An innovative

show, *signori e signore,* that will put the town of Verona on the postmodern map and silence our critics for years to come. Thank you, everybody, thank you.'

Sitting down – and he had spoken for only two minutes, for Christ's sake – Morris smiled benignly into the alarmed eyes of his wife in the front row.

The mayor was on his feet.

'I'm afraid we shall have to call it a day, ladies and gentlemen. Our Arab delegation has arrived. There are important matters of trade and investment to discuss. Let me just say, because I've received a piece of news this very moment, that there is one member of the Dackvert family who hasn't been able to be with us today. Now I understand why. I have just been informed that young Mauro Dackvert, son of Morrees, and *a great fan of our beloved Hellas Verona,* was amongst those arrested, scandalously and without justification, after last night's game in Brescia. I would like to take this opportunity to assure the Dackvert family that they have all our sympathy and will receive our utmost support to ensure the rapid release of their courageous boy from unjust imprisonment. For this too is part of the same implacable campaign against our happy community.'

The young mayor turned and with genuine affection embraced the irate Englishman as he stumbled to his feet.

CHAPTER TWO

MEN OF POWER ARE always vulnerable.

'Isn't that true, Mimi?'

Morris was contemplating Cecil Doughty's *Death of Julius Caesar*. There sits Caesar in his white toga with his laurel crown, ready to deliberate on some important matter, disposing of other people's lives, wives, goods and chattels, and before he knows it he's being stabbed in the back. He feels for his own dagger, drops it and doesn't see that right behind him Cassius already has his knife held high for the next blow. Perhaps one section of the show, Morris reflected, and he tapped out a quick note on his iPad, could be called 'Poised to Strike'. Yes. Jan de Bray's Judith and Holofernes, for example, or Poussin's Abraham and Isaac. Gentileschi's Jael and Sisera. Various Amnons and Abels. Thomas à Becket, David Rizzio. There were so many. And the gesture was always the same: the armed hand raised high, the point of a blade threatening to pierce the top of the picture frame, the intent face of the killer summoning up the will to strike, and the victim sprawled or sleeping, or simply, as in Caesar's case, with his back happily turned; he had been getting on with business as usual until that first blow was struck. Morris particularly admired the way Doughty had painted bright red borders on the elegant white togas of the Roman patricians, as if in anticipation of the blood about to flow. Something decorative and civilised erupting in savagery.

'You struck me from behind,' the painted Mimi murmured.

'I know, love,' Morris replied softly.

'I suppose it is kinder that way,' Mimi acknowledged wistfully. 'I mean, I'm glad I didn't see it coming.'

'I'm glad too,' Morris smiled. 'It was a terrible shame it had to be done at all.'

'I've been looking at Camuccini's Caesar and thinking how much worse it must be when you have time to realise.'

'I've always felt that,' Morris agreed.

She spoke from the far end of the room. She was Lippi's Madonna, copied all those years ago by Forbes. Or Lippi's Madonna was Mimi. The spitting image. She had learned English since she died, something she would never have managed alive. Acquired a baby too, and an impressive knowledge of art history. In Camuccini's painting, or rather the careful copy that Morris owned, Caesar faces his assassins in regal red, raising a bare arm in desperate self-defence against a dozen plunging knives.

'He suffered more,' she sighed.

'Of course some people call it cowardice,' Morris mused. 'Sneaking up from behind.'

'What has to be done has to be done,' she said.

'And if it were done, then t'were well it were done quickly,' Morris echoed.

They mainly agreed on things these days. There was a reassuringly routine, even conjugal predictability to their exchanges. Though Mimi was definitely not in favour of *Painting Death*. She told him that right away, as soon as he came into the room. It was not so much the risk he would be running, drawing attention to his fascination for killing, as the feeling that something private between them was to be exposed to the gaze of others. She feared they would lose the intimacy of these daily chats in The Art Room where Madonna and Child presided over a compendium of carnage. 'This is *my* room,' she told him. 'I've always felt that Morris. That you made this room for me.' Sickert's *Camden Town Murders* were her favourites. She liked the gloomily penitential posture of the man sitting beside the naked girl's corpse with his head in his hands, as if to signify that the murder was a defeat for both of them.

'Not that I ever think of you as defeated, Morris,' the young mother assured him.

Morris liked to think of his first but never really ex-girlfriend as having somehow become the mother of God. What greater recompense could there be? For himself, he found Sickert's canvases rather morbid. Sick Sickert, he thought, getting his models to pose as murdered whores, of the lowest class too, and in slum accommodation. The paintings would definitely have gained from more affluent interiors. In this case, though, since he actually owned two originals, there was no question of asking a copyist to make changes.

'The fact is' – it was important to give her his point of view – 'I feel that if I have anything to offer people, I mean by way of art and expression, it's a fresh perspective on crime and killing: you know, the whys, the wherefores, the consequences' – one of the sections in the show, he decided, should definitely be called 'The Aftermath', showing the butchered corpse and that expression of awful realisation on the faces of the onlookers: Botticelli's *Discovery of the Body of Holofernes*, for example, the general's neck carved like a Sunday joint, surprisingly bloodless, come to think of it, the bedclothes still very white, as if the trunk had been brought out of a freezer for display. It was a strange painting.

'And like I said, it all goes back to the question of vulnerability, Mimi. Great men are always vulnerable. Perhaps vulnerability is a mark of greatness. I feel that more and more.'

This time the girl was silent. Morris would have liked to press the point, it seemed a more interesting line of reflection than their usual sweet nothings, but there was much to do and he had to be careful to limit these dialogues to a post-prandial quarter of an hour or so, otherwise he would have been perfectly capable of frittering away the whole day in her company, talking about paintings and murder and the perils of prominence. He leaned forward to examine Forbes's brushstrokes in the big Botticelli. Impeccable. It was sad the old man had had to go. Nobody had ever really replaced him. The hacks and art students Morris hired these days copied faithfully enough; he could hardly deny them their fees. But there was something perfunctory about their work. In Poussin's *Massacre of the Innocents*, for example, you couldn't quite believe that that sword was really going to come down on the naked babe. Only Forbes had put heart and soul into copying.

'Our children make us vulnerable,' Mimi reminded him, hugging dear little Jesus to her breast and showing once again how well she could read his mind. 'We suffer for our children, Morri.'

'Damn, yes!' Morris looked at his watch. 'Mauro!'

What Cardinal Rusconi had wanted of him in the end was some cut-price construction work on a new Catholic school in the outlying village of Sant'Anna. Red cloak wrapped round red tunic, giving the impression of some expensively festive upholstery, the bulky man had been standing in Morris's path as he pushed through a group of white-robed sheiks to exit his moment of glory.

'As you know, the Curia is asking us to invest first and foremost in Christian education. The future belongs to the young.'

Morris did indeed know all too well how these things went. An outlying congregation was persuaded to vote for a certain ultra-Catholic parliamentary candidate on the understanding that the church would then build them a school so that their precious bambini need no longer mix with hoards of undernourished Moslem immigrants in the state establishment ten kilometres away. The problem being that once their man was elected the school had to be delivered, or at least started, before the next election, this despite the fact that there was not a shred of economic sense or social justice in the project. Still, they must be desperate, Morris thought, to enlist the services of no less than a cardinal to ask such a trivial favour of a devout entrepreneur like himself. Perhaps the interminable paedophile scandals had reduced the flow of cash into the Curia's coffers, though it was hard to understand why, since deep down people had always known about this stuff. More likely the Church itself was spending heavily to buy the victims' silence. In any event, these were hard times. Next thing they'd be obliged to give the infidels a mosque just to attract some foreign investment. Though the rich sheiks usually seemed serenely unworried about the availability of prayer facilities for their immigrant brethren.

After only a moment's reflection, still excited by his announcement, indeed invention, *ex nihilo*, of the Duckworth Foundation's first major art exhibition – himself as curator perhaps! – what Morris asked of the cardinal in return, rather modestly he thought, was just a little flexibility on the sale of artworks held but rarely displayed in the Veneto's hundreds, even thousands of churches, shrines, sanctuaries, baptisteries, chapels, crypts, cathedrals and ossuaries. What was the point, Morris suddenly and rather passionately demanded of this powerful man, realising as he began to speak that he had been waiting years for a chance to express this opinion to someone who mattered – what was the point of the ignorant parish priests locking this wonderful artwork away unsung, unseen, and above all unprofitable, for heaven's sake, and often in the dampest and dirtiest of attics and cellars? Why not sell the paintings before they rotted away and build more schools with the cash? Art, after all, Morris opined, had long since lost its function of drawing people to the Faith, had it not? Especially the baroque art of the Veneto, now decidedly out of fashion when not considered positively grotesque.

The men were standing on the steps of the town hall looking down on all the feverish pre-Christmas activity in the piazza. Morris was frankly impressed how rapidly he had bounced back from the news of his son's arrest, how very sensibly he had chosen to put the matter and its possibly calamitous consequences aside until the big occasion was over. 'And just when the rascal's father has been granted the freedom of the city!' he had laughed with the mayor as the detestable man released him from the kind of proletarian embrace that reminded Morris of his father's bear hugs on those rare occasions he had returned both victorious and halfway sober from Loftus Road. For a moment, picking up his scroll and silver key, Morris had even been tempted to lift the mayor's hand and raise a shout of '*Forza Hellas!*' – it would certainly have been well received by most present – but in the end he feared he might not convince. If there was one emotion Morris had never understood, it was male camaraderie. Much more attractive was the kind of intelligent and strategic exchange between men of cautious wisdom that he had once enjoyed with Forbes, very occasionally with Don Lorenzo, and now rather promisingly, with Cardinal Rusconi.

'Is anybody's soul saved nowadays, Cardinal,' Morris concluded his reflections, 'by meditating on San Sebastian's arrows? Does anyone get on his knees at the sight of Cain slaying Abel?'

The cardinal was quiet for a moment, black brows arching above a bulbous nose. It occurred to Morris those small red skullcaps must have been invented to hide bald spots.

'Is that really the point, Signor Duckworth?' the cardinal eventually asked.

'Well, it was supposed to be the point, surely. What other reason was there for painting all those martyrs?'

A Martyrs' Room would be good.

'Observe our Christmas comet,' the cardinal said quietly, lifting a smoothly shaven double chin to nod towards the square.

Every December, at great expense to the local population, an impressive steel structure was erected in Piazza Bra: sprouting from the top of the Roman arena a great white girder first curved upwards to the wintery sky, then arched rapidly down, tapering as it went, to meet the porphyry cobbles where it exploded, as it were, in a highly stylised, geometric steel star some five metres high. Children in garish bubble-jackets were climbing on its lower 'rays' and sliding down again.

'Observe,' the cardinal repeated.

'I'd rather not,' Morris objected, reflecting once again that Anderton-Dodds wasn't all wrong: Verona's Christmas comet was kitsch of the worst variety.

'Is this extravaganza really intended to give people a sense of the mystery of Christmas? Does anyone think of it as an invitation to lay down their pretensions and riches before the infant Christ?'

'More a case of bread and circuses,' Morris agreed.

'Quite. A question of keeping the masses entertained, getting them through the four seasons.'

'In the crassest fashion.'

'But effectively.' The cardinal smiled. 'And that, alas, is the function our old paintings no longer serve. They don't distract people's attention while their wiser peers get on with the job; that is why they are decomposing in cellars and crypts. At least that steel monstrosity there can be melted down when it no longer amuses.'

Morris hesitated, unsure whether this odd analogy between art and junk was entirely pertinent. But he enjoyed conversations that played out slowly, like a tough game of chess, even if he had never been any good at chess.

'All the more reason, Cardinal,' he decided to probe the churchman's defence, 'to let me do a little snooping and see what's actually there in the cellars and crypts. I'm not interested in buying paintings for resale, you understand. I don't need to make money. I just want to bring them into the light of day. Perhaps something for this show I was mentioning: *Painting Death*.'

'Ah yes, a most unusual idea.'

Lighting a small cigar in the cool winter air, the cardinal smiled indulgently, evidently amused to find himself embroiled in such a delicate discussion. People were always favourably surprised, and challenged, Morris had frequently noticed, when he revealed a little of his true self.

'However, as you may know,' the cardinal resumed, 'all artworks in church possession, valuable or otherwise, have long since been catalogued in files held by the local council's Department of Cultural Heritage. They are no longer ours to dispose of, Mr Duckworth.'

So cheered was he to hear his name pronounced properly for once – the Jesuits still had their standards, it seemed – Morris almost made the mistake of switching to first-name terms. But it was too soon. That would come when Sant'Anna's primary-school foundation stone was laid.

'Naturally I'm aware of that, Your Eminence,' he replied. 'But does anyone ever actually bother to make inspections, to see if the pictures are where they should be?'

And even if they did make inspections, Morris wondered, would the council employees be able to distinguish a well-made copy from an original? Forbes had thought not.

The cardinal blew smoke across the piazza and sighed. He wasn't sure. One would have to ask the clergy 'on the ground'. He pronounced these words as if he himself had long since been raised far above any such earthly contact, along with his cigar smoke perhaps. Morris found it deplorable that a man of the cloth could indulge such boorish vices, but he had learned not to pass judgement.

'I know someone who works in the Heritage Department,' Morris proceeded affably.

The cardinal again arched a shaggy eyebrow.

'She tells me the cataloguing you refer to is, how shall we say, chaotic.'

'I can well imagine.'

'And vulnerable.'

The cardinal dropped his cigarillo on the steps and stood on it. This was something the young Northern League mayor had explicitly banned, along with eating kebabs on the public pavement. A *vigile* was constantly at hand to fine transgressors. But not the cardinal.

'I don't doubt it,' the prelate smiled.

Then Morris said he had a contractor working on a furniture warehouse in the Caprino Veronese area who should be free shortly. That wasn't too far from Sant'Anna. No doubt something could be done. 'To get things moving.'

'The point is they are eager to open the school next September,' the cardinal explained.

'Ah,' Morris observed and added, 'Of course any paintings I buy would be bequeathed to the State on my death, so one needn't feel that anything was being subtracted from the national heritage. On the contrary I would pay for any restoration work required. For the State it's a bargain. For the church an income.'

Pulling out his iPhone to check a text message, the cardinal said that the parish priest of Sant'Anna would be in touch shortly with plans and details. 'I'm afraid I have another engagement now.' He held out his hand. 'Congratulations once again, Mr Duckworth, on your honorary citizenship. You are a credit to our community.'

'Cardinal Rusconi!'

The man in red was at the bottom of the steps, already opening the door of a waiting BMW, when Antonella came rushing out of the town hall followed at a fretful hobble by the long-suffering Don Lorenzo.

'Cardinal Rusconi, please!' Morris's wife called breathlessly, 'I was just wondering' – now she had caught his attention she paused – 'yes,' she took a few steps closer. 'I mean, I was asking myself if there was any chance that you, or someone, I don't know, could put in a word for our boy, Mauro. I mean, you heard he's been arrested. There must have been some kind of mistake. Perhaps a phone call to the *questura*?'

Morris was deeply disappointed; it really wasn't appropriate to address a cardinal so abruptly, never mind to call aloud to him across an open space where anyone might hear. The smallest thing that went wrong and his dear wife completely lost her sense of decorum. In her haste, her silk dress had wriggled up around her considerable thighs and her maroon midriff was pulsing, her great gold crucifix trembling. Antonella generally achieved presentability through stateliness, through the dignity of composed mass. Hasty, wobbling and tearful, she seemed little better than a fat schoolgirl who had outgrown her uniform.

Turning, the cardinal shifted a quizzical eye from the fleshy woman in her mound of fur to the skeletal Don Lorenzo, wringing mummified hands on the step behind. The ancient spiritual adviser was evidently torn between dedication to a wealthy benefactor and respect for his eminent superior. Without a word, the prelate frowned, produced another cigar in his ringed fingers and bent his head to his lighter.

'Absolutely not!' Morris came hurrying down the steps.

Antonella looked up in consternation, as if her husband might have been forbidding the cardinal to smoke.

'The last thing we want,' Morris announced, 'is for the boy to think he can go about behaving like a thug and not pay the price like anyone else.'

'But he's in gaol, Morrees!'

'In a police cell,' Morris corrected. 'If we discover that Mauro really is innocent, then, yes, we might want to appeal to someone who can help. But first we must find out what's happened and give the authorities the benefit of the doubt.'

Hovering at her shoulders, Don Lorenzo said, 'I fear your husband is right, Signora Antonella. We must pray for guidance.'

Sighing, Antonella seemed to pull herself together. 'Do forgive me, Cardinal. It's just so worrying . . . for a mother.'

Her voice appeared to be on the edge of tears, but when she looked over to her husband again there was a cold glint in her eyes. It did not worry Morris in the slightest. This was one quarter from which he was not expecting trouble.

* * *

Morris Duckworth and Antonella Trevisan, for Italian women do not necessarily surrender their surnames in wedlock, had a rather wonderful marriage. For both, of course, it was a second try. Indeed, it was while commiserating each other over the near simultaneous demise of their first spouses that the two had drawn close, an intimacy legitimised by the pain of discovering, from the circumstances of those curious deaths, that both their partners had been flagrantly unfaithful. Comforted by an already decrepit Don Lorenzo, Morris and Antonella had vowed that no such clouds would ever muddy the transparency of their own affections. In the throes, at the time, of a profound religious crisis, Morris had read the Bible morning, noon and night with Antonella and confessed himself daily to Don Lorenzo who eventually advised the troubled young man that there was no need to be so assiduous in one's penitence if the only sin one had to admit was resentment over one's failure to speak perfectly fluent Italian. Morris had been unconvinced. 'Sometimes, Padre,' he muttered, 'I feel that just waking up and breathing is a sin.' Not to mention thinking, he might have added, presiding day by day over the products of Morris Duckworth's busy and increasingly uncensored mind. If he were to be honest, Morris often thought, he ought to spend his days confessing over and over to the mere fact of being alive. On the other hand, there was actually nothing Morris liked better than being alive, than waking in the morning, taking a deep breath and plunging into the day's disturbing reveries. It was because he loved it so much he knew it must be a sin.

Antonella, in contrast, was serenely without sin. In this, Morris's second and, he at once understood, 'real' wife reminded him intensely of his mother. The quietness and absolute reliability of her devotions, whether spiritual or conjugal, was fantastically reassuring after the wayward behaviour of her younger sister, his first wife, Paola, a woman perfectly capable of pleasuring herself in the passenger seat of her Porsche, smearing pheromone-perfumed fingertips across her chauffeur husband's freshly shaven lips as he tried to pass a tractor on a blind bend. Paola had driven Morris crazy and eventually paid the price. If I caught her with Kwame, he reflected, reliving as he occasionally would the moment when he had climbed the spiral staircase of their duplex to see naked black shoulders towering over red sofa cushions, his wife's foxy chin propped on an ebony neck, a beatific smile stealing across her cheeks as she panted towards paradise, and the eyes – those desperate, animal eyes she had! – begging her polite and proper English husband, over the black hunk's shoulder, please not to interrupt until the last drop of pleasure had been squeezed from her corrupt thighs – yes, if Morris had caught his first wife in noisy coitus with his personal assistant of the time, an ungrateful immigrant rescued from the gutter in a spirit of purest Christian charity, then God knows who else she had been with. The good Lord only knew with how many men (and women?) of what social extraction, age or ethnic background, Morris had been sharing Paola's sweet, tight, slippery sex. He could still shudder at the thought, when it suited. I might perfectly well have died of AIDS, he sometimes liked to say to himself.

Had he had any choice but to put an end to it?

There were no such perils with Antonella. Like Morris's mother she was a chaste spirit who put God before self and respectability before both. From the start it had been understood that the pleasures of their union would lie in knowing that they had done all that Upright Society could ever ask of any couple. They would build up the family business and guarantee employment to all those less fortunate souls who had come to rely on Fratelli Trevisan for their sustenance. They would use any excess wealth for charitable works and unimpeachable cultural projects, fitting into the busy routine occasional pilgrimages to Lourdes and to Medjugorje. Sex would be strictly a matter of decorous impregnation, after which the two would catechise their offspring in the age-old Catholic tradition, ensuring them the finest available schooling so that they too could accrue wealth and distribute it to virtuous causes, never missing Mass or confession or the annual trip to the city's monumental cemetery where the Trevisan family's multitudinous dead would certainly not be obliged to turn in well-appointed tombs for any misdemeanour of theirs.

How different things might have been, Morris had sometimes reflected during these fertile years with Antonella, if his own dear dead mother had had a husband like himself, a man who admired and seconded her virtues, instead of a Neanderthal who grew more crass, drunk and violent the more her modesty verged upon sanctity. 'I know of no finer couple in all Verona,' Don Lorenzo had announced over after-dinner brandy one evening in the mid nineties, as Morris wrestled the charmingly hyperactive Massimina on his knee and Antonella winced under the bite of baby Mauro's gums on her nipples. So that if in the end there had been only two children, this was not the consequence of any disobedience of the church's teaching on sexual practices, but because Antonella felt that with booming world populations two little angels were quite enough; that agreed, she could imagine no further reason for inviting Morris between her ample thighs.

The marriage was perfect. Almost. Morris loved spending his days with a woman who was unfailingly kind, thoughtful, practical and prayerful, a Veronese of the old school who had inherited quiet and efficient servants and ran her household as the Trevisan household had been run for generations: profitably, discreetly, even beautifully. It really was as if his beloved mother had returned from the grave richer and younger to become her son's wife, but without surrendering her admirable and only mildly chiding virtues. After the turbulence of his early years in Italy, such a marriage seemed like a well-deserved point of arrival.

All the same, something was missing. Occasionally and despite himself, as they say, the maturing Morris would find himself fantasising Paola's excesses, her sex toys and exhibitionism, above all, that firm finger she loved to plant deep in the

Duckworth fundament; or better still, though he hardly dared go there, Massimina's adolescent tenderness, a delicate erotic love he had enjoyed all too briefly in that heady summer month of kidnap disguised as elopement.

'All too briefly, Morri,' she echoed from her gilded frame, 'but I will never forget.'

'Nor I, dear Mimi,' he shook his head. 'Nor I.'

It was not that Morris ever contemplated leaving Antonella; she gave him the stability and respectability any man would kill for. But five or six years into the serenity his motherly wife provided, Morris had begun to sense that it was only a matter of time before the transgressions began; he was in a holding pattern waiting for the brutal urge to out. Perhaps good mothers naturally bred naughty boys; their virtue became your vice. Casting about, then, for some innocent palliative that might stave off the evil day, because Morris really did want to be good, he had come up with the idea of The Art Room. The family palazzo in Via Oberdan, acquired from Antonella's first husband, Bobo Posenato, son of the homonymous battery-chicken magnate, was far too big for their modest lifestyle and given Antonella's commendable disinterest in grand social occasions she had not resisted Morris's request to convert the first-floor ballroom into a private art gallery.

'Don't you think she looks a little like Massimina?' he had asked, hanging Lippi's Madonna over the great fireplace.

'Our Massimina?'

Their daughter had been four at the time.

'Your sister, silly!'

Antonella wrinkled her nose, narrowed her eyes; Massimina had been dead eight years.

'Not even a tiny bit, no.'

'She's just jealous,' Mimi had told her killer as soon as they were alone, 'she hates it that you still think of me.'

Whenever he was in The Art Room, Morris was trying to decide what the next picture would be. He regularly trawled the net on his MacBook Air, which he kept on a small desk, to see what images excited him, checking all the auction-room info in case something affordable became available in the original.

'*We're* not jealous of *her* though,' Mimi interrupted him.

'We?'

'Didn't you know, Morri? Paola and I are on speaking terms again.'

'Ah.'

Morris was surprised to learn that his first wife hadn't ended up in a quite different place from dear Massimina, but sensed it would be unwise to seek clarification. There are things it is not given to the living to know.

Lippi's Madonna suddenly let out a peal of healthy, youthful laughter. 'Funny that of us three sisters you managed to end up with the only one who doesn't like sex at all! *Povero Morrees*. What bad luck!'

Morris paused. He had been pondering at the time whether Forbes would be up to copying Delacroix's *Death of Sardanapalus*. All that smutty, sadomaso luxury was very Paola. If one mustn't transgress oneself, it surely wasn't wrong to contemplate an aestheticised transgression.

'So what do you think I should do about it?' he had asked her, almost absent-minded.

'Don't ask me,' the girl snapped back. 'It's hardly my problem is it, where I am? With our Lord Jesus as well.'

This was exactly the sort of prickly, unhelpful answer that convinced Morris that his dialogue with the dead girl was a real one; if he had just been making it up, it would all have been mere ego gratification from start to finish.

'I've decided to collect some pictures for you to look at,' he had told her.

'As if I didn't know,' she came back.

'Tell me what you think of this.' He took the laptop over to where she was hanging. The sumptuous Delacroix was full screen in high-res.

'Forbes could never do that,' the girl said at once. 'Nice picture though. Lots going on. Sexy!'

Morris sighed: 'Don't you think the nude at the front looks a bit like Paola?'

'Not at all,' Mimi told him. 'Grow up, Morri!'

After the paintings had begun to accumulate, Antonella asked, 'So why all the murders?'

There was always a motherly wryness in her manner, an affectionate, perplexed shrewdness, as if dealing with an adolescent going through some particularly tricky phase.

'I give Forbes carte blanche,' Morris told her, as if resigned. 'He copies whatever he likes. It keeps him off the drink.'

'*Madonna mia,* that *is* macabre!' she said, the day he hung *Sardanapalus,* 'Naughty too. Don't let poor Don Lorenzo see!'

Morris was delighted with the painting. Even Mimi admitted that Forbes had excelled himself, though it was around this time that Morris had realised that his relationship with the elderly pervert was fast approaching its sell-by date.

'Don't you think the nude at the front looks a bit like Paola?'

'Morris, what on earth is that man doing to the poor child?'

'Knifing her, I'm afraid.'

Antonella shook her head. 'I don't think I ever saw Paola naked. I wouldn't know.'

This was odd, Morris thought, because when she had been married to him, Paola had hardly ever worn a scrap of clothing, that is not around the house.

Inevitably Don Lorenzo did discover the paintings and whenever Morris hung a new acquisition the elderly priest always made a point, after their evening Bible-readings, of dragging his gammy leg up the stairs to pass judgement. In winter, Morris liked to illuminate the grand room with real candelabra: four wonderfully baroque, wrought-iron monstrosities holding eighteen candles each. It took almost fifteen minutes to light them, lifting and lowering each circle of flame with a system of chains and pulleys, but the work was well worth it: the room became so much more exciting in their wayward, smoky flickering, with raised knives, hammers and broad swords quivering all around. Standing in front of *Sardanapalus*, with its bearded sadists and naked concubines, Morris enjoyed the strangely gratifying impression of being simultaneously in church and brothel.

Don Lorenzo stopped in front of Bellini's *The Assassination of St Peter Martyr* and sighed: 'I used to dream of martyrdom myself once,' he said. He had been a missionary in Burundi, back in the sixties, when they were killing Christians right and left. 'I sometimes think it might all have been easier that way.'

'I know what you mean,' Morris assented, with feeling. He was surprised to find himself sharing, with a man he'd always supposed was supremely pious, this odd, persistent desire he had often felt to be spared life altogether, to pass at once into nothingness, delivered from temptation forever.

'Considering how often our old fart in a cassock visits, you'd think he was Anto's lover,' Mimi said cattily.

Morris had to be careful not to reply out loud when other people were around.

'Assuming he could ever get it up,' she insisted.

'Sometimes I think a certain Madonna has a very dirty little mind,' he chided in silent communion.

At which the dead girl laughed so loud that Morris could barely hear what Don Lorenzo was saying about Thomas à Becket.

'I was reflecting,' the melancholy priest repeated 'that it was a great shame England was lost to Catholicism.'

'Indeed it was,' Morris agreed. 'Indeed it was.'

So on the morning in which he received the freedom of the city, the scrolled certificate and silver key, it was natural, on returning home with Don Lorenzo, to invite the old priest up the stairs to see the new Judith and Holofernes and consider together the severed head of another man released from this earthly treadmill of weal and woe.

Antonella stopped him. She was furious.

'What about Mauro?' she demanded. 'What will happen to his schooling if they keep him in gaol? Just think what might be happening to him there! What if he has another of his toothaches?'

Having spent a few months in gaol himself, Morris had a pretty good idea what would happen to his son if they actually sent him there. But, as he again pointed out, the boy was still in a police cell. 'And of course I immediately asked the mayor to arrange for me to see him this afternoon.' Taking Don Lorenzo by the arm, he added over his shoulder, 'How could you imagine that I hadn't already spoken, *discreetly*, to the cardinal?'

Antonella was chastened. 'What time?' she asked. 'I'll get ready.'

Don Lorenzo limped up the stairs beside his host. The morning had exhausted him, he said. His crippled ankle was a constant torment. Nevertheless, after gazing for a few moments at the painting he began to chuckle.

'A man spends his life dreaming of women and then the dear girls pop his head in a basket.'

'Dead right,' Morris agreed. 'I often envy you your vow of celibacy, Don Lorenzo.'

In his eighties now, the priest did not reply.

Then Morris asked, 'I wonder if you could slip downstairs a moment and convince my signora that I should go to see Mauro alone. The boy needs a serious talking to, which won't be possible in his mother's company.'

Acting on a whim, Morris stopped the car in San Zeno to invite Samira to come along. Appearing unannounced, he had often noticed, gave you more information about a person than phoning ahead. You could see how they reacted to your unexpected presence. But the girl was out. 'At work!' So said Tarik through the intercom.

'Buzz me up a moment,' Morris asked. The young man's hesitation didn't surprise him. Nevertheless it was a bit rich when his girlfriend's brother stood defensively in the doorway, as if unwilling to let Morris into a flat he himself was paying for. Morris stood on the landing and smiled. Eventually Tarik backed away and he walked in. The smell of spicy cooking always excited him.

Tarik seemed sullen today. He moved like a peeved cat. Morris needed no explanation for such a mood. Hadn't he too spent most of his twenties in a similar state of mind? There was always good reason for resentment. From being mildly irritated, he now felt a surge of affection. He loved the boy's explosive shock of glossy black hair. Youth and southern vigour. It would be good to brush it off his forehead. If only Mauro had been like this.

'I have to go to Brescia,' he told the young man. 'Would you like to drive me?'

'I'm studying,' Tarik said.

'I wanted to ask you some questions about the Middle East on the way,' Morris invented. 'In particular Syria, and Assyria. I mean, are they the same place?'

That should intrigue the lad.

'No, not at all, or not exactly. Why do you want to know?'

'Come and drive for me,' Morris said. 'The fact is my son has been arrested and I have to go and talk to the police. I'm a bit worried. Help me relax.'

This formula of throwing more meat on the griddle than people could immediately handle usually did the trick. Everyone loves another's troubles. Tarik turned and pulled a light raincoat off the back of a chair.

'Is that the warmest coat you have?' Morris enquired in the street as he gave Tarik the car keys. The young man said it was. Morris nodded, hoping it was understood that the driver would be rewarded with a proper winter jacket.

Tarik drove with measured aggression that suggested a mix of respect for Morris's Alfa Romeo and assertion of his own expertise and personality. His hair really was remarkable. As if all the boy's repressed vitality were thrusting up out of the top of his skull.

'No need to stop for a ticket,' Morris said complacently at the entrance to the autostrada. 'We have a Telepass.'

As the radio contact buzzed and the toll barrier lifted, the Arab's clouded face creased in a faint smile. Is there anyone who doesn't enjoy wealth, Morris wondered? It really was so easy for the rich to seduce.

'My son has got himself involved in some football violence,' he said. 'You know the Verona and Brescia fans have this ancient rivalry. It's ridiculous.'

Tarik settled in the fast lane travelling exactly 10 kph over the limit. To the left the Po Valley was a rigid geometry of concrete vineyard posts, each bearing its little crucifix of twisted trunk and outflung tendrils. To the right, the foothills of the Alps rose steeply in their grey-green winter shabbiness. Had he wished to impress, Morris could have pointed out three environmentally friendly housing developments his money was invested in.

'I mean, I'd have felt better if it was political violence, with real principles involved.' He hesitated, 'Like the Arab Spring.'

The boy kept his counsel, nervy wrists communicating a guarded alertness.

'It saddens me that he would get himself arrested for something so frivolous, you know. Life is a serious thing and there's so much happening in the world today.'

The driver sat silent as a statue. Morris smiled.

Typically, as they neared Sommacampagna, they hit a wall of fog. Equally typically, the traffic hammered on regardless, each car hanging on to the tail lights of the vehicle ahead. Aside from those red pinpoints, all colour and shape was gone; they were in a motorised underworld of mechanical wraiths. Morris felt the boy's concentration winding up. He was relishing the challenge.

'No the reason I asked about Assyria was because I have

recently acquired two paintings that involve so-called Assyrian leaders: Holofernes and Sardanapalus.'

Tarik's grip on the driving wheel tightened.

'It seems the latter, Sardanapalus – I'm sorry, I'm sure I'm pronouncing it wrongly and I know how horrible that can be for a native speaker – King Sardanapalus, that is, when he realised he was facing military defeat, in Nineveh I think it was, decided to immolate himself along with all his concubines.'

Morris had always been attracted to the word 'immolate'. One so rarely got a chance to use it, to the point that he wasn't quite sure what it really meant.

'Well, then, what I was wondering was—'

Suddenly the boy hit the brake, swerved dangerously across the middle lane, then again, amid a storm of protesting claxons, through the near impenetrable greyness between two lorries into the slow lane, and finally on to the hard shoulder beyond the traffic where the car bumped wildly on the broken surface before slithering to a halt.

'I'm getting out,' Tarik announced. He snapped open his belt.

Morris was astonished.

The young Arab turned to him. 'It's disgusting,' he said. He started to open the door.

'Don't,' Morris told him. 'You'll be killed.'

The car rocked as a truck slammed by. To their right, beyond the crash barrier, was only a heavy whiteness.

Tarik turned and glared, eyes smouldering with righteous anger.

'That's how the East is always presented here, isn't it? Decadent, cruel. A cheap horror movie, so you westerners can feel superior. A Jewish woman puts an Arab head in a basket and you applaud.'

Morris was a little concerned that this unscheduled halt might make him late. Not so much for Brescia and Mauro, but the appointment with his contractor in Caprino Veronese that he had arranged to follow. At the same time he was fascinated.

'Go on. Tell me more.'

'You project your own sick perversions on to an Arab nobleman and then enjoy imagining him defeated, suicidal and morally disgraced. To remind yourselves,' the boy was sneering now, 'why you don't have the courage to live out your own filthy fantasies.'

'That's an interesting idea,' Morris said sincerely.

'I'm getting out,' Tarik repeated. The car continued to rock in the rush of traffic. Morris had always felt they cheated on the emergency lanes in Italy; they were too narrow by far.

'Did you ever hear about Marco Donat Cattin?' he asked.

An off-the-wall question to reset the conversation.

Tarik stared. His eyes were magnificent. Liquid tar. More beautiful than his sister's perhaps. His hair stood up like a cat's hackles.

'Donat Cattin was a terrorist in the seventies. Actually the son of a Christian Democrat minister. Well, he served his time in gaol, then, when they released him after God knows how many years, he stopped his car on the hard shoulder in the fog to help a driver who had broken down. On this very stretch of road, as I recall. A passing truck killed him. *Ironia della sorte*.'

'I hate everything you stand for,' the boy said.

'Hmmm,' Morris reflected. 'So why don't you drive on to some point where it's safe to stop. I quite understand you might have issues with me. All the same there's no reason you should risk your life to make the point. Not to mention a long walk in freezing fog without a proper coat.'

Tarik sighed, drew a deep breath, then turned to the road again.

'Do up your safety belt,' Morris reminded him. After a few minutes back in the traffic, he tried a new tack: 'I've been thinking. There's a way you could really help me, Tarik, you know.'

'I don't want to help you.'

'Wouldn't you like a chance to tell the world the things you've just told me?'

Tarik didn't reply.

'Next autumn,' Morris said, 'I shall be curating an art exhibition about murder and assassination – a word of Arabic origin I believe.'

The boy was pretending not to be interested.

'And as you rightly point out, many of the Bible-inspired paintings have some unpleasantly prejudiced content. The Massacre of the Innocents. David and Goliath. Sardanapalus. As you say, the bad guys are always Arabs. And it still goes on today, we lick sheik arse to attract foreign investment and won't even give the local Moroccans and Libyans a mosque to worship in.'

Tarik's jaw was working, as if he might be planning to spit. They were in the fast lane again, dangerously close to the lights ahead. With a flash of nostalgia, Morris remembered the times when Kwame had chauffeured him around the countryside, absolutely careless of any traffic rules or precautions. Tarik on the other hand was focused and angry, wound up rather than laid-back. But Morris's excitement was equally intense.

'My own position,' he said, watching the boy carefully, 'is that the paintings are very beautiful, I mean beautifully made, even when their content and implications are scandalous. What do you think about that? I mean, can you have a beautiful work of art that conveys an ugly or unacceptable message?'

It wasn't clear whether Tarik was listening or had withdrawn into a world of private bitterness. Morris was aware of waves of negative energy.

'The next exit is ours,' Morris said calmly.

If anything the muscles round Tarik's jaw hardened. He was holding his head unnaturally high, his neck rigid.

'Anyway, my plan is to surprise people with some captions that really open up this can of worms, have you got me? I want people to walk into that show and think, hey, wait a minute, these paintings are beautiful but completely beyond the pale. I want people to face that issue. Our culture is built on disgraceful ideas.'

Tarik was working his way across the lanes to the exit, quite sensibly this time.

'It just occurred to me, what if someone like *you* were to write a few of the captions? Sign them in your name. You know? The Arab point of view. "Handsome Jew boy David slays ugly Arab Goliath." Force people out of that mindless bourgeois assent to art they always have.'

'Forget it,' Tarik said. 'I'll never do anything for you.'

'Right at the roundabout,' Morris told him.

As they drove toward the centre, he turned the radio on. It was important to give people the impression you respected their refusals.

Opinionated listeners were phoning in about Berlusconi's trial for abetting underage prostitution. The dominant view was that what a man did in the privacy of his own home should not be an object of public interest. Ruby looked at least eighteen and was clearly asking for it. A woman called from Cagliari to say she wouldn't have minded a bit of bunga-bunga herself.

Suddenly Morris found himself bursting into laughter. 'At least Sardanapalus immolated himself! No such luck with Berlusca.'

Looking at Tarik, he saw the same half-smile that had played on his lips when the autostrada barrier lifted. He would come round. Morris felt thrilled. In the space of a few days, no a few hours, life had become exciting again.

'Herod was Jewish,' Tarik said a few moments later.

'I beg your pardon?'

'Herod was Jewish. It was a Jew who ordered the Massacre of the Innocents.'

'Quite right,' Morris acknowledged. 'How careless of me.'

Mauro Duckworth had a head of curly red hair over a chubby cherub face. Exactly where those tight gingery curls had come from, Morris had no idea. There was no history of curls or red hair in either his or the Trevisan families. On occasion he had allowed himself to imagine that he was the victim of a terrible betrayal: at their time of greatest intimacy Antonella had opened her womb to someone else. But this was so out of character as to seem barely credible. And the boy definitely had Morris's slate blue eyes and inwardly curving little fingers. An alternative might be that he himself was not his father's son, that his own blonde mother had betrayed the monstrously swarthy Leonard Duckworth with some more aristocratic redhead; hence he himself was the unwitting carrier of curly, carroty genes that had then been passed on to Mauro. That would explain all kinds of things and it had occasionally given Morris much satisfaction to fantasise that he was not his father's son, was free as it were from that contamination, and what's more bearer of the no doubt nobler genes required to make an adulteress of a woman as pious as his mother. On the other hand, this version of events implied a complete revision of Morris's faith in Mother's purity, while his father became more sympathetic: a man with a grievance tricked into bringing up a cuckoo in the nest. This didn't suit at all. A less troubling explanation might be that Antonella was not the daughter of the Latin-dark man who featured in all Trevisan family photos, Christian Democrat mayor of the godforsaken outpost of Sanguinetto and dead some years before Morris's arrival in the Bel Paese. Yes, Antonella's mother, whom Morris had always disliked for her unwarranted suspicion of everything he said, had betrayed her powerful husband with a mysterious redheaded *conte*, or even Monsignor, why not? and it was thus Antonella, not Morris, who carried the red genes, so to speak, in background. This, to Morris, seemed more credible. He had always felt that Italians were terribly lax about sexual matters and his time with Paola had amply confirmed the suspicion. What it made you wonder, though, was how many other lamentable or even dangerous traits one might innocently be carrying around as a result of other people's intemperance. How could you ever feel safe with your loved ones, or even yourself? There had been any number of occasions when Morris's own two children just did not seem to be flesh of his flesh at all, as Morris had never felt he was flesh of his father's flesh and often felt alienated even in his own skin. It was tempting, in such circumstances, to imagine that life was such a lottery you couldn't really be held responsible for anything; but Morris knew that that way madness lay. Genes or no genes, for example, his son had definitely committed a severe error of judgement getting himself involved in a brawl with a bunch of football fans. He deserved to be punished for it.

As it turned out, Mauro had a black eye and a bandaged ear. One wrist was in plaster. Morris felt a surge of pity for the boy; he remembered all too well what it meant to wake up after a violent encounter and find one's good looks radically compromised.

But the first thing his son said was calculated to repel any nascent sympathy.

'I'm not going back to school, Papà.'

The police had told Morris five minutes and no more. It was a special favour. So the mayor *had* called.

'You won't *be able* to go back to school, if they put you in gaol.'

Mauro spoke to his father in Veronese dialect, which Morris hated; it was the idiom of thugs and peasants. Morris replied in proper English, using the accent he had made his own at Cambridge, which was also the language they drilled the boys in at Tonbridge School. Rightly so.

'I sent you to one of the world's best schools, Mauro, to give you a better chance in life. It doesn't come cheap.'

'I'm a fish out of water there, *dio bon*.'

'Water?' Morris grimaced. 'I thought you preferred sewage.'

Mauro sucked a swollen lip. He must have taken some kind of blow where jaw met neck. There was a bruise he kept touching with the fingers that peeped from the plaster.

'Where's Mamma?' the boy asked. '*Oddio*, I hope she's not too upset.'

'Too upset to come today, for sure. But not as upset as she'll be when she hears you don't have the courage to finish school.'

'*Ma porco dio*, Papà, it's pointless wasting money on something that doesn't suit me.'

'Until you're eighteen, I'll be the judge of what suits you. And I'd prefer it if you spared me the blasphemies. They're ugly and infantile.'

There was a long pause. The five minutes were being frittered away in an argument they could have had any time.

'By the way,' Morris added, 'this was supposed to be the day when your father received honorary citizenship of your home town.'

'They didn't give it to you?'

'Of course they did.'

'So why did you say, supposed to be?'

Morris took a deep breath. 'I meant, *given* that it was the day, etc., etc., it should have been a day of unsullied family pride.'

Mauro grimaced. Morris wasn't sure he had understood the word 'unsullied'. Evidently it was painful for the lad to move his features. '*Dio povero*, my teeth are killing me.' He seemed to reflect for a moment. 'If you want to talk about courage, though, Papà, I can promise you we gave as good as we got.'

Morris said: 'Tell me the story and I'll get a lawyer.'

The police had started it, Mauro explained. Forced to file between two lines of riot shields as they left the stadium, he and his friends had been systematically beaten. 'With truncheons, *dio boia*! Like it was a production line and we were the pieces on the conveyor. They hit every one of us, *dio can*.'

Morris watched as his son spoke. The seventeen-year-old was relishing the story. His one open eye flashed. On the table, his good hand clenched as he recalled a punch. It was strange to realise that one's offspring had become a menacing physical presence. Meatily built, trained on the rugby field, without his civilising Tonbridge uniform Mauro was the classic English cherub turned lout.

'So we waited for them outside,' he said with grim satisfaction.

'I beg your pardon?' Morris sat up in surprise. '*You* waited for *them*, for the police?'

'That's right.'

'To assault them? Deliberately?'

'They started it, *porco dio*!'

'You're mad.'

'We jumped them at a corner.'

Morris was incredulous. 'And you didn't cover your faces with balaclavas or hoods, stockings, whatever you rabble do?'

'We decided to take them face to face. We knew they wouldn't be expecting that.'

'I bet they weren't.'

'It would have been OK too, if a busload of reinforcements hadn't arrived at the crucial moment. We were doing fine.'

Morris sighed. 'Mauro, you realise they're probably recording this conversation.'

'Then the judges will hear that it was them started it, won't they?'

'That's not the part of the recording that will get played in court. Grow up, kid.'

The boy touched his plastered hand to his cheek again. 'This tooth, *dio bon*.' For the first time he appeared to be struck by the idea: 'You really think they'll put me in gaol?'

'Certainly an institution of some kind. You're still a minor. But what else can they do, if you admit to assaulting a policeman?'

Most surprising of all, though, Morris thought, was that despite the unhappy prospect of imprisonment, not to mention all the physical pain he must be in, his son was evidently pleased with himself; as if being spared a return to Tonbridge School was all he cared about.

'Is there anything particular worrying you about going back to school?' Morris asked. 'It would be crazy to drop out just because a teacher's picking on you or something.'

This time Mauro tried to smile, but again his features froze. 'The only thing that worries me is that I might kill my maths teacher.'

‘I’m sorry?’

‘He’s so sarcastic. I get this urge to grab his neck. A sort of wave of angry heat.’

‘Mauro, for heaven’s sake, you’re not going to resolve anything by killing people.’

‘That’s why I’m not going back,’ the boy said.

For a moment Morris tried to set aside his disappointment and concentrate; his son’s life was at a turning point; and a child’s destiny reflects on the father; this would affect Morris’s reputation. Meantime, Mauro was describing the beating they had taken, even after the fighting was over and they were handcuffed face down on the pavement. ‘They still kept kicking us, *dio boia,* they’re animals!’

‘If I can get you out of this,’ Morris interrupted, ‘will you do what I tell you? I mean obey unconditionally?’

Mauro was pouting. ‘Is there any chance I could get off?’

How much more attractive Tarik was, Morris suddenly thought. How much more cultured. His spiritual children were Samira and Tarik, not Massimina and Mauro.

‘The first thing is to stop telling the truth. They assaulted you, not you them. You did not jump them at a corner. You—’

‘But Papà—’

‘And in future you never take on another person face to face.’

At this point a policeman put his head round the door. Time was up. Without another word Morris got to his feet and left.

CHAPTER THREE

MORRIS WAS ASLEEP AND he was awake. He felt many hands lifting him in his winter pyjamas, carrying him from his bed, laying him down on a table. Where? The only big table on the first floor was the one in The Art Room. They laid him down clumsily and his head took a knock. He felt he could have woken at this point, if he made an effort. He could have opened his eyes and contemplated the beautiful renderings of violent death that hung on the walls. Perhaps I collect these paintings so as not to kill again; that thought flashed through his mind. Or perhaps because I'd love to kill again but don't have the nerve.

A cannibal who wants to have his corpse and eat it.

Morris smiled, then heard the sound of steel on steel, a harsh, rhythmical rasping. Now he was alert. There was a muttering and a whispering. Hands gripped his wrists. Open your eyes, Morris! He couldn't. He struggled, but strong fingers were pressing on his face. The blade penetrated his neck. It sliced across his windpipe and sank straight through the flesh till it met the bone, and began to saw. Morris felt every movement very precisely. They were twisting his head this way and that while the blade sawed at the spine. I'm dead! he yelled. Oh, I'm dead! Mimi, why didn't you warn me? Why have you forsaken me? His head was turning from side to side with the blade in his neck sawing and sawing, until at last the bone gave.

Aaaaaaaaaaaaaaaah!

'*Madonna-mia-madre-di-Dio!*' Antonella cried.

Morris lay in a sweat.

'I thought you'd never wake up. I've been shaking you like mad.'

He moved his head carefully; it had not fallen in a basket.

'You were shouting, "I'm dead, I'm dead."'

'God.'

'And all kind of other things besides.'

Morris was still savouring the pleasure of being in one piece.

'Other things?'

'Lots of other things.'

Morris hesitated; best not to enquire, he decided.

'It must have been seeing Mauro in such a bad way.'

There was a pause. Their bed was the same carved old four-poster that had once been out in the family villa in Quinzano. Trevisan DNA seemed to require that all furniture be massive, dark and at least one hundred years old. The only objects like it that Morris had known as a child were the oak pews in St Bartholomew's, or perhaps the polished coffins when he sang at funerals for half a crown. But he enjoyed the waxy atmosphere of sepulchral wealth in the Trevisan household, and he loved too to think that Massimina had slept on this same hard wool mattress beside her widowed mother right up to the fateful day when she had run away with him. It made him feel close to his first love even as he slept beside her more sensible elder sister.

'It didn't sound like it was about Mauro,' Antonella finally said.

Morris said nothing. The previous evening they had argued. A rare event. After leaving the police station in Brescia – and he had taken care to chat politely to the policemen for five minutes before departing – Morris had asked Tarik to drive him to Caprino Veronese. On the way he had spoken to his lawyer, Carla Cogni, an overweight workaholic in her mid forties. Whenever possible, Morris explained to Tarik, while waiting for Carla's receptionist to put him through, he preferred to work with women: they took more pleasure in his Englishness, had more sympathy for his facial scars and were generally impressed without needing to compete. 'Oh, if all the world were women and me the only man!' he laughed. 'Me and you, that is, Tarik.'

Tarik did not smile. The fog was thicker than ever.

'*Carissimo* Signor Duckworth!' the lawyer exclaimed, her voice far louder than necessary. Morris had to hold the phone some distance from his ear. 'My warmest congratulations on your honorary citizenship. We are all very proud. In what way can I be of service to you?'

Morris loved these Latinate formulas which he still contrived to hear in English, even as they were being pronounced in Italian. They sounded so much more old-fashioned and dignified with only a literal translation, which was just as well, given the tawdry situation in hand. He began to explain.

'Not wise to speak on the phone,' she stopped him.

'I know, I know, Avvocatessa, but I'm afraid he has already said as much to the police. He seems—'

'That's as maybe,' the lawyer told him. 'But nothing is irreversible, Signor Duckworth.' Speaking very firmly, as if addressing someone she knew was hiding behind a filing cabinet, she added, 'The fact is we know that he hasn't done anything wrong.'

'Of course,' Morris agreed. Returning the phone to his pocket he was shaking his head in admiration. If anyone could get the boy out, it was Carla.

They drove in silence until Tarik quite unexpectedly announced, 'I think I like your son.'

This was a surprise.

'You wouldn't if you knew him. He goes around with a bunch of racist Hellas Verona fans. Complete louts.'

'That's rhetoric,' Tarik said complacently. 'When they're supporting their local team they like to shout Verona for the Veronese and feel everybody else is an enemy. It's just part of the game. We do it back in Tripoli too.'

How confusing! Morris took a deep breath. On the outward journey the young Arab had got furiously worked up about

Morris's professional interest in *Judith Slaying Holofernes*, a marvellously conceived and brilliantly executed painting by the incomparable Artemisia Gentileschi, and here he was on the return trip endorsing a bunch of yobs who quite probably tossed bananas at black football players. Meanwhile, Morris noticed how wonderfully sinister Tarik's quiet smile was. It lifted the right side of his face, leaving the left absolutely expressionless. The lips were thin and stayed firmly shut while the eyes lit very faintly as if to suggest that the boy was aware of much more than what had been said. It was splendid.

'Racist or not, he's a fool.'

'You say they ambushed the police and fought them in an open fight?'

'That would be one way of putting it.'

Tarik shook his shock of black hair. 'Quite a guy.'

Morris was irritated. 'But not in a noble cause, Tarik! Out of mere adolescent bloody-mindedness. He's a beefy yob with more energy than sense.'

Tarik continued to make admiring clucks with his lips and little nods of the head. Morris's irritation became exasperation.

'What is the point of paying a fortune for a child's education, if he goes and gets himself put away for a decade? It's not respectful to me or his mother.'

'The police started it,' Tarik objected. 'Didn't they? They're the real fascists.'

Exasperation morphed into amazement. Sometimes it did seem to Morris that he was the only halfway law-abiding citizen on the planet.

'Listen, I'd much rather have you for a son,' he announced bluntly. 'Think how easily you'd get into the LSE if you'd been to Tonbridge School. I can't imagine *you* getting yourself put away for a stupid brawl. You're far too smart.'

In response to this enormous compliment, with its hint of promise too, the boy said nothing.

Amazement hardened into pique.

'Perhaps I'm so upset because I went to gaol myself once. I know what it means to lose my freedom.'

When Tarik showed no interest, he added dangerously, 'They put me on trial for murder, you know.'

The Alfa was held up by a slow van that wouldn't move in from the fast lane. Flashing his, or rather Morris's, headlights, Tarik asked:

'Who were you supposed to have killed?'

'Oh, a business partner.'

Morris didn't mention that Bobo had been his present wife's husband, or that his death had allowed Morris to take over Fratelli Trevisan.

'But they didn't find you guilty?'

'Because I hadn't done it.'

The van moved in and Tarik could accelerate. 'So who had?' he asked, hurtling into complete invisibility now.

'One of the immigrant workers,' Morris said carelessly. 'Bobo treated them rather badly, I'm afraid. Talk about racist! I did warn him.'

Tarik frowned. 'And they caught this man, the murderer?'

'A Nigerian, yes. Not exactly caught. They found out he had done it after he was killed, burned to death by racist arsonists who objected to his sleeping with a white woman. It was most unpleasant.'

Morris didn't mention that the white woman was his first wife.

There was a long pause before Tarik remarked, 'How convenient.'

What was that supposed to mean?

Morris felt irritated, yet at the same time realised he was liking the boy more and more, the expert nerviness of his young fingers on the wheel, his extreme alertness as he drove too fast in the fog.

Morris asked: 'Have you had another think about that show I mentioned?'

Tarik didn't reply. He was negotiating the autostrada exit.

Morris gave him directions and the car started to climb north into the hills above Lake Garda.

'It would be a real novelty,' he insisted, 'to have an Arab point of view on our biblical art. People would be intrigued.'

All at once the fog thinned and then in just a few metres they were above it, driving through a winter twilight of white stone walls, inky cypresses and flaking roadside Madonnas.

'How beautiful!' Morris exclaimed. Turning back, you could see the whole North Italian Plain as a sea of luminous grey with just here and there a campanile or an archipelago of office blocks poking through.

'Isn't Italy marvellous?'

The boy grimaced.

'Do it for Samira,' Morris suggested. 'She'd be proud of you. You'll make a name for yourself, I promise.'

'No.'

They arrived in Caprino Veronese where Morris left Tarik in the car again, to go looking for the contractor he had mentioned to Cardinal Rusconi. In a small overheated cabin amid mountains of building materials on an apparently idle building site, they had talked about the school in Sant'Anna and how much might be done without spending anything at all. 'The important thing for them politically,' Morris said, 'is to get the foundations dug. Send over an excavator when you have one spare and put it on the bill for this place.'

Old Zuccato was a taciturn man who rarely offered more than a grunt in reply. Morris thought of him as one of the world's geniuses in the art of subcontracting; there was not a single task on Zuccato's building sites that was not subcontracted to the most disparate suppliers imaginable, most of them southern, Slav or African, all astonishingly cheap. Morris explained the concept to Tarik as they drove back to Verona.

'Zuccato would subcontract his own bodily functions if it made economic sense.'

Tarik didn't find this funny.

'Call in quotations for getting his wife with child.'
Nor this.
So Morris phoned the boy's sister.
'Sammy.'
'Tesoro!' she whispered. 'What a nice surprise!'
'Bellissima,' he said huskily.
That would show the boy who was boss.

An hour later, crossing his home courtyard in Via Oberdan, Morris was in a classically mixed mood: on the one hand there was the honorary citizenship (if it hadn't gone spectacularly well, the ceremony had at least happened); then the idea of the art show (a startling confirmation of his creativity); plus this curious new intimacy with Samira's brother (Morris felt sure the boy would change his mind) – all that was positive and exciting – but on the downside there was the huge and no doubt time-consuming problem of Mauro who was, like it or not, a Duckworth, and as such capable of dragging the family name into the mud. 'My son, my son,' Morris sighed; he was just giving a wistful caress, as he always did – because sculptures are there for the touching – to Mercury's marbly buttocks, when he was stopped in his tracks by a voice calling:

'Here comes the Honourable Citizen! Hey Morris, man!'

A window creaked open on the first floor and a grinning face was looking down: a middle-aged and very Jewish face, pointed chin and receding, if not terminally receded hairline. Together with the rush of adrenalin that immediately flooded Morris's body, came the alarming reflection that if there was one person in the whole world who should *never* have been admitted to The Art Room it was Stan Albertini.

'I can't believe,' were Morris's first furious words, as Antonella and her guest came to greet him in the hallway, 'that you two are looking at pictures when our Mauro is in gaol.'

No sooner had he said this than he appreciated his mistake. Hadn't he himself taken Don Lorenzo up to see *Judith Slaying*

Holofernes after this morning's ceremony? Hadn't he insisted that it was better that he, Morris, handle police and lawyers alone while his wife get on with life as if nothing had happened? And had he ever used the expression 'our Mauro' before? Never. Then specifically to mention the paintings! Achilles might as well have removed his ankle boots beneath the walls of Troy.

'Where's Massimina?' he went on, almost in panic.

Antonella was confused. 'What's Mimi got to do with it?'

Amazingly, Stan didn't seem to take in the fact that the people around him were going through some kind of family crisis; but then the American was famous for missing the obvious. He had never really registered the fact that he had seen Morris together with Massimina the afternoon she was supposedly kidnapped; nor grasped the coincidence that he had again run into the Englishman at Stazione Termini the very day someone picked up the ransom there. It seemed entirely possible that Stan could be relied upon until the end of time never to smell even the most stinking of rats. On the other hand, could one, should one, allow one's freedom to depend on someone else's crass stupidity?

'How you doin', you old fraud?' The unwelcome visitor embraced him and slapped him on the shoulders. 'Long time no see, eh?'

If only it could have stayed that way.

'I'm just here for a month or so, on vacation.'

A month!

'Taken early retirement,' Stan went on. He waved be-ringed hands around and occasionally clapped himself in his enthusiasm, as if his hosts could have any time for small talk with their son in a cell facing serious charges.

'I was hoping to hook up with old Mike. Forbes. Remember?' The man just wouldn't stop.

'Great paintings by the way. Kind of Tarantino before Tarantino. Pulp baroque. Love the one of the lady hammering the big nail into the guy's skull. Talk about splatter, man!'

If I had a hammer, Morris thought, I'd hammer in the morning.

'We need to persuade Massimina,' he improvised, addressing his wife, 'to talk some sense into Mauro. Sorry Stan, but you've arrived at a tricky moment. The situation is actually worse than we thought,' he said urgently to Antonella. 'Much worse.'

That should refocus her attention.

'I know, I know, my own are the same,' Stan was immediately agreeing.

I'd hammer all day, Morris thought. Fleetingly, he wondered if Antonella and the American had already shared an aperitivo. They seemed altogether too relaxed.

'My oldest,' Stan was babbling, 'totalled his Toyota the day before I flew. Wasn't hurt fortunately.'

'I'm here, Papà.' Massimina tapped Morris on the shoulder. Apparently she'd been standing behind him the whole time. The tall girl laughed at her father's absent-mindedness. 'We've been grilling Stan about how you were when you first arrived in Italy.'

Morris was lost. Why weren't they more worried about Mauro?

'And how was I?' he asked coldly.

Stan couldn't stop chuckling, 'You know those little hermit crabs that kinda nip your fingers if you try to pull 'em out of their shells? Complete recluse! There were people thought our Mo was way way off the rails.'

'Our son Mauro,' Morris announced very loudly, 'has confessed to the police that he assaulted them *deliberately*. He is facing ten years' imprisonment. We have to discuss this *at once*.'

They had moved to the salotto where, sitting together around the monumental fireplace, Morris had insisted that Mauro must be persuaded to lie. Lying was absolutely the only sensible course. He was aware of speaking too much and too fast. The lawyer agreed with him, he said. The boy must say he had given his confessional statement under extreme duress after being beaten within an inch of his life. Massimina must convince him to do this. The best way would be to tell him that his mother was so overcome with shock and hysterics she had had to take to her bed and been put on tranquillisers. 'If you visit looking fit and well,' he added quickly as his wife opened her mouth to protest, 'he just won't realise the harm he's doing. The boy lives in a different world. He seems to take some sort of crazy pride,' Morris concluded, 'in claiming that he would *never stoop to lying*, which is fine if you have nothing to hide. But the truth is there are moments when lying is the only honest course of action.'

Morris finally stopped speaking to accept and immediately drain a glass of prosecco. The ancient maid was hovering with bottle and ice bucket as she had been instructed to do on all occasions when there were guests. Evidently it hadn't occurred to her that this was hardly a moment to celebrate, but given that she had poured a glass Morris decided he might as well take it. He badly needed a drink. Just the presence of Stan seemed to plunge him into agonies of adolescent insecurity, as if he hadn't become a pillar of society at all, but remained a sore thumb in need of a bandage. Sipping the sharp wine as the others stared at him, he was aware of having said something that didn't make sense but, precisely because of that, achieved a certain profundity: *lying is the only honest course of action*. What could that mean? He tilted his head and emptied the glass. Perhaps the contradiction might be resolved through the idea of consistency: if it was noble and honest to be consistent, then once you had lied it was surely noble and honest to go on lying. What good, for example, would Morris be doing anyone if he owned up now to six half-forgotten murders? Or was it seven? No good at all. But Mauro, it seemed, wouldn't even *start* lying. What could you do with a boy like that?

Antonella wore a heavy grey cardigan over a long olive-green gown. Casa Trevisan was never the warmest of environments; there hardly seemed much point in trying to heat such a vast space. She was drinking tea not wine and Morris noticed a quietness and reserve about her as if she were gathering energy for some difficult task. Normally admirable, today the pose seemed threatening. Crucified in her cleavage, Christ was sulking; he wouldn't raise his head to Morris's gaze. Then, smiling wearily and putting down her cup, the lady of the house turned to Stan, who had chosen to sit back to front on one of the room's old wooden dining chairs, and with a heavy sigh said: 'Can you believe Morris gave a talk along these lines at a Rotary dinner a couple of months ago? The importance of lying in the creation of prosperity. I nearly died of shame.'

Leaning dangerously into the creaking carpentry of the antique chair, Stan laughed raucously and slapped his knees: '*Inglese italianizzato, inglese indemoniato,*' he declared.

It was a cliché Morris had heard at least a thousand times, though never perhaps in such an Americanised Italian.

'Why on earth did you tell him that?' he demanded a moment later when Stan hurried off to the loo. 'It's humiliating.'

Antonella sighed over her teacup. 'Because you really mustn't say those things, Morris, and especially not in front of people who are not family. What kind of idea will he have of you? And you never know who he might run off and chatter to.'

'Well then get rid of him! This is a family emergency and he's hanging around as if we were having a summer picnic!'

'He's here for you, not for me, Morris. You get rid of him.'

Morris had been convinced it was the other way round. Hadn't Stan been Antonella's private English teacher, in the old days? Weren't they always in each other's pockets translating Jim Morrison and the Authorised Version? In any event, both husband and wife knew that if the American had not changed his ways he wouldn't take any hints about leaving until absolutely stuffed with food.

'The old prostate,' Stan grinned ruefully, still buttoning up as he came back into the room. 'Did the op, you know, but it seems to have gotten worse rather than better.'

'How interesting,' Morris agreed.

'No, I won't stay to dinner, thanks,' Stan was saying now in reply to Antonella's offer, 'not with you folks wound up over your boy. Just one thing: I was wondering if you could put me on the trail of Old Mike. Forbes. I'm really hoping I can find him.'

For a moment there was silence. Like all the other rooms in the palazzo the salotto was as spacious as it was austere. Silver-framed photos gleamed on a massive *credenza*; portraits from the Trevisan past loomed in the shadows; old books and bottles stood on their allotted shelves, rigorously unopened. Every carefully dusted surface emanated the sense of a promise too long and too scrupulously unrealised to be in danger of disappointing, like an invitation to a ball that should have taken place many centuries before. Made up with handsome logs, the great fireplace was eternally unlit, hence in no danger of requiring replenishment. In the ordinary way of things, Morris loved it. But now, once again, he smelled danger; once again he was obliged to reflect that a murderer's job is never done.

'Forbes went back to England, didn't he?' Massimina asked. The girl was sprawled on the sofa with the cat, her pink blouse the one splash of life defying the decorous embalming all around.

'That's right,' Morris agreed, hoping his face made clear how worried he was, about his son.

'It's weird, because he was writing to me pretty regularly,' Stan said, the wrinkling around his great nose a caricature of perplexity. 'Snail mail, of course. He never got himself a computer. Wouldn't have been Forbes, would it? Then one day, out of the blue, nothing.'

'Oh really?' Morris asked. 'Is that the case?'

Stan's head made a side-to-side movement, rehearsing his amazement. ''Fraid so.'

'Out of the blue?' Morris repeated quizzically '. . . nothing?'

'Right.'

Morris flashed a baffled smile, 'Stan, surely, the celebrated blue is itself that nothing out of which unexpected *things* surprise us when they come. Lightning bolts for example.' Or visits from unwanted crime witnesses. 'You can't say, or am I wrong, one day, out of the nothing, nothing. Get me?'

'*Per l'amore del cielo,* Papà!' Massimina cried.

Antonella's face was set in an expression of dismayed embarrassment. Stan seemed genuinely perplexed, as if trying to grasp what Morris meant, what he was trying to convey about Forbes's disappearance. On returning from the loo, the ageing American had stayed on his feet and his still-scrawny body in jeans and shapeless sweater seemed unchanged from twenty and more years before. Bald and beardless, his head perhaps looked somewhat smaller than it had been, but with, to compensate, larger ears, one of which Stan now tugged in perplexity.

'You got me there, man,' he eventually laughed. 'Yep, you got me.'

'Forbes used to copy paintings for you, didn't he, Morris?' Antonella tried to help. 'I remember you saying he had a drink problem.'

'Did I?'

'That's weird. He didn't mention that in his letters.'

What on earth, Morris wondered, could the ageing Etonian gay and the hip Californian Jew have been writing to each other about? Had they perhaps been lovers at some point? Morris had thought Stan a ladies' man, but nobody knew better than he not to trust appearances. Even if they had been lovers, though, what would they still have to write to each other about fifteen years on?

What, if not me? Morris asked himself, with growing alarm.

'Uncle Michael used to help me with my drawing when I was in the *scuola media,*' Massimina sighed.

'He did?' Uncle Michael?

'He was so sweet, and he had a really good eye. He used to lean over my shoulder and guide my hand with the pencil.'

If the girl's mother had the slightest inkling how dangerous Forbes had been around children, she would have had a heart attack.

'I remember about five years ago,' Morris announced as if making a huge effort to tear his mind away from graver matters, 'he started talking about going back to England. He'd given up the summer school you know. There'd been some, erm, unpleasant accusations and he was getting on in years. He felt nostalgic. I think he was hoping to pick up a state pension and live out in Wales, somewhere cheap, not too far from his ex-wife. That was the last I heard of him. He didn't leave an address. I felt a bit let down to be honest, after all I'd done for him.'

'Weird,' Stan shook his head. Evidently this was the American's favourite word. He pronounced it as if it had two syllables. Morris had always thought it a crime to allow Stan to teach English. The American sighed. 'Well, I guess I'll ask around, in case anyone knows. See if I can smell the old charmer out.'

They all embraced and said goodbye, Stan tripping over the cat and scratching his baldness with a rueful smile. Hopefully, Morris thought, there should be nothing left to smell under the roof of Santi Apostoli del Soccorso where Forbes's body had been keeping the company of the proverbial church mice for some long time now. It was a shame because he would have been a most useful consultant for *Painting Death*.

'What I don't understand,' Morris turned on the others the moment they were alone, 'is why you're not more concerned about talking some sense into Mauro.'

With the guest gone, Antonella has taken up her usual position at the big mahogany table, with her embroidery. Her lips puckered and eyes squinted as she wove in the golden thread that blinded Saul of Tarsus on the Road to Damascus. Finished and expensively framed, her Bible scenes adorned the church hall where Don Lorenzo held prayer meetings and charity raffles.

'The truth is,' he accused, 'you always spoiled him, gave him the impression he was untouchable. And now he's in deep trouble.'

Antonella held her peace.

'So I'll have to do everything, will I?' There was a slight frisson in assuming this tone of voice with his wife. They hadn't argued in a decade.

'Come on, Papà!' Massimina protested. 'Don't be childish.'

'As a consequence he thinks he can confess to attacking the police and be shriven with a couple of Hail Marys.'

'Mousie hasn't confessed himself in years,' Massimina chuckled.

'I *forbid* you to call him Mousie.'

Antonella smiled. 'For heaven's sake, Morris, we've called him Mousie since he was two and twitched his little nose the way he did.'

But Morris was staring at his daughter. 'And who is it you are always firing texts to?'

Lithe and coltish, the tall girl was crouched beside the sofa, stroking the cat with one hand and texting with the other. In this position her low-slung jeans revealed a good hand's breadth of primrose panties. There was a happy negligence about her sexuality that boded ill.

'Not always,' she said.

'Beppe Baguta?'

'Don't you wish!'

'He's a nice enough boy.'

'He's thirty, Papà! You just want me to get off with someone old and rich.'

'If you'd prefer poverty, of course . . .'

Massimina liked to plunge both hands under the cat's furry armpits and splay it out on the floor like a cartoon figure.

'I prefer love,' she told the cat. 'Don't I, pussy, pussy?' She nuzzled her snubbed nose into the creature's black fur. 'Lovey love love!' She used her huskiest voice.

Morris shook his head. More and more these days the family seemed alien to him, as if he were forever the fall guy for others to make fun of. Curiously, the more successful he became, in a business way, the more they made fun of him. Perhaps there was something he hadn't understood. In the normal way of things he would simply have given up at this point and retired to The Art Room to chat to Madonna Massimina. She respected him. But tonight there was an emergency.

'Why aren't we talking about Mauro?' Morris demanded.

'How did you find him?' Antonella enquired.

'A black eye, a torn ear, a broken wrist. Toothache.'

'*O poverino!*'

'Severe toothache.'

'*Povero* Mousie.'

Morris was bewildered. Where was the anxiety that had had her shrieking across the piazza at the cardinal this morning?

'And that's nothing compared with the charges that will be brought. Somebody has to persuade the boy to offer a less damning account of his behaviour.'

Texting as she spoke, Massimina said: 'Tell him, Mamma.'

Morris's wife set down her embroidery. Her mouth was surprisingly small and round in her large pale face and she had a habit of making it smaller still by pursing the lips in a tense little bud of concentration.

'If you had let me get a word in earlier, Morris, I could have given you the good news that just before you got home . . .'

She paused, studying the embroidery where the dazzled Saul knelt on the stony road.

'Yes?'

'Just before you got home there was a phone call.'

'From?'

'Actually, I don't know who from.'

'Ah.'

'Not exactly.'

'And?'

'I mean, I don't know his name. But I think it was the Curia.'

'The Curia? You think?'

'I have that feeling.'

'So what did the mystery Curia caller say?'

Antonella looked up. 'He said: Signora Trevisan, do not worry about your son, Mauro. He is in God's hands. He will come home soon.'

Morris stared at his wife. She was such a wholesome, middle-class creature, a woman who made purity seem as ordinary and achievable as a dull Sunday on the sofa. All the same, when she came out with stuff like this, how could one not wonder for her sanity?

'I assume the number was withheld?' Morris asked.

'Yes.'

'So we can't phone back?'

'I wouldn't want to.'

'And as a result of this, er, anonymous phone call, you feel quite relaxed now about your son being charged with the assault of ten police officers. You don't feel the need to take any legal action to protect him, from himself as much as anything else?'

'I believe the man was telling the truth when he said the boy was in God's hands.'

'We're all in God's hands!' Morris said sharply. 'And they're not always the safest of pairs, are they?' If there was one thing that sometimes threatened his own faith, it was his wife's.

'One reason I believe him is that as soon as he rang off, Mauro phoned.'

Now Morris was impressed.

'Mauro *phoned*? You're joking. From a police cell?'

'He said he was feeling better and expected to be home tomorrow or the day after.'

'He's mad.'

'He said that's what the police had told him.'

Massimina yawned. 'Papà, Mamma spent all day phoning every priest she knows and every organisation you've ever given money to. Seems her prayers have been answered.'

'Prayers!' Morris paced up and down the uneven parquet of the grand salotto. One day he would have it all torn out and a fitted Axminster put in from some carpet warehouse, if there were carpet warehouses in Italy, if there wasn't some obscure government regulation that prohibited fitted carpeting in fifteenth-century housing.

'So I went to Brescia for nothing,' he said. 'With all the work I'm supposed to be doing. And missing the morning too for that stupid ceremony.'

Suddenly Morris felt overcome by a near suicidal frustration. What should have been one of the best days of his life had gone from the sublime to the tragic, and now, inevitably, the ridiculous. Italy was a stupid stupid place, that was all there was to it.

'You went to Brescia to see Mauro, *caro*. How can that be a waste of time?'

Antonella had picked up her embroidery again. She wore glasses for needlework and the light of her table lamp gleamed off the lenses. Framed on a shelf beside her, her own buxom mother smiled down in black and white. Without looking up, Antonella added: 'You were right to go alone. Sometimes poor Mousie gets the impression that it's only me who cares for him. It must have cheered him up no end to see his father.'

'The idiot didn't need cheering up. He was so proud of himself for having attacked a policeman. No, ten policemen.'

'Papà, aren't you pleased it's not so bad after all?' Massimina asked. 'He won't even miss his flight back.'

'He's not going back,' Morris said sharply. 'I'm withdrawing him from Tonbridge. I refuse to go on spending a fortune to breed a thug.'

There was a short silence. Eventually Antonella nodded and said, 'I'm sure that's a wise decision, Morris.'

But this only made Morris feel madder. The truth was that Antonella had never wanted to send their son to England in the first place, or even to have him learn English probably. She wanted the boy to be Veronese, as local as gloomy old sideboards and pompous tombs. Suddenly it was all too much. Declining to join his lady-folk for dinner, Morris withdrew in a huff and spent the evening in The Art Room trawling the net for the best representation of Othello seeing off Desdemona. There was a Chinese company that promised full-size, hand-painted copies of a rather bizarre work by Alexandre-Marie Colin for just $250. Only after he was quite sure that Antonella would already be in bed and sound asleep, did Morris kiss Mimi goodnight and follow, finding his wife snoring lightly under the covers, apparently snug and safe, though in reality, as Colin's picture so charmingly demonstrated, tremendously vulnerable.

Despite these piquant thoughts, Morris had fallen asleep the moment his head hit the pillow and was enjoying the deep sleep of the just, when, quite unfairly, this miserable nightmare stabbed him into wakefulness, the hands fastening on his body, the hard feel of the table beneath back and buttocks, the whispering, the cold steel in his throat, the sawing, then his voice yelling out just before his head must surely be severed. Going over it now in the chill of the early hours, because even a nightmare could be turned into something pleasurable if you went back over it sensation by sensation, he was bound to realise that what Antonella must have heard in the agitated seconds before she had woken him, was his cry of Mimi, Mimi, why have you forsaken me? Something like that. So the question had to be, should he say something to her, anything, invent some story, to explain that cry? Perhaps he could say that he had dreamed of their daughter letting him down? It did seem terribly unlikely, and maybe more dangerous than leaving things be. What could his wife ever really make of an exclamation like that? How could she ever know what lurked behind it? The horror (and triumph!) of marriage, Morris reflected, was that you each lay in the same bed year in year out without the slightest inkling of what was going on inside your partner's skull. Rather than shrinking with time, that distance grew. It began to seem impossible that two people could be so together and so very apart. The thoughts must burst out and overwhelm them.

As if sensing his anxieties, Antonella's foot pushed towards him under the bedclothes and their toes touched, then their ankles, their calves. Her left, his right. She was seeking reassurance, he thought. Or offering it, perhaps. Who could tell? If she didn't know what was in his head, he certainly had no idea what was in hers. Who had she phoned yesterday afternoon, for example, who did she *know*, who was this person who had assured her Mauro would soon be home? Why hadn't she called him at once? Was he really supposed to believe that she didn't know who had phoned her from the Curia? There was definitely a part of his wife's old Veronese social life that she kept strictly under wraps, even though she denied this. 'My old paranoid,' she would laugh if ever Morris accused her of secrecy. As if paranoids were *necessarily* wrong. Then what had passed between her and Stan before he returned? In The Art Room of all places! How could you ever know these things, without perhaps keeping hidden microphones all over the house? Had Forbes been writing to the American about the murderous paintings Morris was getting him to copy, about their playful plans for a spot of forgery? Was it even possible that Antonella knew the truth about her husband, perhaps the whole truth – imagine! – and had known it all along even, but had nevertheless decided to stay with him. Why? Out of love? Out of trust? Could such an angelic thing ever be?

Morris's eyes filled with tears. He reached across the bed and twined his fingers into hers.

Man and wife lay like that for some time, foot over foot, hand in hand. After a while, as their fingers moistened together in silent communion, Morris's mind shifted tack and he found himself pondering the sad and sizeable crucifix just visible, albeit in dramatic foreshortening, above his head. Antonella was determined that there should be a crucifix in every room of the palazzo, indeed every room of every property they owned. All sizeable and very sad. It was quite a collection. There were crucifixes in the children's rooms, the bathrooms, the cubbies. Against the grain, Morris had even allowed one into The Art Room, a late Botticelli, copied, simply to keep his signora happy. Massimina hated it. Understandably so, with the Christ child in her arms.

More imagining than really seeing, Morris began to picture the thorny head on the dark wall above him, its expression of suffering, acceptance and love. *Love despite all,* he thought with a sudden thrill. Such a rare quality. It must be quite a challenge to paint an emotion like that. Quite a challenge to feel it! In general with paintings, Morris reflected now, and this was certainly the case in his murder paintings, it was the relation between facial expression and action that determined the quality of the picture, the expression of the murderer striking the blow, and the expression of the victim receiving it.

Suddenly, lying in this poignant silence between himself and his wife, it struck Morris with extraordinary force that murder was the moment when the dam broke and the truth about your nearest and dearest burst forth. Two people – Cain and Abel, Agamemnon and Clytemnestra, Othello and Desdemona – who had lived together in growing tension and distance, were finally revealed to one another. The horror on the victim's face was not just the horror of one about to die, that was nothing, but of someone who finally understands what has lain hidden for so long in his beloved's psyche. Yes! Or there was Romney's Medea where she is sitting looking at her children and you can *see* what she's thinking. They are playing innocently, naked of course, and she is full of fury, full of murder. And the dam is cracking. The inhibitions are going. If I can't kill my husband I'll kill *them*! Good! Any moment now she's going to jump up and strike.

This was what his art show would really be about, Morris realised: the moment of truth between two people, of awful truth, the rending of the veil that hides our unforgiveable selves from each other. And Morris would be making that statement, talking about that issue, which was supremely *his* issue, but without actually quite giving away his own personal truth.

How brilliant! God!

All at once Morris Duckworth felt so pleased with himself he squeezed his wife's hand tight.

'Oh Morris!' she murmured.

'*Carissima,*' he sighed. Full of affection he pushed his face blindly through the dark and kissed her hair.

'How sweet,' she whispered. 'What on earth was that for?'

CHAPTER FOUR

'IT'S ABOUT CHANGE,' MORRIS said.

The museum director was concerned that a show exclusively focused on killings and death might appear limited. The museum would be accused of morbid poor taste. The public would shy away. It would be hard to find sponsorship.

'Not at all,' Morris assured him. It would be innovative, political, psychological, anthropological, daring. 'And *I* am providing the sponsorship.'

It was as if an electric shock had galvanised a hitherto inert mass. Offensively sprawled in an executive swivel chair, countless kilos of flab shuddered and stiffened. The director almost pulled himself upright.

'All of it, Signor Duckworth?'

'If necessary, Dottor Volpi. Please do not underestimate my commitment to this town and to culture in general, or indeed my desire to be truly worthy of my, er, honorary citizenship.'

Morris smiled through the scars that made him so interesting. Samira sat beside him. Portfolio in hand, she looked smart, glossy and very Arab, her jacket formal and her skirt tight.

Volpi removed his spectacles which, rather than hooking over the ears, seemed to slot into wodges of flesh beside the eyes.

Obesity is a crime, Morris reflected, an insult to the image of God in which we are all made.

Volpi studied his lenses against the light from arched windows. Far too large for an office, the room contrived to be both cluttered and empty. Framed posters advertising previous exhibitions and stacks of old display panels did not make it more attractive. An ancient radiator ticked and bubbled.

'Do you have the slightest idea, Signor Duckworth,' the director sighed, his Neapolitan accent slow with gravelly irony, 'how much these things cost: the transport and insurance of priceless works of art; the restoration of this or that masterpiece in return for its loan; the promotions required to reach any kind of serious national, never mind international public; do you?'

He replaced his glasses, frowned at Samira, then reached toward her across his desk raising a peremptory eyebrow. Without a word or a smile, Samira handed him the portfolio.

Morris kept calm. Do you have any idea, *caro* Dottor Gluttony, he could easily have replied, how much *I* am worth? A worldwide wine export business. Major construction contracts all over the Veneto. A fortune in real estate. Do you have even the slightest notion, he could have gone on, of the depth and extent of my reading and culture? Please do not treat as a crass Veronese entrepreneur a man who has studied English Literature at the best university *in the world* and whose thirty years in Italy have been spent visiting every art exhibition imaginable.

Morris could have thus replied, with appropriate hauteur and icy conviction, and some years ago, no doubt, he would have done just that, in a fit of indignant pique, and with a certain acquired Veronese resentment towards slovenly southerners occupying important posts in the public administrations of the north. There were so many of them. But Massimina had been working hard of late to teach her earthly charge patience. Reaction is weakness, Morrees, hostility is defeat. You must come across as the director's friend. You and he will be working together, you know. Don't let them provoke you.

Morris kept his mouth shut.

Dottor Volpi opened the folder and began to leaf through the pages. As he did so his right knee started to jerk rhythmically on the ball of his foot so that the flesh on thighs and flanks quivered under his loose clothes. Looking at one image, he drew in his breath sharply, grunted and shook his head. His right hand scratched distractedly behind his left ear.

Gross theatrics, Morris thought.

Now the director began to lick his index finger to turn the pages faster and faster, almost as fast as his knee was jerking. This went on for some minutes, then the jerking stopped. Volpi drew a deep breath, closed the folder, rested both podgy hands on it, looked up at Samira again, stared at her for a moment as if at some exotic flower blossoming in a winter window box, then handed it back.

'*Grazie* Signorina, er . . . ?'

'Al Zuwaid. Samira Al Zuwaid.'

'Ah, of course,' the director smiled with avuncular benevolence, then gave a little push on the desk to swivel his bulk toward Morris.

'Bizarre, Signor Duckworth. Quite bizarre, I have honestly never seen a proposal like it.'

Morris smiled generously.

'Bizarre and, alas, impossible.'

Morris sustained his smile.

'Giotto, Botticelli, Caravaggio' – the director rocked gently back and forth as he listed the names – 'Titian, Poussin, Delacroix' – each painter was accompanied by a little shake of the head – 'Bouguereau, Breugel, Cézanne.' He sighed deeply. 'Warhol, Koons, Hirst.' He looked up: 'Plus any number of minor artists.'

'Artemisia Gentileschi,' Morris pointed out.

'Indeed, indeed, the delightful Gentileschi, so we have men *and* women.'

'Men and woman.'

'One is quite enough,' Volpi opined. He frowned, then with belated graciousness added: 'Especially if she is as charming as Signorina El Zaiwud.'

'Al Zuwaid,' Samira corrected.

'Ah,' Volpi coughed. 'Of course. *Chiedo scusa.*' His breasts quivered. 'Where was I? Oils, etchings, sculptures. Wood, bronze, stone.' Again he was shaking his head as if this helped his powers of recall: 'Vases, tapestries, ivory inlays . . . Have I missed anything?'

'Ebony bas-relief.'

'Of course. Then: biblical legend, Greek myth, Roman myth, ancient history, modern history. The Renaissance, the baroque, Mannerism, Romanticism. Colonialism, tribalism, totemism. Impressionism, expressionism, modernism and postmodernism.'

Volpi spoke in a rapid monotone, as if to underline with what wearisome ease he had taken in the mad scope of Morris's proposal.

'Jack the Ripper,' Morris prompted. 'Photography.'

'Indeed. Nothing more murderous than photography. Regicide, parricide, matricide, fratricide, uxoricide, martyrdom, execution, murder with robbery, murder with rape . . .'

'Infanticide,' Morris chimed. 'Pietro Testa's *Massacre of the Innocents* is particularly powerful, don't you think?'

'A skewered newborn is bound to impress,' Volpi conceded.

'Going back to your list, though, Dottore,' Morris asked, 'how would you categorise Pentheus' demise? Can we accuse the Bacchae of lynching?'

'Idioticide?'

'Excellent!' Morris laughed. 'The Paul Reid is a curious version, *n'est-ce pas?*'

'You're a generous critic, Signor Duckworth. Paul Reid is not an artist we've ever shown at Castelvecchio. Or planned to show. So, what else?' Poised to launch into another list the director stopped and frowned.

'Daggers?' Morris suggested. 'Swords, guns, nails, hammers, stones, arrows, and, er, bare hands. Strangling.'

Exactly as he said the word, a thought spoke very clearly in Morris's mind: would *I* have the strength? Could I ever *strangle*? Surely Dottor Volpi's neck was far too thick. It would have to be the dagger.

'Thank you Signor Duckworth. And when it comes to gathering in this, er, curious phantasmagoria, we have, let me see, the Louvre, the Uffizi, the National Gallery, the Metropolitan, the Rijksmuseum.'

'The Prado, the Tate, the Frick,' Morris added.

'Quite.'

The director blew out both huge cheeks then slowly and noisily expired between pursed lips.

'It's too much, Signor Duckworth.'

'For one visit, no doubt,' Morris smiled. 'We'll have them all coming back. Perhaps twice. What was the picture that made you chuckle, by the way?'

'Did I?'

With his elbows on the desk, Volpi was now rubbing his chin up and down against cradled fingertips, as if to test the roughness of his beard. The man couldn't keep still.

'Von Stuck,' he acknowledged.

'Ah. Yes. One of five Holofernes, I think.'

'Rather more Judith in this case,' Volpi remarked drily. 'Stuck never missed a chance to paint the pudenda.'

'It's a bold image.'

'For most visitors "unwholesome" would seem a more appropriate epithet.'

'Needless to say, Professor Volpi' – Morris was determined to insist on his seriousness – 'we'd be looking at a section of the show that compares images of men killing women with others of women killing men, on opposite walls perhaps. Or in pairs. So much of human violence is about the sexes, don't you think?'

A pained expression had formed on Volpi's face. It lingered a while in the creases around his eyes. Morris waited till it rippled away into the hinterlands of temples and jaw, then spoke up again.

'Isn't it curious, for example, Direttore – by the way I'm never sure if I should be calling you Direttore, Dottore or Professore – that whether the women are the victims or the killers, they do tend to be nude. You must have noticed. As if they killed with their . . .'

'Charms,' the director said, nodding graciously toward Samira who remained eloquently mute.

'And there's no need for you to call me anything at all, Signor Duckworth. Anything at all.'

'Delilah, Salome.' Morris was enthusing. He frowned: 'Of course, if we imagine another section dedicated to political conflict, we find ourselves faced with the question: how should we classify the Stuck? What was a political, or even religiously inspired killing in Holy Scripture is now an emblem of women's liberation.'

'Misogyny rather,' the director opined.

'The two are not unrelated,' Morris pointed out. He was still feeling pleased with himself for having said Holy Scripture rather than Bible. A flourish he owed to Antonella.

Rather suddenly Volpi started to shake his huge head from side to side, the way dogs will suddenly stand up and shake themselves free from torpor, or river water, or just the dirt they've been rolling in. Cheeks and jowls slapped. Chest and paunch juddered. He stopped, drew a noisy breath, thrust his chair decisively back from his desk and looked straight at Morris.

'Enough. This is all quite impossible. Castelvecchio is a serious museum, Signor Duckworth. It has, as you know, an international reputation, largely thanks to Carlo Scarpa's restoration of the building in the sixties. People come from all over the world to study the avant-garde arrangement of space here. That said, there is no way a Verona-based institution could persuade so many important museums to relinquish works by major painters for a show that would largely be construed as frivolous, if not morbid or merely sensational.'

Morris uncrossed and recrossed his legs. He seemed lost in thought. 'I'm not sure,' he eventually said, with great circumspection, as if determined not to offend, 'whether the adverb "merely" is really appropriate before the adjective "sensational", Dottor

Volpi. What do you think? Surely, exactly what people are looking for when they come to a place like Castelvecchio and pay their twelve euros or so, is a *sensational* show.' He hesitated, 'Forgive my pedantry, Professore, I began my, er, career, we can call it that I hope, as a humble language teacher. So I have a certain attention to words. "Frivolous", for example. Are we really sure that in an age that has given us the assassination of Osama Bin Laden, of Colonel Gaddafi, possibly of Lady Diana, and going a little further back of Mrs Gandhi, John Lennon, Martin Luther King, Aldo Moro, Giovanni Falcone, President Kennedy – an age, what's more, obsessed by serial killers, sectarian slaughter and genocide, are we sure we can call the subject of murder *frivolous*? There is an important moral message in this show, as I see it: that when a stalled and conflicted society or even just a man–woman relationship fails to change by negotiation, then someone will pull out a knife or a gun, or worse still strap a bomb to his belly.'

Pronouncing the word belly, Morris faltered, so present and grotesque was Volpi's exemplum of the species. Imagine a bomb strapped to that! Then fearing he might start to smile, or be caught exchanging knowing glances with Samira, he hurried on:

'Actually I was discussing this matter on the phone only yesterday with my old friend James Bradburne.'

That should wake the fat slug up.

'Director of the Strozzi museum, as I'm sure you know. James and I were at Cambridge together.'

Over the years Morris had noticed how Italians seemed willing to believe that all English-speaking persons of any note or class had all been to the same school or university. No doubt there were historical reasons for this.

'I'm a great admirer of the shows he's been putting on since he took over there at Palazzo Strozzi, don't you think, rather in the teeth of the traditional old Florentines, you know what a superiority complex they have, very brave man, I particularly enjoyed *Money and Beauty*, you know, the Botticelli, Bonfire of the Vanities thing, overambitious perhaps, and certainly overpraised, but always stimulating – you'll have your own opinion of course. So naturally I discussed what I was planning with him.'

There must be a very considerable rearrangement of mental furniture going on, Morris thought, in Mr Snob Director's prejudiced skull as he tried to process this new information: Morris's friendship with Europe's most adventurous museum director. Two years ago Trevisan Wines had managed to supply their Classico Superiore to a banquet at Palazzo Strozzi, Morris cadging an invitation to the event in return for a gift of a hundred bottles. Whether Bradburne had actually gone to Cambridge or not, he hadn't the slightest idea, having never actually spoken to the man; all he'd learned was that he had a very powerful handshake and wore fussily fanciful waistcoats.

'As I was saying, my friend James raised exactly the objection you've advanced. He thought it might be, what was the word he used, *nobler*, yes, and metaphysically more challenging, to have a show focusing on death in general rather than the particular category of murder. He was worried about questions of taste. To which I pointed out that people have a natural and understandable reluctance to contemplate the event of death, unless packaged in the, er, *alibi* of melodrama, of murder. Or even of political expediency. The recent spate of Arab terrorism almost demands a reflection on killing. Still, to cut a stimulating discussion short, he came on board in the end, in rather a big way actually, to the point of saying that if you and I couldn't do the show here in Verona, which of course I'd much prefer, loving the town as I do, he'd very much like to have a *shot* at it himself, as it were, at Palazzo Strozzi.'

Dottor Volpi was watching Morris carefully.

'Signor Duckworth,' he said quietly, 'I'm aware of course that you have various members of our board of directors on your side over this, not to mention our, er, dynamic First Citizen, the mayor.' He smiled. 'You seem to have a long acquaintance with many people in positions of local power. Otherwise we wouldn't be having this meeting, would we?'

'Presidente Carbone did ask,' Morris acknowledged, 'if I might contribute to the renovation of your East Wing.'

This was not an out-and-out lie. Morris had simply reversed the direction of approach. He had personally offered to pay for it.

'However,' Volpi continued, 'the last word on any shows at the museum I direct remains with me.'

'As it should,' Morris agreed. 'Very much as it should.'

'A serious museum can't allow any Gaio or Tizio simply to *pay* to have their own show.'

'No, of course, that wouldn't be appropriate at all. And let me say, Dottor Volpi . . .' Morris stopped. Finding the right word would be crucial.

'Yes?'

'Let me say I share your, er,' he sighed, '*reservations* as to the, how shall I say, cultural credentials of representatives of the Northern League.'

This was a serious bid for complicity. Two outsiders, one Neapolitan, one English, could join forces against Veronese provincialism. The museum director sat tight. He appeared to reflect, waited, as if to allow a brief indisposition or unpleasant smell to pass, then continued.

'But let's imagine that we did decide to go ahead with *Painting Death*. Just imagine, mind.'

'I'm sure you won't regret it.'

'The first question would be, who would curate such a show? Frankly, given the range of styles and periods covered and the generally unorthodox approach, I can't immediately think of anyone.'

'I will,' Morris said boldly. He hadn't planned to say this. He hadn't supposed the opportunity would come up. But the moment he said it he knew he wanted this more than anything else in the world: *to curate his own art exhibition*. Morris Duckworth! He wanted it more than his business empire, now run largely by others. More than sex with Samira. More than ownership of a palazzo on Via Oberdan. More than the rather silly title of honorary citizen. More than getting his son out of a police cell. Morris *had to* curate this show. If for no other reason than that this was *his* show. The show *was* him. Murder. Suddenly he knew something terribly important was at stake, even if he couldn't quite have explained what.

'Signor Duckworth, the curator of a museum show has to be an academic with years of experience in the field and a proven track record, which is precisely my problem, when it comes to such an unusual theme.'

'You mean you don't know any academic murderers? Or murderous academics?'

'Very witty,' the director nodded. For the first time a real smile curled one corner of his mouth. 'It's not an accomplishment people normally include in their curriculum.'

Morris was now yearning to tell him: *You won't find anyone more experienced than me in this field, Dottor Volpi. For a killer of a show on killing you need a man who's killed and killed and killed again.* Instead he said: 'As I recall James Bradburne had the *Money and Beauty* show curated by some hack English journalist, not an art historian at all, what's his name?'

'No!' The director now made a very vigorous objection: 'No, you are quite wrong there. The *Money and Beauty* show, Signor Duckworth, which to my mind had very considerable shortcomings, was nevertheless curated, to all intents and purposes, I can assure you, by the highly reputed Florentine art historian and academic, Ludovica Sebregondi. Ted Parkes just wrote a few pathetically disrespectful captions. Bradburne brought him in, no doubt, as so-called vice curator, to catch the interest of the Anglo-Saxon press, to whom we are obliged, I'm afraid, to kowtow in the hope of attracting an international clientele. A clever move promotionally, but hardly good for the show as such.'

'Ted Parkes?'

'Sorry, Tom Parkes,' the director corrected himself. 'One of the many Americans making a sleazy living out of pretending to know something about Italy and generally spitting in the bowl he slops from.'

Morris was surprised at this level of animosity, though presumably its real target was Bradburne, a museologist, Morris felt, of real charisma and hence an envied competitor. Or perhaps Volpi just disliked Americans, or foreigners in general. In any case Morris sensed at once that he must second Volpi's grudges if ever he was to have the man on his side.

'I'm sure you're right,' he agreed. 'Like the hack who wrote the attack on Verona that I replied to in the British papers, what's his name, Anderton-Dodds.'

'Quite, Signor Duckworth, there are dozens of them. Tobias Joyce is another. The one who wrote *The Black Hole of Italy*.'

'Unreadable,' Morris agreed, having heard only distant rumours of the tome. What was the point of reading about Italy when you lived the beautiful nightmare every day?

'They just play to the Northern League's position,' Volpi went on, giving himself away entirely now. Morris was delighted.

'All the same, Dottor Volpi,' he said, 'I suggest we take a leaf out of Bradburne's book. Make me a pin-up curator, as it were, or vice curator, to excite the foreign press, and put me alongside a scrupulously respectable art historian who will make it an excellent show. Yourself, for example. It would be such an honour to work with you. I can't tell you.'

Volpi seemed to be aware he had said too much. He settled his bulk.

'Signor Duckworth, one doesn't curate a show in one's own museum.'

'Does etiquette prevent that?'

'Some sort of hierarchy and separation of roles needs to be preserved, don't you think?' Dottor Volpi frowned. 'Am I right, Signorina Wuzid?'

'Zuwaid,' she corrected.

'*Le chiedo scusa.*' The director's eyes lingered on the young woman a little longer than they ought to have. Samira accepted the gaze without embarrassment.

'Actually it's Tim Parkes,' she said then. 'He lives here in Verona.'

'I beg your pardon?'

'It's Tim. Not Tom or Ted. He's English not American.'

'Oh Parkes.'

'I don't think we really need to worry about the scribbler's Christian name,' Morris rebuked her gently. It was the first foot she'd put wrong all afternoon. What was the point of showing up the director on such an irrelevance?

'Signor Duckworth.'

Announcing the name, the director placed both hands on his desktop and with awesome slowness levered himself to his feet. Upright, he was rather smaller, or at least shorter, than one would have expected, and as a result even rounder. 'Let us proceed as follows. I will ask Professor Zolla, the museum's resident art historian, to approach the appropriate foreign museums with requests for loans of, er, some, just some, mind, of the paintings you indicate. Only the paintings. In the remote event that we do get a sufficient number of positive responses, I shall allow the show to go ahead with yourself and Zolla, who is an excellent and meticulous academic, as co-curators. If, on the other hand, as I expect, we get refusals across the board, then we shall have no choice but to shelve the project.'

Morris jumped to his feet to take a hand he thought had been extended but that Volpi now tried to withdraw. Perhaps he had only reached out to steady himself on the desk. In any event, Morris grabbed it, squeezed it and held it tight. 'Thank you so much,' he said warmly. 'That's very generous. However, Dottore, there is one important detail you are unaware of.'

The director waited, his eye straying to Samira who had also got to her feet and was wriggling down the hem of her dress.

'I own all the paintings.'

The director was too bewildered to reply.

'Only a half-dozen are originals, of course. But I have had all the rest professionally copied, in the original dimensions, with identical frames.'

Having made the very considerable effort of fighting himself to his feet, the director now slumped down in his chair again. Morris stood over him, as David over the defeated Goliath.

'So where museums are unwilling to give us the originals,' he said cheerfully, 'we might, er, integrate the collection with copies. So much art is a question of copying, isn't it? All the crucifixions, the Madonnas, scores of Holofernes, scores of Salomes. Often four or five versions of the same painting by the same artist. Or by other artists, imitating this, altering that. We could make it a theme of the show: spot the copy. Like a whodunit. Copying is a kind of murder in the end, don't you think? Killing the original with its double. Killing the first flourish with the follow-up. So the art critics say. Let's call their bluff!'

He paused and smiled radiantly. 'Let's do something really *different* is what I say, Dottor Volpi. Something that will make people sit up and talk about us, about Castelvecchio, about the wonderful city of Verona. The art press worldwide would go crazy.'

The Duckworth Foundation would be global news.

'Signor Duckworth,' the director eventually said, 'you are mad.'

Morris made a small bow: 'Morris Arthur Duckworth at your service,' he said, and taking Samira's arm with ostentatious intimacy, he showed himself out.

CHAPTER FIVE

IT GRIEVED MORRIS THAT he couldn't show Samira The Art Room. In the flat in San Zeno she sat astride him, rocking gently.

'*Caro*,' she whispered. She liked to lean forward and trace a finger along his scars.

From mouth to eye the nerves sang. 'Sammy,' Morris responded.

He wanted her to see that wonderful Stuck and of course Bonnaud's magnificent Salome with the Baptist's head beside the lovely lady, still very much part of the conversation on its golden plate.

'Darling,' she sighed. 'I'm so close.'

Then she would realise that Morris was much, much more than a dull businessman. Or even a generous lover. Morris was one who moved between the living and the dead, between experience and art.

'Let me keep you company,' he murmured, pushing gently.

The problem was not so much Antonella, or the children. There were always moments when he could rely on their being out of the house. The maid was trickier, since Maddalena's loyalty to Antonella was absolute. But in the end Morris could have got round her too. The real hurdle was Massimina. The dear dead girl had made it plain that though she understood Morris's needs in this department, she absolutely would not countenance the Arab mistress on her territory. 'And you must say Mimi when you climax,' she insisted, rather coquettishly.

'It's been nearly thirty years, *cara*,' he had reminded her.

'I'm still *exactly* as *I* was,' she told him. 'The years don't pass for me, Morrees.'

'Sam-mimi,' he gasped, 'Sam-mimi.'

The girl fell forward on his chest and he circled her with his arms.

'What a cute little nickname,' she whispered.

Morris had met Samira at the university. As head of a company that offered frequent internships to local students, he had been invited on Careers Day to say a few words about what he looked for in a new recruit.

'A willingness to do anything the company requires, however menial on the one hand or intellectually challenging on the other,' he said grandly. 'And a talent for thinking outside the box.'

In reality Morris mostly had his interns phoning through lapsed client files, making coffee and photocopies, shredding oceans of incriminating correspondence and queuing in public offices to deposit and retrieve the documents that established the official version of events. All for very low pay or none at all, since these kids were usually from families who had far more than Morris Duckworth had ever had at their age. It was experience they needed, not money. But when someone particularly smart and personable turned up, male or female, then Morris might decide to take the child under his wing and let them work by his side for three or even six months. It cheered life up and gave them a chance to see how hectic things could be at the top. 'You'll never want to be successful after this,' he would joke.

On occasion, over the years, such arrangements had led to a little affair or two, to the mutual benefit, Morris was sure, of both parties. In fact, Morris had been rather scandalised at first to discover how natural and even ordinary these respectable young Catholic girls found the situation. Like ducks to water, he would mutter to himself. Or Duckworths to blood. He laughed and would have feared for his daughter, if Massimina Duckworth wasn't so evidently woven from a stronger moral fibre than the girls her father bedded. In any case Morris would have strictly forbidden her from taking part in any such shady internship.

Scruples aside, it would have been hard to imagine a more ideal situation: the official work relationship gave a cover for being seen in the company of a charming young woman, while the strictly circumscribed duration of the internships put a sensible sell-by date on any developing intimacy. Samira was in fact the first mistress he had held on to after the relationship with Fratelli Trevisan had terminated. This was partly, Morris sensed, because she was also the last of this string of lovers. There would be no more young interns in his bed. It wasn't so much that at fifty-five the managing director of Fratelli Trevisan felt too old to seduce, just that over the years what had started as excitement and evasion had become routine. He knew the ropes too well. All of a sudden everything in his life had to change, Morris realised. He was moving into a new phase. The show was part of it. And so was Samira.

Now she padded about the flat in just her tee shirt and panties, cleaning up in the bathroom, making one of her herb teas in the kitchen. What attracted Morris, beyond the obvious physical charms, were the young woman's poverty, her foreignness and her healthy opportunism. She had milked Morris for all he was worth, in rent and clothes and even jewels, and he had been happy to oblige, knowing that this generosity exonerated him from any responsibility in her regard. It was even encouraging that she had this charming and rather severe younger brother Tarik to keep an eye out and hold her in check, otherwise there were occasions when you felt Samira might have got seriously out of line.

She rolled a cigarette with a little dope. Morris, who never smoked cigarettes, and who actually believed that smoking, like obesity, was a weakness and a sin, nevertheless allowed himself a couple of leisurely puffs in her company.

'By the way, I found three more killing pictures for you to go and see,' she said now. Sitting very erect behind the glass table, there was something of the pharaoh about her, a kind of lush rigidity which Morris immensely appreciated and sometimes wondered if he might not be falling in love with.

'Another Death of Absalom. That's in Conegliano. I've got the details at the office. One Moses slaying the Egyptian. In Ca' di David I think. Pretty rare. And a martyrdom of San Bartolomeo. I can't remember where that was. Ilasi?'

'Excellent.' Morris loved the fact that she kept thinking business despite the intimate interlude.

'Not famous painters, I don't think. But the catalogues are such a mess. Scribbled file cards bundled into cupboards twenty years ago.'

'Doesn't matter. Get the details and we'll go and look. Be a nice day out.'

'Morris!' she smiled and cocked her head to one side. 'I'm learning so much with you. I could take an exam in Christian culture!'

'Sammy. I'm glad! You could be St Sammy!'

There were times, Morris thought, when having an affair was far more a virtue than a vice.

But now his young mistress was frowning.

'About those requests for the paintings, though. For the show.'

'At Castelvecchio?'

'How can you be sure that fat pig will actually make them? I think he'll just wait a while, then pretend they were all turned down.'

Morris hadn't thought of that, but didn't want to show it.

'I'll ask for the requests to be copied to me as co-curator.'

'He really didn't like you, you know.'

But Morris was feeling marvellously confident.

'It's irrelevant. His hands are tied. The government is making big cuts in its cultural budget. The museum needs the money I've offered. What's more' – Morris took a deep puff on her cigarette and beamed through his dizziness – 'it's a brilliant idea for a show. Isn't it? People will come in droves.'

She smiled. 'It is a wonderful idea, Morris.'

He thought for a moment. 'Obviously Titian's big *Cain and Abel* must come right at the entrance, the first thing you see as you walk in, for maximum impact: the murder that set history in motion.'

'Moslems have that story too,' she said.

Morris sensed an idea coming, but had to make an effort to formulate it. The dope seemed to have made his body lighter.

'Which, when you think about it,' he said, 'was largely God's fault.'

Blowing out smoke, Samira twisted her pretty mouth into a question; it was the expression of the smart student asking a charismatic teacher to explain.

'Cain was a tiller of the ground,' Morris reflected, hardly knowing himself what he meant. 'Abel was a shepherd. As I remember. They made an offering to God, Cain of his crops, Abel of a lamb. Sort of vegetarian versus carnivore. God respected Abel's offering, but not Cain's. That's the word in the Bible. Respect. Then when vegetarian Cain asked what he'd done wrong, God wouldn't say. You get the feeling it was just because Cain was a crop farmer and not a shepherd. Simple as that. He didn't have red meat to offer. I mean, the way someone is born poor and someone else rich. Or someone black and someone white. God respects one and not the other. No wonder the man was resentful.'

The girl watched him intently.

'It's the kind of thing they never put in the captions of course.'

She nodded.

'But they should, they really should. If you know the story, it changes the image. Maybe Cain was right.'

She folded her arms and sat straight-backed and perfectly still at the glass table, a faint smile on her lips. Behind her was the kitchen corner where she cooked her Arab soups and stews and on the walls to each side the patterned hangings in shades of earth and orange that she liked so much. Morris felt pleasantly bohemian.

'Did Tarik tell you I asked him to get involved? To write some captions. I thought it would be great to get an Arab point of view. Unusual.'

She shook her head, watching. It was extraordinary how willing she was to hang on his every word.

'Unfortunately, he refused. To be honest, he seemed a bit hostile.'

Samira smiled. 'I'll try to bring him round. It would do him good. But sometimes my little brother thinks he should avoid all involvement, you know, with the West.'

'Hardly possible if he goes to the LSE.'

'He thinks he can learn something like economics without compromising himself, then take the knowledge back home, uncontaminated.'

'I can sympathise with that,' Morris said. 'By the way, did he like the coat I bought?'

'He's wearing it all the time,' she smiled. 'He loves leather. But he'll never say thank you. He's too proud.'

'I get that with my son,' Morris agreed. He was on the sofa, his head thrown back, arms stretched out on the upholstery. They sat quietly for a minute and more. Morris couldn't remember ever having sat like this with a woman before. It was different from the sort of silence he sometimes enjoyed with Antonella where both were simply getting on with their own thoughts as if the other weren't present at all. Here on the contrary there was a strange reaching out, from both sides, across the half-dark of the unlit room at evening. She smiled and smoked and looked at him intently from behind the table, as if something important were happening.

'What are you thinking?' Morris suddenly wanted to know.

Samira leaned forward: 'I was thinking of a game.'

'Oh yes?'

'What if people going to the show had to solve a murder, find clues in paintings that would solve a mystery? Who did a murder or where a body has been hidden.'

Morris was taken aback. He tried to think, but felt disoriented. Dope was definitely a vice. 'That's brilliant,' he agreed. 'That's a wonderful idea. We can fit it in with spotting copies and originals.' He frowned. Why did he feel disconcerted? 'The only thing is I doubt whether Volpi would come on board. He seems hopelessly conservative. There's nothing worse than a southerner in the northern provinces.'

'He's another thing I was thinking about,' Samira chuckled. Her voice was deeper when she laughed. She lit another cigarette and sat back, pushing her dark hair from her forehead. Near naked as she was, there was a triumphant womanhood about her. She was full of life and enjoying it.

'If we need to fix him,' she smiled, 'nothing would be easier.'

'Fix him?'

'Well, you saw the way he looked at me.'

Morris tried to think. 'Not really, no.'

'Oh come on, Mo, it was obvious.'

'Was it?' Morris didn't like this. She seemed amused that he hadn't been aware.

'I'm just saying, you know, if you gave me the word, I could put him in all kinds of trouble.'

Morris couldn't quite grasp what she was saying.

'I mean if he's really standing in your way. I'll just give him the come-on. Then we can blackmail him.'

'We can what? Sammy!'

'Only if you give the word, Morris.'

'I would never let another man touch you,' Morris said sharply. He was upset. 'And most of all not a monstrous beast like Volpi. He'd crush you.'

In his agitation Morris stood up and walked to the window that looked down over a narrow side street where snow had begun to fall through the December twilight. How was it that just when something was beginning to seem idyllic, suddenly it turned out to be exactly the opposite: rotten and putrid and filthy. Only Massimina had never let him down in this regard.

Still looking out into the street, he said in a low voice:

'How can you even think of it? What would Tarik say? He'd be furious!'

Samira cocked her head in amusement.

'My brother is not my keeper.'

'Well, he should be! And you can be damn sure he wouldn't want his sister fucking a greasy old pig like that.'

'Tarik doesn't want me to be fucking you,' she said evenly. 'But it's none of his business, is it? I don't ask him who he's fucking and he's no angel.'

'You can't compare me with Volpi!'

'I'm not, but Tarik would.' She laughed. 'Come on, Mo, I'm not your wife.'

Morris was nonplussed. He hated conversations like this.

Samira sat with her legs crossed, a smouldering cigarette between her fingers. Now it was she who had the confidence of maturity, while he was just an insecure middle-aged adolescent hovering at a windowsill. Morris turned his back to her and stared out at the thickly falling flakes, willing them to mesmerise him with their silent whiteness, to return him to childhood perhaps, to the time he had held Mother's hand in sooty snow singing 'Once in Royal David's' outside St Bart's on the Uxbridge Road. Morris vaguely remembered a certain confusion in his infant mind between the slums of Park Royal and the Royal Jerusalem. What suckers the English were for royalty!

Mother had breathed her last in the Royal Free.

Mother.

Outside the dark cobbles were already white and the street lights had come on. White and pure.

'Fact is,' the voice behind his back was saying, 'a smart young woman can get pretty well all the money and attention she wants these days, if she has a mind for it, can't she? Men will never say no. And I can't see any harm in that. It's her business what she does with her body.'

Shifting his attention Morris found his concubine's reflection in the dark gloss of windowpane. She was bent over her lighter, the flame illuminating a beauty that was pure Caravaggio.

'What she can't get is a respectable position of her own. Independence.'

That was too much. Morris turned: 'But, Sammi, you *have* a job! And at the Cultural Heritage Department, for Christ's sake! Most young people would kill for that.'

'I have an internship that pays 500 a month for a max of six months. I can't live on that.'

'But *I* pay your rent.'

'That won't last forever, will it?'

'Yes, it will,' Morris said. Then he repeated: 'It will. Sammy, I'm a serious person. You must sense that. I'm mad about you.'

She laughed.

'Mo, you've had strings of internee girlfriends, you're not paying their rents now, are you?'

'No, I haven't!'

'But I can tell! Why deny it? I don't mind. It's been fun.'

This was very difficult. All of a sudden Morris wished he was at home in Via Oberdan with Antonella, Don Lorenzo and the children, Massimina perhaps banging out something clumsy on the piano. God rest ye merry gentlemen. He might light the logs in the big fireplace for once. He might even invite Stan over for Christmas sherry.

'Your son, for example,' Samira was saying, 'you're always telling me what a lazy ungrateful lout he is, but he'll still get himself a respectable job easily enough, which I never will.'

Morris couldn't quite see the point of this twist in the debate. She knew how painful it was for him to discuss his son.

'You'll give him a place in your company.'

'I will not!' Morris protested. 'I'll give him one internship like everyone else and nothing more. Same with my daughter. I want them to fight their own way in life, like I did.'

In the end, he suddenly thought, we all, like poor Cain, had to make our offerings and hope that God would find them acceptable, without having any idea what the odd fellow's tastes really were, meat or veg.

'Oh Morris!' With charming impulsiveness Samira suddenly stood up and came over to hug him. She buried her head in his chest and held him tight. 'I only said that about Volpi because I saw how much you wanted this show to happen. You really, really want it, don't you? It's the first time I've seen you so excited. I just thought, I won't let that fat pig stand in my man's way. I'll do something about it.'

In the glass of the window, Morris could now see his scarred face resting against a shock of raven hair above the bronze curves of her shoulders and the plump ball of her neat bum in black knickers.

'What was that lovely nickname you thought up for me?'

She was kissing his neck.

'Sammimi,' he muttered, then declared in a surprisingly croaky voice, 'If anyone stands in my way, *cara*, be sure I'll kill them long before they get their hands on you.'

CHAPTER SIX

THOUGHTS OF HIS OFFSPRING did indeed bring Morris pain. Walking home in the fresh snow, down Via Roma and across Piazza Bra, it occurred to him that he had still to buy them presents for Christmas. What though? What they deserved was a kick up the backside, both of them.

It was *aperitivo* time and the idle rich were steaming the windows of expensive cafés festooned with tinsel and piled high with red and gold boxes of *pandori* and *pannettoni*. People with money were enjoying themselves. Glancing in at the jollity and warmth, Morris remembered that Christmas was supposed to be a time of truce; the white snow fell mainly to remind you to open a bottle and not be Scroogey. In spite of all, then, he should try to please the brats, show his legendary Duckworth generosity. On the other hand the two 'lower-key m's' as he sometimes thought of Massimina and Mauro (minors of a major Morris) already had everything, and anything he gave them that they actually desired – a computer game for his son, what else? a graphic novel for his daughter – would only feed their crassness.

The Englishman stopped where the piazza opened out into a Christmas-card expanse of snowy cedars and old-fashioned street lamps, the eighteenth-century café-culture frivolity of the Liston to his left and the ornamented arch of Porta Nuova like some crusty old Austrian uncle to his right. Behind it all, majestically floodlit, the looming pile of the arena gave a stony substance to that antique past compared with which, Morris thought, this present moment is just the blink of an unseeing eye.

Drifting crystals tickled his nose and ears. Slowing his step to take it all in, he felt at once immensely privileged to live in such a beautiful and above all solemn place – *there is no world without Verona walls!* – yet full of regret that somehow he could never really feel part of it. He was here, but not here. Morris had always felt that. An honorary citizen now, but not a real citizen. Would *Painting Death* put that right at last, put him at the centre of Veronese society, or simply define with even greater finality his condition of resident alien, well-to-do murderer?

Suddenly, Morris desperately wanted to be indulgent, to make amends, bury hatchets. What if he appeased Mauro, he wondered, perhaps, with some football-related gift? Knuckledusters? Morris laughed. What if he gave Massimina a subscription to some awful manga mag? He had tried so hard over the years to make his family into a work of art, to have the children become the wonderful people they ought to have been. Unfailingly, unflaggingly, he had pointed the dear creatures with their unformed minds in the right direction. There had been piano lessons and dance classes, judo and singing. There had been catechism and Sunday school. There had been operas and concerts and art exhibitions. There had been Tonbridge School, for Christ's sake. Culture didn't come more expensive than that. Yet nothing had stuck. Even these fugitive snowflakes in the December dusk had more adhesive power than the great art Morris Duckworth had sought to thrust upon his refractory children.

Morris started to walk again, fast, very fast. For heaven's sake, snap out of it, he told himself. After all, if the children didn't fit the frame, he would simply make his art elsewhere. Hadn't that always been the logic of The Art Room? And of *Painting Death*. Morris had a genius and it would out. On a sudden optimistic impulse he slipped into the palatial splendour of La Costa's, ordered himself a negroni at the bar and pulled out his iPhone.

'*L'Arena di Verona,*' a languid female voice responded.

'Domenico Belpoliti, please, the cultural page.'

'Pronto?'

'Salve Domenico, come andiamo?'

Morris had given Belpoliti interviews in the past about his company's sponsorship of cultural events.

'Discretamente,' the pompous young man told him. *'Discretamente be-ne.'*

'Listen, Domenico, I just thought you might want to know – sort of in advance, if you see what I mean, of the imminent press conference – that today we, er, probably best if I don't say who exactly, we decided on July . . . yes, next July, for this big exhibition we're planning . . . you hadn't heard? . . . at Castelvecchio. Yes . . . *Painting Death,* that's the title . . . Yes, yes, you can definitely say it will be the most ambitious show in the museum's history. Absolutely . . . A hundred masterpieces – give or take a sketch or two – showing mankind's centuries-old inability to do without, well, killing . . . Alas, yes! There you are. Hardly Christmas fodder, I know, though there was the Massacre of the Innocents of course, a glitch in the festive season that tends to get edited out. Do you know Breugel's version, in the snow? . . . Yes, Dutch skaters and all. Hard to believe. Sort of white Christmas with freshly butchered babes. It'll be there! Museum politics permitting. One can't put one's hand on one's heart for every work . . . Oh, entirely sponsored by the Duckworth Foundation, I'm proud to say . . . Extremely contemporary theme when you think about it, terrorism too, yes, suicide bombers, genocide . . . Many of the world's most famous museums . . . This time I'll be taking an active part in organising the show myself . . . Not sure if you could actually say the curator, I'm a bit busy to go the whole hog, but certainly the ideas man . . . Oh no doubt about it, quite a development. Yes. But you were aware I collected works of art in this field? . . . Many years now. No, not suicides. Suicide I find depressing . . . Well, Sickert, for example. You know Walter Sickert's work? . . . Some people actually thought he might be the Ripper himself, painting his victims . . . Truth definitely stranger than fiction . . . A Gentileschi too . . . *Sì*

Signore, the real thing, I have it, right here in Via Oberdan. But there are more than a dozen versions, you know. She couldn't stop beheading poor Holofernes. The face of Judith is a self-portrait apparently. Revenge for being raped early on in life, they say. You know her story . . . Ha ha, yes, very good, the women, any excuse. Watch out for the kitchen knives! . . . A Stuck too. Otto Dix. A Frey-Moock . . . You like Stuck? Hard not to . . .'

When the president of the Duckworth Foundation finally closed the call he was in a savagely complacent mood again. It would feel pretty damn marvellous to be reading all of that in tomorrow's papers, and even better to think of Volpi reading it.

So now, Morris thought, eyeing up the potent orange drink that winked at him from the pearly grey granite of the city's most expensive bar with neatly waistcoated waiters in attentive attendance and a perfumed parade of mink and sable swishing and crackling behind his elegant chrome-and-leather barstool – now for a pleasant evening with wifey at home-sweet-luxury-home after a healthy fuck with my dusky mistress in the icy Veronese afternoon. Here's to living, Morris A. D.!

The negroni went down in a gulp.

Don Lorenzo was dining with them which meant the problem of meat again. Morris had gone vegetarian almost a decade ago after watching a documentary on industrial pig farming in California. 'It's not the actual killing,' he always explained – for some reason vegetarians always had to explain themselves while meat-eaters never did – 'but the fact that they don't even allow these animals a life in the first place. Oh, if I knew they'd been killed in a fair fight, I'd eat 'em up gristle and bone.'

Some months later Antonella had joined him in abstention, though strictly 'for health reasons' she always said, for, as Morris reflected, it would have implied criticism of others if she had taken her husband's moral position; 'others' like Don Lorenzo, who always declared that a meal wasn't a meal without thick red meat on the table and a heavy red wine to wash it down, this despite the man's crippled wraith physique and general aura of asthmatic asceticism.

The charming upshot was that Mauro and Massimina, who had neither of them darkened a church door in years, were more likely to grace the family with their presence when the ancient priest was their dinner guest than at any other time. For if Morris had never been one to force his dietary habits on others and would gladly have eaten whatever was on the family menu, minus the kill, Antonella was made of sterner stuff: healthy food – be it lentils or risotto or pasticcio di melanzane – she declared, was equally healthy for everyone and to have *la povera* Maddalena, whose own health was so poor, slave to produce two different menus merely for the benefit of carnivorous children would be a greater cruelty than shooting an electric bolt through the brain of a fattened heifer. Only in honour of Don Lorenzo, then, did such cruelty become admissible on the Duckworth dinner plates, and only when the limping priest hitched up his cassock and lowered his scrawny buttocks on to one of the stiff wooden seats around the great oak table did the children miraculously appear. Otherwise, while Morris and Antonella scooped up curried chick-peas or rice and khorasan, the lower-case m's would very probably be lolling on benches in Piazza Bra sinking their incisors into mutton kebabs in defiance of the mayor's recent edicts.

Don Lorenzo liked to be indulgent with the children. He had known them all their lives. In general he prided himself on being in touch with his flock, particularly the stray lambs, with always the benign assumption that they strayed only because they were lambs who, once adult, would be sheep enough to know they were better off in the fold. Blinking behind smeared glasses, the ancient priest leaned across the table to Mauro and announced, 'I used to go to football matches too, you know.'

Morris couldn't help but wonder if he had heard correctly.

'When I was in the seminary.'

Antonella smiled warmly.

Mauro, his chubby cheek still bruised, ear torn and right arm in plaster, was forking up chunks of beef that his vegetarian mother had carved up for him. She and Morris were eating a leek and mushroom quiche.

'What team?' the boy asked from a full mouth.

'Used to play, too,' Don Lorenzo went on. 'Right wing. We had matches against the Franciscans and the Dominicans. And the new recruits from Africa. There was even a cup.'

'Is that how you hurt your foot?' Massimina enquired. She too was making short work of a generous steak. No sooner were their plates empty, Morris knew, than the children would be gone. They had never understood the joys of conversation and certainly wouldn't be around for Bible-reading and prayers after sweet and brandy.

'Oh, no, that was later, Mimi.' The priest smiled at the girl as if she were even now still sitting on his knee. 'Juventus!' he told Mauro proudly. 'We used to see them when they played in Verona. Once or twice we even went to Turin.'

'Not Hellas?' Mauro protested. His naturally loud voice seemed to have more meat in it than the ageing priest's entire body. 'Not your home team? You could have watched Hellas every week.'

'Juve played so much better,' Don Lorenzo recalled complacently. He chuckled. 'I remember them putting five past Hellas once. Bettega. Causio. Five!' Still chuckling, the priest drew a razor-sharp knife across half a pound of tender flesh.

'*Juve merda,*' the young man muttered under his breath.

Morris watched the blood ooze.

'I beg your pardon!' Antonella demanded.

Swallowing, pointing his fork, Mauro insisted: 'For me football is about belonging and community. It's about who you are. Veronese. Born here, belong here. My town, my people. Winning and losing is for nobodies.'

Morris was impressed: from the carnage on his plate his son was claiming the moral high ground. With what unexpected gravitas!

'Oh, I was always more of a *sportivo* than a *tifoso,*' Don Lorenzo nodded cheerfully. It wasn't clear whether he had registered the indignation in the young man's voice.

'Anyone can support a winner,' Mauro complained. He had a lamentable habit of eating with one elbow on the table, his head propped on a fist. As he leaned forward over his food, his Hellas sweatshirt could barely contain his barrel chest. 'It takes passion,' he said vehemently, 'to support a side that always loses.'

Don Lorenzo laughed openly now. 'I think if one spends one's hard-earned money to go to a game, Mousie, it's only wise to make sure you get value and see some good football.'

'His *father's* hard-earned money,' Morris remarked.

'You have to remember, *caro*,' Antonella chipped in, 'that Don Lorenzo is not actually from Verona, are you?'

'Oh I'm a complete alien,' the priest coughed apologetically. 'Bussolengo,' he explained.

'Fantastic, ten kilometres away!' Mauro was sneering. 'The boys I'm on trial with were all from Bussolengo. It's one of the proudest Hellas fan clubs.'

Again Morris noted how the whole unhappy episode had stoked up the boy's self-esteem rather than the contrary. If some severe punishment wasn't forthcoming when the judges made up their minds, his son seemed well set for a life of thuggery.

'I suppose it's like supporting God against the Devil,' Massimina observed.

Amid the general perplexity that this bizarre remark aroused it was Morris who now asked, 'I beg your pardon, my girl?'

Massimina drained her wine, shook her long dark hair and giggled. 'I mean, supporting Juve, you're sure to win, aren't you? I bet all the priests support them. Like they support God against the Devil, since He's also bound to win.' Her voice had a tinkle of silver to her brother's booming brass.

'They're the devils, not us,' Mauro protested. 'We just fight our corner.' He began to hum the triumphal march from *Aida*: '*Forza giallo blù, giallo blù, giallo blù, giallo blùùùùùù.*'

Morris was surprised that Don Lorenzo wasn't more concerned

about the blasphemy he had just heard. 'Massimina,' he told his daughter, 'a Christian doesn't choose God because He's a winner but because He's good. It's not like Juve and Hellas. You couldn't say, I'll choose the Devil because he's closer to home.'

'Byron did.'

'Byron was hardly a Christian,' Morris pointed out. He had written his Part One Tripos dissertation on *Childe Harold* and loathed the poem. Making heroism out of defying one's Maker.

'Dante, then.'

The tall girl was swaying from side to side on her seat, raising her right hand, knife and all, to push away the long hair that immediately fell back across her laughing eyes and pouty upturned mouth.

'Dante did *not* support the Devil,' Antonella said with surprising severity. 'You really shouldn't talk such nonsense, Mimi.'

Morris saw his wife's strategy at once; to defuse the tension between beloved son and beloved Don she would lay into her daughter's patent stupidity.

But cheered by the abundant meat and wine, Massimina pressed on. At college, she told them, they had a project to create some modern illustrations for the *Inferno*. With computer graphics. Well it was obvious that when it came to Paolo and Francesca, Dante was on the sinners' side, which implied he was in favour of the Devil who'd made them sin and against God who was punishing them forever when it really wasn't necessary. 'I mean,' she finished, 'it's the only part of the poem with any real emotion. It's so sad that they have to be in hell because they loved each other.'

'They were in hell because they were adulterers,' Antonella said frostily.

'He couldn't help it if he fell in love with a married woman, could he? Or she with him.'

Morris was surprised at her obvious feeling. Could it be that his daughter, who with her slender shoulders and tall nervy neck suddenly seemed very attractive, was having an adulterous affair? With whom? A teacher?

'I can't help it if I was born Veronese,' Mauro chimed facetiously, 'and fell in love with Hellas.'

'Mauro, for heaven's sake, don't be so infantile!' Morris snapped.

'*Giallo blù, giallo blù, giallo blùùùùù,*' the boy smirked. Even his eyelashes were red. Those are definitely not my genes, Morris decided.

Don Lorenzo was smiling indulgently. '*Forza*, Mousie! I like your spirit!'

'The spirit that attacks unsuspecting policemen,' Morris reminded him.

Antonella was making urgent signs that they should change the subject.

'The authorities deliberately provoke us so that then they can demonise our town,' Mauro said. 'It's all set up. Papà, even you've seen how they're always trying to present Verona as a shithole.'

'A what?' Antonella was horrified, mostly for the benefit of Don Lorenzo, Morris thought.

'You should come with us and see. We're *forced* to be violent.'

'What rubbish!'

'Come on. I dare you. Come to a game.'

'I thought you'd been banned from going to games,' Morris objected sharply.

The boy grinned under his red hair. 'There may be ways round that.'

'What Dante was trying to say,' Massimina insisted, 'is that the world is more complicated than black and white. He definitely thought God got it wrong about Paolo and Francesca.'

'In a Christian view of things, God can't get it wrong,' Morris told her, exasperated. 'Because God is good. Isn't that right, Father?'

Having tucked away his meat, Don Lorenzo was sitting back from the battlefield, digging between molars with a toothpick.

'Sorry,' he said, 'there's a gap on the bottom right. It's the crown they put in.'

'I get the same thing,' Mauro agreed. 'I hate teeth.'

'Who says I have to have a Christian view of things?' Massimina asked dangerously.

'Don Lorenzo,' Morris turned to the family's spiritual guide, 'could it ever be right for us to feel sympathy for someone God has sent to hell? Surely after God has judged we no longer have any right to hold an opinion.'

As he spoke the words he was aware of a sudden change of tone in his voice, a sudden personal interest that went beyond rebutting his daughter and restoring domestic order. Hadn't he himself been feeling sympathetic to Cain just an hour or two before? A forebear who was surely in hell. There was silence while they waited for the elderly man to pull out three or four animal fibres from between his teeth and swallow them properly with another full glass of Trevisan's Classico Superiore.

'Well,' Don Lorenzo began wiping his mouth, 'Dante was of course excommunicated and posthumously accused of heresy; I believe Cardinal Rusconi has written a learned—'

'I *told* you!' Massimina squealed with delight.

But Mauro interrupted: 'How *did* you hurt your foot then?'

'I'm sorry?'

'Your foot. How did you get your bad foot if it wasn't playing football?'

Morris sometimes wondered if it was drug-taking that prompted his children's disturbing non sequiturs.

'My foot?' The priest paused, then smiled vaguely. 'But have I never told you?' He looked at Antonella. 'Did I never tell you about my foot? After all these years?'

'No, Padre.'

Don Lorenzo shook his head and dabbed at his dry lips.

'How extraordinary.'

'So how did you get it?' Mauro asked.

'Remarkable.'

They waited, Dante, heresy and Hellas all on hold; Don Lorenzo smiled wanly and wriggled off the purple stole he had so far kept round his cassock against the cold.

'Come on, then,' Massimina said impatiently. Plate clean, she was eager to be gone. Was it this adulterous lover that she was always texting, Morris wondered? Yet he felt certain she was still a virgin. Playing with love, he thought.

'I'll tell, if you promise you won't laugh,' Don Lorenzo eventually said.

'Why would we?' Antonella enquired.

'You'll see,' the Don smiled coyly. Then added: 'But why don't you try to guess first?'

Doesn't the old corpse love drawing attention to himself, Morris thought. Do admire my embalming, everybody.

'I'm sure we never would,' Antonella declared. 'Laugh, that is.'

'A horse trod on it.' Massimina tried.

'*Acqua!*' the old priest cried, as if they were playing hunt the thimble.

'Car ran over it.'

'*Acqua!*'

'You kicked a policeman.'

'Oh Mauro, really!'

'*Acqua freddissima,*' the old priest laughed. 'Or rather,' he added mischievously, 'it wasn't that that did the damage.'

'Savaged by a pit-bull?' Morris enquired innocently.

'*Acqua.*'

'Shot by a jealous husband!' Massimina was giggling again.

'Children, please!'

This Classico Superiore was definitely a couple of per cent stronger than it said on the bottle, Morris thought. They were undercharging.

'I'll give you a clue,' Don Lorenzo teased. 'Something fell on it.'

'A brick,' Mauro said at once.

'*Acqua.*'

Morris shook his head. 'Why would a brick be funny?'

For a few minutes then the Trevisan Duckworths, or Duckworth Trevisans, left aside questions of good and evil and tried to guess what object might have fallen on the priest's foot so many years ago, half crippling him for life.

'A wall,' Massimina said.

'*Acqua*.'

'A breviary,' Antonella said.

'*Acqua*.'

'Hard to see how a breviary could have done the damage,' Morris objected.

'The size of the one in church!'

'An aspergillum!'

Don Lorenzo grinned as he had another stab at his yellow teeth, all the time shaking a hoary head.

'A box,' Mauro tried.

'*Fuoco!* Or rather *fuocherellino*. What kind of box?'

Ah. They were getting close.

'A box of books. Of Bibles!'

The Don shook his head, smiling. But the moment of revelation was at hand, they could all feel it. What went in a box that could be heavy enough to have crushed poor Don Lorenzo's foot?

'A case of wine?' Antonella suggested. 'Not Trevisan's I hope.'

'*Acqua*. If that's not rather a contradiction,' Don Lorenzo quipped.

'Of whisky?'

'I don't think,' the priest observed sadly, 'that I've ever handled a case of whisky. Or brandy for that matter. Alas.'

Antonella folded her arms. 'We give up.'

'No, no,' both children cried.

They all studied Don Lorenzo who seemed remarkably pleased with himself; like a dead man, Morris found himself thinking, asking you to guess how he's died. The door opened with its customary creak and Maddalena came into the room to collect the plates. She too dragged her feet these days; she too had one foot in the grave. Or rather, now one, now the other.

'Shall I bring in the sweet, Signora?' she asked.

In one of those flashes that made Morris the genius he most undoubtedly was he shouted: 'Coffin!'

Don Lorenzo looked at him in amazement.

'Yes,' he said.

'A coffin?' Mauro burst into pretended laughter.

Morris felt a sudden cold prickle of pins and needles running down the inside of his leg. What on earth was funny about a coffin?

'Ma povero Don Lorenzo!' Antonella exclaimed. She was trying hard not to laugh, which Morris found rather endearing.

'I was just waving incense over it before they lifted it into the *loculo,*' the Don remembered, 'when one of the bearers fainted, the one beside tried to grab him and the thing came crashing down right on my ankle.'

There was a short silence while they all tried to imagine the scene. Something like 150 kilos of polished casket skewering the priest's foot.

'Whose?' Morris asked.

'I beg your pardon.'

'Who was *inside* the coffin? Whose was it?'

'Oh,' Don Lorenzo hesitated. 'I can't recall now. A parishioner, I think.'

Lying! Morris thought. For the first time in the thirty years he had known the man Don Lorenzo was lying! Morris was sure. He knew perfectly well who was in that box. Even Antonella had a rather perplexed expression on those puckered little lips.

How interesting!

But the moment was soon forgotten. Half an hour hence, as on every Wednesday evening, they were reading a passage from the Bible. The children had gone at this point of course. The hosts and their spiritual guide had retired to black leather sofa and armchairs in the salotto. His brandy on the low mahogany table by his knobbly knee, Don Lorenzo accepted from Morris's hands the Trevisan family Bible, always carefully dusted and always lying open at some page or other on the same shelf that housed the family photographs. It was Antonella's belief, picked up apparently from her grandmother, that a Bible should never be shut. Open, its pious wisdom was released into the domestic atmosphere like the fragrance of an open rose, or a bowl of potpourri.

'So,' Don Lorenzo asked. 'What shall it be this evening? I don't have the strength to read much, I'm afraid.'

All that meat and wine was hard work, Morris reflected.

They had been reading the Bible together for almost thirty years. At the beginning, as a young couple overcoming bereavement, Morris and Antonella had followed specific Bible-reading courses, to deepen their religious instruction and prepare them for parenthood. But thirty years is a long time and when Don Lorenzo had no more courses to offer, they had begun to read the Holy Scriptures at random. That is, Don Lorenzo shut his eyes, the book was placed on his knees, open, without his knowing which way up or at what point, and he turned over a wodge of pages to left or to right with a quick deft movement. Then, eyes still closed, but swiftly and decisively, as if convinced that whatever the Holy Book turned up it would be exactly the spiritual nourishment they required, the old priest would stab a bony finger on the flimsy India paper.

As the years passed an element of ritual had crept in. Everyone had come to feel that there was some magic or augury involved. Read once a week, the randomly chosen passages became a message, like a horoscope in one of the more serious weeklies. They were aware of course of the heresy in this. They did not talk about it openly in this way. Don Lorenzo would simply read out whatever verses his finger had found in the voice he reserved exclusively for Bible-readings, a portentously wavering, sanctimonious sing-song that seemed to come from beyond the grave, beyond whole cemeteries, Morris sometimes thought, after which the ancient priest would bow his head in a closing vesper, before winding up the evening with a double shot of Calvados. All the same, the moment Don Lorenzo opened his eyes and announced the book, chapter and verse, that his finger had lighted on, Morris always felt a fine frisson of excitement run up his wrists and forearms, as if he might be about to receive important news regarding the future, or even irrevocable orders from On High. Certainly there had been something uncanny in Don Lorenzo's reading Jeremiah 40: 15, less than forty-eight hours before the moment of reckoning with Forbes: 'Then Johanan the son of Kareah spoke to Gedaliah in Mizpah secretly, saying, Let me go, I pray you, and I will slay Ishmael the son of Nethaniah, and no man shall know it.'

Morris fetched the Bible and placed it on Don Lorenzo's meagre thighs. The old priest turned a wodge of pages, waved his mummified hand in the musty air, then brought it down with ominous decision; he swivelled the big Bible around since Morris had given it to him upside down and declared:

'Judges 3: 14.'

Morris stepped dutifully back to sit on the sofa beside his wife. Only when the couple listened to the Bible together did they regress to holding hands and occasionally actually looking each other in unfathomable eyes.

'So the children of Israel,' Don Lorenzo began, 'served Eglon the King of Moab eighteen years.'

Morris always felt excited when he heard the word Moab. Or better still Moabites. The Bible did have its pleasures. He rather wished now he had made the effort to light some candles.

'But when the children of Israel cried unto the LORD, the LORD raised them up a deliverer, Ehud the son of Gera, a Benjamite, a man left-handed: and by him the children of Israel sent a present unto Eglon the King of Moab.'

Massimina had been left-handed, Morris remembered. It perhaps explained her poor performance at school. Or at least gave her an excuse.

'But Ehud made him a dagger which had two edges, of a cubit length; and he did gird it under his raiment upon his right thigh.'

No sooner was the word dagger pronounced, than Morris pricked up his ears. How long was a cubit, he wondered?

'And he brought the present unto Eglon, King of Moab: and Eglon was a very fat man.'

'What was that?' Morris sat up sharp.

It was unusual for the reading to be interrupted. Antonella started from the light slumber she was falling into.

'The present? I don't know. Wheat? Wine? What did these people give each other?'

'No, at the end.'

'Ah . . . he was a very fat man. Eglon, King of Moab.'

'Ah. Curious detail. The Bible doesn't usually get into people's physique.'

Don Lorenzo frowned and went on reading:

'When Ehud had made an end to offer the present, he sent away the people that bear the present. But he himself turned again from the quarries that were by Gilgal, and said, I have a secret errand unto thee, O king: who said, Keep silence. And all that stood by him went out from him. And Ehud came unto him; and he was sitting in a summer parlour, which he had for himself alone. And Ehud said, I have a message from God unto thee. And he arose out of his seat.'

A message from God was good, Morris thought, for a cubit-long dagger.

'And Ehud put forth his left hand, and took the dagger from his right thigh, and thrust it into his belly. And the haft also went in after the blade; and the fat closed upon the blade, so that he could not draw the dagger out of his belly; and the dirt came out.'

The dirt came out! Morris was electrified. The dirt damn well came out! Indeed it did! In thirty years of Bible-reading he had never heard anything more pertinent.

Don Lorenzo read on as if cruising through the beatitudes. A faint snore told Morris his wife was in fact asleep, though oddly her hand continued to squeeze her husband's with apparent affection.

'Then Ehud went forth through the porch, and shut the doors

of the parlour upon him, and locked them. When he was gone out, the king's servants came; and when they saw that, behold, the doors of the parlour were locked, they said, Surely he covereth his feet in his summer chamber.'

Covereth his feet? What was that about? Morris was already yearning to stick Eglon in Google and see if there were any paintings.

'And they tarried till they were ashamed: and, behold, the king opened not the doors of the parlour; therefore they took a key, and opened them: and, behold, their lord was fallen down dead on the earth.'

Two 'beholds' in one sentence was pretty poor, Morris thought. Still, it was an exciting moment.

'And Ehud escaped while they tarried, and passed beyond the quarries, and escaped unto Seirath.'

Don Lorenzo stopped, a puzzled look on his face.

'Yes, Padre?' Morris asked. When they were in Bible-reading mode he liked to call the man Padre.

'I was just wondering about the quarries,' Don Lorenzo said. 'I mean, what kind of things they would have been quarrying.'

'Oh right,' Morris agreed. 'I wonder.' After a moment's silence, listening to the slight rattle of Antonella's indrawn breath, he asked: 'What do you make of a story like that, Padre? I mean, why is it included in our Bible? What does it teach us?'

Don Lorenzo knew the answer. This passage was in all the commentaries, he said. 'Ehud is left-handed. That enables him to hide his dagger on the right thigh where no one would look for it, rather than the left, which was the norm and would have been checked. The moral is that every person, however different and unconventional, has some special gift to offer to the community.'

'Of course,' Morris agreed. 'Why didn't I think of that?'

CHAPTER SEVEN

AS SOON AS THE news appeared in the *Arena*, Morris phoned King Eglon, as Dottor Volpi had now become in his mind, to apologise. He had been chatting to the journalist, an old friend, over drinks and had imagined the conversation was in confidence. It was so irritating the way the press assumed they could turn every casual natter into headline news. With such big photos! When Volpi expressed his wrath in no uncertain terms, Morris agreed that it would be only wise to send a denial at once for immediate and obligatory publication. He would do it himself, this minute. Closing the call he wished Volpi a Happy Christmas. 'Are you going away, Dottore?' 'Tomorrow, to my sister's in Potenzuolo,' Volpi told him. 'How I envy you!' Morris enthused. 'Do give my love to the sunny south.'

'And let the dirt come out,' he muttered slipping the iPhone back in his pocket. His screensaver now was an 1881 woodcut by Ford Madox Brown for Dalziel's illustrated Bible, showing the avenger Ehud with right hand raised, apparently to reinforce some preacherly point he was making, while his left reached under fancifully antique clothing for the dagger hidden on his right thigh (a cubit was an impressive twenty inches, Morris had discovered). The doomed King Eglon, meantime, was fabulously oriental, black-bearded, bare-breasted and brashly bovine on a tubular throne that looked strangely like the National Health wheelchair Morris's father had been decomposing on for the last couple of years in an old people's home by Willesden Junction. How perceptive of Madox

Brown, Morris felt, to have seen that preparations for murder might be covered by a pious flourish. Something to bear in mind.

With that little duty out of the way, Morris's own Christmas proceeded pleasantly enough, though it was precisely at these festive occasions that it could prove hectic trying to satisfy both wife and mistress, not to mention the painted Massimina who became extremely demanding around religious festivals, another sure sign that she really was an independent entity and not just a voice in his head.

'I was pregnant, Mo,' she reminded him when he went to light the candles in The Art Room on Christmas Eve. 'Remember? It would have been a boy.'

Morris remembered. 'Not a Christmas baby, though, Mimi.'

'Well, it was hardly an immaculate conception!' Her laugh was a distant tinkle. Then after a moment's thoughtful calculation: 'More like April. A Taurus.'

'Right,' Morris acknowledged. 'A boy, you said?'

'Yes.'

'How can you know?'

'There are things we know here that you can't.'

A draught in the room made the flame-light from the chandeliers tremble over all the lush and ghastly canvases. Tonight Morris had brought up a bottle of port. He poured two glasses on the table in the centre of the room and walked over to clink them beneath Lippi's portrait. Her face was very alive. Her upper lip puckered and trembled.

'It's a shame,' he said, 'I bet the boy would have been a million times smarter than Mauro.'

'Oh, I don't know about that, Mo. I wasn't exactly the brains of the family, was I? Cheers.'

Mimi took a sip and smiled slyly, cuddling her divine child a little more warmly than usual, Morris thought. Curious that the immaculate conception could have come *after* losing their child like that. He shut his eyes a moment to enjoy the caress of her voice on his ears and the excellent Old Tawny on his pallet.

'Definitely better-looking, though,' she picked up brightly. 'That red hair Mauro has really puzzles me.'

Morris was silent.

'You can go now, *caro*,' she told him in a whisper. 'I know you've got other people to see.'

This sort of generous consideration, so unusual in a woman, only made it even more regrettable that Massimina had met the end she had. Not to mention the loss of that potentially gratifying son. Released from duty, Morris downed both glasses and hurried to take presents to Samira and Tarik: a case of Trevisan Amarone Reserve for the festivities, North Face gloves for Tarik and a charming seal-fur hat for Sammy. The seal fur was rather running against his vegetarian principles, but at least he hadn't ingested the creature.

What surprised Morris most at the flat in San Zeno was that the Moslem brother and sister had set up a Christmas tree almost as big as the Duckworths' and with an impressive pile of gaily wrapped packages under its branches. He felt vaguely envious, both of their easy eclecticism and cosy intimacy. 'I do wish I could be here with you,' he enthused unwisely. I'm always playing benefactor, he thought, without ever really putting my feet up. Kissing him at the door as he hurried off, Samira looked her older lover in the eyes.

'Why don't you make this the year you leave home?' she said huskily.

Morris was taken aback.

'Become somebody new and serious,' she said. 'Give up your double life. Let's live together.'

He tried to smile it off. 'Is this the same girl,' he asked, 'who told me she was only my lover for a month or two?'

'I'm giving you a chance of something better,' the Arab girl told him. There was an affectionate tension in her voice. 'But you'd better decide soon. I won't wait forever.'

'After the show at Castelvecchio,' Morris said instinctively. 'Let's put on a fantastic exhibition, then I'll do the deed.'

To which Samira replied very coolly, 'I love you.'

Morris felt confused. It was some time since he had heard those words on the lips of a beautiful woman. Was it a positive development, or not?

In Via Oberdan the family's handsome Christmas tree stood five cubits high between the fireplace and the sofa in the old salotto. A tad overdressed by Duckworth standards, Morris felt. On the first day of Christmas, roots intact in a terracotta pot, the tree still had something of the freshness and mystery of northern mountain slopes as the parents and two children shared out their twelve presents, each to all and all to each, after a heavy lunch of nut roast, tiramisu and Trevisan Cabernet. On the seventh day, New Year's Eve, victim of the cat's incorrigible fascination with tinsel and the funereal absence of light and air in casa Duckworth, the poor pine had few needles left to usher in a year it would evidently not be seeing out, while come Epiphany, which Morris dedicated naturally enough to Massimina, to the point of burning a little frankincense in The Art Room and buying myrrh soap and gold earrings, the sad spruce was no more than a wire skeleton, as grotesque in its baubles and fairy lights as a desiccated corpse in a wedding dress. *Sic transit*, etc. All the same there was no way, Morris was adamant, that the tree could be removed from the salotto until the Twelfth Night was through.

'Maddalena is wasting half her time hoovering up the needles,' Antonella protested.

It was not time *wasted*, Morris told her rather sharply. Anyway, what else did a maid have to do? It brought bad luck to take out a Christmas tree before the end of the twelfth day of Christmas.

'What is it with you and tradition, Papà?' his daughter challenged him.

Massimina was sitting on the floor, her back against the sofa sketching with one hand and texting with the other.

'Mass Sunday morning, Bible-reading Wednesday evening,

natale con i tuoi, pasqua con chi vuoi, cappuccino at eight, aperitivo at six. Loosen up, Papà. You live in a prison! Be free.'

'Rules are beautiful,' Morris told her curtly. 'Somebody studying art should appreciate that.'

It irritated him that his daughter sat in a tight skirt with her knees up and knickers plumply exposed; but if he pointed this out, he would be accused of voyeurism. What she was drawing was the nth dreamy fantasy of some manga superwoman in militaristic décolleté. It was depressing. The girl seemed to take no interest in life *as it really was*. Fleetingly he imagined a portrait of his mistress accurately drawn by his daughter. How exciting it would be to mix everything up. Hadn't Samira also bade him to be free?

'You should thank your lucky stars you have such a conservative father,' Antonella rounded on the girl. Half her college friends were from broken families, dividing time and loyalties between feckless parents who thought only of their own immediate gratification. 'Everything your father and I have put together has been for your and Mauro's future,' she reminded their daughter.

It was at times like this that Morris felt most satisfied with his choice of wife. Dull she might be, but Antonella always gave her husband the comforting feeling that he was doing the right thing. Massimina, however, wasn't listening; she was smirking over another text message. It was quite disturbing, Morris observed then, how the girl was able to go on drawing with her right hand while texting with her left. That kind of capacity, he remarked later to his wife in bed, to operate in two worlds at once testified to a split personality. The right hand didn't know what the left was up to.

'Mauro is so much more straightforward,' Antonella agreed.

'You mean he has trouble walking and chewing gum?' Morris couldn't resist.

'Don't be cruel!'

'I gave them nice presents.'

'You did,' she agreed: a camcorder for Massimina and an iPad for Mauro. Then she added: 'Hasn't it occurred to you, Morris, that Mousie did whatever he did in Brescia to impress his father?'

'I beg your pardon?' Morris sat up. His wife's reference to 'his father' almost made it seem as though that man might not be Morris. 'Why would I be impressed by my son joining a gang of thugs to attack a policeman?'

'He wants you to acknowledge that he exists, and that he has personality and courage to act. You heard the way he spoke to Don Lorenzo. About pride and identity.'

'It sounded like Northern League talk to me,' Morris said. 'I hoped he'd develop some pride in going to one of the world's best schools, and instead he attaches his affections to a group of racist hooligans.'

There was a long silence before his wife said quietly, 'I'm glad he's home, Morris. But he's not a boy for school or university. He reminds me a little of Massimina that way. I mean my sister.'

Morris lay very still.

'It was a terrible mistake Mamma made pushing Mimi at school when she wasn't cut out for it. I often feel that was one of the reasons for what happened. She must have got into bad company.'

Morris couldn't trust himself to say anything. Antonella sighed.

'Don't you think sometimes Mauro looks a bit like Mimi, Morris? The round, full face and fleshy arms.'

Was she mad? Mimi had been the gentlest, most graceful creature on earth. Their son was an oaf.

'Morris I think the right thing for you to do would be to take Mousie into the company. Prepare him for running it.'

'What! He's only seventeen, for Christ's sake. He's not ready for work.'

Antonella was silent. Then she said very deliberately: 'You're wrong Morris. I think Mauro would flower if you gave him responsibility. It would keep him out of trouble. You have no idea how much he seeks your approval.'

How did it happen, Morris wondered, that people always surprised him with their absurd requests? This was beyond ridiculous.

'Remember, the business isn't yours, or mine for that matter. It's a family affair going back generations. It will pass to Mauro.'

'And Massimina?'

'She wouldn't want it, Morris. You know that. She's more like you, more . . . artistic.'

'But I've run it for years!' he protested.

'You've run the company wonderfully,' she assured him. 'But I've always felt that it's been, well, against the grain, hasn't it? You didn't really *want* to run a company. And you've always been transforming it into something it wasn't before, pushing it here and there, as if you were afraid you might get bored. I've always felt that.' She hesitated, 'Look at this strange art show you suddenly want to put on. I mean, I don't like the subject at all, it's so macabre, but I see you need to do something new. Like the time you tried to write a novel. And to make a film. You've lost interest in the business as such.'

'No, I have *not*,' Morris said flatly. For some reason he felt like a little boy put on the spot. And he didn't want to be reminded of past fiascos. This show was in a completely different league from that awful novel.

'Don't be upset, *amore*. It's not a crime to have ambitions. And it can't be much fun digging foundations for a silly primary school that only a handful of children will ever go to, and all for free.'

'Who told you about that?' Morris was alarmed.

'Don Lorenzo was singing your praises,' Antonella said. 'It seemed Cardinal Rusconi thanked him for suggesting your name. He has a nephew in Sant'Anna, a local councillor. You know everyone's so worried about mixing with the Moslems.'

'I try to do my part,' Morris said virtuously, 'especially where the church is concerned.'

Suddenly he felt quite moved by these observations his wife

had made, by the thought that she had been watching him and thinking about him. So often it seemed the world paid no attention at all.

'If you draw Mauro in, it will give you more time for the things you care about.'

'Could be.'

'Otherwise . . .'

'What?'

She thought for a moment. 'I sometimes fear you'll get so bored with the business you'll, well, throw it away, somehow.'

'What on earth do you mean?' Morris propped himself on an elbow.

Again his wife sighed heavily. They were speaking of course, as always, with Christ Crucified and his virgin mother as their witnesses.

'I don't know, I just get the feeling that you're not an ordinary sort of man, Morris. You won't be content to leave things as they are.' She hesitated. 'That's partly why I married you, I suppose. Because you're special.'

She sighed deeply.

'Anto,' Morris breathed in the darkness of the Twelfth Night, settling on his back again. 'Anto, Anto Anto.'

There were moments when it would have been wonderful to have shared the whole truth with her. She could have offered such useful advice.

CHAPTER EIGHT

AS OF 6 JANUARY Morris began a series of visits to the churches Samira had earmarked for him. Sometimes he took the Arab girl, or, if she was at work, his son, or his daughter, or even on one occasion Tarik. He liked to be accompanied, possibly chauffeured, by someone much younger than himself and despite the fact that these were very different people, with different intellects, backgrounds and attitudes, nevertheless in a way, for Morris, these four youngsters, boys and girls, were all the same person. Despite a little petulance and muscle-flexing from time to time, they accepted that he called the tune. He had the Alfa Romeo. He had the track record. Above all, he had a project, knew what he was doing and why, whereas they were still unformed, unclear about their lives, unsure what fate would bring them. Morris loved this. He felt paternal, protective, munificent. He liked to think he was teaching them, not just about art, or about dealing with people – for there is no stranger race of men than parish priests – but about the whole ethos of purposefulness, of making a life for oneself, pushing on undeterred, however unpromising this or that immediate result might be, whatever obstacle might get in your way. Deep down every artist was a teacher, Morris thought. And the only way to lead was by example, not explanation.

'I believe,' he told a stout little man in his forties, 'you have a martyrdom of San Bartolomeo in your church.'

On his doorstep, the priest blinked. He was wearing contact lenses, Morris guessed. In one puffy hand he held a cheap Nokia and in the other an espresso pot.

'Come in, come in.'

Morris introduced himself and his son. He had Mauro with him today. The house was an ugly modern construction with roll-down plastic shutters and cheap black tiles somehow evoking the contrasting spirits of mass production and mausoleum. There was a cold, biscuity, old-sock staleness to the air that somehow went together with the priest's shiny cassock and a poorly executed Christ above an ancient television. In the centre of the room a low table was a cubit deep in loosely stacked newspapers, including, on top, today's *Gazzetta dello Sport*, which Mauro immediately picked up.

'I wouldn't want to take any more of your time than was necessary,' Morris deferred.

But the priest insisted on making coffee.

'I'd just screwed up the pot,' he smiled. 'Let's drink it together.' Still blinking, he added 'Cardinal Rusconi, you said?'

'We're collecting paintings for a show at the Castelvecchio museum; you may have read about it in the *Arena*. Cardinal Rusconi has been so good as to encourage me to seek out some lesser-known works right here in the Veneto, in liaison with the Cultural Heritage people, of course.'

'Verona or Chievo?' the priest asked Mauro as the boy turned the pink pages, frowning.

'There's only one team in Verona,' the boy replied.

'*Forza* Hellas,' the holy man concurred.

It might have been *Gott mit uns*, Morris thought. How was it that he had never understood the connective glue of football until his son hit puberty?

'San Bartolomeo, you said?'

'Martyrdom of,' Morris clarified.

'Flayed alive, if I rightly recall.'

'You do indeed.'

'But aren't we all in the end?' the little man sighed, waiting for the espresso pot to bubble up. 'Aren't we all?'

'No, Padre,' Morris said firmly. 'I don't think we are.'

If there was one thing that had always exasperated Morris in Italy, it was this habit people had of supposing themselves nailed to some especially awful personal cross. Christianity existed only to give them an inflated image of their own small trials and tribulations, when the truth was none of them had the slightest idea how tough it was for a foreigner to get so much as a bruised toe inside the door of their miserable, mafia-driven society.

The priest blinked energetically. He had a round but severely wrinkled face; the cheeks in particular appeared to have been recently pumped up, then abruptly deflated. Apparently he had a problem keeping his eyelids fully open. Perhaps an asset in his profession, Morris thought.

'Well, not literally flayed of course. Or let's hope not,' he laughed, 'But don't you think, Dottor . . . ?'

'Duckworth.'

'Don't you think, Dottor Dackvert, that these paintings of martyrdom make, er, explicit, *symbolically*, the sufferings many of us feel? That's why they're interesting.'

Morris had no time at all for this sentimental imprecision, and he wanted his son, deeply immersed in the sports news, to be aware of his position and to learn from it: 'I'm sure being flayed alive, *literally*,' he raised the volume of his voice, 'would be suffering of a quite different order from any you or I are likely to undergo, Padre. *That's* what makes the picture interesting *for me*. That someone inflicted, and someone else underwent, such intense and special pain over a question of faith.'

Mauro looked up from the *Gazzetta* and asked blandly what flayed alive meant. When the priest explained, he muttered: 'I wish someone would do that to Galliani.'

Morris had no idea who this hated fellow might be, but was taken aback when, instead of rebuking the boy's bloodthirsty spirit, the priest said, 'Ha, I know *exactly* what you mean!' His ensuing chuckle merged quite demonically with the gurgle of the coffee bubbling up in the pot.

As they now sugared their espressos the priest explained that the church of Santa Chiara in Ecstasy had moved ten years ago, just before his time actually, from an older building which had become unusable when spring water began to rise through the floor. The Curia still hadn't decided what to do with the place. If the picture existed it would be there, not in the new building almost a kilometre away where there were no paintings at all.

'It must exist,' Morris said, 'because it's in the Heritage Department archives.'

The priest smiled. 'Not everything in print corresponds to reality, Dottor Dackwert.'

'The *Gazzetta*'s a scandal,' Mauro agreed, munching a second stale biscuit. 'I only read it to get angry.'

The old church stood on the bank of a big square millpond and, to Morris's surprise and, for some inexplicable reason, pleasure, there was indeed spring water trickling out from under the splintery old door; it sloshed along a little rut in the gravel path and down into the pond.

The priest wrestled with a rusty padlock and let them in. Inside, the damp mustiness could not have been more powerful. In the gloom something started, scratched, scuttled, and fell silent. On the far wall a frescoed Deposition was velvety with spreading mould. Morris breathed deeply and felt a strong welling of affection. It was the kind of place where he would gladly have set up house.

'What a stink,' his son said. 'I'll wait outside.'

'As you see,' the priest remarked, picking his way through puddles across the floor, 'no San Bartolomeo.'

Indeed the walls were mostly frescoed with somewhat saccharine accounts of Christ's passion. But Morris had spied a door beyond the altar and behind it, as he soon discovered, there was a wooden staircase.

'I've been told not to go up there,' the priest warned. 'It's unsafe.'

Morris didn't hesitate. The first two steps looked dangerously rotten and halfway up another was simply gone, but he picked his way past them and hurried up before the priest could stop him. At the top, waiting for his eyes to grow accustomed, he realised he was in exactly the sort of under-the-roof gloom that had served for the deposition of Forbes some years ago. It had amazed Morris that nobody had found the body. As the days and weeks had passed and no one raised so much as a murmur over the old fool's disappearance, he had felt unaccountably lucky, blessed even, exonerated it seemed by the same fate that had allowed a heavy candlestick to sprout in his hand at exactly the moment the idiot had made his threat explicit. Now, six years on, here he was gazing into another dark attic that no one had bothered to check for decades, and with a smell so over-powering it could have masked any misdemeanour.

'It's dark. I'd need a torch,' he shouted down to the priest.

'Use your mobile,' the man shouted back.

Of course! Morris shook his head and laughed. How odd to have a priest as an accomplice! He pulled out his iPhone, pressed a key and at once the space declared itself in a steady fluorescent glow; a long low attic with sloping roof choked with cobwebs and stacked with dusty packages and forgotten liturgical para-phernalia. Was the floor safe? Morris advanced a step or two. There were squeaky, splintery sounds.

'Are you all right?' the priest called again. 'I'm afraid you shouldn't be up there, Dottor Dackwert. We're not insured.'

Morris had seen a stack of canvases, at the far end.

'Just taking a quick look,' he shouted.

If he walked directly down the centre of the space, he thought, there would surely be a solid beam beneath the rotting boards. Holding the phone low in front of him, he walked swiftly down the length of the small church. Cobwebs caught at his lips and there was a dead bird, feather, bone and beak, in the deep filth to his left. A crow. How had that got in?

The paintings were wrapped in thick polythene sheets. A stack of five in massive old frames, all about four feet by three. Crouching, Morris held his phone close and brushed off the dust. Was this a boat? Yes, but comically undersized for the three big men standing up in it hauling in their nets. The miracle of the fish. Nice, but not what Morris was after. Though, cast your net on the other side, he thought, was always good advice. An invitation to bisexuality, perhaps? Smiling, Morris stood up and with some effort shifted the heavy canvas along the wall. The boards groaned. 'Are you all right,' came the prompt shout from below. Ignoring it, Morris crouched again and peered through a veil of polythene grey. Three men walking side by side. Two in brown robes, one in white. Our Lord? The Road to Emmaus? Damn.

Again Morris moved the painting aside, again he crouched down, rubbed away the dust with his sleeve, again he peered. A kneeling woman embracing a seated man's naked foot. Mary? Martha's sister? The overpriced anointing oil? What a mixed bag the Bible was!

Then at last, there it was in all its gory glory, or glorious gore. Once again Morris held the glowing phone to a dusty grey transparency and, bingo! The victim was precariously balanced on one leg, hands thrown up in the air, apparently in danger of falling over backwards, while the expert killer leaned over him with a long knife that had already stripped the skin from one vividly red arm, leaving a gleaming anatomy lesson of biceps and triceps. San Bartolomeo, patron saint of tanners!

Morris stood, reflected, then shifted Martha, Emmaus and the fishes back into the stack. He turned 180 degrees, held the phone in front of him and followed his own footsteps through the dust back to where he had started.

'Alas, nothing,' he declared, shaking his head as he met the priest's anxious blinking at the bottom of the stairs. Making a great show of carefulness he jumped over the last two rotten steps and stood up slapping the dust from his hands. 'Just dead mice and a broken lectern,' he elaborated with evident disappointment. For fun he added, 'Not even a brass candlestick.'

'I'm not surprised,' the priest observed as they went out into the daylight. 'Anything halfway valuable was no doubt sold to help pay for the new church.'

'You know that's illegal,' Morris told the priest with sudden formality. 'The painting is registered as part of the national cultural heritage.' He hesitated, 'I'm afraid I shall have to report this.'

They were at the church door. The small man turned, touched Morris's hand and looked into his face with his own rather gentle, half-closed eyes: 'I'd be extremely grateful if you didn't, Dottor Dackvert,' he said. He blinked. 'Why stir up trouble, for myself and the parish?'

Morris sighed, perhaps too theatrically, and for a few minutes, they watched Mauro skimming stones across the pond which was clogged with weed. A rusty bicycle was just visible in a mass of green. The chubby boy, who had taken off his coat to reveal an untucked shirt and trouser bottoms hanging almost below his buttocks, made little grunts of pleasure and frustration depending on the number of times a stone skipped.

The priest was smiling and blinking indulgently. 'Extraordinary hair your son has,' he remarked. 'Quite unusual.'

'I won't keep you any longer, then,' Morris announced brusquely. 'In any event, thank you, Father, for your help.'

'So, all that for nothing,' Mauro chirped as they climbed into the car. Already he was turning on his Game Boy.

'Not at all,' Morris said coolly.

'I suppose at least you know you don't have to come back again.'

Morris left a pause of perhaps two minutes, negotiating the road out of the village. 'On the contrary. I'm sure we will be back.'

'How come?'

Responding to a sudden whim, instead of heading home, Morris turned right off the main road, heading north into the hills of Lessinia.

'Why come back,' Mauro repeated, 'if the picture isn't there?'

'It is there.'

Mauro was puzzled. 'You said it wasn't.'

'It's wrapped up in the attic, and rather more interesting than I hoped.'

'So why didn't you say?'

Morris didn't reply. It seemed to him that the experience of driving was perennially that of finding someone else in your way. There was always some car or van going slower than you wanted to. This was why in general he liked to be driven by others, so that he could watch their reaction, rather than have to react himself.

Mauro sat up. 'Come on, Papà, why?'

Miracle of miracles, Morris thought, the kid had paused his computer game. He honked, accelerated, moved out to overtake, then braked fiercely when a *furgoncino* appeared.

'Papà!'

Morris shook his head. 'I'm too old for this. Time you learned to drive,' he told his son. 'You can start lessons at seventeen, can't you?'

'I'm not interested in driving,' Mauro said.

This was unexpected.

'I thought all young people wanted to drive. Power, freedom, car sex.'

Mauro laughed. 'You don't know anything about young people, Papà.'

Morris wasn't going to rise to that kind of bait. 'You can hardly think of running the company without driving a car,' he pointed out.

'Why not? Cars will soon be obsolete for personal travel.'

Behold, the utopian football thug.

'Why did you say the painting wasn't there, if it was?'

Morris finally got round two Vespas travelling side by side, their four riders laden with overstuffed shopping bags.

'If the priest doesn't know what's in his own church, I don't see why I should tell him.'

'But what happens when he finds out? He'll know you lied to him.'

'He won't find out.'

'But how—'

'Oh for Christ's sake!' Morris spluttered. 'Use your head!'

Mauro was nonplussed. For a while the two sat in uneasy silence as the car climbed out of the Val d'Illasi, beyond Tregnago. Then Morris asked more affably, 'Do you know where we're going now?'

It was Mauro's turn not to reply. The boy had slouched lower down into the passenger seat, his meaty knees against the dashboard.

'You've forgotten your seat belt.'

Mauro said nothing.

'It's illegal to travel without a belt.'

'But OK to lie to a priest,' his son came back. 'What would Don Lorenzo say? Will you confess to him?'

Morris was patient. He even smiled at his son's impertinence. The fact was he had begun to feel rather excited about going back to Montecchio di Sopra. He hit the accelerator as they climbed the winding road.

'When's your trial again?' he eventually asked.

'The 20th.'

'We'll see who'll be lying then,' Morris said.

'Not me,' Mauro chimed. 'You can't complain about match-fixing and players diving and newspapers pretending games are clean when they're not, and then go and lie in court, can you?'

How on earth, Morris wondered, in a country like Italy, and in the most Catholic of Catholic regions to boot, the bleeding heart of the Veneto, had his son come out with such a strong vocation for truth-telling? Then he reflected ruefully that it must have been the three years at Tonbridge. From England and public school his son had brought back the one trait of polite education that was of no use at all back home, and certainly not if he was to occupy an important position in Fratelli Trevisan.

'Know where we're going now?' he asked again.

'To – tell – the – truth,' Mauro said, 'no.'

He had found a penknife and was scraping under a fingernail.

'You know that painting I have in The Art Room, *The Death of Jezebel*.'

'I haven't been in there for a while.'

'The one of the woman falling from the window.'

The boy yawned. 'Vaguely.'

'We're going to the church that has the original.'

'How interesting.'

'Isn't it? Actually, if you'd taken a close look at the one at home it would indeed be very interesting to me to know if you could tell original and copy apart.'

'The original is in the church.'

'But is it?'

'Bound to be.'

'But imagine you weren't sure. Would you be able to tell by studying the paintings?'

'God, Papà. Who cares! Is this the sort of stuff you spend your time thinking about? I thought you were a business genius or something.'

'Because you might not be able to,' Morris went on regardless. 'You might even think' – he was definitely enjoying himself now – 'that the original was the one at home.'

'I wish you'd slow down,' Mauro said abruptly. 'These bends are bringing my toothache back.' After a moment he asked: 'Is it worth anything?'

'What?'

'The picture. What's it worth?'

'The original or the copy?'

'God. Whichever.'

'Things are worth what you decide they're worth.'

Mauro thought about this for a moment. Morris was pleased. It was probably the most sustained exchange the two had ever managed. Eventually the boy said: 'The money is real when it's handed over.'

'The money is real, you're right, but the perception of *worth* is not the money. Maybe the buyer thinks he paid too much. Or maybe he's gloating that he got a cheap deal. You asked me what the painting was *worth*.'

'That's not true with football players,' Mauro said solemnly. 'You can only measure how much a striker's worth by how many goals he scores, not how much they paid for him.'

'I wasn't talking about football players. I was talking about a painting which has been around for 300 years.'

'And how many assists he gives,' Mauro mused on. 'I think Gomez is really undervalued, for example, when you consider—'

'Actually,' Morris interrupted, trying to force the boy to appreciate that the visit was important for him, 'this was the last painting that Forbes copied for me.'

He accelerated into the final hairpin before the village. Mauro pressed a hand against his cheek.

'Remember Forbes?'

'Sure. I used to see him at the stadium.'

'You what!'

'That old English guy, right, who had the summer school? For posh boys.'

Morris nodded. He was flabbergasted.

'Yeah, he used to bring a bunch of kiddies to the Bentegodi. Disadvantaged or something. Immigrants. They had places down in the parterre where the schools go. He was a bit creepy if you ask me. And bringing them there with all the racist chanting and everything. It was odd.'

Mauro shook his head, but this seemed to disturb his teeth even more.

It occurred to Morris that the whole city of Verona might have a double life he knew nothing of: by day in the workplace, by night and on Sunday afternoons at the stadium, up to God knows what.

'How do you mean, creepy?' he asked.

'He was always offering sweets and treats, you know. Like Don Lorenzo that way, actually.'

'He was an excellent painter,' Morris said severely.

Mauro thought about it. 'Not if all he did was copy.'

The car fretted behind a garbage truck up the last slope to the village square. What was growing old for, Morris asked himself, if not to learn patience? In just a few moments he would be back where it had all happened. He knew this would give him a big shot of adrenalin.

'It takes a special genius to copy,' he told his son. 'A determined suppression of your personality. But of course, only people with a bit of personality know how important it is to curtail it.'

Obviously this was way over the boy's head.

'So why did he stop if he was so good?'

'Good question. Very good indeed, why did Forbes stop?'

So saying and smiling, Morris twisted the wheel sharply to the right and, with a little yelp of nice new tyres, braked hard into a parking place against the cemetery wall. The boy's computer game shot off his lap and into the darkness beneath the dashboard.

'Christ, Papà!'

Morris wondered how this could be the same boy who laid in wait for well-armed policemen.

The church of the Santi Apostoli del Soccorso stood among tall cypresses at the top of the hill with the cemetery to one side and the *canonica* to the other. The priest, it turned out, had changed since the days when Morris had come out here with Forbes to ask permission to set up an easel in the nave and copy the painting they were interested in. Why, he wondered, was the Curia moving its priests around so much? The sprightly young man who opened the door of the *canonica* was too pleased with himself by half and putting on airs beyond his age. But more and more this seemed to be the case with everyone under forty. Morris was damned if he would call him Padre.

'How very strange,' Don Gaetano said after hearing Morris's request. 'No one in the four years I've been here, and then all of a sudden two in as many days.'

'I beg your pardon?'

'Two people in as many days to see "Jezebel Defenestrated". I had no idea anyone rated the painting.'

'Who?' Morris demanded.

The priest wanted them to come into the house now. Perhaps they would 'break bread' with him, he suggested. A door opening to the left of the living room emitted wisps of steam and there was the sound of someone knocking pots and pans together.

'I've always thought it a rather strange painting myself,' the gangly priest went on. 'It has a sort of raw look for its age. Too aggressively restored, perhaps. I'm not an expert on these things.'

'Who came to ask about it?' Morris asked with brutal directness.

'Maddalena,' the young priest called, half enthusiastic, half apologetic 'we have guests. Could you lay the table for three?'

Another Maddalena. They were a race. And what a lonely bunch these priests must be, Morris thought, inviting every casual visitor to drink coffee and break biscuits together at the drop of a biretta.

'We've probably just got time for a quick viewing before the food is on the table.'

Don Gaetano took a black overcoat from a hook and ushered them out of the door, lowering his voice to say, 'The poor dear gets upset if we don't eat our *minestra* piping hot.'

Who was we, Morris wondered?

They walked round the side of the house to the priest's private entrance at the back of the church and Morris repeated his question, 'But do tell me who else has been here to see the painting.'

'An elderly American.'

Morris relaxed. Surely Stan Albertini could hardly be described as elderly.

'It was a curious story,' Don Gaetano went on; he held the door to let them in, then headed for the light switch. 'Apparently he had a friend who had been making a copy of the painting some time ago, they had been corresponding about it, some technical detail or other, then they lost touch. He hoped maybe I knew the man.'

Suddenly it wasn't exciting being here at all. As if exposed to a blast of intense heat, Morris felt the same acute anxiety that had always beset him when he feared Mother would catch him stealing cash from her purse or, worse still, penis in hand on the brink of orgasm. Chest tight, it seemed he must faint. He had to put a hand on a stone pillar. Life was so *unfair*. He had no desire now to see Jezebel Defenestrated, no desire at all to stand a few feet beneath Forbes's remains. The ceiling would surely crumble, he thought, and the rotten old corpse come tumbling down to point a skeletal finger.

Mauro joined them this time. Had he seen his father's reaction to the priest's tale? Wouldn't he be surprised that his father hadn't acknowledged that he too knew the man who had come here to copy a painting? Morris felt he was inside a house of cards at exactly the moment someone removes the central support.

'I insist on having genuine candles,' Don Gaetano was confiding as they walked into a cold airy nave. 'The truth is that for many people prayer does require a certain aura, don't you think, the same way a book needs a good cover, one might say.'

What on earth was he on about?

They reached the small side chapel toward the back on the right and there was Jezebel Defenestrated exactly where Morris had rehung her before leaving the church that winter morning five, or was it six years ago: a woman in a bright blue dress plunging head first from an upper floor into a group of armed horsemen on the street.

'An unusual subject for a small church like ours,' Don Gaetano observed. 'You see what I mean about the aggressive restoration work? Bits of it look like it was painted yesterday.'

'I'll need to be paid a lot more, old chap,' Forbes had observed, 'if you're going to swap the canvases. *Satis superque,* if you know what I mean.'

Morris didn't.

'Enough,' the Eton man grinned crookedly, 'and *more* than enough. *Superque!* Lovely word.'

He stood there paintbrush in hand and artist's beret on his head, far far far too pleased with himself.

Morris had offered double. Forbes still wasn't satisfied.

'But you don't *need* all that money,' Morris had insisted. 'I've given you a house. I've guaranteed you an income. Haven't I?'

'*Decet verecundum esse adolescentem.*'

It was infuriating, but also rather wonderful how effortlessly Forbes trotted out these tags. Morris had waited.

'It befits a young man to be modest.'

'Michael,' Morris did his best to show the old pervert some respect, 'I simply meant that I'd relieved you of all practical worries. How can you need so much money?'

Forbes had answered slowly, as though to someone who was having rather too much trouble seeing the obvious: 'Morris, at my age it isn't, er, quite so easy as it used to be to get what one, er, wants. But I assure you that I still do want it. Such is life.'

The pig.

Then Forbes had said casually: 'I know quite a lot about you, old chap, actually. And I think you know I know. Don't you? What really happened to young Posenato, for example.'

That was when the candlestick jumped into his hand. What else could one do? Accept a lifetime's blackmail from a self-confessed insatiable pederast? And now here it was again, eighteen inches of lumpen brass, standing exactly where Morris had left it on the white altar cloth in this quiet side chapel. He had washed it, of course. He had washed and wiped its polished curves with immense care. He had washed and wiped everything. The floor in particular. There was a big sink in the bathroom beyond the vestry. He had filled tin buckets. But doubtless with the tools they had today some minuscule particle of DNA could easily be found, if ever anyone started to look.

The priest was telling Mauro the story of Queen Jezebel. She had allowed the people of Israel to worship foreign gods, notably Baal.

'And as a result she got the push?' Mauro grinned.

'That's right. It seems she knew it was going to happen and made sure she was well dressed for the occasion. Hence the fancy dress in the picture.'

Morris was fighting to stay compos mentis. There were times when reality fizzed with such chemical intensity that the only real choice seemed to be between lying down under the already hissing blade of the guillotine or grabbing a Kalashnikov and slaughtering every last soul in sight. For a moment he thought he heard the noise of bony fingers and toes scraping their way out from under a pile of builder's rubble above his head.

'Guy fell from the upper ring of the terraces last year,' Mauro observed. 'Neapolitan. They reckon he was pushed. Seems he'd brought some Napoli fans right into the Hellas *curva*. Crazy.'

How, oh how to organise the same fate for Stan Albertini!

'You see what I mean, about the brushwork seeming too fresh for something from the seventeenth century?' Don Gaetano was bending forward across the top of the altar to look carefully at the work. 'Your American friend thought the same.'

Friend? How could these idiots not put two and two together? Surely Stan would remember the rather duller and dustier Jezebel he had seen in Morris's Art Room.

Morris went to stand beside the young priest, his body pulsing with a dangerous heat. 'Typical, I'm afraid,' he said. He made a massive effort to stay calm, or at least give the impression that his anger was to do with the supposedly poor condition of the painting. 'Just the sort of invasive restoration job that was in vogue back in the nineties.'

However, looking at the canvas across the marble top of the altar, his cheek almost touching the candlestick, Morris couldn't help feeling that Forbes had indeed improved on the original, sharpening up its Vaselined baroque into something more urgent and almost hyper-real. You felt you could hear the doomed queen's cry. No, the better of the two paintings was definitely the one here in the church of Santi Apostoli del Soccorso, not in The Art Room in Via Oberdan. How ironic!

'Heavens, we'd better hurry back,' Don Gaetano exclaimed with a sudden violent rustling of his cassock. 'Or Maddalena will make mincemeat of us all.' He laughed out loud as if this were an excellent joke.

Morris lingered a moment in the porch to text Samira. 'Phone me in ten minutes. Please!' He set the ringtone on loud and hurried after the others.

The call came just as Don Gaetano was winding up his Latin grace with Morris tucking a fiercely starched napkin under his chin. Sammy knew the routine by now and put down as soon as Morris picked up.

'*Pronto?*' Morris frowned. '*O santo cielo!*' He stood abruptly and walked into the porch to talk in low and urgent tones, then returned and announced that there was a crisis at the bottling factory, a man had been seriously injured, they would have to leave at once.

The old *perpetua* was livid.

CHAPTER NINE

MORE THAN ONCE, DURING the most intense periods of his life, it had occurred to Morris to think of himself as a juggler. Now, crossing Piazza Bra at carnival time, a bright cold morning in February, his attention was caught by a street artist juggling. Dressed as a convict, standing in the midst of a field of cobbles, Roman ruins before him and Austrian pomp behind, the man began with large rubber balls, including, with regular jerks of his knee, the larger ball, evidently hollow, attached to his foot by a long red plastic chain. It was amusing enough, but nothing special, until his sidekick, who had thus far pretended to be one of the gathering spectators, began to pull all kinds of odd objects from a large rucksack and lob them at the juggler: first a knife, then a gun, now a chisel, now a torch which he first set aflame, and finally, miracle of awful miracles, a small electric chainsaw that the man actually turned on before tossing it, to a sigh of general amazement, at his friend.

Morris was riveted. His apprehension of imminent catastrophe was so powerful he had to look away. It seemed extraordinary that the crowd, many of them masked as sheiks, popes and leering Berlusconis, could enjoy the sight of a man taking such frightening risks to earn a few coppers. How callous! At any moment blood would spurt, clothes would catch fire and the air would be full of grief and pain. Yet, when he found the courage to look again, the juggler was laughing, exhilarated, the centre of rapt attention and loving every moment of it.

Each time something new was thrown at him he let one of the rubber balls drop into a capacious bag between his feet until, at the end, there were only these frightening objects plus the larger ball at the end of its chain, circulating around his steady hands and rhythmically jerking foot, while his eyes lifted in a smile of faint amusement to watch the missiles arching over his head.

How long could it go on? Morris found himself sweating. And how could the man ever free himself from the slavery of keeping so many threats in the air? Most of all that whining chainsaw. The crowd had begun to clap. Little children, dressed as penguins and fairies, were getting dangerously close. It was surprising that the local authorities would allow such perilous performances in an open public space. At last the sidekick, himself masked as a policeman, took a hand grenade from his bag, pulled the pin with his teeth and lobbed the grenade into the air. Up it flew. It looked terribly real. The juggler caught it, apparently without looking, spared it only a passing glance as it circulated a second time, seemed merely, momentarily intrigued, until, suddenly understanding, his eyes and mouth opened wide in theatrical alarm. The grenade was *smoking*! In two seconds of frantic dexterity, he caught the knife between his teeth, contrived to have the whirring saw intersect the plastic chain that held his convict's ball, slicing it in two, and, suddenly free, torch in one hand, gun in the other, was firing blanks into the crowd as he stepped back from the grenade which fell, neatly, into his performer's bag, whence, with a loud bang, it sent a shower of confetti into the air together with a plume of orange smoke.

Enormously relieved by this innocent conclusion, Morris pushed brusquely through a cheering group of dwarves, Snow Whites and cackling harlequins to place a hundred-euro note in the policeman's upturned cap. At his friend's side, the juggler looked at the contribution in amazement. Their eyes met: escape artist and multiple murderer. That man is me, Morris thought.

I wish I had his panache. I wish I could make such good use of every weapon they throw at me.

The truth was there was rather too much going on in Morris's life now: to the point that his normally frantic job of running a major business seemed a mere rubber-ball routine compared to the new and urgent claims on his attention. The formal charge at his son's first appearance in court had alarmed him; they wanted to send Mauro down to some juvenile institution for five years and more. It would be a serious stain on the family's reputation. It would compromise Morris's influence in the town. Meantime, Tonbridge School insisted that the Duckworths pay the year's fees, despite withdrawing the boy. Morris refused. They could take whatever legal action they liked, but he was damned if he was going to pay to support a privileged class that had always excluded him.

In Sant'Anna, Zuccato's third-rate, drunken Moldavian subcontractor had backed his bulldozer into a war memorial for which the local council was seeking damages, from Morris. Nor had there been a word of gratitude from Cardinal Rusconi, which was all justification enough, Morris decided, if any was required, for recovering the Martyrdom of San Bartolomeo *scorticato* from San Briccio free of charge. All he had to do was to find the time and the right accomplice. Samira perhaps? Week by week the girl was becoming more affectionate but also more demanding. She wanted him to accompany her openly to the theatre, to concerts, to restaurants, to cinemas. In Verona that was tricky. Morris drove her to Milan and Bologna. It was time-consuming. Her brother too had grown more deferential, apparently accepting Morris as a fixture in their Libyan lives, inviting him to holiday in Tripoli. 'Perhaps one day you will convert to Islam,' he had said rather disquietingly. 'I think it would be a better religion for you.'

Massimina (Morris's daughter) was increasingly locked into some interminable exchange of text messages which had begun to make Morris worry for her studies and sanity, while Massimina (the murderer's guardian angel) complained constantly that The Art Room was too cold for her poor baby and that Morris was making a terrible mistake with this proposed exhibition at Castelvecchio. 'It's the beginning of the end,' she kept repeating, 'the end of our life together, Mo.'

On Antonella's warm invitation, Stan Albertini had come to dinner three times in as many weeks and spoken anxiously of his old friend Mike and the man's mysterious disappearance, asking Morris to show him the paintings Forbes had copied, as if these might hold precious clues. Did they? Could they? Had Forbes perhaps written what he knew about Morris on the back of a canvas? Or between canvas and frame? On one occasion Mauro had been at the dinner table with them, and Morris had been concerned that the boy might mention their visit to Jezebel Defenestrated. Meantime, he had removed the painting from The Art Room and filled the empty space with a decidedly below-par Tarquinio and Lucrezia. Sooner or later these worries would make him ill. To cap it all Don Lorenzo had remarked between mouthfuls of roast that Forbes had come to confess himself – and it had been the first time in a decade – shortly before his abrupt departure, but of course he, Don Lorenzo, would never abuse the secret of the confessional by revealing what had been said on that occasion. Morris made a mental note that he must find out who had been in the coffin that had destroyed the priest's foot.

Above all there was Volpi. On return from Christmas in Naples the museum director must have realised, Morris supposed, that the *Arena* had not published a correction to his interview about the forthcoming show. In the town's cultural circles people were talking about nothing else. It was getting harder and harder for the museum to back out of the project. So how would King Eglon react? It had surprised Morris when the man did nothing. What he had expected was some heated but inconsequential argument that would have got the issue out of the way and cleared the air. It wasn't forthcoming. Instead, Volpi made himself scarce, leaving a secretary to put Morris in touch with Professor Zolla, the resident art historian who was sending out the loan requests and would eventually co-curate the show, assuming it came off. This should have been promising, but Morris couldn't believe the director wouldn't strike back, and the longer he waited to do so, the more Morris feared that the strike would be decisive.

Approaching Castelvecchio for his first encounter with Zolla, the building's rust-brick parapets and extravagant crenulations, the medieval moat, the drawbridge and the grand arched gate, had something fantastical about them, Morris thought: it was a castle of fairy-tale encounters, a place where he might undergo some defining trial of courage or *vertù*, in mortal combat perhaps, with King Eglon. He smiled, but felt a shiver about his neck too. The last thing he wanted was to kill again. Whether Volpi or Stan. Actually, he had never *wanted* to kill. All the same, it was Castelvecchio, he sensed, this show at Castelvecchio, *Painting Death*, that would ultimately determine how Morris was to be remembered: as a minor eccentric collector with more copies than originals, or as a major force for reflection and renewal in the world of European art!

If only he could be sure that the show would really come off.

Professor Angelo Zolla was both a mystery and a disappointment. Younger than Morris had supposed, perhaps not even forty, he had an impressive, well-equipped, over-tidy office all to himself, from whose open door he could, if he so desired, keep an eye on the half-dozen staff the museum employed for management and marketing. Trim as the institution's director was lardy, Veronese as Volpi was Neapolitan, the young professor must, Morris at first assumed, be at least potentially hostile to the older, more powerful man. Casting about for complicity, the Englishman had made a few casually condescending remarks about southerners and complimented Zolla profusely on his smart, silver-grey suit, pastel shirt, Rotary-look tie and finely toned physique. Smiling blandly from a perma-haze of deodorant and aftershave, his small moustache clipped to rhomboid perfection,

Zolla seemed pleased enough, but deaf to any implied criticism of his boss. Because he hadn't picked it up, Morris wondered, or because he chose to ignore it? It was hard to know whether the man was completely stupid or very shrewd. Morris felt vulnerable, as great men must.

About the show, however, the art historian was enthusiastic. 'Our Beppe does tend to play the old pessimist,' he reassured the Englishman, who had expressed concern that Volpi might not be a hundred per cent on board.

'I'm sorry?' Morris said. 'Our Beppe?'

'*Il direttore,*' Zolla laughed. 'Giuseppe Volpi. Not to worry. I'll bring him round. He's actually a wonderful man.'

Again, this should have been encouraging, but Morris sensed there was something wrong. It was evident that Zolla genuinely wanted to curate the show. Studying the man's curriculum on the museum's website, Morris quickly realised that in the past he had merely played dogsbody to other curators, collecting and ordering the appropriate artworks, editing and publishing the catalogues. To be a curator in his own right would represent a significant career breakthrough. This had to be positive. On the other hand, Zolla seemed unable to grasp what Morris intended the show to be or why he had proposed it in the first place. Experienced art historian or not (but how else could he have got a full professorship so young?), Zolla seemed to know only one basic formula for any exhibition: meticulous classification plus fulsome rhetoric: you arranged a group of paintings by artist, school or chronology, and then declared them sublime. Mission accomplished. 'An exhibition bringing together the finest representations of violent death,' was all he had offered by way of description on the letter calling in loans from such august institutions as the Louvre, the Met and the National Gallery. Were the serious folks in those places likely to part with their marvellous artworks to support such a banal proposition from a provincial backwater like Verona? More was required.

Over the following weeks Morris tried and tried, talked and

talked, about his ideas, plans and theories, the psychology of the show as he saw it, the implied cultural critique, the institutionalisation of violence, the aestheticisation of horror, and Zolla had listened politely, apparently patiently, but still didn't get it. Not that he countered Morris's arguments; he rarely expressed disagreement. He just didn't seem to appreciate how profoundly the subject of murder connected with the depths of the collective psyche and the organisation of contemporary society. Above all, he wouldn't hear of sending a second email with a detailed account of their/Morris's plans for the show.

'These are busy men, Morris,' he shook his head. Somehow they had been on first-name terms almost from the start, something unusual in Italy, though without any real familiarity. Frequently Zolla hazarded a few words in schoolboy English, then waited, smiling, for Morris's compliments. 'We are not wanting to try hard their patience, do we?'

'What about using conflicting voices in the captions?' Morris hinted. 'We could give aggressively opposing views of some of the key images. "Was Cain framed?" Or: "To start history rolling, a good man has to die." That would force people to look at the pictures in a new way. What we want is to get them thinking.'

Zolla sat very straight behind his polished desk. He was always perfectly groomed. His papers were in order. His PC had a magnificent screen without a speck of dust. His nails were manicured, his cuffs immaculate.

'That might be confusing, Morris,' he eventually said. Surely it was best to keep the captions simple: the artist, the date, the work's ownership history, and a brief comment on the genius involved, so that people knew that they were looking at quality. For more complex considerations – the school of painting, the particular brush technique, the circumstances of the commission – there were the audio guide and the catalogue, for which he was already drawing up a list of highly respected contributors. Obviously the public's understanding would be facilitated by hanging the canvases in strict chronological order.

'You've forgotten to ask for Caravaggio's *Sacrifice of Isaac,*' Morris complained.

Zolla was always affable, confident, generous, deodorised.

'Since Isaac is not actually killed,' he explained in careful English, 'I decided that this painting is not being included in the show.' He switched to Italian. 'I'm afraid we would be accused of a methodological error, Morris. You cannot imagine how ready other art historians are to, how do you say in English, "poke hole" or "pick hole". They are a murderous crowd.'

He smiled at this little joke.

To Morris's mind the dramatic image of a bearded old man with a knife at his child's naked throat could not have been more devastatingly on theme. Foolishly, he pleaded his case: 'The point is, it's a murder *about to happen*. The fact that the whole disgraceful scenario was instigated by Jehovah Himself speaks worlds, don't you think, Angelo?'

Zolla nodded sagely: 'We have to be a bit careful, Morris, you know, on that front, Verona being such a Catholic town.'

For the first time Morris felt some sympathy for the Hellas Verona fans and their choral blasphemies. Walking out of Zolla's room, he began to notice how the regular office staff would glance up with quiet smiles on their lips. They thought something was funny.

It would occasionally happen during these visits that Morris ran into Volpi, leaning on a walking stick, perhaps in the corridor, or taking some visiting dignitary round the museum, and he too smiled the smile of someone who knows something that the recipient of the smile does not. What was it?

'You don't have the charming Signorina Al Wazid with you today, Signor Duckworth,' Volpi remarked, his chins resting on his collarbone like a pile of Assyrian cushions.

'Miss Al Zuwaid is at work. In the Cultural Heritage Department.'

'Ah, of course. Fine people, fine people.' There was a perennial dampness about the fat man's dewlaps. He was breathing heavily.

What was the 'of course' about, Morris wondered? Had he ever mentioned where Samira worked? He seemed to remember having presented the girl as his secretary.

Volpi used the lift to go downstairs, even if it was only one floor. Out of politeness Morris joined him, though the space was so tight he had to flatten himself against a metal wall to avoid contact with the man's grotesque paunch. 'And the haft also went in after the blade,' he remembered. What a nice word haft was.

'She has a brother, does she not?'

Now Morris was alarmed; it was another threatening item tossed into his juggling mind. Volpi laughed.

'Oh, not to worry, Signor Duckworth, I just ran into the two of them in the piazza and the pretty lady was, er, kind enough to introduce me to the young man. A charming couple.'

Couple was a strange word to use, Morris thought. For a brother and sister. If he could never decide whether there were any brain cells at all in Zolla's head, he felt sure that Volpi had too many.

'Your concern for them does you honour,' Volpi went on charitably as the lift doors opened. He scratched behind his ear and took a deep breath before propelling his bulk into the corridor.

Morris decided to say nothing, as if the matter were of the utmost indifference to him. He had been right to stop bringing Samira here. The brute had his eyes on her.

To reach the street they now had to walk through the ground floor of the museum's permanent exhibition. First a room of medieval sculpture and statuary, then some second-rate seventeenth-century paintings, then the display of the so-called *armi bianche*.

'You know the story behind the Arch of the Saints?' Volpi enquired. He took off his glasses and began to polish them on his handkerchief.

Morris nodded. He had no idea.

'I suppose beheading was a relief after walking for miles with nails in your feet.'

'Undoubtedly,' Morris replied at random.

Volpi sighed, then suddenly shook head and jowls vigorously from side to side. Evidently this was a tic, the spirit's instinctive urge, Morris interpreted, to free itself from a mountain of flab.

'And do you know why they were called "*armi bianche*"?'

The director was waddling between a line of showcases displaying short sharp swords, long stilettos and dangerously pointed pike heads.

Morris hesitated.

Volpi raised his heavy eyebrows.

'I have no idea,' Morris said, perhaps aggressively.

'Nor do I,' Volpi laughed. 'But it does seem odd to call something white that is essentially made to get very dirty, doesn't it?'

Morris tried to laugh. Was the man reading his mind? Was he aware of the story of King Eglon? The dirt came out. Morris had added the murder to Zolla's list of requests. There was a painting in Budapest. And Madox Brown's woodcut of course.

For a moment they stood by one of the cases and contemplated the weapons. The business of arranging scores of swords, knives, spears and pikes in neat long lines according to type and date made them seem rather harmless, Morris thought. Even boring. Yet the moment a man picked one of these things up, he realised, and closed his fingers round the solid haft, felt the weapon's weight and purpose, ran a finger along its keen blade, touched the killing point, then the heart would start to pound and the blood to throb, he had no doubt. Morris suddenly shivered.

'Perhaps, Signor Duckworth,' the fat man's voice seemed to bubble like oil through sludge, 'we could include a few of the more, er, evil daggers in the show, what do you think? And a pike or two, for good measure. Perhaps a spear. To give people a hint of what it would mean to use such things. Actually, I can't see why we shouldn't have some kind of situation where they are allowed to pick one up and get a sense of how they feel. The more modern shows do that kind of thing these days. For example, beside *The Massacre of the Innocents*.'

Morris breathed deeply.

'No doubt you have seen the research on how people's response to paintings intensifies when exposed to the objects depicted in them?'

Morris hadn't. But how stupid, he suddenly thought now, to be so anxious; the evident truth was that Volpi had finally recognised what a brilliant idea the show was. He had come on board and was offering his expertise.

'It is an interesting thought,' he said carefully: 'The murder weapon beside each painting, yes. Though I suggest we seek Professor Zolla's opinion first. Angelo has a strong sense of what is appropriate or not.'

Volpi turned rather brusquely. His paunch quivered.

'I should have asked, how have you been getting on with our resident professor?'

'Very well,' Morris said neutrally. With the museum's director actually favourable now, it suddenly seemed even more important to send a convincing account of the show to those museums that held the goods.

'You appreciate, do you, what a fine collaborator I have found for you?'

'I've been very impressed,' he said, 'by Professor Zolla's grasp of detail.'

Volpi laughed. 'Angelo's is a very special mind. He was telling me about your idea of introducing contrasting captions. I think it might work well.'

'Why, thank you, Angelo seemed worried that—'

'I've reassured him.'

This was too good to be true.

Volpi now rotated his bulk towards Morris and extended his chubby hand.

'I'll go so far as to say, Signor Duckworth, that inviting the

Arab boy, I can't recall his name, Signorina El Zidow's brother, to be involved is both provocative and, I hesitate to use the word, but I have to say it, brilliant. Yes provocative and brilliant. A delightful young man. Many charms. *Complimenti*. We shall have to think about the details very carefully, of course. Verona is, as you know, a supremely bigoted and provincial town. Anything perceived as an offence to the Catholic faith, or an encouragement to the Moslem, would be condemned without trial and boycotted at once. On the other hand, it could be the kind of idea that puts this show on the world map. Local immigrant commissioned to caption international show. Could anything be more politically correct?'

Morris moved in a daze. Was he dreaming? He usually hated it when the separate parts of his life were allowed to meet without his being present to check that they did not conspire against him. How did Volpi know about his invitation to Tarik? On the other hand, with things going so well it would be churlish to complain.

'You've been interceding for me, haven't you?' he remarked to Massimina later in the candlelit Art Room. He had been wondering whether perhaps it was too late to ask for Goya's *Saturn Devouring One of his Sons*, or *Cannibals Contemplating their Victims*. Goya was special.

'No more than usual,' she told him. 'You're always in my prayers, Morris.'

'By the way, do you know what's wrong with Mimi?' he asked, meaning his daughter.

'Of course I do.'

'And so?'

'I think you should ask her yourself, Morris.'

'But—'

'I wish I'd had a father when I was first dating boys,' she interrupted, rather heatedly. 'Then maybe I wouldn't have ended up here on the wall. You ask her. Before it's too late.'

Was she just being melodramatic to keep him anxious? He wouldn't put it past her.

'What do you think's going on with Massimina?' Morris asked his wife the following afternoon. 'She's at home all the time. She does nothing but send text messages.'

'Maybe she's in love.'

Antonella was picking one or two dead heads from a vase of lilies on the table in the salotto. 'Aren't they nice?'

'People in love are usually happy and full of energy.'

'You just need things to worry about, Morris, *caro*,' his wife smiled. 'Speaking of which, how's Mousie getting on?'

For a month now Morris had taken Mauro into the office every day. The company occupied the seventh floor of a commercial building block near the Verona Sud autostrada exit.

'Everybody loves him. It doesn't matter who I put him next to, they end up spending the day talking about Hellas Verona.'

Antonella smiled indulgently.

'It was nice of Stan to bring these,' she said, changing the subject. 'It's an expensive time for flowers.'

Morris hardly winced. With nothing to do during his extended holiday of Veronese nostalgia, Stan had been buzzing around Palazzo Duckworth like a tired blowfly, the kind that drone themselves to death in dusty corners. Fancifully, Morris imagined the sound emanating from one of Sickert's *Camden Town Murders*. Buzz buzz buzz, around the corpses in those squalid bedsits. Wasn't there some audio technology, he vaguely remembered, they had developed for museums that allowed you to have sound triggered and localised around each exhibit. You could have children whimpering, women shrieking, saints groaning. Bring death alive.

'Stan's mellowed with old age,' Morris agreed. 'Invite him this evening. He's always pleasant company.'

'He's gone to England for a couple of days.'

Shame!

'To visit Forbes's ex-wife, if he can find her.'

Damn. A virtual hand rose from Morris's alarmed mind to catch yet another dangerous missile. Sooner or later, something was going to explode in his face.

'I had no idea they were such close friends,' he said.

Antonella frowned: 'It seems Stan had lent him quite a lot of money.'

So that was it! So much for friendship. Immediately it occurred to Morris that perhaps the American could be bought off. If only he could think of some delicate way to propose it. Send him away with the money he had come to recover. How much could it be in the end?

At Samira's, Morris gave Tarik a list of the paintings he would require captions for. Samson and Delilah. Sardanapalus. Absalom. Judith and Holofernes. Jael and Sisera. King Eglon. The Death of Agag. The Levite and his Concubine. Othello and Desdemona. And St Bartholomew.

At the table they went through a PowerPoint together. Samira sat close to Morris, absently stroking his left thigh, while to his right Tarik had his chin in his hands, elbows on the table, shaking his head as image after bloody image popped up before them.

'Just study what happened,' Morris told him. 'Wikipedia has the background. Then write whatever you feel in response. Maximum 500 characters. Including spaces. That's six or seven lines. Then I'll edit.'

'Why The Levite and his Concubine?' Tarik asked. 'Are there any Arabs in that?'

'I thought you might want to comment that this, hmmm, shameful story, entirely within the Jewish community, has so few images, while a triumph over their Arab enemies, Judith decapitating Holofernes for example, is endlessly celebrated and reproduced.'

'What was the story?' Samira asked.

The woodcut they were looking at showed a man raising a

rather splendid axe, over a woman's body already cut into six or seven hapless chunks.

Morris explained.

'Poor concubine,' the girl breathed. She pulled her head away from Morris's shoulder. 'Gang-raped, left to die, then cut to bits. I hope that's not supposed to be a warning.'

'For heaven's sake!' Morris was alarmed.

'She sacrificed herself to save her man,' Tarik said, clucking his lips, apparently impressed.

'Not *willingly,*' Morris pointed out. 'The Levite just pushed her out in the street to satisfy the hoodlums who'd actually been after him.'

'Typical,' Samira complained, 'a man gets tired of his woman and throws her to the sharks.'

'But darling—'

'Interesting,' Tarik said, 'that the hoodlums first thought they would rape *him*, then raped his whore instead.'

Right. It was the kind of detail, Morris agreed, you just never heard from a Church of England pulpit. But the Bible was clear on the point. They had wanted the Levite's butt.

The young Arab was smiling that marvellous smile that lit up just one half of his face. 'Perhaps our Levite was good-looking.'

'Trust you!' Samira said.

Uncomfortably, Morris remembered the days when he himself had been an object of sexual interest to other men. Forbes for example. He'd never have guessed if Massimina hadn't warned him.

'Not at all,' he said firmly. 'It was because they had issues with him.'

'Issues!' Tarik laughed unpleasantly. 'What issues?'

'The Bible doesn't say.'

'Was that how they used to deal with issues? Forcing their opponents into anal sex?'

'I've no idea.' Morris became aware of a wave of heat rising as if from the seat, through intestines and belly. 'Anyway,' he hurried on, 'when the Levite cut the corpse up and sent the twelve pieces of concubine to the twelve tribes of Israel – see the messengers standing round with baskets to carry the bits? – they agreed that her death had to be avenged and about 100,000 people were killed in the ensuing battle.'

'Christ!' Samira said.

'No it was BC,' Tarik laughed.

Morris began to dislike the boy.

'Quite a lesson!' Samira was still shaking her head.

'How am I supposed to get all that plus an opinion into 500 characters?' Tarik demanded.

'If you don't feel up to it, I can find someone else,' Morris said coolly.

'Easy,' Samira sang, 'they wanted to fuck *him*, he tells them to fuck *her*, then *everyone* gets fucked!'

Tarik laughed out loud. As he did so his left hand dropped carelessly from his neck to fall on Morris's right thigh. Morris looked down and glancing through the glass tabletop saw the boy's strong fingers brush Samira's for a moment. The heat in his bowels intensified. He pushed back his chair and sat up.

'By the way,' he announced, 'are you two busy Sunday morning? I'd like you to help me move a painting.'

CHAPTER TEN

HE REALLY COULDN'T WAIT any longer. Between a meeting with American buyers and another with Tunisian suppliers – it was important to keep the two well apart – Morris had stepped out of the office to pick up his now soberly framed honorary citizenship scroll from the *corniciaio*, and then, in the hardware store in Corso Milano, something to break a stout padlock. 'A garage on a property we have in the country,' he explained blithely. 'I'm afraid I lost the key to the padlock.'

Then coming out of the hardware store, reflecting, as he so often did when he found a heavy object in his hand, that this bolt cutter could definitely kill, and break fingers off too if you were that way inclined, he was simply overwhelmed by the need to *solve this business of the loan requests once and for all*. What was the point of all this mental ferment, this constant thinking about the various paintings, their arrangement, their captions, the overall effect on the public, if the show was never going to happen? What was the point of grabbing San Bartolomeo if the saint flayed was not to be a saint displayed? Rather than waste time walking a hundred yards back to the office for his Alfa, Morris stepped into the street and hailed a cab.

'Castelvecchio, per favore.'

Sitting in the back, Morris was again overwhelmed with indignation that a worm of a man like Zolla could call himself an art historian. The pedant didn't want to take on board that these paintings Morris had put together were throbbing with life, heavy with death. The real thing. And instead Zolla was talking chronology and framing history, school of this, school of that. And as a result the Louvre had already said no. Other museums had asked for more information. And Zolla had replied, giving, he reassured Morris, 'full details of air, humidity and temperature inside the museum and the travel and insurance arrangements'. For Christ's sake! When what any serious museum director would want, Morris felt, was some compelling reason for lending his priceless heritage to this out-of-the-way show! He, Morris, had to sort this out *now*! Life is now.

'*Grazie*,' he told the taxi driver, tipped him generously and ignored his gratitude. He had to explain to those directors why they would one day be proud to have contributed to a *ground-breaking exhibition* which would bring together in the most explosive and illuminating fashion the beauty of form and the ugliness of murder. Otherwise Holofernes had been killed in vain. The Baptist had been decapitated to no end. Christ crucified for nothing.

Morris marched into the museum, assured the guard on the door that he was not about to break the locks on the display cases and steal their swords and daggers, left his package and bolt cutter in the cloakroom and hurried through the permanent exhibition, then up the stairs to the offices.

Zolla's secretary seemed flustered.

'Did you have an appointment, Signor Duckworth?'

She blocked him outside Zolla's door, which, unusually, was closed.

Affable, if breathless, Morris explained that something had just occurred to him that made it *imperative* he have a word with Professor Zolla *at once*. A lot was at stake, he said. He walked past the young woman's desk.

'He's not in,' the secretary said, sidestepping to block him again. She was a cheerfully plump creature, dark-eyed and demure, but her suddenly brilliant smile now, as she stood with her shoulders to Zolla's door, was oddly unfathomable. Morris stopped and stared at her. The secretary was smiling, as it were *determinedly*.

Morris raised his right scar-brow in a question. The secretary smiled harder, as if willing Morris to *please* understand, but simultaneously withholding the information that would get him there. The burden of it must be, Morris thought that Zolla *was* in his room, but had told the secretary to say he wasn't. She, in her zealous ignorance, had not understood that such an order could hardly apply to so important a visitor as himself. Again he made for the door. Again she blocked him.

Morris sighed.

'I'm sorry I've never asked you your name.'

'Tosi.' She cocked her head to one side. Her breasts were generously maternal.

'I meant your first name.'

'Mariella.'

'How lovely,' Morris said graciously.

'*Grazie*.'

'I'll wait, then.' He looked around to see if there was a free chair.

The big girl still wasn't happy. 'I'm afraid he may be a long time.'

Morris thought a moment.

'OK, why don't we do this? I'll just pop down to the museum for half an hour. I have to check a couple of wall measurements. In the meantime, if you have a chance to be in touch with him, can you let the professor know that I need to speak to him urgently?'

'I'll see what I can do, Signor Duckworth.'

'Morris,' Morris said.

The secretary smiled still, but was too canny to use his first name. Her smile was a smile of power now, and obvious relief, and as Morris walked back through the office he was intensely aware that they *all*, yes, all five of the other workers, were wearing that same smile on their busy, dutiful and utterly hypocritical faces.

Down in the museum he needed to check whether the door

that led to the basement storerooms was usually kept locked or open. He walked past the arch of saints, and along the line of stony trecento dukes and knights to the double door in the far corner that bore the legend *'L'ingresso e severamente vietato ai non autorizzati'*. Morris smiled. He still loved the way it was never enough for Italians to forbid something. It had to be *severely* forbidden. Which only made it the more exciting just to press the handle down and see if . . . yes, it opened. There. But now he could hardly just close it again. How suspicious would that look? He breezed through, shut the door behind him and found himself in the pitch dark.

Damn. Morris stood still for a moment and noticed at once that the air quality was different from that in the display rooms. It smelt dank. No humidity control. Hardly ideal for storing things. Running his hand over rough plaster to the left and right of the doorway, he eventually found a switch that lit a descending staircase. In for a penny. Morris walked down and discovered a large shadowy space dustily cluttered with what must be sculptures under heavy plastic sheeting and, along the wall to the right, stacks of canvases, some protected, others not. Morris picked his way over there. One rather charming stone griffin squatted under a coating of grime. Were these things valuable or not? Morris had often wondered whether the storerooms of museums might not be used by art traffickers, with a little internal collusion, as the ideal places to hide stolen artefacts until a buyer was found. The police would hardly go looking in the vast reserves of the V&A for stolen paintings. It might be interesting to know exactly what was under all these wraps. Of course it would be the merest prejudice to imagine that because Volpi was Neapolitan he might be up to something. Yet why do we have prejudices in the end? Because more often than not experience bears them out.

Morris frowned. Exploring a little further in the room, he found a row of metal cupboards. He moved along the doors. Padlocked. Padlocked. Open! Inside were a dozen swords and daggers in a loose pile. Morris stopped. This was interesting. He stared. The light wasn't good. Just naked bulbs strung along the central vault of a low ceiling. All the same, these were clearly antique pieces, presumably an extension of the collection on permanent display upstairs. It was strange that they weren't even labelled. He picked one up. The haft felt a little small for his grip. But the weapon was pleasantly heavy. 'A dagger which had two edges, of a cubit length.' Morris smiled. 'And he did gird it under his raiment upon his right thigh.' Morris stood up, opening his jacket, and tried to slip the thing under his belt. Damn it was sharp! The point caught his thumb. He had a nasty scratch. Morris sucked the wound to stop the blood staining his clothes. How irritating! He put the knife back in the cupboard. There was something wrapped in a cloth and he unwrapped it one-handedly – a tiny stiletto – then thrust his thumb into the cloth which felt as if it had been gathering dust for years.

He squatted in front of the cupboard, lost in thought. The weapons seemed rather pathetic, piled haphazardly in an old cupboard in a dank, gloomy room, like any junk people no longer have any use for; yet ready to flash out too, he knew, like genies from a bottle, ready to spring into the willing hand and accomplish some awful destiny. Weapons call to the willing hand. There was no doubt about that. Morris chuckled, savouring that moment when suddenly all indecision is behind you, you have the knife by the handle, you are going to strike, and the Devil take the hindmost.

Hindmost. Another wonderful word.

Then he was furious with himself. What on earth was he wasting all this time for, gloating over rusty swords? Once again the impulse that had driven him to the museum an hour or so ago returned with renewed force; he must head straight back upstairs and simply force Zolla, who was no doubt skulking in his office – masturbating quite probably, or entertaining a girlfriend – to write the kind of letter that might still save his exhibition. That was the *only thing that mattered*. Do it now.

Hurrying back up the stairs from the storerooms, Morris banged out of the severely forbidden door, almost knocking over a dozy museum guard who had chosen precisely this quiet corner to while away the next sleepy but salaried hour. Without stopping to apologise, he rushed straight back upstairs and in no time at all, wounded hand thrust in jacket pocket, was striding between the desks of the office staff whose faces once again broke into smiles as he appeared. Zolla's door was open now, but again the secretary stood up and shook her head. She wore too much eyeliner, Morris thought. It was vulgar.

'I'm afraid, the professor's still out.'

'I'll wait in his room if that's OK, Mariella.'

'I don't think he'll be back at all this morning.'

Her nails were a luminous turquoise.

'I'll take the risk,' Morris said.

He pushed determinedly forward and into Zolla's office. Behind him he had the impression that everybody in the room was about to burst into laughter. The Six-Dagger Massacre, he muttered a headline to himself: When it came time to close the offices, wrote *Corriere della Sera,* the museum caretaker found the institution's entire administrative staff skewered to their swivel chairs and drenched in blood.

Morris plonked himself in the armchair in the corner. The computer was on, he noticed. Zolla's deodorant was in the air. How far away could the guy be?

The secretary had followed him in and now stood helplessly at the door.

'You really shouldn't insist, Signor Duckworth,' she said.

'Morris,' Morris smiled. 'Call me Morris.' From the wall beside him he picked out an old catalogue entitled *L'onore delle armi*. A show in 2004. *The Honour of Arms. The Castelvecchio Collection.*

Since the young woman was watching him, he couldn't pull his left hand from his pocket with its bloody rag. He could still feel the thumb pulsing. All the same he managed to rest the catalogue on his knee and, holding the bulk with his right hand, let the pages open one by one. There were tribal spears and shields from the Congo. Italy's colonial wars. A sabre from Turkey. Rifles and bayonets from 1917.

'The portrait gallery,' he read on one page, 'of gentlemen in armour at the turn of the sixteenth to the seventeenth century includes exponents of the Sagramoso and Pompei families from Verona. The finest portrait, that of Francesco Sagramoso, by Felice Brusasorci, is also the only one of a contemporary personage.'

The secretary was still standing in the doorway.

'Did Professor Zolla write this?' Morris asked innocently.

'Yes,' she said, 'he always looks after the catalogues.'

Morris glanced up and saw that she understood what he was thinking: the text was dire.

'Lots of stuff about honour and gentlemen,' he laughed, 'but not much indication of what these unpleasant little jiggers actually did to people's insides.'

The secretary didn't reply.

Morris flicked leisurely through the catalogue. The woman hung on.

'So, do I take it that all these weapons are held here at the museum?'

'Not everything,' she said. 'But a lot of them. There are all kinds of things in the storerooms.'

Morris put the catalogue down.

'Tell me,' he said.

'Oh,' she frowned. 'I really couldn't recall. There's an inventory of course. We could have two or three permanent displays, if we had the space.'

'An inventory? If you have it on Excel or something, could you email it to me?'

The secretary looked helpless now.

Morris smiled his most reassuring smile.

'*Cara* Mariella, you really don't need to stand guard over me like an anxious mastiff. As co-curator of a forthcoming show, not to mention a major sponsor of the museum, I have some urgent business with the professor. So, if you don't mind, I'll just sit here reading catalogues until the professor shows up.'

The woman sighed, lifting her ample breasts in an almost cartoon gesture. The moment she turned and retreated into the main open-plan room, Morris was on his feet and standing at Zolla's computer. The screensaver was Donatello's David. Naff. Pulling his left hand from his pocket, shaking off the rag and giving his thumb a good suck, Morris opened the search window in the bottom right of the screen and typed in 'passwords'. A huge list of documents scrolled down. Morris looked at their file names. *Spasso alla spiaggia. Il diritto e la privacy. Le leggi suntuarie nel* 400 *fiorentina* . . .

Too many. And his thumb was still bleeding. How ridiculous!

Another hard suck and Morris went back to the search window and typed 'skype email username banca biblioteca codice fiscale pin login'. Again various names appeared. But this time *Le leggi suntuarie nel* 400 was dominant. Morris clicked the file and, bingo! There they were, all Zolla's passwords in a neat list. So much for fifteenth-century sumptuary laws. What an idiot imagining he had hidden the file by giving it an oddball name. Morris selected and copied the lot, closed the file, switched to Explorer which was already open on Zolla's email, addressed a message to his own email account, MAD@duckworth.com, pasted in Zolla's passwords, sent the mail, then deleted it, first from *Posta inviata* then from *Posta eliminata*. He opened the *Documenti recenti* folder to delete *Le leggi suntuarie* from that. Done? Yes. All in less than a minute. He really could have been a professional criminal. Morris returned the email window to *Posta in arrivo* and noted that the most recent message was from Volpi. Twenty-five minutes ago, but already read. He moved the cursor to it and a preview appeared. 'Gioletto, get your sweet ass into my office now!'

Gioletto? Sweet ass!

'Signor Duckworth!'

The secretary was back.

'Just leaving Angelo a message, Mariella,' Morris smiled. 'I'm afraid I'll have to go now. Or I'll miss a meeting.'

'Please leave any messages with me, Signor Duckworth.'

Glancing down Morris saw a drop of fresh blood on the white keyboard. So much for the professional criminal. But who uses white keyboards? He sighed, picked up the rag, wiped the space bar, wrapped his thumb in it again, pushed his hand back into his pocket and walked straight towards the plump woman at the door.

'What would you like me to say to the professor?' she insisted.

'Just tell him to call me as soon as he can.'

No sooner had Morris passed the line of desks – and he didn't even bother to check whether people were smirking or not this time – he turned right rather than left, down the corridor that led to Volpi's office.

'Signor Duckworth! *Per favore!*'

The secretary was coming after him again, running. He could hear her high heels clipping on the stone floor.

'Dottor Volpi is also out, Signor Duckworth!'

But Morris was at the door. He knocked and pushed. It swung open.

For a moment it seemed the secretary had been telling the truth. The huge desk at the other end of the room and in particular the upholstered swivel chair were not occupied. Evidently Volpi had called Gioletto to his office and the two of them had gone out together for lunch.

Then Morris heard a quick intake of breath. More than that. It was a sob. Without thinking, he stepped forward into the room and saw Zolla to his right *sitting on the floor against the wall.* The man's carefully groomed head was in his hands and his body was shaking, uncontrollably. Morris stared. Zolla seemed completely stricken. What on earth was he doing on the floor? On an old display panel leaning against the wall beside him, red on black, were the words: 'Devotees of the Bianchi made their pilgrimages barefoot, slept on straw, abstained from meat-eating, and scourged themselves while calling for mercy and peace.' Why Morris should have taken the time to read this odd relic of a forgotten show and even to try to understand it, he couldn't have said. But the unhappy man weeping in his smart suit and the old display panel with its strange caption somehow struck Morris as forming a single picture. Who were the Bianchi? Why did they scourge themselves? Above all, why was Zolla in this state?

Morris hesitated. Behind him, too, he heard the secretary's heels scrape to a halt, as if the fact that Morris had opened the door made any further intervention on her part superfluous. Clearly he had arrived at the heart of whatever it was made the office staff at Castelvecchio smile their interminable smiles. But what was it?

'Signor Duckworth,' a gravelly voice enquired, 'did your good mother not teach you to knock *and* wait before entering?'

Turning to his left Morris saw Volpi standing with his back to the room, looking out of the barred window. The fat man was so perfectly still, his eye hadn't travelled that way. But how did he know it was Morris if he was looking out of the window?

'Please be so kind as to leave at once,' the director said. Still without turning, he added drily: 'If you don't want to end up like one of the victims in this ridiculous show of yours.'

At which someone somewhere else in the room laughed. It was a rather unusual yet at the same time, Morris later felt, rather familiar laugh. But since he was already withdrawing and closing the doors he had no occasion to find out who that person might be.

CHAPTER ELEVEN

WITHOUT HIS CAR, MORRIS walked back to Via Oberdan, feeling perplexed and unsteady. At least he would now be able to access the addresses of the appropriate people to write to in the various museums. And now he knew things which of course other people would not want him to talk about. That was always useful in Italy. Next they would be asking him to join in whatever perverse nonsense they were into. Perhaps his morning had been more fruitful than it had seemed. Turning from Via Roma into Piazza Bra he became aware that someone was calling to him.

'Morris!'

Someone with an American accent.

'Hey Morris, man.'

'Stan, what a pleasure.'

'You're not going to believe this, Morris.'

The Californian was breathless. He was carrying a small backpack.

'I came straight from the airport.'

Morris stiffened. All over his mind battle stations were ringing.

'To see you.'

'On foot?' Morris enquired.

'Bus,' Stan explained. He was breathing hard. 'You're not going to believe what I found out. About Forbes. We've got to go to the police.'

'Tell me,' Morris said. He took the American's arm. 'Let's sit and have a drink.' As he moved toward the blue tables of La Costa, Stan was already talking ten to the dozen and far more loudly than was wise. Morris was struggling to imagine what was the properly innocent response.

'*Due prosecchi,*' he said, when the waiter passed. It was one-fifteen.

'Incredible names they have in Wales,' Stan was saying. 'Pwllgwyngyll. Something like that. The old bird was about a hundred. The wife. Turned out she was much older than Mikey. Twenty years and more. Shades of the mother syndrome, I reckon. Anyway she was quite gaga. Couldn't get anything out of her at all. Hardly seemed to know what I was talking about.' Stan leaned forward across the table. 'Fortunately, just as I was leaving, the daughter turned up.'

Fortunate indeed. Morris looked around to see when the drinks were coming. 'Forbes never mentioned a daughter to me,' he said carefully.

'Nice lady. Our age.' Stan grinned. 'Bit of a drinker, I'm afraid. Took me straight to the pub. Said there were things couldn't be said in front of the mother.'

'Who was gaga.'

'Right.'

How was it possible, Morris thought, that in the midst of all his other troubles he now had to deal with this?

'So what did you learn?'

The proseccos arrived. Morris sipped, looking at Stan over the rim of his glass. He was struck then by the leanness of his old acquaintance's neck, the shiny bulbousness of the forehead. Not a handsome specimen.

'From a psychological point of view, this is one of the weirdest stories you've ever heard.' Stan scooped up a handful of the peanuts the waiter had brought.

'I'm all ears,' Morris assured him.

'First thing is, although he hadn't been back to Pwllwynwhatever for more than twenty years, Forbsey used to phone his old lady for about an hour every day, or rather night. Around midnight. *An hour!* Without fail.'

'Astonishing,' Morris said calmly. At least it explained where some of that money had been going. An hour a day from Verona to Pwllgwyngyll year in year out would run up quite a bill.

'Wait till you hear why,' Stan grinned, taking more peanuts and swallowing the wine.

'Why?' Morris obliged.

'To *confess,*' Stan munched. 'To confess and be shriven.'

'Confess what?' Morris was steeling himself.

'The daughter said her dad was an accident waiting to happen, the way he behaved. She said everyone knew.'

'May we have the daughter's name?' Morris enquired.

'Molly.'

'Are you sure?'

'That's what she said.'

'I can't imagine Forbes calling a daughter Molly. You'd have thought at the very least Lucrezia or Cleopatra.'

Stan scratched his thinning hair and shook his head. It was fascinating how easily he was distracted.

'Weird,' the American finally agreed, at random, Morris thought. 'The thing is, Mo, it seems Forbes was attracted to boys. Can you imagine? Worse still, young boys. He'd been in trouble even. Anyway he confessed this stuff every day to his wife, his urges, if you get me and she . . . she . . .' Stan seemed at a loss.

'Shrove him. Shrive-shrove-shriven.' Morris smiled faintly.

'Well . . .'

'Perhaps in America they accept shrived.'

'Well . . .' Stan had got stuck again.

'Anyway,' Morris interrupted, 'yes, I knew Forbes had this vice. That's why I tried to keep him busy with the paintings.'

'You knew?'

'Yes.'

'And didn't say?'

'I didn't want a friend to go to gaol. I tried to keep him out of trouble.'

Stan shook his head. 'But think of the damage a guy like that could do.'

'The older I get, Stan, the more it seems to me that all living is about damage. People have to learn to look after themselves.'

Morris looked the American straight in the eye. Stan was undeterred.

'But get this. It seems, according to Molly at least, that he was also working for some guy he knew was a criminal. Someone was giving him money just to keep him quiet. Apparently he had it on his conscience, but he needed the money. Anyway, she, the daughter, was convinced that something bad must have happened to him, otherwise, why would he just have stopped calling from one day to the next? He needed to make those calls and feel his wife had forgiven him.'

Morris frowned. 'He found some other confessor perhaps. Without the need for the expensive phone call.'

Stan had already emptied his glass. He shook his head. 'He was zapped, man. Must have been. You don't change a twenty-year habit just like that. The daughter thought it would be one of these boys he was after. Or this guy he knew about.'

Morris sighed. 'I wonder who that can be.'

'Maybe explains why he was in with so many priests,' Stan said. 'Maybe it was a priest even. The criminal guy. He knew about some priest who was more into the paedo stuff than he was. Anyway, we've got to go to the police.'

'Do you really think they'll be interested?' Morris asked.

Stan was surprised. 'We're talking about a disappearance. Possibly a murder.'

Morris sipped. He still had more than half a glass. 'It was five years and more ago, Stan. An awful lot happens in this country every single day. And Michael was not even Italian. Why should they care about him.'

'I think we owe it to him to report it at least,' Stan said. 'A guy goes missing and no one even reports it.'

They had finished their drinks. Morris stayed silent.

'You know I went out to look at that last picture he copied. The Jezebel. That you have in your room.'

'Oh right,' Morris smiled. 'Did you? How interesting.'

'Amazing the job he did making it look even older than it was. I mean, quite a technique. The thing in the church looks new in comparison. Restored, the priest said.'

'Michael had special skills.' It occurred to Morris that if only Stan would drop the idea of going to the police, he could indeed rely on him never to put two and two together.

'The nearest *questura* is along the river beyond Ponte Nuovo, right?'

'That's right,' Morris agreed. 'If you like, I'll go for you. In the end your time here's nearly up, isn't it? You don't want to get drawn into some long drawn-out legal thing.'

Stan sucked his lips. 'No, I'd better go myself. I've got some photographs and stuff. And some letters the daughter gave me.'

'I can take them,' Morris said.

For the first time Stan gave him a queer look. 'No worries, man,' he said. 'You're a busy guy. And I'm kind of into this now. Nothing like this ever happened to me.'

Morris slowed down his responses to disguise any suggestion that he was a man thinking fast. He raised a hand to get the waiter to bring the bill, then with a heavy heart said, 'Let's go together. I'll get the car.'

'But it's so close.' Stan hesitated. 'Good of you though. My Italian's pretty rusty these days.'

When the waiter returned, the American added, ''Fraid I'm out of cash.'

Wasn't that ever the way, Morris remembered. And wasn't it amazing that thirty years ago he had been sitting at a table in this same café with Massimina when Stan saw them together. Perhaps this very same table. The day she decided to run away with him, the day it all began. It was as if something that should have happened many years ago was finally coming to pass.

'Thinking about it,' Morris said reflectively, 'we'll probably have more luck with the police if we drive out to where he was last resident. When he was painting the Jezebel. The local police won't have so much to do out there.'

Stan hesitated.

'We could even take a look at the picture again. Maybe see if the priest there knows something.'

'That's a point,' Stan said. 'He was eating when I went. Wouldn't leave the table.'

Morris thus had perhaps an hour to take his decision. First a short cab ride to get the car, then a forty-minute drive round the city and up into the hills. At the wheel he told Stan about his concerns for his daughter. She seemed to have stopped going to the university and spent all her time texting. It was so disappointing seeing a young person throwing her life away.

'No worries,' Stan said, for perhaps the third time in an hour. 'Adolescents do that stuff. You should stay cool. I'll speak to her if you like.'

'You're so relaxed about everything,' Morris said appreciatively.

'Not about this Forbsey thing,' Stan admitted. 'I really think he must have come to grief.'

It was as if the man were asking for it, Morris thought. He found it fascinating how some people would suspect him even when he hadn't done anything at all, while poor Stan seemed genetically incapable of suspicion. The problem would be when the police realised that yet another person close to Morris Duckworth was missing in mysterious circumstances. There must be a limit to one's luck. Meanwhile Stan was complaining how expensive everything had gotten in Italy these last few years. Morris nodded sagely.

'In the end,' he suddenly interrupted, 'the last place we know of Forbes ever going was the church.'

'There was the flat he rented,' Stan said.

'Of course.'

'I went there last week.'

'You did?'

'Obvious place to go. Naturally someone else was living there. The landlord is an agency so the staff have all changed. From the records it seems when he didn't pay rent for a few months they went to check and found all his stuff gone. So they just rented to someone else.'

'There you are,' Morris said. 'So he did a flit. Typical. He's probably safe and sound in China or somewhere. I know he'd had offers to teach in other parts of the world. It isn't easy to get a good Latin teacher these days. Dying breed,' Morris added, enjoying the expression.

'How do we know it was him took his stuff out of the flat?' Stan asked. 'What if he was killed and the killer took it all, to give the impression he'd done a runner.'

That did it. Morris drove on, up into the hills toward the church where he had been so recently with his son. Santi Apostoli del Soccorso. He parked in the shade against the cemetery wall. What he needed, he thought, was just a little bit of luck. Who visited a church on a Wednesday early afternoon? No one. At the same time he wondered if he could really go through with this. He'd prayed so much the cup would pass from him.

'Let's look at the picture again, first,' he said. 'The priest will be having his siesta. I read a novel once,' he went on, 'where a painter had left a message on the back of a canvas.'

'We can't start turning it round,' Stan laughed. 'They'll think we're stealing it.'

'Actually, I remember Forbes telling me it was amazing the sort of stuff you found in church attics. Maybe we should check if there is one in the place. There's just a chance he could have come to grief up there.'

'I already checked,' Stan said.

Morris tripped and almost fell.

'Pure curiosity. But there's only rubble up there.'

'Rubble?'

'Some builder's leftovers they didn't bother to bring down and chuck away. Sacks of cement and so on.'

They had reached the church.

'What if he was under them?'

Stan whistled softly. 'Quite a mind you have Ducky! But they wouldn't have killed him in the church, would they? Most likely it was a reaction to some hanky-panky, or something.'

The good thing, Morris thought, pushing open the door, was that having visited the place recently he knew that everything was there, everything was in place. And so it was. For a few minutes they stood together and stared at Jezebel crashing down from the window.

'It was because she was a foreigner, you know,' Morris said. 'Seems that's why they didn't trust her.'

'Typical,' Stan laughed. 'You kind of wonder if she couldn't maybe have survived a jump from the second floor, though. Don't you reckon?'

'Speaking of which,' Morris allowed himself an embarrassing non sequitur, 'let's go take a look upstairs at that rubble.'

Making his invitation, Morris barely trusted the sound of his voice. It all seemed so obvious, so easy. How could Stan not see what he was walking into? Morris moved purposefully to the altar table. 'We can light the way with one of the candlesticks.'

True to his word, Don Gaetano had put real wax candles in the big brass sticks. Morris took the heavy thing to the little battery of votive candles in the nave and lowered it to the flames. The thick smoke curled up round the white flesh of the wax.

'Baroque!' Stan laughed.

The man was a fool, Morris thought. An utter fool. He deserved it. Afterwards, he would light a votive candle himself and beg forgiveness.

Stan showed him the door at the back of the chancel and led the way along a short corridor, then up steep stone steps. At the top in the gloom was a small iron door that groaned in exactly the way it had five years ago. As if a switch had turned, Morris felt his body thrill with anticipation.

'I reckon it would have happened in his flat,' Stan was saying.

Morris was too tense to respond. The low space under the roof was lit by light filtering through the tiles. The air was curiously fresh; evidently any smell here escaped upwards rather than down. All the same, it would be wise to bag the body. There were plastic sacks against the wall.

'I suppose the problem is that with other people renting there the last five years, any traces will be gone.'

Stan stepped forward and examined the heap of rubble in the middle of the floor.

'There could be somebody under here, come to think of it.'

Now!

Morris raised his arm and he was glad, glad to be killing again. Glad to be back in the saddle. Come what may.

He raised the heavy candlestick but then was overcome by a sudden desire to vomit. Cain, Judith, Brutus, they all flashed across his mind. He had a terrible feeling of déjà vu. Hadn't he collected those paintings precisely so as never to kill again?

Do it!

Absolutely determined, Morris raised his arm violently and the big candlestick with its fat burning candle struck the low attic ceiling. He hadn't thought of that. The candle tumbled out of its heavy brass base before the latter could be brought down on the faint gleam of Stan Albertini's bald spot. The light shifted drastically, the flame guttering as it fell from ceiling to floor, then flaring again as, in its now horizontal position, the candle found a generous supply of wax. Morris felt the room spin, a whirl of shadow and flame. Stan swung round. 'Whoa, careful there! You'll start a fire.' Both men went down, Stan to grab the candle, Morris because he had fainted. He was out cold.

PART TWO

CHAPTER TWELVE

All'Avvocatessa Carla Cogni

Carissima Carla,

You ask me to send you a full account of my movements in the month leading up to my arrest and imprisonment, to help you in my defence. I shall do my best and just hope you won't mind if I digress now and then. Solitary confinement is solitary indeed and without phone or Internet I may as well pass the time this way as any other. Then what appears to be digression may actually turn out to hold the key to the case, who knows; to date I remain as bewildered as anyone else as to who could have carried out such a strangely brutal, yet, in a curious way, as I felt at once when I discovered the body, beautiful murder.

A month before my arrest takes me back to where? 22 March? I don't have my diary with me, so I might get a few days mixed up. Do you want to hear how I got my honorary-citizen's scroll framed and was all set to hang it on the wall when I discovered they'd spelt '*imprenditore*' wrong, with a double 't' '*imprendittore*'? I was with my daughter trying to nail the thing up over the piano and she laughed and said they must be taking the mick out of my accent because I always got the doubles wrong, not pronouncing them when they were there and introducing them when they weren't. Actually, I don't think that's the case at all. I've always taken great care over the pronunciation of double letters, which alas the English in their general linguistic slovenliness ignore and simply pronounce as one letter. And no, Carla, this is not one of the digressions I was warning of. I'm not digressing at all. I mention the language issue because it has frequently occurred to me that I am always considered the first suspect for a crime because I am a foreigner, I have an accent, or, even worse, because I have only the *very slightest* of accents. We've all seen in recent years how easy it has been for the police to accuse blacks, Arabs and Slavs whenever there's some violent street crime, or even a perfectly ingenuous American like Amanda Knox, and how satisfied the public always is to suppose that a foreigner must be responsible for every ugly calamity on Italian soil. You should definitely ask yourself if this isn't an issue in the way I'm being treated. A murder occurs within a relatively closed community – a state-run museum – in which there is just one foreigner, and what's more a foreigner who more than any other has camouflaged himself as one of us, has demanded our approval for his achievements, has become a major benefactor of all kinds of civic institutions, has distinguished himself, we could say, as exactly the kind of cultural product we would wish our own nation to produce, if only we educated our children properly. Damn him! He puts us to shame. Obviously he is guilty! I should say here that the first time I met Dottor Volpi he made his distaste for foreigners, and in particular Anglo-Saxons (he appeared unable to distinguish between Americans and English) all too evident, passing the most disparaging remarks about a respected English novelist who had curated a prestigious art exhibition in Florence and criticising out of hand all foreigners who wrote about Italy in any way, as if they were somehow terrorists and should be repatriated at once. That, Carla, is the kind of cultural context that Morris Duckworth has always had to contend with in Italy. I shall elaborate on this a little further when we come to the matter of my son's trial. However, right now I have my break for some prison-yard exercise. Just fifteen minutes and completely alone. Under the rain by the looks of it. Why they need to keep me away from the other prisoners I can't imagine. Perhaps they think I will crack sooner this way. The Italian judiciary always spends more time trying to persuade people to confess than actually building a solid case against them. I suppose it's cheaper and easier. Of which more after my break. I shall let some rain run down my cheeks and imagine the drops are tears. The truth is I'm beyond crying. The world is too absurd. I must be the only man who ever lived to have been wrongly accused of murder twice. Perhaps – I return to my pen to scribble a last word – having given me that honorary citizenship, they had to find some way of marking me out as foreign again. Having given me the freedom of the city, they felt obliged to put me in gaol. I was set up for a fall.

To the Mayor of Verona

Egregio sindaco, onorevole Dottor Lunardi,

Forgive me for writing to you out of the blue, not the vast and wonderful blue of God's heavens either, but the deep mental indigo of this suffocating prison cell. I have time on my hands.

Forgive also the miserable quality of this notepaper and biro. It is all I have.

I write first and foremost to thank you, for the honour you conferred upon me in granting me the freedom (!) of the fair city of Verona, for your solicitousness in coming to my son's trial, and, more generally, for having run the city so well over the past five years, facilitating the work of businessmen like myself who, without your attention to efficient infrastructures and your abhorrence of red tape, would be even more hard-pressed than we already are.

Congratulations are also in order, I believe, and I extend them gladly. It is not easy for me to get news here in solitary confinement, but a guard was kind enough to confirm that you have indeed been re-elected, and at the first round of voting. Frankly, I would have been immensely surprised by any other result; nevertheless it was a relief to hear that a man of your stature and wisdom remains in Palazzo Barbieri and I can only send you my warmest compliments. Your success is richly deserved.

I won't deny of course that I write as a petitioner and I appreciate at once that very likely my plea may not and perhaps cannot be granted. As you know, I am being held on charges of murder. The injustice of my arrest seems so evident that I struggle to enter into the mentality of one who needs to argue his case. I write, then, simply to beg you, as you prepare for your second term of office, aware of course of the many pressing demands upon your time and energies, to pay a little attention to my plight. What grieves me most about being in gaol is not so much the physical constriction and mental loneliness, which I hope I bear with dignity, but the fact that my being here prevents me from comforting my wife at a time when our daughter has left home leaving only the briefest of notes and no indication of her whereabouts. If the police show as much incompetence in their search for her as they have in their investigations of this murder, I fear we may never see her again. There is also the simple fact that once out of here I can set to work to find the real murderer and so clear my name. Any influence you can wield in encouraging the magistrates to grant me bail would be most welcome.

I remain your humble servant,
Morris Duckworth (an honorary citizen dishonoured)

Carla, I'm back. It's pouring out there. So much for spring. Where was I? The truth is that last month I was distracted by a situation that had been developing with my daughter. Do you remember Massimina? I think I brought her along once many years ago when we had to defend ourselves against those fanciful claims that we were adulterating our Cabernet with methanol. Remember? She was a charming ten-year-old at the time, all giggles, ribbons and curls. Now she's a young adult studying art at university. I was in two minds about allowing her to do this. Not that she doesn't have talent. There's definitely a creative streak in the Duckworth psyche (excluding my son I'm afraid). But I was worried that she might be forced to experience my own disappointment of approaching the artistic life only to be expelled from it, denied access, forced to apply my creativity to the rather more prosaic world of wine-making and provincial real estate. I say this so you get a sense of how important this art exhibition at Castelvecchio is for me. Doubtless the prosecution will say, Duckworth killed because he was deeply, pathologically attached to this pet project which the victim was threatening to deprive him of.

Anyway, since February or so I had become concerned because Massimina, who is usually very lively and always out seeing people, clubbing, dancing and so on, had fallen to staying indoors, draping herself moodily on one chair or another, paying exaggerated and morbid attention to the cat, or simply wriggling on the floor, and texting all the time. Antonella supposed that she must be in love. The girl is twenty after all and tolerably pretty, as Jane Austen would have put it. She has an indolent, teenage coltishness, between innocent and femme fatale, always showing too much midriff and cleavage. I know we men are not supposed to notice such things, but it is rather hard not to worry for one's daughter when she all too readily lets her parents' male friends glimpse her knickers or even nipples. There was an occasion when a friend of ours, Stan Albertini, had come to dinner and Massimina turned up in her bathrobe, slumped on the sofa and was so busy with her text messages she wasn't even aware of how much she was showing, top and bottom, without knickers on this occasion. Stan is in his mid fifties, but anyone can see the kind of frustrated old goat he is. Maybe the police would have a real murder to accuse me of if Stan ever laid a finger on my daughter.

I said to Antonella, if it is love it seems to me an unhappy, possibly sick love and we should do our best to warn or help. I began to quiz the child a little more about her college and teachers and eventually evinced, in the kind of teeth-pulling conversations one has with one's teenage children, that she was rather taken with her art history professor, who, on further questioning, turned out to be none other than Professor Zolla.

This is rather extraordinary, is it not? I mean, that I could have been dealing with a man for some months without appreciating that he was also my daughter's art history professor. I often wonder how many tie-ups there are in our lives that we know nothing of and that might completely alter the scenery for us if we did learn about them. What, for example, if it turned out that one's partner, brother or sister, or even oneself, were, without knowing it, the natural offspring (unbeknown to the legal father of course) of some high-flying personage, a cardinal, say, or a politician, or a business magnate – the sort of plot Dickens loved to dream up – and that this notable fellow were keeping a watchful and protective eye on the family, from a safe distance; one would thus tend to have a positive view of the world as rather benign and generous, because everything would tend to go well with this man tirelessly pulling the strings for you. Alternatively, one could imagine an implacable enemy one knows nothing about, a powerful public figure who wishes you ill for reasons that lie beyond your ken, or perhaps began long before you were born. In my case that would explain so much.

But back to Massimina and Zolla. I found it hard to understand how a lively girl like my daughter could entertain an attraction for this boring, besuited, bureaucratised academic. To test the water, I put it to her that her art history professor, my co-curator, was an utter nobody without a shred of imagination, citing, as proof, his decision not to request Caravaggio's *Sacrifice of Isaac* for our murder show merely because 'Abraham didn't actually go through with the killing.' Can you imagine such literalism? She seemed indifferent to my indignation, remarking that she was glad the painting wouldn't be shown because the story of Abraham and Isaac was too obscene for words. At least Zolla, she said, was always modest and sweet and didn't see himself as God. Unlike a certain *celebre impredit-tor-re*.

I was astonished. Under the pretext of being concerned as to the real extent of her artistic talents (though of course I am extremely concerned), I asked Zolla directly what he thought of my daughter, her performance and prospects. This was perhaps a week after I had caught the man sobbing in Dottor Volpi's office but two weeks before the hasty and ill-advised announcement from Volpi that I was to play no further part in an exhibition that I myself had conceived and devised. But I'm running ahead of my story. Thus quizzed, Zolla made an entirely unconvincing show of

a) pretending not to know who the girl was,
b) pretending not to be aware that I had a daughter, and
c) pretending not to know that there was a Massimina Duckworth in his class.

'There are more than fifty students, in Module 1 Art History,' he said.

My feeling is that it is impossible not to be aware of Massimina, however many students there are in the class. The way she dresses simply forces two very generous breasts on every male beholder. 'She speaks very highly of you,' I told him. 'I think she may have a crush on you.' He smiled with dimpled false modesty and said that amazing as it might seem at least half of the students had a crush on him, a story so improbable I let it pass without comment. The man is an amoeba. In any event, at this point I felt it imperative – it had now been more than a month since my daughter had ceased all activity except messaging – to get into her mobile phone.

And I did. I took her with me one day, forced her to join me I should say, if only to get her out of the house, to look at a Last Judgement in a rather remote village called Gorgusello (near Sant'Anna). I'd started thinking that a good way to close *Painting Death* and send people home with something to think about would be an image of the Just being separated from the Damned, something the subject of murder naturally inclines one to think about.

I persuaded her to drive, since she only got her licence last year and needs practice, and to drive of course she had to stop texting and put her phone in her handbag. Since the bag was between us as she drove and she was concentrating on the road, it wasn't hard to slip a hand in the bag, pull the phone out and drop it into my jacket pocket. The things we do for love! I tell you all this, I suppose, Carla, to give you a sense of how completely preoccupied I have been with my family, how utterly unlikely it is that I would have found the time, never mind the mental energy, for murdering anyone (do people realise what hard work that must be?). We got out of the car to go into the church, little more than a barn really, but with this extravagant three-metres-by-four image of fiery demons poking forks up the backsides of the good burghers and merchants and, yes, priests of the early sixteenth century, when suddenly Massimina lets out a yell because her phone is missing. I told her it must have fallen between the seats in the car and she slithers off on her heels to find it. Finally I had time to see what these messages were.

There were none. She must cancel each one as it arrives. Who does that? But just as I was slipping the thing back in my pocket a message arrived. I knew that if I opened it and left it in the phone she would realise something was up. But there was no time to reflect. I opened the message. The name of the sender was Gio. The text read. 'Ahhhhhhhh, how I miss you!' I read it and cancelled it, relieved that it was the kind of contentless ejaculation that didn't require or deserve a response. I had been lucky.

But the name, Gio?

I had already slipped the phone back in my pocket when it occurred to me that Dottor Volpi sometimes called Angelo Zolla, Gioletto (Out of affection? An-gioletto? Or ironically? Because of his being such a dandy? I don't know.) Of course Gio would normally be Giovanni, or even Giovanna, but there was an outside chance that Angelo actually liked to be called Gioletto. The thing to do would have been to check the number to see if it corresponded to Zolla's mobile. But in my anxiety not to be discovered I had cancelled the message and the number with it. I could perhaps have checked the calls made and received but Massimina was already coming back into the church in a panic because she hadn't found her phone. I gave a last glance at the Devil opening his fiery mouth to chew on women disfigured by syphilis and hurried out to the car where, in a grand flurry of search and concern, I eventually produced the phone from under the maps in the glove compartment. Grudgingly, Massimina accepted she must have slipped it there herself. 'Who else, if not?' I ribbed her and got her to drive me back to Sant'Anna.

I mention Sant'Anna because, as you know, I had asked one of my subcontractors to ask one of his subcontractors to dig the foundations there for the prefab school that the Christian Democratic Union had promised to voters in order to stay in power. I had to visit Sant'Anna because not only was there an issue of a damaged war memorial, but it now turned out that an underground stream passed right through the site, so we had to assess the feasibility and cost of moving it, or alternatively shifting the whole project 200 metres up the hillside, filling in what we had dug so far and starting from scratch.

I pointed out to the priest, a rather splendid man, tall, austere, moody, a real man of God, that the monument (one of those fifties' bathroom-mosaic-on-cheap-cement things) was so ugly that they should have thanked me, or rather the dozy dozer man, for giving them this golden opportunity to replace it. But the reason I mention all this to you is that, looking into the foundation excavations, then boiling with muddy water after the spring rains, it occurred to me that if ever anyone wanted to hide a body, then this was the place to do it. It could be buried four metres deep where no one would ever suspect anything. Why I should have thought such a thing I cannot imagine. A presentiment perhaps. All this anyway to underline the fact that the police must be mad to imagine that someone of my extensive resources would kill a colleague in the hole-and-corner way this murder was carried out without disposing properly of the body. Only a loser sticks a knife in a man in an empty building and runs for his life. Can't the police understand that if someone of my wealth, knowledge and proven organisational abilities had decided to commit murder then there would have been no trace of a body and no leads at all to go on? A little respect, please!

So much for Sant'Anna. I suggested to the priest that if he wanted a new monument, perhaps my daughter, who was an artist, could design one for him, something more in line with the way young people now saw these things. When we got back to the car, Mimi said, 'You must be completely crazy, Papà,' and insisted I drove because she had some messages to send.

'Who to?' I asked.

She didn't even bother to ask me to mind my own business.

Then about five minutes out of Sant'Anna she shouts, 'Stop, stop the car.'

'For why?'

She was smiling brightly at me as if she'd just got good news.

'What's the point,' she says, 'of coming out into the country, if we don't take a walk, Dad?' Suddenly, she was full of warmth and pleasantness.

We took a path to the right of the road that looked down over the Valpolicella towards the cliffs of Rivoli. All very beautiful. I had just started to explain Napoleon's crushing tactics at the battle of Rivoli – there's a marvellously melodramatic painting by Philippoteaux – and then to reflect that like 'em or hate 'em the French might have done a better job of unifying and running Italy than the Italians ever did, when she asked, 'Papà, tell me, why did you come to Italy in the first place?'

Her voice was rather dreamy and friendly. I sensed a new openness. What was that message she had received?

I hesitated. You must have wondered yourself, Carla, why I came to Italy, why anyone comes. The truth is this was the fatal decision of my life. Had I stayed in Acton I can't imagine I would ever have found myself charged with third-degree murder.

'It seemed important to get away,' I said.

'But why?'

We were on a path that ran along the hillside, a tall white stone wall to our left and the dramatic drop to the river as it plunges into the Rivoli gorge on our right.

'Everything seemed so small-minded in the UK. Starting with my father.'

'It wasn't to do with a girl?'

'Escaping someone, you mean?'

'Papà!' she laughed. 'No, I mean you didn't run off for a girl.'

'Oh, heavens, no.'

'I'm thinking of leaving,' she said. 'Italy that is.' She sounded rather solemn.

I thought about this. The logic of the conversation was that she was about to tell me that she was leaving Italy for/with a boy, or man, and had been looking for an instance in my own past that would soften any eventual criticism I might have had for such a move.

'Not before you've finished college, I hope,' I said innocently.

She didn't answer for a while. And here comes one of the reasons why I'm telling you this. There were trees overhanging the wall to our left and sunlight was dappling through the leaves. Cobwebs kept catching my face. Then because of this dapple of sunshine and shade I finally noticed that they weren't just cobwebs. There were tiny worm things hanging from threads. They were caterpillars, small green caterpillars dangling like so many hanged convicts right at eye level. Just as when I had looked into the excavations an hour or so before, I felt a powerful shiver of presentiment.

Massimina had noticed them too. 'They do it to escape a predator,' she said. 'They're baby moths. They drop off a tree when something's trying to eat them and dangle on a thread.'

Life is nothing if not resourceful.

From being very chipper, Massimina suddenly turned gloomy. 'Actually I wouldn't mind being able to do that,' she said. 'Dangle a while.'

The change of mood surprised me. 'I thought you were telling me you were in love and planning to run off with some handsome boy.'

She thought about this for longer than seemed necessary.

'Have you never had a strange love, Dad?' she asked.

Now I was going to get the truth, I thought.

'As you know,' I told her, 'I was once married to your mother's younger sister, and some time after that I married your dear mother. Which is about it for me.'

'Nobody else?'

'Twice is enough,' I said.

'But weren't you Massimina's boyfriend too, Mamma's youngest sister.'

'Briefly,' I said.

She waited a moment. 'Isn't that a bit weird, three sisters in the same family?'

'Not at all,' I told her. 'I imagine you know your Svevo. Zeno was in love with three sisters.'

'Why did you name me after her? Did you want me to be like her?'

'Actually, that was Antonella's idea. To keep her sister alive.'

She suddenly burst out laughing, 'And if there'd been a brother?'

What do you make of that, Carla? It really threw me. I had no idea at all what to think. In fact I begin to wonder now if I'm not wasting your time telling you all this. I should get back to the hard facts. Yet I feel there is something here that has to do with it all, some important connection, or imminent. Or perhaps it's just the solitary confinement getting to me.

'Being attached to three sisters,' I tried, thinking of Zolla, 'is not so strange as falling in love with someone twice your age.'

Immediately she swung round and I thought, got her, it's true!

'Has that happened to you?' she asked.

I sighed. 'Normally, with men, it's someone half their age.'

She was clearly trying to decide whether to tell me the truth. 'You mean like Forbes,' she said, 'and his little boys?'

Again I was taken aback. 'You hardly need to think of a perverse old goat like that to imagine a man with someone half his age. Do you?'

She giggled. 'Oh Forbes was OK. Maybe the boys liked it.'

'Forbes was evil,' I told her. I will not hear any defence of paedophilia.

She bit her lip. 'Let's go back, Dad,' she said. 'I've got stuff to do at home.'

In the car she put her headphones on and spent the whole trip texting. I drove in silence and felt sure I was right. She was having a love affair with an older man. Most likely Zolla. My task must be to make sure that she stayed on the rails and completed her studies without undue distraction.

To His Eminence Cardinal Rusconi

Dear Cardinal Rusconi,

Forgive me, Your Eminence, for occupying a little space in your mailbox and a moment of your precious time. I'm not unaware of the pressures on a Father of the Church charged with the care of so large and needy a flock.

I had been meaning to contact you before this little catastrophe of mine (you will have heard, no doubt, of my farcical arrest for a crime I could not even imagine committing). The fact is that the building project in Sant'Anna has run into serious trouble. I don't know if you have been informed, but a stream was discovered about two metres below ground running diagonally across the site. I must say it does seem odd to me that the architect was unaware of this geological feature.

I am willing of course to have the foundations re-dug elsewhere, but we will need precise instructions. I will do my best to cover the cost through Fratelli Trevisan, though I'm not entirely sure given the present financial crisis how feasible that will be.

May I, in the meantime, be so impertinent as to ask two favours, something I do only because I know what a generous man you are, and because I am truly in need. First, as you know, my spiritual guide Don Lorenzo is seriously ill and hence I have no one to whom I can turn in my present moment of discomfort. My question is, how can I avoid bitterness and resentment, Your Eminence? What prayers can I pray, what part of the Bible should I read? I see the danger of falling into a deep pit of bile. I fear for my soul.

Second, I would be very grateful if you could take my wife into your pastoral care. I'm not sure if you are aware but our family has also been struck by a second catastrophe, the disappearance of my twenty-year-old daughter. These are extreme circumstances and I am concerned for my wife's sanity.

As for my own legal position, I ask nothing, knowing that any help with attaining bail is beyond the mandate of the church.

All I can say is that I am glad to have met you, Your Eminence, when I was at the zenith of my career and can only beg forgiveness if I write to you now from my nadir.

The humblest member of your flock,
Morris Duckworth

Carla. What next? (I just took a rather arduous toilet break. No, don't worry, I shan't trouble you with a description of the lavatory facilities here, not unlike the Last Judgement in Sant'Anna.) Anyhow, slow going though it may be, I hope I am building up for you an idea of my mental state in the weeks immediately preceding the murder. As we get nearer the fatal day I will give you all the necessary details about the painting of San Bartolomeo, the presence of the two young Libyans, and exactly how it was that I came to discover the corpse. But first we must spend a moment on my father's funeral and of course my son's trial. Again, the picture I am seeking to establish is that of a man so overwhelmed with duties and preoccupations that he simply would not have had time or interest to carry out such a primitive and senseless crime. Why, by the way, was the knife thrust in so deep, and actually left inside the body? I cannot remember such a circumstance in all the crime stories, fact or fiction, that I have read over the course of my fifty-five years. Imagine the violence that struck such a blow! I do not think I would be capable of it.

To recap. In early March I had, as I told you in our interview, the strange encounter in Castelvecchio with Volpi, Zolla and a third, unseen person, who laughed, offstage as it were, in the most sinister fashion. I remain convinced that whatever was going on in that room is central to the murder. Yet when I tried to explain this to the police they refused to pay attention. They had already made up their minds in response to the two or three pieces of 'evidence' they have – the fingerprints, the timing, my being in the basement, the traces of blood on Zolla's keyboard, and so on. All the merest coincidence and easily explicable with a quite different narrative than the one they have so morbidly constructed.

Shortly after that incident in Volpi's office, then, despairing of the way Zolla was organising the show, I wrote emails to all the prospective lenders for *Painting Death*, explaining both the philosophy behind the show and specific accounts of the importance of each single item in the topical mosaic of the whole. It was three days' intense, creative work, but it was immediately rewarded by the first affirmative answers. From the National Gallery, the Frick, the Met. I was overjoyed and felt vindicated, to the point, I confess, that I thought no more of the scene in Volpi's office, or my daughter's strange behaviour, and was even beginning to assent to the general serenity surrounding Mauro's trial when I received – I believe it was a Sunday afternoon – the news that my father had died and my presence was required in London for the funeral. This meant I would miss the opening morning of the trial. In fact it was while I was in the taxi driving to the funeral from Gatwick, that, in order to see if my wife had emailed me about the hearing, I checked for messages on my iPhone and found a mail from Volpi. Just four lines:

'Signor Duckworth, given your devious, disloyal behaviour and your unwillingness to work in line with standard museum procedures, it has been decided you can have no further role in the organisation of the exhibition *Painting Death*. This decision is irrevocable.

'The Director, Dottor Giuseppe Volpi.'

You can imagine my sense of injustice. I was being turned away for having taken the initiative and made the show possible!

Obviously they were embarrassed by their inefficiency. Perhaps Volpi had never believed that Zolla would be able to persuade the serious museums to give him the paintings. He had been humouring me. Now all of a sudden the permissions were arriving and the show would have to go ahead.

A word about my father and the funeral. I shall keep it brief. My first memories are of a small, wiry, violent man slapping my mother. I remember her pallor, her quiet courage, her prayers. He smelled: of drink, of factory clothes, of, forgive my crudity, farts. Mother instead had an aura of wilting flowers. She manipulated me with a terrible pathos that intensified, never to be dispersed when she was killed – I was fifteen – by a drunk driver who lost control of his Jaguar and crushed her against the wall of Lloyd's bank. I wasn't allowed to see the body. Dad remarried in no time, a woman more than twenty years younger than himself, only five years older than me. I took all Mum's old things, even her underwear, her perfumes, and doted over them for years. Later, when I became a successful businessman in Verona, I invited him to stay with us in Via Oberdan. By this time his second wife had left him, though he didn't seem unduly concerned. He said Italy was too hot and the beer crap. He knotted a handkerchief on his head and wore socks with his sandals. The only thing he enjoyed was taking Mauro to the stadium. So in just a few weeks, he managed to pass on to my son the curse of his violent ways and his inexplicable vocation for the mob. I should have broken off with the man altogether. But I find it hard to break with people. Even the dead I keep talking to. I offered to buy him a nice place in Chelsea, but he refused and went of his own accord to an old people's home in Willesden. When I visited, which I did religiously every time I was in the UK to visit customers for our wines, he invariably made fun of my clothes and scars and insisted on pouring me Johnnie Walker Red Label (I hate Red Label) from a bottle hidden in his bedclothes.

I had expected to be alone at the funeral and instead the church was packed. Shabby and malodorous, all kinds of ancient creatures offered their bony handshakes and told me in croaking voices what a wonderful, gentle man my father was, and how he had always spoken well of me and excused my not visiting because I was such an important, busy person. Of this I believed not a syllable. Clutching walking sticks and Zimmer frames, they tottered up the chancel steps to make fulsome speeches about this extraordinarily kind man who had so loved the cats in the old folks' home he might have been St Francis of Assisi. And how patriotic he was! He would have gone to Afghanistan himself, on crutches, if they had let him. Someone told a Good Samaritan anecdote about how Dad always bought the *Big Issue* from him. They used to stand together on the corner of Acton Vale, rain or shine, Saturday morning doing the pools and drinking Scotch from Dad's hip flask. He was the soul of the community.

Then out of the blue the vicar asked me if *I* wanted to say something before we committed the body to the flames. It's hard to feel nostalgia for the Italian priesthood, but an Anglican clergyman can do it for you. The man had that stooped, thin-nosed sanctimoniousness they can never caricature enough in soaps and sitcoms. Having reached the top of the steps and turned to the congregation I didn't know what to say. I'm usually quite resourceful in these situations, accustomed to speaking at board meetings and Rotary Club dinners, but of course when I do that, in Verona or Milan, it's in Italian. All at once, facing this English public, I was struck by a powerful awareness that my real centre of gravity now is Italy, my real language, however much it plagues me still, Italian. Words of pomp and circumstance just won't come to me in my native tongue. I opened my mouth and nothing came out. Below me the rabble of pensioners were expecting me to speak. Coffin fodder, I thought, gazing down on their wrinkled faces, grey hair, grey eyes, grey teeth. I tried to speak but couldn't. I realised that if words did begin to flow they would be about Mother. You killed her, I was thinking. You bastard. You shit. You killed my poor mother long before the drunk driver did. Sarah Ann Duckworth née Winchester is gone and utterly forgotten by everyone but her obedient boy Morris. I am my mother's son. Quite likely you're not my father at all. I never wanted you to be my father. I . . .

I opened my mouth and closed it. The coven of crones and codgers beneath me had begun to murmur. The clergyman took my elbow and said, 'Mr Duckworth, these are difficult moments, if you don't feel up to it, we do understand.' Then I simply yelled. 'Dad! Daaaaaad!' It was blood-curdling. The sound bounced off the stone walls. I felt the air vibrate and my chest quivered. 'Daaaad!' As I stumbled down the steps towards the shiny coffin a dozen pairs of arms enfolded me. The women were crying. The men were croaking, 'Good on you, lad.' Overwhelmed by foul breath, I fainted.

Is that the kind of man who could plunge a knife into a fellow human being, a man who faints at a funeral?

To Mauro Duckworth

Dear Mauro,

You are too young for the tasks I am about to place on your inexperienced shoulders, but if, despite my hectoring in the past, you have any affection for your much aged and misunderstood father, can I beg you to see to the following:

1) *First, take care of your mother. She is a strong woman, but these are hard times indeed. Should you see any signs that she is unable to cope, be in touch at once with Dr Bagnoli who has prescribed tranquillisers in the past.*
2) *Please be in daily contact with Alvise Bersi who will be overseeing Fratelli Trevisan. Normally I would ask your mother to do this, but she will be too worried about Massimina to look after company affairs. I know it will be impossible for you to grasp everything about the many projects that are ongoing but try to get a sense of whether anything untoward is happening in my absence. When the cat is away, the mice will play.*

3) *Above all, I need your help over my legal situation. The single thing most likely to bring about a rapid end to my imprisonment would be the identification of the real murderer. I am convinced that Professor Zolla, an art historian who works at Castelvecchio, and two young Libyans ('friends' of the murdered man) Samira and Tarik Al Zuwaid, who live at Via Dietro San Zeno 21, apartment 5, know more about the death than they have told the police. Perhaps you and your many Hellas friends could keep an eye on those Libyans. Since Zolla is also Massimina's art history professor at the university and since he knew her and she professed privately to me to have a crush on him, there is just a chance that he has information as to her whereabouts. I leave it to you to decide how to proceed.*

So, Mauro, that is the situation. You are being asked to grow up rather quickly. I can only pray that you will show the same courage and wisdom now that you showed in the witness box at your trial. I also beg you to close your ears and eyes to all the ludicrous speculation and accusations that are no doubt being made against me in the press. Be assured that they have no foundation.

Your much maligned father,
Morris

Sorry, I broke off for the afternoon there, Carla. Sheer depression. Sometimes I feel I should just let them condemn me to however many years it will be and the hell with it. But enough self-pity. Onward. So, the morning after the funeral, flying back to Italy, I felt determined to establish better relations with my children and to be kinder and more attentive to Antonella. Come hell or high water, Mauro must be saved from gaol, I thought, and given his chance in Fratelli Trevisan. I would not let the family I have struggled for all these years go to pieces. As for the email I had received from Volpi, I decided to ignore it and continue as before. The museum needed my sponsorship. All the trustees had stressed their support for the *Painting Death* initiative. I would simply smile at Volpi as if pretending not to have noticed an unpleasant smell.

Speaking of which, Carla – I know you'll forgive me – the diet here, at least for the vegetarians amongst us, is truly awful. All I get is beans. Raw, boiled, baked, fried. No wonder I'm suffering from wind. Is there anything you can do to help? Are prison systems sensitive to lawyer's complaints?

I flew back from England just in time to see my son cross-questioned by the prosecution. The big surprise, as you can imagine, was the presence of the mayor. He was in jeans and an old sweater, looking more like a defendant than the town's first citizen; all the same I thought it was a generous gesture on his part, obviously undertaken with the intent of putting political pressure on the judge, showing his willingness to defend a citizen of Verona against the brutal Brescia police.

I took my seat between Massimina and Antonella and tried to hold my wife's hand to comfort her, but she seemed perfectly relaxed, chatting away to Don Lorenzo on the other side of her about the Sunday flower arrangements.

'Mauro Dackwert, do you accept,' the prosecutor began, 'that on the evening of so and so on the corner of so and so and so and so in the town of Brescia, in the company of etc., etc., etc., you attacked six policemen identified as etc., etc., etc.'

My son pronounced an emphatic no. I was thrilled. He has decided to lie, I thought. He has a chance! However, when the prosecutor then read out the boy's original statement confessing that he had 'purposefully and deliberately attacked the police' and asked him if this 'no' meant he was retracting that confession, my son replied:

'Not at all, but you have taken the word "attacked" out of context. You forget that we boys, all seventeen years of age, were attacked first by twenty and more heavily armed grown men. If you repeat the question with the word "counter-attacked" I will reply in the affirmative.'

I must say, mad as it was, I was rather impressed. Perhaps Tonbridge had had some positive effect after all.

'Counter-attack is considered a legitimate form of defence by the United Nations,' Mauro added.

As you can imagine the prosecuting lawyer was taken aback. He had been expecting a cretin, had reckoned without the Duckworth gene(ious). The mayor actually clapped out loud. I hadn't realised clapping was permissible in a court of law.

'Is it or is it not true that you and your fellow thugs were armed with sticks?'

Mauro seemed to think for a moment. He had slipped off his jacket, probably he was sweating, and you could see his thick shoulders and bull neck. He said coolly. 'I am not a thug and do not keep company with thugs.'

Now he really has decided to lie, I thought.

'Is it true that you and . . . bla bla bla . . . were armed with sticks?'

The boy actually smiled. 'I wonder if the court is aware that regulations for flag-bearing poles brought into football stadiums require that they be no longer than one metre and be made from flexible polythene weighing no more than eighty grams.'

'Mauro Dackwerth please limit yourself to answering the question. Were you and your companions armed with sticks, or not?'

'I'm sorry, but in that case I need a definition of the word sticks. Meantime, I take the word "armed" to be ironic. As in, "armed with a toothbrush".'

There was some laughter in court. The lawyer appealed to the three presiding judges, a man and two women. They consulted. The middle judge, an elderly man in a red gown eventually said: 'Avvocato Falletti, I think it has been established that the defendants were carrying flexible polythene poles intended for flag waving and weighing eighty grams. Whether we refer to them as sticks or not is beside the point.'

'*Grazie*, Signor Giudice.' The prosecuting magistrate cleared his throat. He didn't seem as upset as you might have expected by this lack of judicial support. 'Is it true,' he continued, 'that you and your fellow Hellas Verona "brigades" so called – I hope you are not going to deny that you are a member of the brigades, Signor Duckworth – share a deep hatred of the police?'

'I am proud to be a Hellas fan,' Mauro said very seriously. 'There is no formal membership of the brigades, but we are a tight-knit community with a strict code of honour. We do not hate the police. But we reserve the right to defend ourselves and counter-attack against discrimination and violence whatever quarter they may come from.'

'*Alé!*' the mayor called out loud.

'Brescia, Bergamo and Vicenza in particular,' Mauro added.

'*Alé!*' repeated the mayor.

There was a general murmur of approval. What I was thinking was this: if my son was capable of such lucidity and articulation, such effective timing too, and even irony, why had he never bothered to display these qualities in my presence? Why hadn't he joined the debating society at Tonbridge? Antonella was smiling quietly. It was as if she were watching something unfold exactly as she had expected. Massimina glanced up, shook her head and went back to her texting.

But now I had missed some of the questioning.

'If we had intended to do serious harm,' Mauro was saying, 'we could have armed ourselves with stones, or bottles, could we not? Our plan was just to show them they hadn't intimidated us with the beating they gave us as we left the stadium. Two of our friends had been taken to hospital. We felt we would be letting them down if we didn't make some statement.'

It was a tough story to swallow, but the boy did have a chubby adolescent charm about him. My own feeling was that the prosecuting magistrate was incompetent. He kept leaving long spaces between questions, reading through his notes as if he'd never seen them before. It was during one of these embarrassing pauses that I noticed that the main presiding judge had red hair. Oh, not flaming red like Mauro's. More a sort of coppery brown. But curly too. I turned to Antonella and saw she was watching with shining eyes. However, since, from where we were sitting, Mauro in the witness box and the judge on the dais fell into the same rising line of vision, it was impossible to tell who she was looking at, the boy or the man, both red-haired.

But enough. I really am wasting your time now. The more I write the more I realise I am paranoid, deeply paranoid. It was probably inevitable that the little hooligans would be let off with a caution. Elections were imminent and the mayor needed to grab some xenophobic consensus by painting the picture of a Verona besieged by the malice of jealous neighbours. Hence my honorary citizenship. The trial of these stupid kids fitted his plans perfectly. Two of the other boys turned out to be sons of a leading banker and a top urologist (a useful man for an ageing elite). Why should the judges make themselves unpopular? There was probably never any doubt the young thugs would win their case, and certainly no need for some kind of Jesuit conspiracy to fling open the prison doors. Which doesn't mean there wasn't a Jesuit conspiracy. The only downside to an acquittal was that my son had been somewhat encouraged in a life of lawlessness. After consultation with Antonella I decided to act at once to get him involved in the company, if only to keep him out of trouble. I urged him to accept a worker's position full-time in our bottling factory and report back to me after a month with ten cost-free measures to improve productivity.

But I have wearied you and you are eager to hear about the events leading up to my discovery of the body.

To Signora Antonella Trevisan

Carissima Anto, mio amore,

My heart bleeds. It is only now that I've been away from you for so long, cara, that I appreciate how much I count on you for companionship and wisdom. Forgive me if I have been a less than attentive husband in recent years. There is nothing like a spell of enforced loneliness and silence to alert one to one's multitudinous shortcomings. As for the legal situation, I have a good idea who might be responsible for the murder, but as long as I'm in prison, what can I do? Paradoxically I cannot get it out of my head that all this has happened to us because we have been too good for too long. Do you know what I mean? We have, as it were, defied the gods with our goodness. Perhaps a little transgression on our part would have spared us this ordeal. It's a strange thought. Such is the effect of solitary confinement.

Has there been no news at all of Massimina? When the magistrates start allowing it, please visit at once. I miss your eyes and the reassuring purr of your voice.

Do give my regards to Stan. Hopefully he is offering you some support through this difficult time. Has he made any progress with his search for Forbes? I'm eager to hear of any new details.

Un abbraccio appassionato,

Your Morris

PS, trouble with constipation and haemorrhoids again. The food is awful and I am not getting enough exercise. I shall take advice about suing for damages when they let me out.

Here we go then, Carla. The final helter-skelter.

With the trial over and having spent a couple of days in Fratelli Trevisan and on various construction sites, I went to see Zolla to discuss progress with the loans for the show. Judging from the faces of the museum staff as I walked through the offices, they had no notion that my role had changed in any way. I was admitted at once to Zolla's office, he rose and shook my hand and commiserated me on the tragic loss of my father. I asked him how the loan requests were coming on and he said the confirmations had been flowing in 'theeck and faster'. He seemed completely unaware of the email Volpi had written to me.

We sat down to a discussion of which paintings should go where and how exactly the space should be divided and designed. The walls might be re-clad in a satiny black, I thought, to have the strong red pigments of the blood stand out. Or perhaps we could have different cladding for different sections in line with the themes they featured, fratricide, infanticide, uxoricide. I must say I found it all very exciting to be working on the details of the show at last. I asked him if I could move a painting we were planning to use from a church in San Briccio into the museum storeroom because the storage situation in San Briccio was primitive to say the least, and he said, why not. (This is an important detail, Carla!)

As I was leaving, Zolla said, 'About your daughter.'

Well, I must admit that the combination of my father's funeral and Mauro's trial had rather led me to take my eye off the ball as far as Massimina was concerned.

'The fact is that she hasn't been present at any classes since Christmas. I just wanted to be sure that you were aware of that.'

He spoke as if to excuse himself.

'Naturally I was aware that she is mainly at home, these days,' I said, 'though she appears to be in constant communication with the world, via her iPhone.' I tried to make the remark as pointed as I could.

'It's a plague,' Zolla agreed. 'Students text all the time during the lessons.'

'Would you have any idea why she is not coming to lessons?' I asked him. 'Especially since she spoke so, er, enthusiastically about you.'

Zolla shook his head. 'These young people are very unpredictable. With their love lives and so on.'

'And so on?' I asked him what he meant.

'They fall in love,' he sighed. 'And they fall out of love. They take it badly perhaps and lose heart.'

Was it an admission?

Then he added: 'Why don't you tell her to come and discuss the matter with me in my tutorial hours. Tuesdays at 4.30. Perhaps I can help.'

'Thank you,' I told him. 'I'll do that.'

Was the man now trying to use me as a go-between to patch up an affair that she had wisely pulled out of, but at the expense of her university career? I decided to confront the matter head on with Massimina. However, when I went to dinner that evening I found that we had a guest, Stan Albertini.

I must explain in a few words my relationship with Stan. Stan was the sort of unofficial leader of an 'alternative' English-speaking hippy community in Verona back in the eighties when I arrived and briefly courted Massimina Trevisan before her unhappy disappearance. Later, when I was married to Paola Trevisan, he was teaching English privately to Antonella and her then husband, sadly deceased of course. Stan also became close friends with a man called Michael Forbes, an Old Etonian whom I had helped to set up a summer school in the Valpolicella for English public-school boys. Forbes was a good amateur painter and after the school was closed I kept him alive financially by commissioning copies of paintings from him. Then some six years ago, Forbes left, leaving no contact details. However, it turned out that Stan, who had long since returned to the USA, had been keeping up a regular correspondence with Forbes, and having taken an early pension he came back to Italy shortly before Christmas, in part, it seems, to look up Forbes. He was so upset not finding him, particularly as he'd lent him a considerable sum of money, that he had insisted on reporting him as missing to the police.

Forgive me, Carla, but once again I'm having difficulty keeping my account short and to the point. One of the problems is working on paper. If I had my computer here I could do a bit of editing. Instead I'm condemned to scribbling in these school exercise books. Never mind. The fact is that the very evening I had planned to speak to Massimina, Stan came over to complain that in the month since he'd reported Forbes's disappearance the police had done – surprise surprise – absolutely nothing. He wanted to ask us if we knew anyone who could pull a string or two.

A visitor at table meant meat for dinner, which in turn meant the children were present. Mauro and Massimina love their steak and both seemed extremely pleased to see Stan. They're too young to appreciate how superficial he is. He cultivates an easy Californian manner and cracks lots of innocuous little jokes in his atrocious Italian, sexual innuendos more often than not. They love it. I notice they never correct him the way they do me. After a third or fourth glass of wine, he started to tell us he was convinced the police knew more than they let on but wouldn't take action because Forbes had been implicated, along with various members of the cloth, in molesting little boys.

'Italy is a can of worms,' he announced. 'I'm glad I didn't stay.'

'It's not a country for faint hearts,' I told him. I really couldn't understand why he was pursuing the matter so insistently. I had already told him that if he was out of pocket over the matter, I was willing to come to his assistance.

Antonella was just saying it was too easy to imagine all priests were paedophiles, when who should hobble into the room but our spiritual adviser, Don Lorenzo. On hearing what we were talking about he immediately seemed troubled; he went white in fact. We had to help him to the sofa and find some quality port. Finally he said that given the kind of confession he had heard from Forbes shortly before his disappearance, he was sure Stan had done the right thing going to the police. 'Though it was wrong,' he added, 'to imagine it had anything to do with priests.'

For my own part, I think if confessions are to be confidential, then frankly they should be so one hundred per cent, without the confessor tossing out hints and titbits left and right. I don't know why – and again, you will see now the point in my telling you this – but at that moment, hearing Don Lorenzo reflecting that Stan had done well to go to the police, I had a blisteringly clear foreboding that very soon I would be arrested for murder. It's crazy isn't it, but whatever goes wrong I feel that people are always going to point the finger at me. This is what Italy has done to me, Carla. It must be a syndrome.

Anyway, I was so paralysed by all this unpleasantness, and frankly rather disgusted with the overheated way my children were chattering about these deeply distasteful matters as if they were the merest entertainment, that I forgot to pursue the question of Zolla with Massimina and by the time I remembered she and Mauro had been spirited off by our Californian calamity to listen to live music in some hip/cool pub he'd discovered in, of all miserable places, the sad suburb of Chievo – Stan was always one for the music scene, flowers love dope and multiple partners (perhaps he had more in common with Forbes than he lets on). After the noisy brigade departed I remember Antonella enthusing to Don Lorenzo, who still seemed extremely troubled, how nice it was to see Mimi in such a good mood again; she must invite old Stan more often, she said. He had really cheered the girl up.

To Stanley Albertini

My dear Stan,

I do hope this missive finds you. I remember Antonella telling me you were staying at the Piccolo Hotel.

How strange life is, no? Once again I have been arrested for murder. I wonder if I'm fated, or if some evil spirit moves in my vicinity, commits crimes and arranges for me to carry the can. I just wanted to ask you as you seemed to be getting on so well with Massimina recently. I know you went out for a drink with her and Mauro a couple of times. It's not possible, is it, searching hard in your memory, that you could find some clue as to where she might be? I don't know why I write this, since of course Anto will already have asked, but there you are. A control obsession, no doubt.

How long are you planning to stay in Verona now? Perhaps you have already departed. Have the police finally come up with anything on Forbes? Again allow me to thank you for looking after me when I fainted on you in the church attic that morning. Un apostolo del soccorso, no less! You know I still can't remember how I got down the stairs. No recollection at all. Very strange. The French tourists must have thought we were ghosts.

Let me know your news, if you can. I'm afraid it's rather lonely here.

Your old pal,

Morris

However, Carla, one aspect of these recent months is how I have never been allowed to get myself properly scalded by one hot potato before another is tossed at me. One moment I was elated about the progress of the show, the next anxious for my daughter, the next unsettled by vague talk of police and missing paedophiles. In short, a couple of days later I had just concluded a fruitful discussion with Zolla about the local paintings that we had decided to bring in alongside the international masterpieces, to give the show Veronese roots as it were, when Mariella, Zolla's rather sweet secretary, tells me Volpi wants to see me in his office. I was glad. It was time the old bitterness between us was cleared up once and for all.

Here then is the crucial conversation on which, or rather (this is important) on Volpi's *preliminary notes* for which, my police persecutors base so much of their case. As you will see, those notes do not at all match what actually took place between us.

It's true that Volpi started by telling me he wanted me out of the building that minute and for good. So his intention was as indicated in those notes. However, far from leaving I sat myself down, uninvited, on a sumptuous swivel chair, confronting him across his preposterously large desk.

What on earth could be the problem, I asked him?

Volpi, as was his way, tried to use his obscene bulk and a sort of unfocused intemperance, to intimidate me, sprawling backward on his chair and pushing up his mountainous paunch.

After a few moments' awkward silence I pointed out that the success of the museum in the immediate future was not unconnected with the Duckworth Foundation. There were four paintings to restore for the show, work that I had pledged to pay for.

Volpi had a strange way of playing with his lips, as if it helped him to think, pouting and popping and puffing. Suddenly he hauled himself up, planted his plump elbows on the desk and made me an offer. My name, he said, would appear as co-curator and sponsor for the show, I would get the credit; in return, however, I must agree to have nothing more to do with the practical organisation of the event and to keep away from Castelvecchio until the show itself opened. He pointed out that I had never been formally invited to curate the show and had no contract to do so.

I had no idea how to respond to this provocation. Playing for time, I pointed out that a number of canvases from my own private collection would be in show and I wished to have a say in their arrangement. A Gentileschi, two Sickerts and an anonymous baroque Jezebel Defenestrated. If there was no contract, I said, it was because I had generously foregone any fee. I hesitated. At the very least he owed me an explanation for his extraordinary animosity in my regard.

'Delving into one of the institution's computers is not acceptable,' he said bluntly. 'You are poison, Duckworth. You have been writing behind our backs and in our names to important representatives of foreign museums.'

Zolla had protested that I must have illegally accessed his email to get hold of the addresses of the people responsible for lending us the paintings. Naturally, it took me no more than a minute to refute such a mad accusation. I explained that I had long had a friendship with a member of staff at the Fitzwilliam, a museum in Cambridge, England, and this man had forwarded to me a round-robin email that Zolla had sent to all the museums involved in our requests; he, the Fitzwilliam friend, wanted to know whether this was the show I had mentioned to him when recently in Cambridge to visit my alma mater. It was true that, having come into possession of these addresses, I had then taken the liberty of sending on some supplementary explanation of the show to the various museums rights' departments, but I did this only after long discussion with Zolla. 'With all respect, Dottore,'

I wound up, 'it seems to me that our Angelo is a little . . .' – I hesitated – 'sometimes a little . . .'

Volpi raised a caterpillar eyebrow. 'A little . . . ?'

I said nothing.

'Erratic?' he suggested.

'I just wish he had raised the matter with me before complaining to you. With me he's been acting as if all was well. Frankly, I don't understand. There seems to be a lack of trust, and a lack of sincerity. Perhaps we should call him in here now.'

Volpi then leaned forward across the desk and, popping his lips again, asked me why I thought Zolla had been weeping in his office that day.

I told him I had no idea and that I didn't concern myself with matters that were none of my business. I was only interested in the show.

He looked at me. 'Signor Duckworth,' he began, but I suddenly found myself interrupting to say that what I *had* thought intriguing that morning was the panel on the wall, which I hadn't noticed before, about the Bianchi scourging themselves on their pilgrimages.

Volpi grunted and sat back. The panel was still there, on the right as one came in the door, and we both turned to look at it.

'What exactly did these Bianchi do?' I asked.

Now he laughed. 'Mice also,' he said, 'have a great ability to change direction when being chased, Signor Duckworth.'

When I refused to respond to such a pathetic provocation, he said: 'The Bianchi were a religious confraternity. On their pilgrimages, they dropped the stoles from their backs, so that they hung on the cord round their waists, then whipped themselves repeatedly with . . .' – he hesitated, smiled, then opened a drawer and with evident relish pulled out what looked like a black stick about eighteen inches long with half a dozen barbed leather lashes attached to one end – 'something like this.' Raising his eyes and flaunting a fat smile he lifted his hand abruptly to his shoulder so that the lashes fell down on his back where they presumably made contact with his damp shirt.

'Ah,' he sighed.

I honestly didn't know what to say. Either the scourge was a museum piece, in which case it had no place in his desk, or it was something modern, of the variety I can only presume people purchase from shops dedicated to the enhancement of erotic pleasure. Why was Volpi showing this to me? Was it an invitation of some kind?

'Fascinating,' I finally agreed. To cover my embarrassment, I remarked how interesting it was that the official church had entirely discontinued this penitential practice.

'I wouldn't be so sure of that,' he said drily. Then very abruptly he demanded: 'Signor Duckworth, why were you in the museum storerooms without permission? How do I know you are not planning to, er, supplement your personal art collection from ours?'

This again indicated such an extraordinary lack of trust that I could only put it down to the man's being raised in Naples. I explained to him that, as agreed with Zolla, I would soon be collecting, for the show, a painting of San Bartolomeo (flayed) from a church in the village of San Briccio. It was precisely to avoid anyone's imagining that I was appropriating the painting for myself that I had organised with Zolla that we would house the work in the storeroom here in Castelvecchio. 'I had not realised I needed permission to check the conditions down there,' I concluded.

Volpi watched me. In retrospect, I realise he must have feared I had stumbled on some kind of activity going on in the storeroom. Why else would he have been willing to recognise me as co-curator so long as I *stayed away* from the museum?

'It appears communications between yourself and Zolla are not what they might be,' I threw in.

He didn't answer. So then I said I needed his advice about San Bartolomeo. Here things get a trifle complicated, and again you will have to bear with me. I had been alerted as to the existence of this painting and its possible suitability for the show by the young Libyan woman Samira Al Zuwaid, who presently works in the archive of the Cultural Heritage Department. I should say for the record that I was familiar with Signorina Al Zuwaid because she previously did an internship with Fratelli Trevisan. As you know, Carla, I have always had a policy of employing immigrants where possible since I feel I share with them a common and thorny destiny here in Italy. However, rumours that I have been having an affair with Signorína Al Zuwaid are ridiculous and frankly more damaging to her than to me. On her suggestion, then, I had gone – with my son (if someone is eager to check up on all these facts) – to look at this and other paintings. But the priest at San Briccio pretended he knew nothing of the canvas and it was only my perseverance that eventually allowed me to discover it, unbeknown to the priest, in a church that had fallen into disuse. I had explained all this to Zolla and now I explained it again to Volpi and asked him for guidance. My plan, I said, was to send a team to remove the painting, if possible without saying anything to the priest, since very likely the cleric was hiding the picture with the intention of selling it, one of the more common if less opprobrious of the priesthood's vices.

Pertinently, Volpi pointed out that it would not be possible to use the museum's regular removal organisation since they would require complete documentation in advance, thus giving the priest all the time in the world to have San Bartolomeo disappear, skin and bone, for good. He asked how many people would be required to remove the painting. I told him three. There was the problem of a narrow wooden staircase with rotten steps. The painting would have to be lowered with a rope.

'Do it yourself,' he said.

I was astonished.

'Obviously, you will need to go with someone from the Cultural Heritage Department,' he said, 'but it must also be someone who can guarantee maximum confidentiality.' He tipped his face to the ceiling and stroked his jowls reflectively with fat fingertips. I had the impression that it was a pleasure for him to think about little problems like this and I must say that for the first time my heart began to warm to him. 'Since Signorina Al Zuwaid already knows about the painting,' he decided, 'perhaps she could be present.'

'It will take three people,' I reminded him. 'At least two men.'

'Take her brother,' he said at once.

I appreciate that in retrospect this conversation hardly seems credible. Why didn't Volpi suggest someone from the museum, someone with the required expertise? Moving heavy old paintings can be a tricky task. As for this brother of Signorina Al Zuwaid, Tarik he is called, I was aware of his existence, in part because his sister had mentioned him when she was working as my intern, but also because quite recently, when I had spoken of getting a Moslem, or at least an Arab, to comment on some of the biblical paintings we were planning to exhibit, Volpi had proposed that we invite Tarik. Quite how a museum director might have got to know two Libyan immigrants I really have no idea and certainly didn't think about it at the time. I presumed that his dealings with the Heritage Department inevitably led to his meeting Signorina Al Zuwaid from time to time. In any event, when he said 'Take her brother', I was so delighted that we were finding common ground in these arrangements and that he had stopped talking about breaking off our relationship, that I immediately said OK.

The conversation had thus been turned on its head. Walking into Volpi's office I had been confronted by a man determined to be rid of me (as indicated in his preliminary notes); now I was walking out with an understanding that I would secure a painting for the show that we both believed to be at risk and bring it to the storeroom beneath the museum, whence it would go to a restorer as soon as possible. What's more, I had a very strong impression that Volpi was now intending to draw me in to whatever was secret in the museum, rather than keep me out. Some balance of power had shifted and I, rather than Zolla, who was my real enemy, and who he now understood had lied about me, was to be the privileged one.

'How soon do you think you can get the painting?' he asked, 'Because the restoration work will have to be scheduled at once. Also, it's important to know when you'll be accessing the storeroom so someone can be there to receive the painting.'

We talked about it. I was feeling elated. He reflected very reasonably that the only time one could be sure that the priest would not interrupt would be when the man was saying Mass in the village's new church. I thus suggested I pick up the painting the following Sunday morning.

'Sometime you and I should explore the storeroom together, Signor Duckworth,' Volpi told me, offering his hand as I stood to leave. At the time I felt absolutely sure that he meant it.

To Professor Zolla

Dear Angelo,

How are you and all my friends at Castelvecchio holding up? It must be hard for you all to carry on normally in these distressing circumstances.

You will also be aware of my arrest. I am not allowed to see newspapers or television here but no doubt they are full of lurid speculation in my regard. I did not, as I'm sure you understand, do the deed. Indeed, I write this letter to appeal to you from the bottom of my heart to do all you can to find out who is responsible. I did wonder if perhaps the two Libyans, Samira and Tarik Al Zuwaid, might not be involved. They seemed extremely wary of coming into Castelvecchio when we brought San Bartolomeo that morning; they spoke of having had 'a rough night' and suddenly invented a lunch appointment they couldn't miss.

Meantime, are you proceeding with arrangements for the show? I hope it hasn't been called off. I can imagine one's first reaction in such circumstances is just to say, a show on murder, forget it. Yet, as you know, art is never more appropriate than when close to reality. Have you taken a look at San Bartolomeo yet? What do you think? Quality? Condition? Extent of restoration required? If you are in doubt about anything, I have every aspect of the show very clearly in my head. When other thoughts oppress me here between these narrow walls, I let my mind wander, and indeed wonder, over those fantastic images, moving in my imagination through the exhibition rooms, observing the excitement of visitors from all over the globe as they see how the old masters understood the marriage of terror and spectacle.

With my warmest regards,

Morris

So much then, Carla, for the situation at Castelvecchio. Here, hour by hour, is the fatal day of Sunday 29 April.

Antonella and I rose early, shortly after six, she to spend some time in quiet prayer, I to sit and meditate in The Art Room where I love to commune with my paintings and reflect on the many tumultuous circumstances of life that they so beautifully express. We dressed for church and then, observing the Eucharistic fast obviously, as is our wont, set out to walk across Piazza Bra to San Nicoló. It was now around seven-forty and it would be hard to express the charm of the piazza in that moment, the air still fresh, but not too cool to sit out, the morning blissfully calm, yet full of airy promise, the cobbles, stone and stucco so decorous and settled in time, yet truly alive and present now, echoing to footsteps, young and old, brisk and plodding, the jingle of bicycles, the clattering of early morning crockery in a dozen delightful cafés. Forgive me this purple prose, Carla, but I mean, would I really have been able to notice these things if I had just carried out a brutal murder? I think not.

Arm in arm, my wife and I proceeded to early Mass at San Nicolò where to our amazement and consternation Don Lorenzo did not appear. We had been coming to San Nicolò for nigh on thirty years and this must have been the first time that Don

Lorenzo was not present to say Mass. The few good folk who attend early service sat in attitudes of prayer, then when the delay became significant began to exchange whispers of concern. Only after half an hour or so did his *perpetua* turn up to explain that the good Don had been taken to hospital in the early hours after some kind of collapse.

Obliged to leave San Nicolò without partaking of the host, my wife found a taxi and rushed off to visit the sick man. I promised I would visit in the afternoon, after my mission to San Briccio. It was thus around nine when I arrived at the Al Zuwaids' apartment in San Zeno. Since I was early, I accepted their offer of a coffee; they had had a late night they said, an ordinary thing for such young folk, I suppose, and had only just dragged themselves out of bed. In fact, they were not yet properly dressed.

After some discussion of the logistics of our mission, we left the apartment around ten. We drove to the Trevisan headquarters where I exchanged the Alfa Romeo for a company van; then Tarik drove us out to San Briccio. As we arrived in the village it was evident from the cars double-parked outside the new church and blocking all but one lane of the main road that Mass was under way.

A few minutes later we parked ourselves, or tried to, in the small square outside the now disused and deconsecrated Santa Chíara in Ecstasy and here ran into an unexpected problem. The fact is I always reckon without the Italian love of Sunday sporting events. Not only were a group of cyclists showing off their shiny machinery and embarrassingly elastic outfits as they assembled in the space outside the church, but another, larger rabble had gathered for the annual Palo della Cuccagna contest in the *laghetto*. They had already erected the pole, or rather tree trunk, a good six metres of it, coated it in an ugly orangey soap and planted in I don't know what slimy mud in the middle of the filthy pond. Already the local hunks were stripping to their tattoos to swim out and scale it. This would all have been excellent fun of course – a deafeningly loud P.A. system was making ironic dialect announcements and there was a smell of sausages in the air – if it hadn't meant that we had to park fifty metres away from our goal and then positively muscle our way through the mob to the church door where a trickle of water was gurgling steadily over the ancient flagstones. However, since we were doing nothing wrong and indeed operating on the express and explicit instructions of a local museum director, I decided to go ahead anyway.

We had brought a bolt cutter and I invited Tarik to break the padlock on the door, something he did with disquieting competence and without raising the slightest interest from the crowd squeezed between church and lake. With their backs towards us, people were intent on watching the first poor fools try to climb the pole. There were so many yells, curses, splashes, oohs and ahs and raucous remarks on the goose-pimpled flesh of prettily shivering maidens as they tumbled into the water that I realised we were actually less likely to be noticed than if the area had been deserted. Once inside we lit our torches and bolted the door behind us.

It was at this moment that I received a phone call from my son to tell me that Massimina had not come home the previous evening. How was I supposed to respond to this? In the end it's not unusual in this day and age for a twenty-year-old girl to stay out on a Saturday night. But Massimina, as I have explained, had hardly been out of the house for the last month and was apparently in a state of, if not depression, then some intense internal conflict. What was particularly surprising, however, was that her oafish brother should show such real concern as to his elder sister's whereabouts, as if he knew something I didn't. I decided that if Massimina was not at home by the time I returned, I would find out where Zolla lived (with his mother *and* grandmother it seems) and drive straight round to demand an explanation.

I had moved to one side to speak to my son, idly playing my torch over a Deposition that left much to be desired. Turning to the others, then, it was to find Christ's dead face, luminous in its affliction, floating in the air not a yard away. My heart skipped a beat and my jaw must have dropped because Samira immediately burst out laughing. It was Tarik playing the torch over his face. The likeness to the Semitic features in the ugly old painting was remarkable. Delighted that they had made a fool of me, the two of them flashed their torches around poking fun at the Christian images on the walls and cackling together in a most unpleasant way. For some private reason that had to do with their late night, they were in extremely high spirits. I was anxious that if we didn't go about our task with a little more decorum we might come to grief in some way.

Behind the altar of Santa Chiara there is a small vestry with a rotten wooden staircase leading up to a low attic. Tarik and I picked our way up the stairs with a length of rope. The paintings, five of them, were at the far end, each about a metre fifty square. Since on my first visit here I had hidden San Bartolomeo at the back of the stack we now had to move the others aside. To tell the truth I almost lost my temper with Tarik who insisted on making rude remarks about the devotional images just about visible through thick plastic sheeting. *The Miracle of the Fish,* in his estimation, was a capitalist fantasy of exploiting natural resources beyond all sustainability. *The Road to Emmaus* was about gay threesomes, *Mary Anointing Jesus's Feet* was pure fetishism. When we got to San Bartolomeo I asked him rather sourly what smart-ass remark he was going to make about a man willing to undergo pain beyond belief for his faith. 'Beyond belief!' he laughed. 'You said it, Boss.' That 'Boss', I thought, was especially uncalled for.

'You do know who did this to him?' I asked sharply.

'I've no idea,' he said.

'Arabs. He was flayed alive by Arab infidels.'

We were still standing with our torches shining at the plastic sheeting, so that the flesh laid bare on the saint's chest looked rather like meat under cellophane. Tarik sighed. 'Let's get moving,' he said. But as we were turning the painting round, he remarked matter-of-factly that it was a good job I was so enthusiastic about martyrs because I could expect to see a lot more of them in the near future.

Naturally I asked him what on earth that was supposed to mean.

'The West is utterly corrupt,' he said. 'People here deserve to die.'

I asked him to whom in particular he might be referring.

'People like you,' he said coolly.

'Look,' I told him, 'I don't know what your problem is, young man, because everyone here in Verona is being extremely nice to you.'

We were now sliding Bartolomeo in his bubble wrap along the wooden planking.

'Volpi himself speaks highly of you,' I added.

'Volpi is another,' Tarik said harshly. 'And Zolla. They'll get what's coming to them.'

'Another what?'

'Sex pig.'

I asked him what in God's name he was on about, but he just laughed, and when I asked him how he knew Zolla, he said anybody who knew Volpi inevitably knew Zolla.

I told him I didn't understand. He said if that was really the case I was more autistic than he had imagined.

'Planning to start a jihad, are we?' I enquired as we began to tie the rope round the frame at the top of the stairs.

'To finish one,' he said grimly. 'Expect a slaughter.'

Out of sorts as I was, I kept in mind that the only important thing right now was to get Bartolomeo's flayed flesh safely down the stairs, and off to the museum. Leaving Tarik at the top, I picked my way over the rotten planks to Samira and the two of us prepared to receive the painting as it was lowered slowly down in its rope cradle. In the event, everything went very smoothly. We got the painting to the porch, unbolted the door and pushed out into the crowd. It had started to rain and people were jostling their umbrellas trying to get a glimpse at the idiots whose efforts on the slippery pole had now washed the soap off the first six feet or so. Fortunately the cyclists had gone to test their synthetics against sweaty saddles. With some effort we lifted the martyred saint into the van where I had put foam sheeting on the floor to receive his tortured remains.

'To Castelvecchio,' I said.

There was silence. We were sitting side by side up front. I was between the other two.

After a few minutes, Samira said: 'I thought we were taking it to your house.'

I laughed. 'If we did that it might seem I was stealing it.'

A little later, Tarik said: 'The trouble is we can't leave the van parked outside the museum blocking all the buses on Via Cavour, can we?'

I said I would phone ahead. The museum was open to visitors on Sunday and one of the guards could open the gate for deliveries at the side of the building beside the river. Obviously I had informed the director and they were expecting us.

'Where are you planning to leave it, exactly?' Samira asked.

'There's below-ground storage,' I explained, though of course Samira would know this, doing the job she did. In any event, it's only in the last few days that I have begun to wonder about all those questions the Libyans put to me during the trip from church to museum. They seemed unnecessarily anxious. And Tarik had seemed extremely belligerent in Volpi's regard.

At a certain point, Tarik said to Samira, 'The trouble is we'll be late for . . .' and he mentioned a name I have forgotten. Apparently they had arranged a lunch with an uncle who had recently come over from Libya.

At this point I was feeling more relaxed. 'Let's do this,' I said: 'we get the painting to the service lift and I'll take it from there. If you're running late for your appointment, by all means use the van.'

As we approached Verona I phoned the museum. On arrival we found the barrier guarding the delivery bay already lifted and the big double door unlocked. We slid the painting along the corridor to the service lift, pushed it inside, and said our goodbyes. Of course I have not seen them since, but all I can say is that as we parted I remember noting a very peculiar look on Tarik's face: it was as if to one side of his nose there was a most sinister, Machiavellian grin, while the other side was a mask of the childish innocence. Samira on the other hand was entirely natural, apparently already focused on their meeting with this uncle, who, she had been explaining in the van, was in some kind of political trouble with the new regime in the country. But then women, as is well documented, are far better at dissembling than men, I suppose because they enjoy so much more sexual opportunity than we do.

Dear Samira,

No doubt you will have heard of the bizarre fate that has fallen me. I write to you from gaol where all my post is being strictly monitored. I just wanted ask you if, from the vantage point of your position in the Cultural Heritage Department, you could focus your mind on everything to do with Castelvecchio and this terrible murder. The fact is that I have heard rumours that the storerooms in the museum were being used as warehouses in an extensive art-trafficking business that was also part of the Camorra's endless need to launder dirty money. If that is the case then it seems quite likely that the murderer was some hit man from the world of organised crime. Again I appreciate that it's unlikely that you would have any pertinent information, but my present situation obliges me to clutch at straws.

With all best wishes and my deep gratitude for our past collaboration and friendship,

Yours sincerely,

Morris Duckworth

* * *

Still without having seen any museum staff, I took the lift down to the storage rooms, slid out the painting and leaned it against the nearest wall, as previously agreed with Volpi and Zolla. My task was now complete and had I had an ounce of good sense, I would have left at once. There was, after all, the question of my daughter not having returned home the night before, a matter of some concern, if not yet alarm. On the other hand, I was naturally excited to have secured the painting and thought it would be a good idea at least to have a quick look at it and check whether it would be useable, once restored. It then occurred to me that if by chance Volpi or Zolla were in their offices, they would also like to come and see it. They knew I was bringing the painting, after all. In fact, it was surprising that they hadn't arranged to have a member of staff on hand to meet me as agreed. In any event, my best chance for working harmoniously with them was to appeal to our shared enthusiasm for art.

Rather than take the lift back to the service entrance, I started to walk through to the other end of the storeroom where a staircase leads up to the museum and the offices. At once I had the impression, if not certainty, that a number of objects had been moved since I was last down there some weeks before. In particular there was a small upright bronze which had been standing then and was now on its side, almost blocking the corridor of free movement among the objects stored. This struck me as odd, since it would have been impossible to knock such a thing over without being aware of it, in which case why wouldn't you take the very short time and effort required to turn it upright again?

The storeroom at Castelvecchio is actually something of a labyrinth; it spreads out in all directions around the old bulwarks and dungeons with doors here and there leading into rooms that might be no bigger than a cupboard or as large as a whole apartment. I reached the stairs and went up to the museum. Again I was struck, finding the door open, at the lax security in the place. A member of staff did nod to me, an elderly lady who knows me by sight. The statuary room was full of Asians surreptitiously photographing things they didn't understand. I hurried up to the offices, to see if by chance Zolla and Volpi were there. In parenthesis, I must say, I noticed the police found this part of my story particularly hard to take. They could not imagine that I really supposed anyone might come into his office on a Sunday. I could only plead with them that, to my shame, I often work on the Lord's Day. Morning *and* afternoon. After Mass of course.

All the doors were open, but nobody was around. I walked through the open-plan section to Zolla's room. I know the police claim that I turned on his computer, but this is not true. I did glance at the papers on his desk, though, among which were insurance documents for the shipping of Titian's *Cain and Abel*. This cheered me up no end.

I took the corridor at the end of the open plan and went to Volpi's office. This was closed. Remembering what had happened on my previous visit, I knocked and waited. I knocked again. Nothing. Why, then, the police asked me, did I go in? And once in, having seen that there was no one in the room, why did I go to Volpi's desk? The answer, at least as far as entering is concerned, is simple. Habit. One knocks, one tries the handle, one enters. I make no apologies. It was not a bedroom. I opened the door and at once saw the office had been turned upside down. It is not true that I turned it upside down myself. Why would I do such a thing? Searching for what? My only interest at Castelvecchio was the organisation of the exhibition *Painting Death*. Sometimes I think the police just don't use their heads, but I thought the same throughout the Amanda Knox case which I followed quite closely. They get excited by whatever lurid solution has popped into their skulls, then move the facts around so as not to be disappointed.

Seeing the room in disorder, I naturally went to the desk as if there might be some explanation there of what had happened. In the event there was nothing but scattered papers. A low hum alerted me to the fact that, though the screen was blank, the computer was on. I went round the desk and pressed the space bar. After the usual delay the screen came to life. It was a video platform. I looked but couldn't understand at first what I was looking at. Only after perhaps thirty seconds did I appreciate that it was an anus seen from close up. I mean two or three centimetres. I was appalled, but for some reason I found the mouse and clicked replay. I hardly need describe what I saw. The police have stored the video as an exhibit. I stopped the film and it was then, as I moved away from the desk to head back towards the entrance, that I noticed faint footprints on the stone floor.

As you know already, I had blood on my shoes.

One says footprints, but the truth is they were barely stains and I only related them to my feet because they occurred at regular intervals crossing the room, though quite long intervals, since it turned out it was only my right foot that was involved. At first, I didn't realise it was blood. I thought I had brought in some dirt on my shoes, perhaps from the wet gravel outside the church. So it was entirely natural that my first thought was to wipe them off so as not to dirty the office of the museum director. There was a pack of tissues on the desk and I crouched down. It was as I was wiping the third or fourth print that it occurred to me that this must be blood. I smelt it. Yes. At that point I simply cleaned off my shoe, just my right shoe, as I said, and with a growing anxiety retraced my steps, through the open plan, and into Zolla's office, then back downstairs and through the museum.

You will no doubt want me to explain my reasoning and my actions at this point, but I honestly can't. On the one hand I just wanted to clean up behind me, like anyone who feels guilty of making a mess. This is the way I was brought up. On the other, I was aware that that blood must have come from somewhere. There was also the problem that I could hardly go down and start cleaning the museum floor with all the Asians touting their cameras and the museum attendants trying to pretend the rules weren't being broken. Undecided, I froze for some minutes.

Then as if to avoid the issue – but who knows why we act as we do? – I took out my mobile and called my son.

'I've found a note,' Mauro said.

'Oh yes?'

'It just says, Dear Mamma e Papà, I'm going away for a while, don't worry about me, Mimi.'

I didn't know how to respond.

'So I guess she's OK.' He seemed dubious.

Eventually I asked: 'What does your mother think?'

'I haven't told her yet.'

'But why on earth not?'

My wife, he said, or rather, his mother, was upset about Don Lorenzo. The priest was in a coma. Mauro hadn't wished to make matters worse.

'I'll be back as soon as possible,' I promised.

At this point I felt extremely eager to get home where my family needed me. I decided to identify the source of the blood, make sure it was nothing serious, then leave at once. The idea of a murder, or even a crime of any kind, still hadn't occurred to me. I was more concerned about having made a mess or being accused of trying to get inside people's computers when they weren't in their offices. Seeing a pack of wipes on Mariella's desk, I hurriedly cleaned up all the prints first in the office, then the corridor. Here it is truly hilarious that the police accuse me of having committed the murder, then tried to eliminate these traces, as if, having knifed a man to the most violent of deaths, I wouldn't be aware that modern forensics is more than equal to a quick scrub with a Kleenex Moisty Wipe. The fact that I behaved in a way entirely natural for someone who has merely brought in a little dirt from the street is rock-solid proof that at this point I knew nothing of the murder.

At the same time it occurred to me now that when the other Massimina, Antonella's younger sister, had left home with such fatal consequences many years ago, she too left a note in which she said she was going away for a while and not to worry about her. That thought changed my mood drastically. From this point on I was, to put it mildly, in a frenzy of concern for my daughter.

Coming out of the lift and re-entering the museum, I lost patience with cleaning the prints, elbowed my way through the tourists, pushed open the service door and hurried down to the storeroom. Turning on all the lights it was evident that there were patches of blood all over the place. I must have been blind not to see them earlier. The stains grew darker the more you moved to the far wall. I followed them and eventually found a door I hadn't noticed before, perhaps because it stood behind two or three ugly stone statues from the twelfth or thirteenth centuries. Opening the door, which I noticed had a large key in the lock *on the inside*, I found myself in a corridor with other doors leading off either side. Again it was all too easy to see where the blood was coming from since the handle of the second door on the right was thickly smeared with red. I was so breathless to get to the bottom of it I simply put my own bare hand on the handle and opened.

There he was.

You've seen the photos, Carla, so there's not much point in describing the scene. What I rather have to explain, I suppose, is my response. I would like to tell you that I was totally disorientated, and in a way I was. But there was also a way in which I was terrifyingly *orientated*: I mean, I knew *exactly* where I was; it was a scene I was familiar with.

How can I explain?

You must remember that for twenty years I have been collecting paintings showing scenes of murder. This has been my specialisation, the way some philatelists collect stamps showing flowers, others wildlife, others famous public buildings. And of course I had been thinking about these representations of lethal violence much more intensely in recent months as I selected the exhibits for the forthcoming show. Among the biblical murder scenes, one that is rarely depicted but extremely quaint is the murder, or rather political assassination, of the Moabite King Eglon by the Jewish hero, Ehud. There is a nineteenth-century woodcut of the scene by Ford Madox Brown which appears in Dalziel's illustrated Bible (published in the 1880s), a copy of which I had procured through an Internet auction room only the month before, having decided to lend it to the museum for the show. What makes it relevant is that King Eglon was hugely fat and the Bible speaks of the long knife that Ehud used sinking right into his belly, to the point that the haft disappeared. Madox Brown's woodcut shows Eglon in his oriental finery sitting on a handsome throne, just before Ehud attacks.

What can I say? I suddenly felt an extraordinary wave of heat welling up, as if my bowels were on fire. It was the throne that most struck me. What had this room been furnished for, with its antique chests and tables, its gilt chaises longues, its plush drapes, its lush and obscene tapestries, its bizarre oriental symbols and strange instruments (I recognised at once the scourge Volpi had shown me in his office and various weapons from the museum's collection). This must be the place the director had been concerned I might discover, I realised, when he objected to my visiting the storeroom. And there he was on his throne, or a least a huge regency armchair, naked but for the red robe on his shoulders, and with that deep gash in his lower stomach. I took a step towards him and became aware of the smell. The room stank. Because out of his belly had come not just blood but faeces. I made the mistake of taking a step closer, seeing the intestines and just the tip of the haft thrust right into the deep blubber. Immediately I wanted to be sick and indeed I was. I retched on the red carpet already thick with blood (would a murderer do this?). It was as I was trying to wipe my mouth that I realised there was a sticky redness on my hand. From the door. With terrible clarity I knew then I was going to be charged with this murder that I had not committed.

This must be the reason why I delayed informing the police. The moment I told them, I felt sure they would arrest me. It was a mistake, but I wasn't thinking. I panicked. How had Volpi come to such a brutal end? Who had done this terrible thing? Why did it correspond so closely to an image on a woodcut I had recently bought, and a copy of which I had emailed to both Zolla and Volpi, but also, come to think of it, to the Arab, Tarik who had been invited to write some captions for the show? One can see a million paintings, read thrillers and watch horror films, but the real thing is different, it's impact incomparably greater. Yet the fact that this real corpse did seem to have come out of one of those paintings, or even in a strange way to be the painting, somehow made things even worse, both real *and* unreal. Most awful of all was the way Volpi's small eyes were open, amazed; the head lolled back, with a strange expression of bewildered lust about the slack lips. I couldn't stop looking at him. The blood must have drained down through his naked body so that the fat feet, on the gold footrest, were a dark bruised blue. The chromatic effect was most curious. On instinct, I took out my mobile and snapped a couple of shots. What was I thinking of? Then somehow the idea of death reminded me of my daughter. I turned, walked out of the room, along the corridor, took the service lift to the back door, and with blood still on my hand walked back to our house in Via Oberdan.

Antonella was lying on the sofa with a perfumed silk scarf over her face. Having washed my hands and drunk some water to clean the taste of vomit from my mouth I drew up a chair and sat beside her in respectful silence.

'Poor Don Lorenzo,' she murmured. She reached out and took my hand and we sat, or I sat and she lay, in silence.

'It seems he went out late to visit a dying patient. He was too old for such duties. When he came back he fainted and struck his head. Who knows if he will ever wake up? I hope he flies straight to Paradise. I know Purgatory terrified him. Oh poor Lorenzo.'

I couldn't help feeling this was rather an overreaction to the plight of a man who was surely old enough and pious enough to be ready to meet his Maker. All the same I felt the same difficulty my son had had in announcing Massimina's disappearance. I squeezed my wife's hand and went looking for my son, but he was nowhere to be found. Then I remembered it was Sunday afternoon. He must have gone to report at the police station as he is obliged to whenever there is a home match. After which, no doubt, he would go straight to the stadium to catch the second half of the game.

I went into the kitchen and found a saucepan with a mix of lentils, ginger and vegetables on the cooker. I heated up a few mouthfuls, washed down my meagre lunch with a glass of Cabernet and retired to The Art Room. Here I sat for an hour and more contemplating my paintings and reflecting on what I had seen at Castelvecchio. I couldn't make head nor tail of it. All too soon of course the police were banging on the door. In less than an hour I was in a cell.

That's it, Carla. I'm exhausted. I have written into the early hours. Every ten minutes the guard peers in to check that I am not trying to commit suicide. They do well. During the day I sketched a Madonna. I've been praying to her that Massimina may be found. So now a last plea to the Almighty, then sleep.

CHAPTER THIRTEEN

THE DEAD BECAME YOUR allies, they really did. It was not unlike those games of tag where, once touched and caught, the victim joins your team and helps you chase the others. Over the years it had become a regular occurrence for Morris to appeal for their help. Massimina most often of course; her ghostly, sweet-smelling presence was always beside him. Then Paola; Morris's first and wilder wife had provided no end of useful tips when he was trying to seduce young interns, and her experience proved even more invaluable when the time came to wind up these affairs. Genital Giacomo, the lascivious photographer bludgeoned to death with his telephoto lens in a two-star Rimini hotel, had been generous with his know-how on many occasions when Morris was photographing artwork in the disobliging gloom of a medieval nave or transept, the man's grating Veronese dialect croaking aperture settings in his murderer's receptive ear. Antonella's dear dead husband, the once ferociously hostile Bobo Posenato, had softened up considerably after his interment and thence fed Morris all kinds of avant-garde strategies for maximising company profits, and indeed for getting a bit more mileage out of the wife Morris had taken over from him. Years later, when the inevitable showdown was looming with Forbes, the Nigerian Kwame had helpfully come back to brief his one-time employer on the full extent of Forbes's paedophilia, something that allowed Morris to feel assured he was only dispensing justice in seeing the man off. Even Forbes, after a few years in the attic at Santi Apostoli del Soccorso, had put unpleasantness behind him and would occasionally let Morris know which paintings would and wouldn't copy well, which priests could be trusted when he bought works that weren't strictly supposed to be on sale. All in all, Morris reflected, bent over a notepad in his prison cell, it was quite a team he had put together for his riper years. There was so much talent and experience there. 'If you lot can't get me out of gaol,' he muttered, 'I want to know who can.'

Morris was drawing now. They had let him have a notepad with plain paper. At first he sketched to fill the time, but soon it became a form of invocation: carefully, deftly, he called the dead into being with his pencil. Pausing a moment from this effort and recalling his previous imprisonment of twenty and more years ago, Morris marvelled at the feverish mental crisis he had gone through in those weeks and months, the tortured religious images he had conjured up. This time, on the contrary, he was absolutely calm. He plied the long penitentiary hours as a steady, well-laden ship plies the empty ocean, unhurried, unimpressed by waves and weather, absolutely confident he would bring his cargo safely to port. Perhaps it had to do with his being innocent, he thought. That must count for something. Even the occasional *interrogazione* hardly unsettled him. They had put a woman magistrate on the case, Ilde Grimaldi. Not an unpleasant lady, Morris had thought when he first found himself sitting across the table from her, though he couldn't help noticing a drab tweedy skirt on square hips. Cool as the occasion would allow, he decided not to insist on having his lawyer present; hopefully this would indicate he had nothing to fear.

What the police were most concerned about were his movements on the night before the murder. Or of the murder perhaps. Presumably they had now established the time of death. Morris explained that he had spent the Saturday evening at home, for the most part in his Art Room. His wife went to bed early and barely noticed when he joined her.

'I know it's not the perfect alibi,' he confessed, 'though I do fear this is all too common a state of affairs in most marriages.'

'I'm not here to collect your pearls of wisdom, Signor Duckworth,' the older woman coughed drily, turning over typed pages on the table before her. 'You were not, then,' she eventually went on without looking up, 'the middle-aged man seen walking down Via Roma, from Castelvecchio in the direction of Piazza Bra, at approximately 2.30 a.m. Eh?'

Morris was not going to rise to bait like this. 'Hardly,' he remarked, and after a pause, 'middle-aged man would not seem an entirely conclusive description.'

Avvocata Grimaldi studied the page in front of her. 'Balding . . . blond, wearing a tweed jacket.' She looked up. 'Eh, Signor Duckworth?'

Morris had always disliked people with the lazy habit of tossing out inarticulate question tags. He didn't trouble himself to repeat his denial. The magistrate sighed:

'Walking unsteadily,' she read from her witness report, 'perhaps drunk or stunned in some way. Occasionally leaning a hand on the walls for support.' She looked up. 'Eh?'

Morris gave her his most friendly smile: 'Scars?' he enquired. 'Birthmarks? Cornflower blue eyes? Carnation in the lapel?' He waited a moment and just as the lawyer opened her mouth to speak, added 'Eh?' She frowned but did not appear to have caught on.

'I hold my drink pretty well,' Morris concluded. 'Ask anyone who knows me.'

The questioning dragged on for three hours and more, the focus shifting to the suspect's relationship with Volpi. Grimaldi refused to believe that Morris had told her all there was to know. Morris noticed she had poor teeth and was evidently a smoker.

'Do you imagine,' he said at one point, 'that I am the kind of person who would have wanted to get naked with the good Dottor Volpi, as the murderer presumably did?'

Pouncing at once, Grimaldi asked how Morris knew that the

body hadn't been stripped and arranged like that *after* being killed? 'Eh?'

Morris reflected: 'I would have thought murdering people would be hard enough without removing their underwear. Why would anyone want to do that?'

'Are you a Freemason, Signor Duckworth?'

Morris frowned. 'I believe the Freemasons observe a vow of secrecy. You will hardly trust me if I tell you no.'

'Not these days,' the magistrate told him.

'I beg your pardon?'

'They are not so obsessed with secrecy these days,' Grimaldi repeated.

'Evidently you know more about these folk than I do,' Morris told her sweetly, and added, 'But going back to the body, if it was stripped after death, I presume such a thing would have required at least two people, two Masons that is.'

The taller of the two policemen standing at the door smiled.

Abruptly, the magistrate again asked why Morris hadn't contacted the police immediately on discovering the body. Again Morris explained that ever since he had been accused of murder many years ago he had felt insecure and vulnerable as far as police and judiciary were concerned. He was simply scared of having anything to do with them.

'When I first saw Volpi I couldn't believe my eyes, Dottoressa.' Morris was at his most sincere and straightforward now. 'And the moment I walked out of the room I couldn't really believe I *had* seen it. That was why I hurried back in and took two photos, to prove to myself that the corpse was there. To see that it registered in the technology. Even then I wanted it not to be true. I suppose I feared I would be held responsible somehow. That's what I'm like, Dottoressa, sorry Avvocata. Crime annals are full of slightly unhinged people who feel guilty for crimes they didn't commit. Just logically though, if I had done it the evening before and walked, er, what was it, unsteadily home at two or three o'clock, I would have had to be stark raving mad to go and fetch a painting, bring it to the museum and then go tramping bloody footprints all over the place only ten hours later, getting myself seen by tourists and guards to boot. Eh?'

The grim Grimaldi countered that if Morris claimed the right to have behaved irrationally in not reporting the crime, then she hardly needed to prove that his visit the following morning was rational. Did she? 'Eh?'

Morris smiled. 'Fair point,' he acknowledged

'You could have returned to remove important evidence from the scene of the crime,' Grimaldi went on. 'You could have brought the painting to provide an excuse for your fingerprints being down in the storeroom, eh?'

The two watched each other over the plain tabletop.

'Signor Duckworth,' Grimaldi said, 'I have to inform you that your fingerprints have been found on a knife in the cupboard of the museum storeroom, a knife in every way similar to the knife in the victim's belly.'

Morris sat tight. Eventually, he said, 'Avvocata Grimaldi, I was waiting for you to frame a proper question for me, but apparently life is too short for such luxuries. So, you found my fingerprints on any number of knives down in the storeroom because I sorted through them a few weeks before. Indeed it was my visit to the storeroom that led to the misunderstanding with Volpi who, I now realise, far from fearing I might steal something down there was actually concerned that I would come across this strangely decorated room where doubtless he and his cronies got up to all kinds of disgraceful stuff with their whips and scourges. Freemasons all, if not worse. They are not the only secret organisation after all. Italy is full of them.'

'All the staff at Castelvecchio knew about this room, Signor Duckworth.' Grimaldi paused, turned a paper and read: 'The underground location . . . signalled on the building plan as *interrato* 7b . . . erm . . . houses an exhibit used in a show . . . in 1993 . . . a mock-up of the decor in the court of Cangrande della Scala, Signore of Verona, in the early fourteenth century. Why are you pretending you didn't know this, Signor Duckworth?' She stopped and looked up. 'Eh?'

Calmly Morris pointed out that he was *not* a member of the Castelvecchio staff. 'And honestly, Avvocata, medieval statuary has never been of the slightest interest to me. It's just not the kind of show I would ever bother with.' He paused. 'However, even if everyone knew about the place that hardly explains why Dottor Volpi would have been down there in such fancy undress, does it?' He opened his mouth to say eh, but then chose not to.

Ilde Grimaldi lifted her papers and started lining up their untidy edges with quick sharp stabs on the tabletop.

'Signor Duckworth, we believe you carried out this disgraceful murder, together with your mistress Samira Al Zuwaid. We believe you used a knife from the museum store. We believe the motivation had to do with disagreements about the prospected show, *Painting Death*, or perhaps an attempt on your part to blackmail Volpi over his homosexual relationship with the art historian Angelo Zolla.'

Morris sighed deeply. 'Avvocata,' he said, 'if you insist on this silly story of my having a mistress less than half my age, I shall get ideas into my head. Am I to take it that the young lady is in gaol?'

But the lawyer was on her feet, where Morris was pleased to note that she was even shorter and tubbier than he had supposed. Without so much as looking at the suspect she turned and left the room. Morris shook his head, and shook it again an hour later as he sketched out Massimina's face on the rather poor quality paper they had given him. 'Gesture of supreme rudeness,' he muttered. 'Especially when one is supposedly innocent before proven guilty.'

'No one is as well mannered as you,' the dear girl assured him; her whisper felt like a caress.

'It takes so little effort,' Morris mused. He was propped up on one elbow on his bed. It was strange this dreamy calm he felt, with so much precious time passing. Almost three weeks now.

Three weeks of solitary confinement. Perhaps it was a question of age, he thought, of the cerebral temperature falling, the pulse easing off. He turned the pages of the sketchbook, working first on this little portrait, then on that, comparing them, studying them. Without actually deciding to, he had embarked on a plan of conjuring up all their beloved faces at exactly that moment of knowledge, of mutual recognition, the last breath before the killer blow, when each victim had become part of his life, forever. He was looking at them again as they had been in that instant, the most intense of their lives, about to die. And they were looking at him: Giacomo and his gawky English girlfriend Sandra, Massimina, Bobo, Paola, Kwame, Forbes, in sketch after sketch. They knew they had become part of the Duckworth team, the Duckworth Foundation, no less. They rejoiced in their common destiny, smiling from the cheap paper and the blunt pencil point. They were happy together. Astonishing, Morris marvelled, how clearly he saw them.

'By the way, you haven't changed at all,' he whispered to Mimi. He had got exactly the glance in her eye.

'I want to stay beautiful for you, Morris.'

'I wish you'd still call me Morrees. I loved that.'

'Silly, it's one thing staying beautiful, another staying ignorant.' She hesitated. 'Everybody speaks English up here, you know. It's the lingua franca.'

'Naive, *cara*, you were naive, not ignorant.'

'Oh Mo-rrees,' she indulged. 'Mo-rrees. *Baci, baci.*'

He chuckled. After a few minutes he mused: 'I would never be able to draw Volpi like this.'

Massimina was silent.

'Despite the fact that he looked like a picture ready-made.'

He was drawing her lips now, but they wouldn't assent.

'I suppose that's because I didn't do it,' he added.

Still she said nothing.

'Though I rather wish I had, in a way. He deserved it. And the scene-setting was fantastic. I mean, if the museum had any commercial sense they'd have had him stuffed like that and put in the show.'

Pencil between his lips Morris sat up on his bunk, the small pad of paper on his knee. From along the corridor came a clanging of doors and echo of voices. Finally, right beside him, he heard the girl sigh rather heavily.

'Are you sure, Morris?'

'What do you mean?'

'That you didn't.'

Morris laughed. 'You should know, Mimi, where you are.' He added: 'I mean, if I couldn't do for poor old Stan in the most favourable of circumstances, it's hardly likely I could have pulled off a masterpiece like that.'

Again there was a long silence.

'How long do you think they can keep me here?' he asked Bobo, 'Without even a hearing or official charge, without visits or news or anything?'

It was the kind of thing a practical fellow like Bobo might know.

'Indefinitely,' was Bobo's discouraging opinion.

Morris looked at his sketch. The difficult thing with Bobo was combining a snub nose with chinlessness, then making the whole thing sufficiently sullen and grumpy.

'The magistrates can do anything they want. You know that.'

'I suppose I could ask to see the British consul,' Morris reflected.

'They'll make you pay if you do.'

'You're right. I wouldn't want to give them an excuse for treating me as an outsider.'

Paola giggled: '*Povero* Mo, such a paranoid.'

Morris shifted his gaze to contemplate her laughing face. With Paola it was a question of delivering symmetry and neatness, but bereft of Mimi's pathos. Paola was a pin-up.

'Always thinking them-and-us,' she mocked. 'Or rather them and poor Mo. You'd have killed dumb Stan for nothing. See it made no difference at all him going to the police.'

'Might have been fun to have some company,' Forbes cut in. 'Though I suppose poor Stan didn't really deserve it the way Volpi did.'

'It's not about *deserving,*' Mimi interrupted shrilly, 'but being *chosen*. If you haven't understood that, Michael, you haven't understood anything.'

Massimina grew restless when the others tried to take centre stage.

'That may very well be, *carissima,*' Forbes condescended, 'I was merely observing that on this occasion Morris has no cause to feel guilty. Volpi was an obscenely obese, arrogant man, and had clearly abused his position of power as museum director to bring his incompetent *innamorato,* Princess Zolla, into a senior position he wasn't equal to, just so they could go on arsing around among the antiques.'

'You saw the video he was watching?' Giacomo laughed rather unpleasantly.

'Hmmm,' Paola simpered. 'Whips!'

Morris concentrated on putting the dimple in her smile.

'*Minatur innocentibus qui parcit nocentibus*.'

'Beg your pardon?' Bobo asked.

'He threatens the innocent who spares the guilty,' Forbes intoned.

'Fair enough,' Morris acknowledged, emphasising the pointiness of the Old Etonian's nose. 'Except that I didn't do it, folks. I really didn't.'

Again there was an uncanny silence.

'The fact is you all *want* me to have done it!' Morris protested. 'Rather than helping me find out who did. You're supposed to be on my side!'

'Zolla, Boss,' Kwame offered. Morris rubbed his thumb on the black cheeks to give them a shine. 'Got to be Zolla. A raving closet queen. I bet those tears that day were about Volpi threatening to out him in front of his own mamma. Or the fat freak had found a new lover boy. So Zolla sticks him with the giant blade.'

'Reminds me of Jabba the Hut,' Sandra chuckled unhelpfully.

'What about the other guy in the room?' Paola mused. 'The one with the sexily sinister laugh. Could have been him.'

Morris looked up from his pencil.

'If I'd done it, surely he'd be here now. Right? One of us. I'd be drawing him.'

'Too soon,' Paola muttered.

Forbes assented. 'Too soon, Morris. Death takes a while to metabolise, you know.'

Morris lay back on the bed and closed his eyes. For a while no one spoke. But even when they held their peace, he knew the dead were all there, beneath his lids. Then he remembered.

'Does anyone know where Massimina is?'

They would know he meant his daughter. Every time he tried to draw her face, she refused to come out. Or rather, it was always the old Massimina he drew, not the living one. But what if Massimina were dead? Morris sat up.

'Don't any of you know where she is?'

As he spoke the judas hole slid rapidly back and forth, a key clunked in a lock.

'Talking to ourselves?' the guard asked.

'Since no one's popped in for elevenses,' Morris smiled.

A minute later he was swallowing lukewarm polenta. They had melted some cheap white cheese on it which had congealed into something like damp flesh. There were mad murderers who ate their victims, of course. He'd read about that. There were even would-be victims who sought to contact people willing to eat them, on the Internet. Imagine! Volpi, for example. Eat me! Was that why the body was stripped? In preparation for a royal feast. Morris thrust the plate away from him.

On the tray underneath was a piece of paper.

At first he thought it must be an extra napkin. But no, it was notepaper, there were lines. Someone had written on it.

Morris hesitated. Should he read?

'Why on earth not?' Mimi asked.

The guard's footsteps were returning; Morris slipped the paper into his back pocket. The door opened; apparently in a hurry, the guard removed the tray without looking for eye contact. He must know the paper had been there, Morris thought. Perhaps he was expecting the prisoner to have written a response. In any event the guard was gone now; immediately afterwards two others came to march him off for his postprandial exercise, right when he might have liked to snooze.

First there was the short corridor of the solitary cells, then the longer walkway of regular inmates who could rattle their doors and insult him as he passed.

'Hey, *inglesino,* can't you kill a few more southerners for us?'

'Tired of waiting for the old fatty to get it up, were you?'

Obviously these people were not deprived of newspapers and their lurid gossip. But Morris was learning to enjoy his walk down the corridor between his stalwart guards. He concentrated on staying erect, head up, chest thrust out. He even slowed his pace a little so the animals in their crowded cells could appreciate his solitary dignity. Then a door was unlocked and he was free in the yard, for fifteen minutes, albeit with the two guards leaning against the wall, smoking and watching.

Morris walked at a brisk pace, clockwise, anticlockwise, figures of eight. Who did he want the note to be from, he wondered? Antonella, Mauro, Samira, Tarik? Or even Zolla. Or Stan. Stan who he just hadn't been able to kill. And what did he want it to say? 'I love you.' 'We will blow a hole in the wall of your cell at 6 p.m. precisely.' 'The name of the murderer is . . .'

Morris frowned. What exactly had happened that Saturday afternoon and evening? With Samira? With both of them? It was so unlike Morris to lose control, yet evidently he had on that occasion. Had he fainted again at some point? He'd lost pretty much an hour when he'd fainted with Stan, it seemed. But one hour wasn't twelve. Not for the first time he was bound to reflect that the Arab couple might have drugged him. But if that was the case, he couldn't recall when or how. He couldn't recall eating or drinking anything. What *did* he remember, then? The strangeness of Samira starting to make love in her brother's presence. That really was very weird, but it hadn't seemed so at the time. Why not? Was it something he himself had already been fantasising?

Morris shook his head. If he had wanted *that*, he had certainly never been aware of it. Or rather, his being aware of how handsome a young man was, how fine his arms and legs, how attractive and loose-limbed his movements and posture, how intelligent and fierce his eyes, was not the same as desiring him. Was it?

And afterwards?

Morris couldn't remember anything!

Then, despite the two guards lounging against the wall watching him, Morris was so confused, so unhappy, so impatient, he simply pulled the scrap of paper from his pocket, unfolded it and stopped still to decipher the spidery handwriting.

'Dottor Duckworth, we can tell you things that will be useful for your defence. We are all so grateful for what you have done. M.'

Morris put the note back in his pocket and resumed his walking. M must be Mariella, he thought. The only other Ms he knew were Mauro and Massimina. But why would Zolla's secretary make an effort like this – was she married to a prison guard? – an effort that was hardly even *on his behalf* since she seemed to share the general aberration that he had done it? Nor did she actually give him the info she claimed to have. It was a trap.

Or could it be, Morris wondered then, that he had done *something else* that had made them – the people in the office – grateful? So grateful they wanted to express their gratitude by helping him with his defence. Like what? The fact was that with a twelve-hour hole in your memory it wasn't easy to make much sense of anything. How can these things happen? How was Morris going to fill that gap? Hypnotism? Not with a police doctor for sure. Had he perhaps done something so absolutely awful that his mind had blotted it out? Some major psycho thing? But what could be more awful than the seven murders Morris Arthur Duckworth had committed in the past?

CHAPTER FOURTEEN

BACK IN HIS CELL Morris assembled his helpers again and asked them if perhaps he was being set up. Could the note be some sophisticated Italian trick to encourage him to confess by getting him excited about mitigating circumstances?

Lying on his side as he waited for a response, he flicked through page after page of his sketchbook: there were Kwame and Paola embracing, one big black hand on one even bigger breast. There was Bobo looking up from his open desk drawer, his fingers pulling out a blackmail letter Morris had mailed years before. There was Forbes beside his easel, paintbrush hovering over the defenestrated Jezebel. Finally someone spoke.

'That magistrate, what's her name?' It was Paola's voice.

'Grimaldi.' Morris turned and lay on his back, holding the notebook in the air.

'Right. She didn't tell you the others had already confessed, did she?'

'What others?'

'The Arab bitch,' Massimina said in a bored voice.

'But . . .'

'That would be the usual trick, wouldn't it? They say your accomplices have confessed so you cave in and tell the truth.'

'But I didn't do it!' Morris frowned. He hesitated. 'Were Samira and Tarik involved? Is there something you know?'

Again there was silence.

'Go over the whole weekend again,' Paola said coolly.

'Do I have to?' Morris protested.

The dead waited. Morris sighed.

'So, Saturday morning there was the nth argument with Massimina. I objected to her locking herself in her bedroom all day, said she should be helping her mother who was trying to put the winter clothes in mothballs and bring out the summer stuff. She slammed the door in my face and said if I kept bothering her she knew things about me she could tell her mother.'

'Nice,' Kwame said.

'Why do you think I always preferred to live alone?' Forbes asked.

'I then spent some time in The Art Room, moving around the paintings on the virtual exhibition I've set up on the Mac. The real problem is to get the balance between an intellectual or thematic arrangement and an aesthetic organisation that suits the space and the light. For example, to my mind the Gentileschi Holofernes would go well with any of the Poussins, but they're not thematically linked.'

This interesting reflection was met with complete silence.

'Tell us about the afternoon,' Forbes said.

'Had lunch around one or one-thirty, I suppose, I mean, that's when I always have lunch on Saturday.'

Morris Duckworth's legal team waited.

'Then a snooze with Antonella. She's been having trouble with her knee recently and—'

'Morris!' Paola snapped. 'Get to the point! Around five o'clock you set off to see your dusky little whore.'

'First I dropped in at Trevisan Wines to make sure there would be a van available for the following morning. To pick up San Bartolomeo. I also took a little time to read Mauro's report on ways to speed things up at the old Quinzano bottle factory. I was honestly surprised how practical and clear-sighted it was, especially the bit about allowing the Moslem workers—'

'Morris, for Christ's sake!' Forbes objected.

'It isn't enough to kill us,' Paola observed drily, 'now he has to bore us to death.'

'OK, so then I went to see Samira.'

There was a brief silence.

'Was she expecting you?'

'No.'

'So why did you go? Or why didn't you call ahead?' It was Paola conducting the interrogation.

'I like to surprise her.'

'You like to act the boss. You like to check up on her. It's sick.'

'The truth is,' Morris conceded, 'I wanted to find out exactly what their relationship with Volpi was. I was uncomfortable about him knowing them so well. I hate it when people I know know each other.'

Silence. It was strange, Morris thought, how the dead questioned him in little flurries, then backed off, as if there were somewhere he wasn't supposed to go.

'Anyway, I rang and they buzzed me up at once.'

'Without asking who it was?'

Morris hadn't thought of this. 'Right. You're right. As if they were expecting me. Though they weren't, because then they were surprised.'

'Tell the truth, Morris.'

'They were both naked.'

'Ah.' The narrow prison cell was alive with sighs.

'Tarik answered naked?'

'Starkers.'

'And you didn't wonder who they might have been expecting if not you?'

'They were high. Maybe they weren't expecting anyone. No one else arrived.'

'High on what?'

'They offered me a smoke.'

'Hadn't you said you never would again?' Mimi asked.

'The flesh is weak,' Morris acknowledged.

'The spirit is non-existent,' Paola added.

'Perhaps they sent a text message warning whoever it was not to come,' Bobo suggested. 'Do you remember them texting?'

'I can't recall.'

'Boss,' Kwame chirped in cheerfully, 'why not just describe the whole thing and we'll sit back and listen.'

Morris sighed deeply. He didn't want to, but sooner or later he would have to go over this. Eyes closed on the narrow bunk he began to tell the story out loud in a muttered monotone. So . . . when he had arrived he had seen at once that the apartment was not in its usual state. All the windows were wide open. It had been the first warm spring evening. Mild air was drifting into the smoky room. The bright cushions Samira liked to keep on bed and sofa were scattered over the living-room floor together with discarded clothes, yoga mats, bowls, plates, glasses and playing cards. A half-eaten cake had been on the table. There were glasses and bottles. Music was playing on YouTube. Modern Arab music, jingly, festive and repetitive. There was a laptop on a chair. Arab babes dancing in jeans and jowly youngsters smarming round the mike. Tarik, usually so sullen and reserved, had burst out laughing when Morris appeared at the door. 'Welcome to Nineveh, Meester Duckworth,' he had shouted. 'Wanna play Sardanapalus?'

'Oh Morrees,' Mimi shook her head.

'Makes me life-sick,' Paola muttered.

'And I just thought, well, the hell with it!' Morris told them.

'Damn right,' Kwame agreed.

'Snoozes with Antonella had that effect on me too,' Bobo acknowledged.

Anyway, he had asked the two of them what all the celebration was about.

'We got good news!' Samira had laughed.

'From Libya,' Tarik added quickly.

Their favourite uncle's faction had prevailed, it seemed, in some complex negotiation in Benghazi.

'And for that they had to get naked?' Giacomo enquired.

Morris remembered feeling at the time that the story had sounded rather improvised: something about a feud in the souk between different suppliers of essential commodities. They had been laughing throughout. Meantime, he had found himself in his underwear on an orange cushion, sucking on a fat joint, something he always promised himself he would never do again.

'What were you thinking of?' Mimi demanded. 'What if they're drug dealers or something? What if this whole Libyan thing is about trafficking? Here in Italy.'

'Arms,' Bobo suggested.

'Paintings,' Forbes thought.

'Prostitutes,' Paola volunteered.

It was Morris's turn to be silent. Eventually, he muttered, 'From the moment Stan went to the police, I'd felt I was living on borrowed time. Then that evening there was spring in the air, and Samira looked so good.'

'Liar,' Paola said. 'You'd seen her naked a thousand times.'

On his back on the bunk, Morris's forehead knitted into a painful frown.

'It was the boy.'

There was a sharp intake of breath.

'It was the first time you'd seen Tarik naked.'

'That's true,' Morris acknowledged. 'Usually he was rather unfriendly. Surly. And instead, all of a sudden . . . It was new to me. I don't know.' He hesitated. 'Having chosen not to kill Stan, I'd been feeling rather virtuous. Like I deserved a treat.'

'Chosen?'

His friends didn't seem impressed.

'It was only the low ceiling,' Bobo said drily.

'Is the Arab well hung?' Forbes enquired.

'Oh for heaven's sake!' Mimi wailed.

Then, pulling a blanket over his face, one arm underneath lolling indigently across his belly, Morris told his seven old friends in unsparing detail how it had all happened. The moment when, eyes closed, he had realised that the lips kissing his possessed an unusual beardy roughness; the moment in the shower kneeling between the two young bodies as the water streamed off them, and then the beautiful moment, dancing together, shoulders closed in a circle, hands on buttocks, to the languid wail of some Arab compilation. Marijuana and sandalwood in the air. Until, a couple of hours later, or perhaps longer, all memories abruptly ceased.

'Wow!' someone breathed.

'Morris dancing!' Sandra giggled.

'Well I'll be buggered,' Forbes remarked with fruity indulgence.

Then the frivolity faded and there was a long silence in the tiny cell. It was rather like at the end of the Communion service back in St Barnabas when everyone had partaken of the body and blood and knelt in their pews to reflect.

Finally Paola said softly: 'Dear Mo, sometimes it feels like you've had to do the living for all of us.'

Morris accepted this interpretation. Then remarked, 'But it's hardly going to help with my defence.'

There was a general shuffling, a certain embarrassment even.

'Well,' Sandra said thoughtfully. 'Now you've had the good grace to tell us what really happened that evening, let me ask this: have you ever heard of TGA?'

'TG what?' Morris sat up.

'Temporary global amnesia,' the English girl said. 'I read about it in some magazine. There was a famous case. In America, of course. It happens to people in their fifties; you get about six to twenty-four hours of total amnesia. It's triggered by some mind-blowing experience. Often sexual.'

Morris was very alert now. And yes, dimly, distantly, he recalled that he too had read about this. It rang a bell.

'So, I have wild sex and lose my memory for a few hours, is that it? Right when the murder happens.'

'I only read the article,' Sandra said. 'I'm not an expert.'

'But what would it mean?' Morris asked. 'That I could have done things I don't know about?'

'I've no idea. You'll have to do some research. Get on the net.'

Which of course was impossible in a prison cell. The problem was that Morris needed to know now. Otherwise, how could he ever put together an alibi?

'Perhaps there are clues in what happened the following morning,' Bobo suggested.

'In what sense?'

'When you went to get the picture, did Samira and Tarik give some hint about what happened the evening before?'

Morris wasn't sure. He would have noticed.

'You didn't know the old fat boy had been skewered at that point, Boss,' Kwame pointed out. 'You weren't looking for hints.'

'Go over it again,' Paola told him.

'But it was exactly as in my report to Carla.'

'Not altogether,' Mimi said severely.

'OK. Early morning Antonella woke me in The Art Room and asked me when I'd got home. That's when I realised I couldn't remember anything.'

'And did you tell your wife?'

'Of course not! I felt confused, and rather guilty too, for what had happened the previous afternoon.'

'What a useless hypocrite you are,' Paola said with an intensity of contempt that Morris found both humbling and exciting.

'Then we went to church, only to find that Don Lorenzo wasn't—'

'Could he be involved?'

'Who?'

'The priest.'

It was Sandra again. Morris was rather surprised at the extent of her participation.

'After all, why was he out in the middle of the night, and why did he have a heart attack when he got home?'

'Because he was visiting a deathbed,' Morris said.

'Yeah, Volpi's!' Sandra insisted.

'Hardly a death*bed*,' Kwame quipped.

'He's a strange priest if you ask me,' Sandra said. 'How did they get your boy Mauro out of gaol in the end, Morris? Whose coffin was it fell on his foot that he never wants to confess?'

Morris felt lost.

'I was molested by a priest,' Sandra said. 'I was only twelve. It was after choir practice in—'

'For Christ's sake, Sandy,' Giacomo interrupted.

'Anto hurried to the hospital,' Morris resumed, 'while I set off to San Zeno again.'

'And . . . ?' Paola took over the questioning.

And Morris had had to ring the bell two or three times before he was buzzed in. They were barely out of bed.

'No mention of the previous evening's antics?'

'Not at all. Or not at first.'

Over breakfast – Morris had brought the Libyans cappuccinos and pastries from the café in the piazza – Samira had rather unexpectedly said something about their relationship being at a crossroads. Either he, Morris, was man enough to leave home and make an honest woman of her, or they had to stop seeing each other. It was too painful for her to get any deeper in a relationship if it was just going to end.

'An honest woman,' Mimi objected. 'That's rich.'

'Obviously I have no intention of leaving home,' Morris reassured his seven servers. He had always understood that the Duckworth ghosts were profoundly conservative.

'Anyway, enough of my relationship with Samira, since it's got nothing at all to do with Volpi's murder.'

'It might have a lot to do with it,' Bobo said, 'and it certainly will have a lot to do with how those two kids responded when the police questioned them.'

'For example,' Paola resumed, 'what you didn't tell Carla in your statement was that at the church in San Briccio they weren't just making fun of the paintings, they were making fun of *you*.'

Morris said nothing.

'Of your sexual prowess to be precise,' Paola said. 'Or lack thereof.'

'Of how you *struggled,*' Mimi said quietly.

'Did not your dusky damsel say,' Forbes chuckled, 'and I quote: "I thought Methuselah was going to blow a gasket"?'

Morris tried to be patient. 'I just don't see what this has got to do with Volpi's death.'

'Why didn't you *tell* the two of them you couldn't remember anything?' Paola enquired. 'It might have been a more honest way to deal with the situation. Look guys, what on earth happened to me yesterday evening? I can't remember. Maybe they'd have told you. Maybe you'd have an alibi now. Or at least you'd know you did it.'

He hadn't asked because he had felt insecure, Morris confessed, anxious that he would come across as incipient Alzheimer's. Anxious that he was Alzheimer's maybe. After all, he'd already fainted once and forgotten an hour or so. 'Anyway, whatever I did when I wasn't remembering, it clearly wasn't anything with them or they would have referred to it, wouldn't they?'

'So, your position,' Paola summed up, 'is that if you killed Volpi when you weren't remembering anything, you didn't do it with the Arabs, or things would have been different Sunday morning, because surely they would have referred to it.'

'Right!' Morris said.

'So if *they* did it,' Paola went on, 'they did it in your absence.'

'Right,' Morris agreed again.

'Unless of course they *knew* that you were in a special state and wouldn't remember anything.'

'Hard to imagine,' Morris shook his head. 'But surely it's far more likely that someone quite different did it, someone I know nothing about and who has nothing to do with Sammie and Tarik.'

Silence.

'I mean, about this famous *mise en scène,* the Eglon cameo, supposedly so damning, in that I had just purchased the woodcut and so on.'

'Yes?'

Morris hesitated: 'Well, I may have been a warm advocate of using the image in the show, but I certainly never did any of that unhealthy stuff when I killed in the past, did I? I mean, I just killed because I had to and got out fast. Without arcane messages or perverse theatricals.'

There was an awkward pause.

'So a murder like this would be a major departure for me, wouldn't it? I mean, in a way, it would have been something to be proud of. I almost wish I had done it. But given my performance with Stan, it hardly seems likely that . . .'

More silence.

Finally, in a very low voice, Mimi said, 'I wish you'd shown a bit more respect with me, Morris. Stuffing me in bin bags. With my bottom hanging out as well.'

'In the boot of a car,' Bobo reminded him.

'Under rubble,' Forbes protested.

'Sent up in flames,' Kwame sighed.

'OK, I was rushed, but I mean, precisely because of that I didn't go for the big *symbolic* display, did I? That's just not me. Not my signature. I only kill because I have to then I get out fast.'

'You've changed a lot over the years,' Paola pointed out. 'You've acquired this art obsession.'

'And you were high on dope and group sex,' Mimi added.

'Unfortunately, Morris,' Bobo observed caustically, 'the police don't know you have a record as a different kind of killer, do they? I mean, Grimaldi's not going to say, Ah, no, this *can't* be Morris Duckworth; when our honorary citizen kills he just bashes his victim over the head, bundles the body into any filthy hole he can find and gets the hell out.'

There was some tittering.

Morris felt exasperated, and exhausted. In a way it was exciting, but there was only so much you could take. He yawned. His legal team chattered on. They were discussing the chances of uncovering seamy aspects of Volpi's life. 'He didn't end up nude in the museum basement by accident.' Morris was too drowsy to keep track. They wondered what Zolla's alibi might be. They worried whether the Arabs would tell the police about the intimate nature of their relationship with Morris, or whether Morris was right to assume their *omertà* over this point. Had Morris considered the idea that they might *not* be brother and sister? What if they were members of the Libyan secret services? And being Neapolitan, was Volpi perhaps a *camorrista*? What if the police did now finally make connections to the disappearance of Forbes? Bobo complained what a shame it was the dead didn't have access to the net to check up on the causes and consequences of temporary amnesia. Was it something that regularly happened to killers? Was this fainting habit Morris appeared to have a blood-pressure problem? The last thing Morris heard before falling into a deep sleep was Kwame's voice offering the common-sense reflection that in the end it hardly mattered who had actually killed Volpi; their only concern should be to concoct a credible alibi that shifted the suspicion on to someone else's shoulders. 'Pass the buck, Boss. Pass the buck.'

CHAPTER FIFTEEN

MORRIS WATCHED FROM THE window. Hidden behind a removals van, two policemen had pulled over yet another car making the illegal left into Via Quattro Stagioni from the busy Viale Venezia, the main Verona–Vicenza trunk road. There were the usual angry gesticulations, protests no doubt that there was no reason to forbid the left turn at this particular junction, that if the police really wanted to enforce the rule they could have put a barrier in the middle of the road, that if they hadn't put the barrier the only reason must be to collect fat fines from those who understandably made the turn to avoid a kilometre and more of pointless and polluting driving. And so on. Morris admired the patience of the police officers as they ignored these remonstrations and filled in their forms. He had always, he thought, been on the side of law, order and civic obedience. Not once had he been fined for a traffic offence.

Yet despite all his best efforts Morris had come to this: a lonely man in his mid fifties, bereft of position and purpose in life, gazing emptily through the smeared windowpane of a poky one-bedroom flat in the nondescript suburb of an insignificant northern Italian town.

A man stripped of his power, Morris muttered to himself. Deprived of his authority. Deprived too of the groundbreaking show he should have been curating. A man bereft of all belongings. Prospero without his magic books. Bereft of all affections. A man abandoned even by the Dead. His ungrateful Dead. Abandoned even by Mimi. They and she had stopped speaking to him.

Morris Duckworth had confessed. The public prosecutor was satisfied that the case was closed; house arrest could now be granted. On an unpleasantly hot day in June, Morris found no one waiting for him at the prison gates. How was that possible? Not even the press. One expected at least notoriety. He had to beg the guards to reopen the gates, walk back to reception and ask them to call a taxi. Returning to the road, he waited under hazy sunshine. Frogs were croaking in the ditches. The word unruly came to mind. Rowdy, refractory, rebellious.

Morris frowned. Why was nobody here? Why wasn't there even a pavement beside the high prison wall? Grass grew through cracks in the asphalt. Not even a white line in the middle of this provincial road. Perhaps he really should have stayed in England, which, for all its faults, did offer some basic services in return for taxes. Just as the taxi drew up from the left, Morris saw his own elegant Alfa Romeo approaching from the right. 'Not me,' he told the taxi driver, casting a quick glance around. 'Must be someone waiting inside.'

'Ciao Papà.'

It was Mauro. The big boy was sitting in the back, chauffeured by an Indian Morris didn't recognise, someone fished up from the bottle factory floor, no doubt. In jeans. The man got out and put Morris's suitcase in the boot.

'He ought to be wearing a uniform,' Morris observed.

Mauro raised a quizzical eyebrow, but didn't reply. During the awkward silence as they drove, Morris was acutely aware that something important had shifted between them. It was like returning to a room to find the furniture moved.

'How's business?' he asked.

Mauro frowned. He reflected. The crisis was squeezing profits, he said. The English were buying less wine and were obsessed by pricing and quality. On the building side, the banks were starving the contractors of credit. 'The whole country is grinding to a halt,' Duckworth Junior finished. 'We're in a deep recession.'

Morris tried to pay attention, but suddenly none of this seemed important. The empire he had built was anyway slipping away from him; what happened to it when he was definitively behind bars hardly mattered.

'And Hellas?'

'Going into the play-offs for Serie A.'

'You must be excited.'

Mauro shrugged meaty shoulders in a smart linen jacket. His hair was neatly parted, which somehow made it seem slightly less flamingly red than his father remembered it. 'At the moment, I hardly have time to think about football.'

They imprison you unjustly, Morris reflected, and lo and behold your son comes of age in your absence. The young man was wearing a sober tie, he was speaking Italian rather than dialect. Morris felt proud, resentful.

'And Massimina? Any news?'

'I'll tell you when we arrive.'

Apparently there were things that couldn't be said in the presence of the driver. Speaking of whom, Morris realised that the man was going the wrong way. He leaned forward and tapped his shoulder.

'You should have taken Via Montorio,' he said. 'It'll take forever this way.'

The Indian half turned for confirmation. He was unpleasantly pockmarked, Morris thought. There was a gold tooth.

'You're doing fine,' Mauro told him, 'continue as instructed.'

Having driven south to the Verona–Vicenza Statale, the car now turned west toward the city.

'We're not going home, Dad.'

Thus did Morris learn that his pious wife would be playing that role no longer. Indeed, in his absence she had set wheels in motion to claim that they had never been man and wife at all; Antonella had applied to the Sacra Rota to have the Duckworth's twenty-two-year marriage annulled.

'Just like that!'

Morris was appalled. He couldn't take it in. And appalled too by the suffocating room in which Mauro eventually explained all this: just four metres by three, including sofa, table, two chairs and a few spartan kitchen accoutrements. The bedroom was even smaller, with a single bed, the bathroom minuscule. Since Antonella was sole owner of the palazzo in Via Oberdan, it seemed she had the right to lock him out. Or she was assuming that right, whether she had it or not. This was where Morris must spend the months before his trial. There was no air conditioning.

'But surely she understands that my confession was strategic!' Morris protested. 'Hasn't Carla told her?'

'Carla who?'

Mauro had found a coffee pot and was making an espresso. When he opened a cupboard Morris saw it was stocked with the bare essentials. Rice. Pasta. Salt.

'The lawyer. Carla Cogni. They must have been in touch.'

'Mamma has her own lawyer. I don't think she's interested in your defence.'

'But just because I *confessed*? Surely she realises that that was the only way I could get out of gaol a while and find who the real murderer was! The actual killing couldn't possibly have happened the way I confessed to it. Give me your phone and I can sort this out in a second.'

Mauro stood with his back to the cooker. Morris was struck by a new gravitas in the boy's posture.

'It's not about your confession,' he said quietly. 'She decided weeks ago.'

Morris sat heavily on a chair that creaked. The place was sweltering. For some reason his mind went back to his first meeting with the Trevisan family all those years ago, when Massimina had taken him home and he had massaged the truth about himself, his career, oh just a smidgen, to gain the hypercritical Mamma's acceptance. She had checked up on his story at once and forbidden him to see his beloved any more. That was where it had all begun, all his woes, with their ungenerous, unwarranted suspicions. If they had afforded him even a grain of credit, even a husk, nothing need ever have happened. And now the wife whom he thought he had convinced, the woman he believed was his faithful partner, was betraying him in the same way; she was pulling the plug on Morris Duckworth, ignoring all the work he had done to turn a plonky wine business into a major construction company, declaring all their years together null and void. Cutting my head off as surely as Judith decapitated Holofernes, Morris thought. Was this what those terrible dreams had been about?

Mauro watched his unhappy father.

'Apparently Don Lorenzo said something to her.'

'Don Lorenzo?' Morris jumped to his feet. 'Let's go and talk in a café. I can't sit in here. I'm suffocating. It was cooler in prison.'

Mauro didn't move. 'You're under house arrest, Papà. You can't go out.'

Morris had forgotten. The arrangement was a half-hour's fresh air mid morning and another towards evening. At any other time the police could come to check whether the accused was present. If he broke the rules, they would send him back to his cell.

Mauro poured the coffee. Morris was struck by the poor quality of the espresso cups. If this place had been furnished specifically for him, the intention was hardly to keep him in the manner to which he was accustomed.

'I imagined Don Lorenzo would have passed to a better world,' he said.

'He's dead, yes, if that's what you mean. But before he died he said some stuff in his coma.'

'People don't speak in coma,' Morris objected. 'Or it wouldn't be a coma, would it?'

Mauro raised a wry eyebrow. 'You're so weird, Dad,' he said. 'It's like you never focus on the thing that matters.'

Hearing this, Morris was acutely aware that three months in gaol had left him out of training for the abrasive back-and-forth of domestic conversation.

'Whatever state he was in,' Mauro continued, 'Don Lorenzo said things that upset Mamma so much she decided to go to the Sacra Rota.'

'What things?'

'She wouldn't tell me. Said no son should ever hear such things about a father.'

'Let me call her,' Morris said. 'Have you brought me my phone?'

Mauro frowned. 'Papà, you're not supposed to communicate with the outside world. You're under house arrest.'

As in the whole silly saga of the boy's trial for assault, Morris was struck by his son's literalism when it came to rules. The police knew perfectly well that they couldn't stop a man in his own home from using a mobile and writing a few emails. Probably the whole purpose of house arrests was to monitor the accused's calls so they could get some more evidence.

'At least I should know what it is I'm supposed to have done wrong.'

Mauro drained his coffee and looked at his watch.

'You wanted to know about Massimina.'

'Yes. Of course.' But as he acquiesced Morris was wondering how many blows a man could take without going mad. There was a speech along those lines in *Lear*. Another father who had lost a daughter and been betrayed by everyone.

'I did as you asked in your letter,' Mauro said. He was standing at the window now, his back turned towards his father. 'I went to see Zolla. And for a couple of weeks I paid someone to follow your Arab friends.'

'No friends of mine,' Morris said quickly. 'Just tell me. Is Mimi OK?'

'Well, we had a postcard from her. Her writing, signed by her. About ten days ago.'

'Thank God. What did it say?'

Mauro turned round and shook his head. '*Sto bene.*'

'That's all? She just tells us she's well and that's it?'

'Yes.'

'Could be worse,' Morris observed. 'Where was it sent from? What was the picture?'

Mauro hesitated. 'San Diego,' he said.

After his son had gone, Morris stood at the window for hours. He was in a daze. It was so strange to have even this restricted freedom. On the other hand if he wanted to eat, he would have to prepare his food himself, something he hadn't done for literally decades. Not that he felt hungry. He felt numb. When the police car pulled up across the road behind the removals van, he imagined it had come to keep watch on him, then had to smile when the two men started flagging down illegal turners. Unless they *were* there for him and this traffic duty was a cover, or something they did for amusement while really keeping watch on the front of the apartment block. Killing the proverbial two birds. With the state of police finances, it would be an excellent idea to hand out a few fines while actually involved in surveillance.

His flat was part of a large block. He was on the first floor, over the entrance, but there were five floors above and a row of windows both to left and right. It was a Chinese wall of humdrum social endeavour, without grace, without distinction, the kind of place his father should have lived in, not Morris. Now the police had stopped a top-of-the-range BMW and a uniformed man climbed out and remonstrated, gesturing to the back of the sleek black vehicle. Morris didn't understand. A policeman bent to peer inside, then, suddenly respectful, almost bowing, backed off. The car looked vaguely familiar. No! As it roared away Morris caught a glimpse of scarlet on the back seat. Vatican plates. He shook his head. What a country! When an old Cinquecento with a Hellas pennant on the roof now made the same illegal turn, the two policemen were ferocious. They got the young man to put his arms and forehead on the roof of the car. They frisked him. They crouched down to check the tyres. One of them got inside and began emptying the glove compartment. Morris would have liked to phone his son to give him this confirmation of his views on police prejudices, but he didn't have a phone, or a computer for that matter. There was nothing for him to do but look out of the window and reflect how strange it was that Cardinal Rusconi should be turning into Via Quattro Stagioni.

And how bizarre too that Massimina had run off with Stan Albertini. Could that really be true? In which case who was the Gio who had sent the miss-you message on her phone? Mauro had explained that Stan hadn't returned to the States for almost a month after Morris's arrest. On the contrary, he had been constantly round the house in Via Oberdan. So what had Massimina been doing in the meantime? Getting a passport and visa? Where had she been staying? In Stan's hotel? What was the age difference between them? Thirty-five years? It was outrageous! I really should have killed him, Morris thought. I should have done it. And yet if there was one thing that made him happy from time to time it was that he hadn't killed Stan. Why, he had no idea. Perhaps secretly he actually liked Stan, or felt some kind of deep connection with him. In any event, a Stan wrapped around his daughter's long legs on some Pacific surfing beach was not a Stan who would be standing up in court remembering moments in Roma Termini twenty and more years before. The day Morris picked up the ransom for Mimi.

The news Mauro had brought his father about Samira and Tarik was also puzzling. The girl continued to work at the Cultural Heritage office. She must have got her contract extended. But the boy rarely left the apartment they shared. When he did so, it was to be driven off in a black SUV with Arab plates that invariably headed for the autostrada at Verona Sud and sped off west. It seemed the boy returned in the early hours, always driven by the same portly Arab, in his fifties.

'You know there's been stuff in the paper about some arms-for-oil deal with the new Libyan government.'

'And?'

'Apparently one condition is that they allow Moslems to open more mosques here.'

Morris frowned. 'So?'

Mauro had shrugged. 'I suppose I just started noticing the word Libyan. The church has been complaining. And the Northern League. They're furious.'

'Oh for heaven's sake!' Morris interrupted. 'What about Zolla?'

Mauro shook his head. 'Talk about creeps!' He had gone to the man's office in Castelvecchio. 'Is it a poker he has up his backside?' Zolla had said he couldn't understand why anyone would come to talk to him about the matter. 'And if you're thinking he might have killed the guy,' Mauro added, 'I doubt he would have had the guts.'

'Whereas I would?' Morris said drily.

'More than him, for sure.'

'I'll take that as a compliment.'

'Take it any way you like.'

For a moment father and son had looked at each other very frankly.

'You think I did it,' Morris said.

Mauro sighed and frowned together. 'Honestly, Papà, I don't know what to think.' He hesitated. 'People say so many things about you.'

'You believe them?'

'It doesn't matter whether I believe them or not, does it? Let me go now, I've got appointments.' The boy smiled at his father. 'A last check-up with the dentist in fact. I've finally had my teeth fixed.'

* * *

At five, Morris set out to the shops. It was still hard to believe how completely he had been abandoned. Mauro had left him a debit card and some change and that was that. He walked in the warm evening down a drab street: miserable seventies' apartment blocks, dusty asphalt, untidy balconies, stout women with too many bags, pensioners wobbling on ancient bicycles. Who *am* I without my fine house, he wondered, without my wife, without The Art Room?

'Mimi,' he enquired out loud. There was a flaking Madonna beside a grey gate. But he already knew she wouldn't reply. It was as if Morris had abruptly been kicked out of his own life, his own self-narrative. All the dead had left him. The police weren't even bothering to keep him in a cell any more. He was a complete nobody.

In the supermarket he found he had no idea what to buy. A pasta sauce. There had been some penne in the cupboard. A bottle of wine. Suddenly, he found himself gazing at the familiar Trevisan label. Classico Superiore. No. He would boycott the brand. He chose an expensive Piedmontese Grignolino. Mauro hadn't told him what account the debit card drew on, only the pin. Were they legally in their rights to chuck him out of the house and the company he had built up? Morris had the strange feeling that if he just walked away along the street, away from this meaningless suburb, away from Verona and his Italian past, no one would stop him. If he just marched northwards and over the Alps he could perhaps put these thirty years of madness, his adult Italian life, behind him. He would wake in a bed in East Croydon and find it had all been a bad dream and he was still in time to get the 8.12 to Victoria and put in an ordinary day at the Milk Marketing Board.

Aimlessly, Morris filled his trolley. At the till the girl asked if he had a loyalty card.

'Loyalty?' Morris repeated.

'Have you need the bag?' the girl asked, apparently in English.

'*Sì, grazie*,' Morris told her.

* * *

Back in the flat he was too tired to cook. He missed the guards, the prison routine. For a moment he thought he might draw, but couldn't find pencil or paper. Why wasn't there a television at least? A radio? He sat at the table, nonplussed. The idea that he might, on his own, find out who had committed a crime that had occurred two months before now seemed ridiculous. Added to which he might well become the first detective to find out he had committed the crime himself. But if there was nothing he could do now, why had he confessed? To what end? This is really happening, he kept telling himself. He was tempted to go out again and visit someone, Samira perhaps, just to see if they really would arrest him on the way and take him back to gaol.

Having put on a pot of pasta, he forgot about it and stared out of the window. Forty minutes later it was gunge. He threw it away. The room was unbearably hot. Eventually, he discovered a magic marker in a kitchen drawer. Sitting on the bed he began to draw on the white wall. The flat had been recently white-washed. Without thinking, he drew a large throne and a fat man slumped across it. That cameo ended my life, Morris thought. Then it occurred to him: if Don Lorenzo hadn't read out the famous passage from Judges that evening – the Eglon and Ehud story – would the murder have taken place weeks later in the way it did? Although he felt sure he hadn't done it, nevertheless Morris couldn't help but feel there must be a connection. As if he had done it, but in a dream. Speaking of which, what awful truths, or perhaps fictions, had Don Lorenzo muttered in his dying sleep to Antonella? Idly, Morris sketched in lines for the murdered king's four or five bellies, then a black gash for a wound. Magic marker poised, he tried to imagine the scene around the victim at the moment of the crime. Had there been other people in the room? 'I went to the museum just before it closed on Saturday,' he had told Grimaldi. 'I was hoping to identify one or two artefacts to take away for my own collection. In particular, a knife. Volpi surprised me. Why he was there I have no idea.' Morris had chased the fat man back into the throne room and stabbed him. Then removed his clothes and surrounded him with fetishist items to make it look like some ritual or other.

'How did you get the body on the chair?' Grimaldi had asked. 'Eh?'

'With great difficulty,' Morris replied.

'Why did you dispose of the clothes?'

'Instinct.'

'And where?'

'In the river.'

'Why did you return the following morning?'

'The recovery of San Bartolomeo was already scheduled. I deliberately got rid of the Arabs because I wanted to go up to the offices and look through Volpi's computer. Unfortunately I didn't realise I'd stepped in the blood.'

What a stupid story! Yet Morris started to think he might somehow have been there when it happened. He even had moments, inklings, when he felt he was beginning to remember. A knife, the movement of the hand. It was strange.

Staring at his drawing on the wall above the bed, he wondered again who were the other people in the scene. It was like trying to imagine a whole painting from a fragment. Remember the way the throne was turned when you found it, he told himself. Remember the position of the mats and cushions in the photos you took. Draw, Morris suddenly told himself. Just draw, damn it! Trust to inspiration, to the artist in you. At random he traced a vertical line, and at once it was a back, a man's rigid back. Kneeling. It was Zolla! There were his knees, his bare feet. The meeting was organised to punish Zolla! Yes. To scourge him. The thought came to Morris's mind. Am I a psychic? Even without my ungrateful dead? He definitely saw Zolla. Very quickly he sketched him in, supplicant at Volpi's feet. There was something round his neck. What? A sort of halter? Morris drew it. Attached where, to what? The ceiling? Some iron ring set in the wall? No. To Volpi's hand! Like Pozzo and Lucky in *Godot*.

The gross fat man and the elegant forty-year-old. The Dominant and the Submissive. They had been playing a game and something had gone wrong. Perhaps because of the third person in Volpi's office that day, the one who laughed. I knew that laugh, Morris thought. He shook his head, drew one line, then another. There was definitely some force guiding his hand, he thought, in the darkness behind closed eyes. He put in four, five confident lines. A squiggle here, a squiggle there. He stopped, eyes still closed. When I open them I'll know who the murderer is. I'll have drawn the murderer! He felt convinced. He was definitely psychic. He prayed, briefly. When he opened his eyes the wall was a complete pig's ear. Morris went back to the sitting room/kitchen, opened the Grignolino and drained two glasses in quick succession.

CHAPTER SIXTEEN

'DOTTOR DUCKWORTH. DOTTOR DUCKWORTH.'

Morris knew he must be dreaming. He was alone in the apartment. He was in bed. The door was locked.

'Dottor Duckworth!'

It was a low urgent voice. Morris felt a hand plucking at his pyjama sleeve. Were they going to cut off his head again?

'Wake up! *Per favore.*'

'I am awake.'

That was a funny thing to say when you knew you were dreaming.

'It's Mariella.' The name was whispered.

Morris whispered back, 'Ah. Is that so?'

'From Castelvecchio.'

'I know, Mariella with the magnificent breasts.'

Perhaps it was going to be an erotic dream.

'Dottor Duckworth, *per l'amore di Dio,* wake up!'

Responding to a brusque tug on his sleeve, Morris sat up abruptly and clashed heads in the dark with the figure leaning over him.

'For Christ's sake!'

'Shhhh, Dottor Duckworth, the place is bugged.'

'Mariella!'

The woman was there in the flesh. All of it.

'I have a key. Follow me. Don't put the light on. Don't worry about clothes. Just follow.'

He was being liberated, Morris thought. Fantastic. But why?

Still holding his sleeve, the woman led him through the small apartment to the front door which was ajar and out on to the landing. There was a key in the lock and very carefully she pulled the door to, turning the key slowly to prevent any clunking. Morris was in just a pyjama top and underwear, but the night was warm.

'We can't use the lift,' she warned.

'It's only one floor,' Morris said.

'No, we're going up.'

A rooftop escape? Morris was so far outside normality anything seemed possible.

They climbed the stairs, flight after flight. On each landing a small window was open, letting in the moist air of Verona's summer night. The stone steps felt cool under his bare feet. Ahead of him the woman was wearing a loose grey tracksuit. Her bottom seemed pleasantly mobile.

'What time is it?'

'3 a.m.'

On the sixth floor, at the end of the corridor a door was ajar. Mariella slipped in and pulled him after her. At once he was aware of air conditioning, comfortable freshness and a soft hum. A moment later the light came on and as he blinked she was already draping him in a dressing gown.

'Are we escaping?' he asked. The gown was black and silky.

She smiled the same mocking smile he had seen in Zolla's office. 'Someone wants to speak to you. Come in here.'

It was a much larger apartment than his own, occupying one of the top corners of the building. Morris was led down a passageway past sombre doors with rather attractive brass handles, then into a spacious sitting room with fluffy rugs, blue sofas and regiments of silver-framed photographs on low cabinets. Double French windows led to a rooftop terrace; one could sense the glow of the city beyond.

'Would you like a drink while you wait?'

'Wait for what?'

'The person who wants to see you.'

'Do *I* want to see *him?*' Morris asked, collapsing on the sofa. 'If it is a him.'

'I think you do,' Mariella said. She smiled all the time, as if he were a poor innocent who would never understand.

Could it be Zolla? Stan?

'I'll have a malt, if you've got one. No ice, no water.'

What she brought back was Jack Daniels. Morris let it ride. Innocent he might forever be, but he did know the difference between sour mash and malt. As she leaned over him with the drink, Morris felt an enormous desire to touch her. How many times was he likely to have sex again if they condemned him for Volpi's murder?

Mariella was moving away.

'It was you who sent me the note in gaol, wasn't it?'

She looked back, smiled, then left the room.

Morris waited. The Jack Daniels was disappointing, but better than nothing. How strange that he had been brought to an apartment *in the same building*. And that she had a key to his apartment. So who had chosen to lodge him here? His son? Antonella? On whose advice?

He looked around to see if he could learn anything from the room. It seemed very lived in. Newspapers, fruit, empty coffee cups, a scatter of books, a woman's cardigan over the arm of a chair, a very poor painting in the cubist style. Call it style. Morris stood and went to the French window. There were a couple of lounge beds on the terrace, the usual plants and, beyond the railings, the streets and apartment blocks of the eastern part of the city, thousands upon thousands of people breathing quietly in their beds and others sitting in the softly glowing cockpits of their cars, winding their devious ways through the sleeping metropolis. Was there still any place for Morris in this world?

'Dottor Duckworth, *benvenuto!*'

The voice was gravelly, familiar, and evidently speaking around some object in the mouth. Morris turned and saw a balding head bent over a flame. Cardinal Rusconi, in a bright red dressing gown, was lighting himself a thin cigar.

'Surprised to see me here, I imagine.'

Morris was indeed struggling to suppress his astonishment.

'Your Eminence,' he said quietly and walked round the sofa to take the cardinal's hand. 'What a pleasure.'

Plump as Christmas pudding, Rusconi insisted on drawing Morris into a brief embrace, cheek touching cheek. Cigar smoke poisoned the air. Morris sat on the sofa, crossed his legs, pulled his own dressing gown over his knees, and waited. Rusconi stayed on his slippered feet. He was drinking something from a brandy glass. At each sip his heavy eyebrows puckered and his bulbous nose seemed to redden. Between the lapels of his dressing gown, chest hair frothed. He waddled across the room revealing varicose ankles, tapped contemplatively into an ashtray, and came back.

'Your very good health,' he said, raising his glass.

'To Your Eminence,' Morris replied.

'And those who can't be with us,' Rusconi went on. 'Lorenzo, and of course poor Giuseppe.'

It took Morris a moment to appreciate that the cardinal must be referring to Don Lorenzo and Giuseppe Volpi.

'Indeed,' he agreed, 'to Lorenzo and Giuseppe,' but was struggling to grasp the implications of such a toast. Could Rusconi believe he had killed Volpi, if he was inviting him to raise a glass to his memory? Perhaps yes.

His brandy drained, the cardinal again waddled across the room, this time to pick up a decanter on a distant sideboard. He seemed entirely familiar with the room and happily accustomed to being on his feet at 3 a.m.

'You are wondering of course, why we have brought you here, Dottor Duckworth.' Rusconi spoke between sips, puffs and satisfied exhalations. 'But before we go into detail the first thing I must do is extend to you my thanks, or rather, the gratitude of all those involved, for your admirable reticence. It must have been extremely tempting for you, during those long days in solitary confinement, to tell the truth about what happened, name some names and win yourself concessions in return. You chose not to do so. This honourable, er, reserve on your part, will not go unrewarded.'

Morris sat very still and wished again that they had given him something better than Jack Daniels to imbibe. He drew a deep breath, as if about to reply, then chose not to.

The prelate paced back and forth, head slightly bowed, apparently deep in thought. Mariella popped her head round the door that led to the passageway and asked if 'you men' needed anything; if not, she was going back to bed until it was time to take Dottor Duckworth down. 'By all means, *cara,*' the cardinal said.

Were they lovers, Morris wondered? Or was she his niece or something? Did the cardinal assume that Morris knew what the relationship was? If it was compromising, why wasn't the churchman afraid of revealing it?

'Dottor Duckworth,' the cardinal's voice was velvety with catarrh, 'I'm sure you won't want me to return to the events of that unhappy evening which took our two, er, friends from us. No doubt you are expecting me to reprove you for your, er, how shall I put it "intemperate" actions on that fatal night.' The cardinal frowned and shook his head. 'And perhaps I should. No, I *certainly* should.' He smiled. 'On the other hand and although of course it goes without saying that I would never, er, wish anyone dead, and least of all a man of the vast, er, culture and wit, of Professor Volpi, nevertheless . . . well, yes, nevertheless there are reasons for supposing that this is God's handiwork.' He stopped and looked Morris straight in the face. 'Volpi had overstepped himself.'

'Quite,' Morris agreed.

'The, er, outcome might even be described as an answer to prayer.'

'God moves in a mysterious way,' Morris acknowledged.

'I also found it rather touching that you insisted Don Lorenzo shrive the old beast.' The cardinal frowned, chuckled, shook his head. 'How many men would have been concerned about the last rites amid such mayhem?' Again the cardinal paused and paced. 'However, beyond the loss of two such different men and in such different ways, that evening has left us with quite innumerable and, er, most distasteful repercussions, and it is this which I am hoping you can now help us with, to your own considerable advantage of course.'

As long as I don't say anything, I can't put a foot wrong, Morris thought. He needed another drink. Rather than ask, he gathered the dressing gown around him, got to his feet and walked to the same sideboard where the cardinal had found the decanter. Among a row of noxious *digestivi* and *amari* there was a rather dusty Oban; the bottle had that untouched look of the misguided Christmas present. Morris had no qualms about breaking the seal and pouring generously.

The cardinal waited. Lifting the glass to his lips, Morris noted a photo showing a younger and even more joyously prosperous Mariella together, in bathing costumes, with a paunchy man who was not the cardinal, but certainly a good thirty years older than herself. Was the lady a gold digger?

Full glass in hand, Morris returned to his seat, sat, sipped, concentrated. But now the cardinal seemed to be having trouble proceeding. The man turned around on himself two or three times, bluing the air with his cigar. At which, reflecting on their two dressing gowns, one satiny black, the other taffeta red, Morris was suddenly reminded of dubious illustrations in a childhood edition of *Wind in the Willows* that showed Badger and Mole in their bedroom wear. 'Upper-class faggots,' had been his father's inevitable comment, on seeing the books Mother read to him.

'Do you have any questions before I go on?' the cardinal asked abruptly. Disconcertingly, he took his nose between thumb and forefinger and gave it a good squeeze, as though it might be bursting with pus.

Morris hesitated. With a flash of intuition, he risked: 'Actually, now that I have the chance to speak to you face to face, Your Eminence, I'd like to thank *you* for what you did for my son. I was going to mention it in my letter from gaol, but I thought it might be, er, inappropriate, in black and white, so to speak.'

Letting go of his nose, Rusconi smiled. 'Not at all. Not at all. With D'Alessio heading the judges it was hardly going to be a challenge, was it?'

'D'Alessio was the judge with the red hair?' Morris enquired.

'That's right,' the cardinal chuckled. 'I believe dear Mousie,' he added, 'is doing very well for Fratelli Trevisan now.'

'That's right,' Morris agreed, then tried: 'Though I'm afraid he won't be able to do much to resolve the situation at Sant'Anna.'

'To the contrary!' the cardinal laughed. 'Didn't he tell you? The pesty little Styx has been, how do they say, "canalised", put in a pipe; the foundations are now laid and the school should be up before winter.'

Morris was shocked. There was no way a lively underground stream seeping through heavily weathered limestone could so easily have been contained. Who was Mauro taking advice from?

'How kind of you, though, Dottor Duckworth,' the cardinal conceded, 'to be sparing a thought for my little projects at such a difficult time.'

Morris nodded. Suddenly, conveniently, he felt tears pricking.

'As you can imagine, I'm extremely upset about Antonella.'

The cardinal allowed a pained look to cloud his eyes. 'That is, at least in part, Morris, what I would like to talk to you about.'

Again Morris was surprised. 'Do you think you can help me reverse my wife's decision?' He hesitated. 'I'd be so grateful.'

The cardinal, Morris now supposed, would surely be impressed by a man more worried about his marriage breakdown than an imminent life sentence. But this time the churchman assumed a rather severe expression.

'Dottor Duckworth,' he sighed. He was pinching his nose again. 'Or may I call you Morris?'

'Please do,' Morris said.

'Dottore, er, yes, sorry, Morris.' Suddenly, the cardinal sank down on the armchair opposite and leaned towards the Englishman. 'I have to tell you, Morris, that we have known for some time about certain, er, remains, yes, under the roof of Santi Apostoli del Soccorso in the outlying village of, er, what's the name of the place, Montecchio di Sopra. The church with the rather remarkably, how shall I put it, *well-preserved* painting of Jezebel Defenestrated.'

The cardinal sat back. Morris watched him. What a miserable tic this nose-squeezing thing was, he reflected.

'Nor did it take very long,' the cardinal continued, 'to connect those remains with the painting, and indeed, the other extant, how shall I put it – copy? – of the same in the house of Don Lorenzo's dear friends in Via Oberdan.'

How pathetically roundabout all this was! Phlegmatically, Morris remarked, 'Sounds like someone's been talking to Stan Albertini.'

'Not at all! Not at all!' the cardinal cried. 'We have been aware, as I said, of those remains for, er, some years now. If anything young Albertini has been an irritation. The last thing we need is for the police to start snooping around under our church roofs.' The cardinal laughed. 'There would be no end of secrets coming out.'

'So why was nothing done?' Morris asked politely.

How on earth could the cardinal refer to Stan as young?

The Churchman shook his head. 'Such matters require prayer and reflection. One has to ask what is really in the interests of the Church, and indeed, more generally the Faith, or, dare I pronounce the word, humankind. Some of the, er, dead man's behaviour had been unseemly, had it not, even criminal, and some of that, er, behaviour was undertaken with the connivance, perhaps more than connivance, I'm afraid to say, of men of the cloth.' The cardinal sighed. 'How can I deny it? The flesh, as we know, is weak. Proverbially so. Even when clad in the finest vestments. The good Lord made us thus. But was it really in anyone's interests to have those sordid details emerge? There has been quite enough talk, don't you think, my dear Morris, about ecclesiastical paedophilia, I mean, enough to put people on their guard. One more case would hardly be instructive. There was also the not inconsiderable, er, yes, not inconsiderable concern that the person, er, shall we say *responsible* for the presence of these remains was the husband of a dear friend of ours and, what's more, a most reliable and *generous*, yes, *extremely* generous benefactor of Christian causes.'

At this point the cardinal arched his tufted eyebrows with friendly complicity. 'Don Lorenzo was always adamant on this point, I mean, that such generosity is rare, very rare, and not lightly to be, er, sacrificed to, how can I put it, naive and fundamentalist conceptions of justice and propriety. How many people, do you think, have benefitted from your charity over the years, Dottore . . . er, Morris. Countless, countless men and women. Well, they owe that charity in part to our indulgence, our silence.'

At this point Morris was sorely tempted to ask the slimy hypocrite who exactly he meant when he kept saying 'we', 'us', 'our' and 'ours' – the church? A bunch of Freemasons? A group of sadomaso perverts? – but he knew he mustn't. The cardinal obviously imagined that Antonella had told him far more than she actually had about her ecclesiastical contacts and their jolly get-togethers. Morris mustn't disabuse him.

'So why was nothing done to help when I was arrested?' he said bluntly. Then added for good measure, 'And what about the young Arabs?' He drained his Oban and looked the cardinal straight in the eye. Sooner or later, if only by inference, some kind of truth would emerge.

'*Young* Arabs?' The cardinal seemed puzzled but alert. 'I'm afraid I only know the, er, one or two older ones.'

'You're not aware, then, of Volpi's contacts with Libyan art traffickers?'

'Dottor Duckworth, I don't think we need—'

'Morris.'

The cardinal stopped, thought, appeared to change his mind. 'Obviously there were all kinds of . . . aspects, yes, aspects of Beppe's, er, approach to the world that had become . . . unsustainable. Otherwise it wouldn't have . . .'

'Why wasn't I helped?' Morris repeated. 'It's a disgrace.'

The cardinal was not unsettled: 'We *are* helping you, *caro* Morris, really we are. And more help would have been forthcoming if a certain prominently placed individual had not put very considerable obstacles in our path, testifying repeatedly against you and offering the inspectors a very strong narrative of motivation, apparently oblivious to the consequences if you really began to speak about what happened that evening. Alas, some people lose their heads in these situations. They choose to live in denial and the rest of us have to carry the can. Of that, more anon.'

The cardinal smiled. His teeth, Morris noticed, as the man bit his cigar, had an unhappy, gummy look about them.

'However, you must admit, that if a person blunders into a cellar where he knows there is a freshly butchered corpse, gets his feet dirty with blood, walks it around miles of stairways and corridors, puts his fingerprints on every visible surface, has himself seen by attentive museum guards and hordes of tourists, then to cap it all gets himself arrested with photos of the said corpse in his mobile, this despite the fact that he hasn't bothered to inform the police, well there's not much even *Dio onnipotente* can do to help, is there?'

The cardinal raised his eyebrows in rhetorical interrogation and sighed deeply.

'Why did you do that, Morris? To be quite honest your behaviour both the evening and the morning after rather bewildered us.'

Morris ignored the question. 'Not even if that *person* hadn't done the butchering?' he asked evenly. He felt proud of himself for having finally framed the question, so beautifully non-committally too.

In response the cardinal shook his head and found it necessary to squeeze his nose again. He seemed exasperated. '*Caro* Morris, from the video footage that I've seen your, er, involvement in the matter seems undeniable. Though how actually you came to be there I'm not quite sure. I had only heard advance proposals of your initiation. All the same, as far as the police are concerned, they have their man. Nor is it easy, as I said before, when we have someone, er, working against us, or rather, against you.'

Morris wished to heaven the man would be a bit clearer. Video footage! The cardinal now stood to fill their glasses. Doing so, his red gown briefly fell open revealing to Morris the furriest inner thighs imaginable, plus a squat wodge of swarthy wedding tackle wedged between. The Englishman was disgusted.

'But to return to your question of a moment ago,' the cardinal continued, 'the fact of our not being able to help you once arrested and the rather drastic decisions your consort has taken in your regard were not, I'm afraid to say, unrelated. You see, it seems that the, er, mystery of Santi Apostoli was not the only thing that poor Don Lorenzo in his delirious deathbed state revealed to the good lady. Hence we were briefly afraid that it might prove pointless trying to help you, if all this, er, rich background, were to fall into the public domain.'

Morris sat absolutely still. In the end, the hell with it, he thought. Let them lock him up in a tiny cell to the end of his days. It would be a relief.

'Morris' – the cardinal was sitting again – 'Morris, I know you English have a rather poor opinion of the Italian intellect, but you can't really imagine that there are not one or two people among the elite in this town who are, er, *cognisant* of your past. News does get around you know, and then of course we clerics have the advantage of the confessional, do we not? Things come out. This is very largely where our power resides. No, no,' – he raised a hand to postpone what he imagined was Morris's indignant interruption, whereas in fact the Englishman had merely started to splutter when a drop of Oban went down the wrong way – 'please, let me explain. There are times when a man with a, I think we can fairly say, tormented curriculum, becomes an extremely valuable and productive citizen, precisely because of that torment. Murder does tend to make a man solemn, does it not? Or at least a certain kind of man. It makes him think, reflect. Aware of the gravity of his, er, misdemeanours, this fellow recognises his good fortune in being allowed to continue his life of liberty and, as the years pass and he is blessed with worldly success he may become a major contributor to the community. He feels he should give back what he has taken, as it were. Such has been the case, Morris, with yourself, and those of us who have, over the years, allowed this, er, *virtuous circle* to develop, rather than crudely rushing to have you walled up for a lifetime at considerable public expense, those of us, I was saying, here in Verona, who felt clemency was in the public interest, can feel justified now, Morris, in seeing everything you have accomplished for the town over the years. I know Don Lorenzo in particular was extremely proud of his part in your, er, *rehabilitation* and its felicitous consequences. At the last count, as I recall, charitable contributions from the Trevisan estate were reckoned at several hundreds of thousands of euros. So we all felt, after much prayer and heart-searching, yes, many an evening spent on ageing knees, that what we were doing was of great benefit to the community and altogether in line with our confraternity's goals. But alas, at the end, poor Don Lorenzo, perhaps under the influence of powerful modern pharmaceuticals, or perhaps burdened with guilt over the fate of poor Beppe, Volpi I mean, at the end Don Lorenzo let something slip. At the same time you were arrested for what looked like the nth crime.' The cardinal sighed. 'In short, we felt it might be wise to wait a month or two before trying to come to your aid.'

'I'm appalled,' Morris said flatly.

'I can imagine. It must be very hard to accept that someone close to us knows all the truth of our hearts.' The cardinal appeared to shiver.

'I meant,' Morris corrected him coldly, 'appalled that you could imagine that I was ever responsible for anyone's death.' This was a lie. What really appalled Morris was that these worms had been letting him *buy* his liberty. He had been a cash cow.

'Tut tut,' the cardinal laughed. 'There are no bugs in this apartment, Morris. We can be quite frank with each other here. Would you like a cigar by the way? I should have offered.'

'I suppose,' Morris said, waving away the offer to indulge in a vice as ugly as it was harmful, 'that since I no longer have control of the Trevisan wealth there is now no reason for keeping this sinner out of gaol.'

The cardinal had his head bowed over his lighter. He looked up, breathed out a cloud of smoke, appeared to reflect. 'Money is not everything,' he eventually said. 'In fact, often more highly appreciated than money are good works.'

Morris waited.

'Which brings us, as you will have no doubt guessed,' the cardinal sighed, 'to the purpose of our late night meeting. What we would like you to . . .'

Morris had a revelation.

'*You* were the one in the room that morning.'

'I beg your pardon?'

'Your laugh a moment ago. I've heard it before. You were in Volpi's office when Zolla was weeping on the floor and I walked in.'

'Indeed I was.' The cardinal looked puzzled. 'I assumed you were aware of that.'

'Ah.' Morris had merely given away his ignorance again. 'So what do you really think about these meetings?' he demanded.

'What meetings?'

'Scourging. What do you think of all this scourging?'

The cardinal smoked. He had a way of holding his cigar poised as it if was a pen with which he was about to jot down some extremely intelligent idea, or sign some historically important document.

'Morris, I do appreciate your eagerness for debate, but I'm afraid we really don't have all night. I wouldn't like the police to become aware of our meeting here. As for scourging, what can I say? You must distinguish between the old *confraternità* proper, in plenary session, and one or two rather grotesque offshoots and appropriations, for private interest perhaps. The *confraternità* as I have always known it, meets, as it has done since the fourteenth century, once a month, and, traditionally, the members engage in a general mea culpa before getting down to business. Do we really need to discuss such matters? One is rarely well advised to change an ancient ritual, however strange it may seem in the modern world. Quite possibly what Volpi, Zolla and his Arab pals were up to was quite a different matter. What disturbs me is the presence of those three or four regular members, whom I would never have suspected of getting themselves involved in such unacceptable activities. Though, Don Lorenzo, poor fellow, has paid the price. Indeed, in a way, the confraternity has to thank you, Morris, your extraordinary, er, rashness that is, or whatever it was that, er, inspired you on that unhappy occasion, for, however erm unwittingly, bringing this disgraceful splinter group to light. There is no doubt that Volpi was seeking to appropriate the authority of the confraternity for dealings that went far beyond his, er, remit, or even,' the prelate acknowledged, 'the admittedly remarkable scope of his libido.'

Morris had had enough. He drained his second Oban and set the glass down on the coffee table with a sharp click. 'Let us by all means hear your sermon on good works,' he said, 'before the day dawns. What is it that I have to do to be free?'

CHAPTER SEVENTEEN

WHEN HE RETURNED FROM his morning trip to the supermarket, they were already there, in a plastic bag outside the door. A laptop and a phone. Mid afternoon the paintings should arrive, as requested: Lippi's Madonna, in Forbes's excellent copy; Gentileschi's *Judith Slaying Holofernes*. Hopefully this would encourage Mimi to start talking to him again. 'I can't think without them,' Morris had explained to the cardinal.

Having bought himself a handsome squash, the first thing he did when he had the computer online was look up a recipe for squash soup. An onion, a potato, half an apple, a small squash, vegetable stock, black pepper, coconut milk, curry powder. Coconut milk he hadn't thought of, but the hell with it. Morris worked methodically, chopping up the squash with a bread knife. The kitchen needed more equipment. The weather was warm again, though there was thunder in the air. As he sliced, he tried to come to terms with all that had been said and proposed last night. Essentially, it seemed, he had become a debt slave: his past crimes were a kind of overdraft he had taken out, offering his own person as security. Now the debts were being called and there were just two ways of paying back: go to prison, or do the 'work' they asked. Unfortunately, prison would be prison for life; and the job they wanted him to do was . . . beyond me, Morris thought. Quite beyond me. They hadn't understood Morris Duckworth's psyche at all.

The onion had his eyes streaming. But the truth was he was

beyond tears. It was too baroque. How can I know, he had asked the cardinal, that after I have done what you require, assuming I do it, that you won't have me gaoled *anyway*, and gaoled *for that as well*? Also: how can I know you won't ask me to do something else equally abhorrent further down the line, or all kinds of abhorrent things for the rest of my life, since I'll hardly be in a position to object?

'I give you my word,' the cardinal had said, 'as a man of God.' He spoke drawing on a cigar in the corner of his mouth and added, 'You have no choice, Morris, don't you see? And I'm afraid this, er, intervention, has become absolutely necessary for us. Meantime, we will do our best to convince your dear spouse that Don Lorenzo in his agony was raving about things he couldn't possibly have known and that you are the same old innocent, much maligned Englishman she had always supposed you to be.'

Basically they were promising to put Humpty together again, if only he would be a good egg and kill the red queen. Talk about Wonderland.

All the same it wasn't unpleasant, Morris thought, to be preparing a squash soup for oneself in a tiny proletarian *appartamentino*. One had to live in the moment, forgetful of past and future. The colour of the squash flesh in particular was rather beautiful: a firm, pale orange. There was a pleasure too in the precision of the little peeler he'd acquired. The neat strips it tore from a knobbly spud put him in mind again of poor San Bartolomeo. It was a shame not to have had a good look at the picture.

Later, while the veg was simmering, he opened Word and tried to jot down what he had understood from last night's conversation. Clearly he had been there when the deed was done and most likely done it himself. There was video footage, though the cardinal, who it seemed hadn't been present, had been a little evasive as to exactly what this footage showed, no doubt imagining that Morris knew perfectly well. Then again, if the video hadn't been given to the police it could only be because it showed other people who mustn't be implicated in such goings-on. Don Lorenzo for one. No doubt the ugly melodrama had brought on his stroke. And Zolla too, of course, though the cardinal hadn't actually said as much. The cardinal was head of some kind of fraternity, or confraternity – what was the difference? – and as such was trying to sort things out on behalf of the others present, also confraternity members. Morris had read something about this confraternity tradition in one of those potboiler, Christmas-gift history books on the glamorous Medici. That scribbler Parker again. Or Parkes. *Medici Cash*, some such crass title. Rich men, politicians and priests got together in secret, away from any official institutional framework, justified and absolved themselves with a few leisurely lashes, pious paternosters and noxious notions of divine entitlement, then proceeded to carve up the city's wealth between them. A dictatorship of the Catholic bourgeoisie. Occasionally, no doubt, such gatherings would be transformed into jolly *festini* of the bunga-bunga variety. Is there anything new under the sun?

Morris cut himself a crust of bread and started to chew, watching his pot simmer. Don Lorenzo, he thought. Hadn't the man made some remark, in The Art Room one day, that had suggested his position on women and celibacy was not quite as pure as it ought to have been? Meantime, Antonella must surely have known about this Rotary of Rotaries, this inner sanctum of ageing patricians baring their chests together for the pleasures of the scourge. Wouldn't her father, as Mayor of Sanguinetto, have been a member? Might it not even have been the case that their whole married life had been a sort of theatre of Morris's naivety; his wife constantly smiling over her husband's charming ignorance? That discussion about how Don Lorenzo hurt his leg, for example; what if that had been an elaborate private joke between them? Antonella knew from the start it was a coffin that had crushed the priest's foot and knew, what's more, whose coffin it was. *Her father's? Was Don Lorenzo, then, the mother's lover? Perhaps Antonella's real father?* Morris stirred vigorously. In any event, imagine Antonella's anger when it turns out that Don

Lorenzo has been keeping secrets *from her,* secrets he *shared with Morris,* and that made a mockery of their whole marriage. No wonder she didn't want to see him.

Morris lowered the flame and covered the pot. One felt virtuous cooking greens, he thought, in a way one did not, for example, grilling a steak or roasting lamb. Perhaps that was why he had become a vegetarian in the end. One built up a sort of moral capital with the lentils and sorghum and hummus, which could then be carefully invested. But how many years of squash soups and lentils would be required before he could offset, as was now required of him, a contract killing?

But back to the death of King Eglon. Why *had* Morris been there? Had he blundered into the situation? Towards midnight? In Castelvecchio? Surely not. Or had he been invited? If so, why? To make him some kind of offer? The cardinal had heard proposals for his initiation. You can be involved in the show, Signor Duckworth, if you agree to help us in our shady dealings with . . . the older Arabs, the cardinal had said. Did that mean the Arab trade delegation? Nothing was impossible. But in the event Volpi had provoked him. Why? Morris had hit back. With the cubit-long knife. Or was that part of some initiation ceremony? This time he hadn't fainted. But he had lost his memory. Or perhaps he *had* fainted. Perhaps the video, if he ever got hold of it, would show Morris falling back in a faint as the filth began to flow from Volpi's gaping wound. Fainting and banging his head on the floor. That would explain so much. The unsteadiness of his walk as he proceeded along Via Roma in the small hours. For example.

Morris stirred the thick soup. There was something very beautiful about speculation, he thought, beautifully provisional. Like the simmering pot, everything was ahead of you, everything possible. It was definitely preferable to fact and truth. He prodded a spud. Then returning to his computer, he opened Google. What had Sandra called the condition? Temporary global amnesia. But why had the dead deserted him? One day they were there. There had been almost too much conversation. Then he was on his own. Had he said something to upset them? He couldn't think what. His confession? Sitting down, listening a moment, hoping for Mimi's whisper, hearing only silence, Morris found himself reflecting that this was the rather sad state most ordinary folk lived in; a monotone consciousness, empty of voices. Hopefully, the paintings would bring them back. Perhaps it was one of the functions of art to facilitate communication with the dead.

'Transient global amnesia (TGA),' Wikipedia's entry began – how much more attractive 'transient' was than 'temporary'! – 'is a syndrome in clinical neurology whose key defining characteristic is a temporary but total disruption of short-term memory.'

It existed!

But at once Sandra's theory about his sexual exploits went out of the window. Crucial to the idea of TGA was that the victim/sufferer *forgot the event that had brought on the amnesia.* So it couldn't have been the wild threesome with Samira and Tarik, which Morris remembered all too well. What had brought on the forgetting, then, must have been the violence sometime later. 'While seemingly back to normal within twenty-four hours,' Wiki concluded, 'there are subtle effects on memory that can persist longer; in particular a complete lack of recall for the period of the attack and an hour or two before its onset.'

A smell of burning dragged Morris back to the oven. Talk about amnesia! He turned off the flame and left the pot to cool. Back at the screen Wiki surmised that the probable cause of the memory loss was a small stroke; a tiny blood vessel gave way in a very particular point in the brain. Well, if he had fainted trying to club Stan over the head it was quite possible that worse would have befallen him when that dagger plunged into King Eglon.

But suddenly Morris realised he hadn't checked up on the show. For heaven's sake! *'Painting Death*, Castelvecchio, Verona,' he typed. And what was the image that sprung up: a Poussin? A Caravaggio? A Titian? No. *A photograph of Professore A. Zolla.*

'Curator of a daringly innovative show that is attracting attention from all over the world.'

Morris was livid. His jaw set hard. With grim meticulousness, he went through all the blurbs, the teasers, the quotations on murder from famous writers, the list of masterpieces to be shown. It was all *his* work, all part of the package he had prepared to encourage those snob museums in Paris and New York to lend their bloody masterpieces. Yet, at no point was any name mentioned but Zolla's.

Morris stared at the man's photo, above a pale pink tie, the overly neat moustache conferred a sort of fake virility on simpering lips. Zolla had been so friendly that last time they had discussed the show. Hypocrite. He gets himself promoted way above his abilities – the ancient freemasonry of the gay – then kicks away the ladder that got him there. Volpi is killed, Morris is accused of killing him. Perhaps he had been *invited* to do the murder. The dagger put in his hand. Then filmed. Framed. In any event it was perfect, for Zolla, who now took all the credit for one of the most extraordinary art shows of recent memory.

Morris shifted the cursor to the little cross at the top right corner of Zolla's enlarged image and clicked. Gone. When you thought about it, he realised, there was really no need for him to understand what had happened between himself and Volpi that night. There had been some kind of weird event. Stuff had happened. This was Italy. All he had to do now was accept the cardinal's offer, do what was asked of him and earn back his certificate of virginity. Think about the future, Morris, not the past. This was a world of every man for himself, and the Devil take the hindmost, who, if Morris had anything to do with it, would be Zolla.

In the event it was Mauro who arrived towards three with the paintings. What a curious line of communication, Morris thought, through a cardinal to my son. No doubt via Antonella.

The copy of Lippi's little Madonna was quickly unpacked, but the other canvas, alas, was not Gentileschi's *Judith Slaying Holofernes*. 'They took a few things away for the Castelvecchio show about ten days ago,' Mauro explained. He had brought Forbes's copy of Delacroix's *The Death of Sardanapalus* instead. 'It looks the kind of thing that might cheer you up,' the boy said.

The Indian driver with the gold tooth was again in assistance, leaning the big painting against the wall behind the sofa. There would barely be room to hang it. Morris waited till he was gone to tell his son that all the paintings in The Art Room had been bought in his, Morris's, name, and required his written permission to be lent anywhere.

'You spent too much on cultural sponsorships,' Mauro reflected. 'I'm cutting back.'

Morris stared at him, was about to object, then reflected that he didn't give a damn. Instead he found himself saying: 'And please make it clear to your mother that I will not cooperate with the annulment of our marriage in any way. Those whom God hath joined together let no man put asunder. Or at least not until there has been a proper discussion of the motivation.'

'Dishonesty,' Mauro said.

'I beg your pardon?'

'She says you didn't tell her some important truths about yourself at the moment of the marriage. She said if you wanted to argue the point in court she'd be happy to offer plenty of evidence.'

'Court! A few old priests?' But Morris decided to shift attention elsewhere. 'Anything more from Massimina?'

'No.'

'She doesn't even keep up her Facebook page, that sort of thing?'

'It's been a while since I looked,' Mauro admitted. 'I mean, now we know she's safe, her life is up to her.'

'Isn't your mother furious about her running off with a man

thirty-five years older than her? A man who pretended to be her friend? Talk about dishonesty!'

Mauro was hovering at the door. He looked more handsome these days. His nose was thinning; the chubbiness of adolescence was drying out.

'According to Mamma there is a lot to be said for older men.'

'Is there indeed? And what is that supposed to mean?'

Mauro shrugged. 'Actually, I'm not sure Mimi is with Stan.'

'I beg your pardon? Why else would she have gone to San Diego?'

'Maybe Stan was just facilitating . . .'

Only a few months ago Morris would have been delighted to know that his son could use a word like 'facilitating'.

'In what sense?'

Neatly dressed in a coal blue linen suit, the young man seemed possessed of an authority beyond his years.

'She wanted to escape.'

'Don't we all?'

'She wasn't happy.'

Morris was sobered by the boy's solemn tone.

'I thought you didn't care about her.'

Mauro shrugged. 'I had my own stuff to get through.' He hesitated. 'Actually, she had a friend, Dad. *Un'amica*.'

'Ah. *Un'amica?*'

'I think they left together.'

'Not *un amico*?'

'No.'

Morris drew a deep breath. A 'strange love', the girl had said.

'Giovanna, would that be?'

The boy frowned. 'How did . . .'

'And you've known all along?'

'She thought she would be criticised if the truth came out with you and Mamma. Stan told her things would be easier in San Diego.'

'You knew all along she was safe and didn't bother to tell me!'

'You've been in prison, Papà. Since the morning it happened. By the way, Mamma still thinks she must be with Stan. I haven't told her yet.'

'And she's not furious?'

'She's furious with you,' Mauro said.

As soon as his son was gone, Morris went back to the computer and opened an email account, holofernes@hotmail.com. His own would be under surveillance. He would write to Zolla. Of course the police might perfectly well be checking the professor's email too, but the hell with it.

Dear Angelo,

Finally, I have use of a computer. But don't worry, I won't bother you with my vicissitudes. No doubt the misunderstanding will be cleared up soon enough. I just wanted to congratulate you on the web pages for the show. It looks like it is coming on wonderfully. Only a month to go now! You must feel proud and excited. I was hugely impressed by the number of important paintings you managed to get in the end. If only I could be there to watch them arrive!

I did have one question, or rather one offer to make. Are all the captions ready? I have time on my hands and could easily write some for you. Let me know.

With respect and best regards
Morris

CHAPTER EIGHTEEN

MORRIS STARED INTO THE dark. For a moment he hoped he had woken in response to a voice, a touch. Mariella was there, perhaps. Or Mimi had finally spoken. He had hung her on the wall opposite. Instead he just needed a pee. Returning to bed, he lay awake. He waited for sleep, knowing it wouldn't come. The darkness had that feel to it. The air was fresh after a summer storm, laden with a kind of urgency. He was intensely aware of being here, really here, mortal flesh and blood, a precarious, vulnerable Morris in a world where everything had gone wrong. His wife had abandoned him. His beautiful daughter was lesbian. His son despised him, assuming Mauro was his son. The great art exhibition that was to have redeemed his life had become a trophy for a man he loathed. '*Caro* Morris,' Zolla had replied instantly to his email, 'much thanks for your generous proposing. However, having myself too many duties consequent to poor Giuseppe's decease, I invited our local English author, Timoty Parkes, to prepare the captions. I am hoping very much you can be able to come and see the success! With my regards. Angelo Zolla.'

Damn Parkes! It was curious, Morris thought, that after so many years in the same tiny town of Verona he and this odious compatriot had never met. Pious Parkesie has everything, Morris thought: money, celebrity, freedom; and I have nothing. He lives a privileged life while I am hounded by the furies. I have a brilliant idea and he gets the recognition, when the only difference between us is that I was once obliged to kill someone. It was the mark of Cain. Parkes's sacrifice had been found pleasing to God. He was a meat man, no doubt. Duckworth's, the vegetarian's, had not. Suddenly it seemed to Morris that it was actually Parkes's fault that he had suffered as he had, as if there were only two roles an Englishman in Verona could possibly occupy and by claiming the other for himself, the lauded role, the respectable role, the artist's role, Parkes had condemned Morris to a life of deviousness and villainy.

For perhaps an hour Morris lay on his bed piling as much fuel as possible on the pyre of his misery. The window was open and the fresh night air brought wafts of oxygen to the coals of his unhappiness. Fact was that in Via Oberdan, with his wonderful art collection, his respectable wife, two rebellious children, a dusky mistress, a peevish maid, not to mention his position at the head of a major local company, Morris Duckworth had had an identity. Not an easy one: he had been living a lie, of course, multitudinous lies; but he knew what the lies were and what they added up to and how to give them direction and purpose. Actually it was the lies, the needing to be simultaneously both this and that, both the upstanding head of a prosperous household and the philandering multiple murderer, that had given Morris his deepest sense of self. But here in Via Quattro Stagioni, deprived of both duty and depravation, he was lost. Life had no consistency beyond the reality of his ageing body, tossed on this bleak, proletarian shore. He was flotsam after the wreck. There was nothing his mind could attach to and build on. No wife, no work, no mistress, no project, unless you counted the gun they wanted to put in his hand. He would become a hired killer. At least Cain killed for himself.

Morris rebelled. 'Mimi!' His whole soul cried in anguish.

Lippi's Madonna was just visible through the dark. Beautiful, serene, devout.

'Mimi, Mimi, Mimi!'

Why wouldn't she speak?

Morris sat up. 'If you don't talk, I'll call Sammy,' he threatened.

Distant lightning flickered across the painting. The Madonna would not stir. It was as if there were a direct relation between his wife's request for annulment and her long-dead sister's abandonment. It was both or nothing.

'Not only will I call her, but I'll give myself to her *forever,*' Morris insisted. 'I'll leave you *and* Antonella, for Sammy! I'll start a new life.'

Nothing.

This, then, Morris thought, as the minutes passed, was the famous dark night of the soul. No, that too was an illusion, too noble and transformative to be true. In reality it was just another dark night.

Samira, then. Morris turned on his new phone, but of course the girl's number wasn't there. Where could he find it? On the net? A pretty girl like Sammy wasn't so stupid as to put her number on a chatline.

How?

Then Morris remembered that there were such things as online mobile accounts. Once, no doubt, he must have logged on to his. Naked, he padded back to the living room and the laptop. Waiting for Windows to boot up, his eye wandered to the tumble of bodies and bedclothes in Delacroix/Forbes's *Sardanapalus*, the jewellery, weapons and carved elephants, the prancing horse, black slaves and white breasts. Everywhere coiffed hair and bare buttocks, a lush panic of drama, sex and death. At the top of the painting, behind and above the mayhem, stretched on his bed in a white nightgown and about to enjoy the carafe of wine that a young slave was bringing on a wicker tray, the bearded Assyrian king surveyed the orgy in much the way a modern insomniac might watch a porno film in bed. His trusty servants were slaying his cute concubines before the foreign soldiers broke down the doors. That is the difference between this scribbler Parkes and me, Morris thought. He watches it all onscreen, remote in hand, sipping his wine, courtesy of Grub Street; but I'm the man in the action, the man who plunges a dagger down a pretty woman's throat, who slaughters on command, before himself being overcome by slaughter. Morris shivered with excitement and fear. 'Parkes is just a frustrated spectator,' he muttered. 'I'm the one who's really in there.'

And now Morris was in the Vodafone website. He typed out his old phone number for the username. The password?

mass1m1na.

No.

ma221m1na.

No.

ma223m4na.

No.

a1n1m1ssam.

Yes! Welcome to Vodafone, Morris Duckworth. It took a while to work out how to get to a calling list, but finally he had it: *Dettaglio costi e traffico*. He called up the month of April, the last days of his freedom. He would recognise her number at once, he thought. It ended with 33.

Got you!

Morris began to key Samira's number into his new phone. What would it be like to speak to her again? Had she too betrayed him? But now another idea occurred. Why not check the details of that fatal Saturday evening, 28 April? He went back to the screen and scrolled down. There had been various calls through the afternoon. Work no doubt. The site gave only numbers, not names. Then a break after six, when the phone would have been turned off. That made sense. Then, yes, at ten-thirty a call to him, to Morris. He didn't recognise the number. How interesting. And towards eleven, another number. Also unrecognisable. But how many numbers did one actually remember these days? Then there was just one other call, at 1.30 a.m. That was late. This number was familiar, though. Morris glanced up at the Assyrians, carousing in paint. Think! He looked again and remembered.

Massimina. Departing for her alternative life, his daughter had called him. Damn. How sweet. The conversation had lasted three minutes. What did Morris say to her and she to him? Did the exchange have any bearing on what happened? Did she tell him of her decision? Was it possible that Massimina might be able to tell him something about his own movements that evening?

Morris stared at the calling list. Why hadn't the police asked him about this? What were they thinking of? Two calls just before and one perhaps just after the murder. Three people who might be able to tell him where he was around the crucial time. Always assuming he had told them, truthfully, where he was, during the call. His daughter would have ditched her Italian phone, of course, but why not call these other numbers now? Did he have anything to lose?

He dialled the first. Waited. *Numero inesistente,* the recorded voice said. He checked that he had dialled correctly and dialled again. *Numero inesistente*. He called the second number. *Il numero da Lei chiamato è inesistente*. It was maddening. And again. *Inesistente*. Two numbers that had called him and only two months ago, and now both of them were . . . dead.

Don Lorenzo and Volpi?

Morris dialled Samira's number, but then decided against and hit the red button. He couldn't face a conversation of possibly negative outcome. Better a text.

> Dear Sammy, do you still love me? I have left my wife. I am all yours. Come and find me in Via Quattro Stagioni 18, staircase b, #4. Don't ring from outside or be seen. I'm under house arrest. Enter through underground garage when a car goes in and KNOCK SOFTLY on my door. REPEAT DON'T RING.

An hour later, she arrived, though it seemed she had been knocking, softly, for fifteen minutes before Morris woke and heard. He was amazed she had come so soon and most impressed that she had had the patience not to hit the bell.

'The apartment is bugged,' he whispered.

'My darling old paranoid,' she cooed.

So much for the rules of house arrest, Morris thought.

As soon as she was there and he saw and smelt and touched her, all doubt evaporated. Samira was his girl. She too asked for no explanation. As if there had been no two-month silence, no charge of murder. Or perhaps it was precisely these things that made this present moment so exciting. In silence they went to the bed and made love. Once again, Morris found himself switching between despair and delight in a far shorter time than he could have imagined possible. Afterwards, they sat on the single bed, drinking beer and whispering.

'So you're mine,' she smiled. 'You've promised now. I have the text.'

'I'm under arrest,' Morris reminded her. 'I'm accused of murder. And leaving my wife I will lose most of my wealth.'

She shook her raven hair. 'Morris, you never believed I loved you, did you?' She had a marvellous way of narrowing her bright eyes with teasing affection. 'You always thought it was just for your cash.'

'A question of modesty,' Morris said carefully. 'You're too beautiful to love a scarred old man like me, Sammy.'

'I never think of you as old,' she murmured. She ran the tip of her tongue down his cheek along the line of his scar. 'You're more like a mischievous little boy who's always getting into trouble.'

This all seemed too good to be true.

'What's the real story about you and Tarik,' he demanded. 'Tell me where you went when you left me at the museum that morning. The uncle story was obviously rubbish. You knew something about Volpi, didn't you?'

She sat back. 'Morris! You really don't want to be happy, do you?'

'I need to know,' he said. 'Especially after what happened with Tarik the previous evening.'

The Arab girl chuckled. 'You were fantastic.'

Morris felt confused. 'Come on, tell me. You're not really brother and sister, are you?'

She shook her head. 'I hope this room *is* bugged, or we're going to feel really stupid having whispered all night.'

'It is, definitely.'

'But how do you know?'

Morris decided to tell her about Mariella's visit and the conversation, carefully edited, with the cardinal. 'I don't trust them,' he wound up some minutes later. 'But I do *believe* them. If you see the difference.'

'Italy!' Samira frowned. 'This country hasn't changed since Cesare Borgia.'

Not for nothing, Morris realised then, was he choosing a foreigner as a companion. He was through with Italians. Or was this all a dream? Forty-eight hours ago he had been in solitary.

'Pinch me,' he invited.

She reached manicured nails beneath his scrotum. Morris giggled.

'Shhhh.'

'OK, trial of love!' he announced.

The girl leaned forward to put the tip of her hooked nose against his. 'Do I have to walk through fire?' She giggled. 'Or just, hmm, swallow a litre of sperm?'

'I'm going to tell you the truth about the evening when Volpi was murdered. Or at least, my truth.'

Samira moved away, pulled the sheet over her waist and became extremely attentive.

'I have no idea what happened,' he said.

She pouted. 'Don't tease!'

'I'm not. The truth I'm telling you is that I lost my memory.'

'Don't bullshit me, Morris.'

Then Morris Duckworth at last succumbed to a need that had been growing for many weeks. He exposed all his vulnerability to the girl. He told her about the memory gap between their Saturday evening threesome and the Sunday morning awakening. He explained that a couple of weeks earlier there had been another memory loss after fainting in the company of his American friend Stan. But this was drastic. Twelve hours almost. Morris admitted that he had even suspected that Tarik might be responsible for the murder.

'You didn't.'

'I did.'

Finally, he told her what the cardinal had proposed last night. To get him off the hook.

'Can you imagine? Me, killing?'

Samira didn't hesitate. 'Absolutely,' she smiled. 'You're a special person, Morris. That's why I love you.'

As she pulled him into her soft strong arms again, Morris realised that the night was growing old. The girl should be going. On the other hand, it seemed perfectly likely that the apartment wasn't being checked at all. The police had just parked him here without his passport till the trial. They thought their case was cut and dried.

Twenty minutes later, after Samira had taken a trip to the bidet, making a detour to the fridge on her way back to fetch another beer, her mood had changed. She was matter-of-fact, practical.

'Tarik is an old boyfriend,' she said, as if this had been obvious all along. 'I pretended he was my brother so you wouldn't mind his sharing the flat. He had nowhere to go.'

'But . . .'

'You don't think I'd get involved in a threesome with my own brother, do you?'

Morris remembered a Bertolucci film where this had indeed happened, but decided not to go there.

'I won't deny that we occasionally consoled each other. That stuff happens when your man's always away, *and* married, *and* has children, *and* runs a major company, *and* an art show, *and* thinks he's God. Shhh!' She put a finger on his lips. 'But I always knew the one I really loved was you, and Tarik accepted that. After all, he has his jihad to think about. He's too serious.'

'How come you two got to know Volpi?' Morris asked.

The girl sighed. Outside the window, a sky of scattered cloud was paling.

'When I told Tarik about our visit to Castelvecchio, it seemed he'd already heard of him. He said he wanted to get to know him.'

'Why?'

'He thought he could pick up some easy money. And introduce him to friends.'

Morris stared at her.

Samira spelled it out: 'Tarik has a rather unpleasant little strategy for paying his way in the world. That's one of the reasons I left him. I guess he realised that Volpi was a sex pig.'

Morris was shocked. 'I always thought he was a holier-than-thou Moslem in an evil Western world.'

She frowned. 'What you have to understand about Tarik is that the more he degrades himself, the more solemn he becomes about Islam. Between imams and perverts he has a lot of odd friends. The idea is that one day he'll use one lot to make the other pay.'

'Pay?'

'He fantasises gunning them all down.'

'Why were you naked when I arrived that evening?' Morris asked.

'It was warm!' she laughed. 'Actually, Tarik was expecting someone. He asked me to help him get in the mood. And there was the dope of course.'

'Was this someone Volpi?'

'No, not Volpi.'

There was a pause. Daylight was stealing over her brown body. She should have left ages ago.

'Actually, I thought it was great when we all three made love together. You shouldn't be upset. It was just one of those strange things that happen.'

'You made fun of me the following morning.'

'It's fun to make fun of you!'

Morris was determined to stay calm. 'Please,' he asked, 'tell me everything you remember about that evening. After the threesome. When did I leave your flat? Did you two go to Castelvecchio that night?'

'For heaven's sake, Morris. Why would we do that?'

'Just tell me what you know about that evening.'

'What's the last thing you remember?'

'We all made love, then I fell asleep. Next thing I know I woke on my sofa at home.'

She sighed. 'While you were sleeping, Tarik's "friend" came. The guy he'd been planning to see when you arrived. We were worried he'd see you, so Tarik pulled on some clothes, met him at the door and headed out.'

'It wasn't Volpi?'

'I told you! Then after about half an hour—'

'You really have no idea who it was? Didn't you see him?'

Samira frowned. 'Tall, slim, early forties, maybe. A suit. Oh, a moustache, embarrassed-looking. I thought, Tarik has got lucky.'

'Ah.'

She cocked her head. 'You know who it is?'

'Maybe. But you were saying, after about half an hour . . .'

'We made love again . . .'

'Impossible!'

'It was the coke, Morris. I gave you a little coke. Actually rather a lot. You were wild.'

Oh this strict Moslem youth. Morris shook his head.

'Anyway, then we went out to dinner. At the trattoria in Piazza San Zeno. You kept saying you were definitely going to leave your wife after this show. And I was saying why not *before*, and you said because you didn't want to have a scandal *before* the show and I was saying that that was just an excuse and that after the show you'd find some other reason for putting it off. It was a lovely evening and people kept looking at us and for once you didn't seem to mind. It was the coke I suppose. Perhaps coke can cause amnesia. Actually I seem to remember we both sniffed another line in the bathroom, and then . . .'

'I got a phone call.'

'You *do* remember!'

'I checked on my Vodafone account. Did I say who it was from?'

She frowned and tried to remember. 'You did, yes. You started telling funny stories about an old priest you thought had been your wife's lover. We were laughing our heads off.'

'My wife's *mother's* lover, surely.'

'You definitely said your wife's.'

Morris was perplexed. 'And?'

'After the call you said you'd have to go,' she went on. 'Apparently he wanted to see you pretty urgently. Something about a painting he wanted someone to paint.'

'A painting!' When had Don Lorenzo ever called Morris about a painting? This couldn't be right. 'Not about joining a club?'

'Not that I recall. I asked if I could come along and you said no and we had an argument about it.'

'What time was it?'

'You went around eleven, I guess,' Samira said. 'I was pretty pissed off to be honest.'

CHAPTER NINETEEN

THE POLICE ARRIVED AT eight o'clock. By the time Morris let them in Samira had gathered her clothes and was sitting in the bottom half of the bedroom closet, the only possible hiding place in the tiny apartment.

'How are we this morning Meester Dackwert?' asked the older of the two.

'I was sleeping,' Morris said, to explain his slowness. Turning round he swept the phone off the table into the pocket of his dressing gown. 'Can't tell you how much I'm enjoying being out of gaol!'

'*Complimenti*,' the officer said, hitching up his pants a little. He was well built, lumbering and overfamiliar, Morris thought.

More diligently, the younger of the two was looking round the room.

'You're aware that you're not supposed to use email or chat-lines, Signor Dackwert,' he remarked, indicating the laptop.

'*Naturalmente*,' Morris said. 'I've been playing chess with myself.'

'We will need the IP,' the policeman told him.

Morris asked if he could offer them a coffee. 'Do sit down, gentlemen.'

The younger man, who had a strangely earnest, intellectual look, was now opening the door into the rest of the flat.

'Look anywhere you like!' Morris called gaily.

'I'd like a coffee, yes,' the older man said. He sat on the sofa and twisted his neck to study *Sardanapalus*, still propped on the floor. 'Quite a scene,' he remarked.

'An Assyrian version of house arrest,' Morris laughed.

Preparing the espresso pot he began to tell the officer the story. The other man was opening another door. Through to the bedroom?

'Encircled by the enemy, he decided to have one last orgy.'

'Sounds like Berlusconi,' the officer laughed.

'With milk or without?' Morris called. Exactly as he spoke he noticed Samira's handbag on the low table by the door.

'Do you want me to put some milk on as well?' Morris repeated innocently.

Came the sound of furniture being shifted, or perhaps a window opened.

This time the older man responded. 'Not for me.'

'Biscuits?' Morris called.

'We expected,' the officer said, 'with your reputation, Signore, that you would be in a, er, grander place.'

What on earth could the other policeman be *doing*?

'Unlike the Assyrian king,' Morris said cheerfully, 'I do not own the family home, which is actually my wife's property; she has taken advantage of my absence to ask for a separation.'

'Very wise,' the officer said disconcertingly. Had he understood? 'Niki!' he called out, 'Niki, come and look at this crazy painting.'

There was no reply.

Do not go and check, Morris ordered himself. He was washing coffee cups in the sink. Do not try to do anything about the handbag. Or the cigarettes. Samira had left a pack of Diana on the table beside the computer. Would they know he didn't smoke? And since when did any man ever smoke Diana?

Just as the coffee began to bubble up there was the sound of the toilet flushing. Morris took a deep breath and savoured the relief, though it was irritating the man hadn't asked.

'Cigarette?' He suddenly decided it might actually be useful if they supposed him effeminate.

'Thanks, but I'll smoke one of my own, if you don't mind.'

The younger man returned and seemed a little more relaxed. Morris offered to check the computer IP while the two smoked and chuckled over the painting.

'Shag that,' one remarked of the Paola lookalike with the knife at her throat. The younger policeman made a gesture of gathering a handful of arse in his hand. Neither seemed to think it odd that Morris had offered them a saucer as an ashtray.

'*Centonovantenove, trecentosessantadue, zeroventisette,*' he sang. 'But let me write it down for you.'

As soon as they were gone, he undressed again and opened the wardrobe just a crack so that the first thing Samira saw . . .

'Hmmm, cock,' she laughed.

After this near-miss, Morris decided to calm down. He must. For hours at a time, day after day, he surfed the net. What else was there to do? He was surprised how little the newspapers had written about the murder. Usually the Italian press went to town over such macabre melodramas. The fact was that Morris's arrest was universally understood to have resolved the case; there had been a bitter quarrel over control of the museum, journalists wrote, and a deep personal animosity. The corpse had been left in an attitude that recalled an etching the Englishman owned. Morris Duckworth was known to have bizarre psychological quirks and might well be asking for a psychiatrist's examination and reduced responsibility.

What complete and utter nonsense! Morris shook his head. Bizarre psychological quirks! Like what? Running an efficient business? Could it be, he wondered, that the entire Italian press was censored and controlled? To avoid mention of the *confraternità*?

More avidly, he read all he could find about *Painting Death*. The Castelvecchio website gave a full list of the works in the show. Morris downloaded photos of the paintings and set up a PowerPoint presentation. What kind of captions would be most effective, he wondered? 'First men, first murder,' he typed beside Titian's *Cain and Abel*.

'Not everyone can please God and it's hard when your younger brother becomes the Almighty's favourite. Strike him down! Titian adds a stormy sky and gives us the action from a low angle. Bloody and brutal, but aesthetically exciting. Now God can banish Cain, the world has its first refugee, and history is on the move.'

Morris liked this. 342 characters. Succinct and provocative. A little information panel beside could give the technical details. He called up *Judith Slaying Holofernes* and wrote. 'Dressed to decapitate! There are two weapons here, female beauty and the sword. In fancy jewels and make-up, Judith strikes with God's blessing. Holofernes deserves it because he wants to destroy the Children of Israel and seduce a pure woman. Raped in her teens, Artemisia Gentileschi painted this murder over and over with increasing relish. We all love a lady who kills in a good cause.'

Morris adjusted a word here and there, reorganised a little phrasing. 390 characters. A little long perhaps. Could he whittle it down a word or two? It was such a pleasurable way to spend the time.

Sickert was next. The *Camden Town Murders* should definitely be hung in juxtaposition to Judith, he thought. It was intriguing how the artist's pointillism meshed with an atmosphere of defeat and sadness, quite the opposite of Gentileschi's lethally bold brushstrokes.

'Whodunnit!' That was how to start. 'The Ripper sits beside his naked victim, head bowed, face and identity hidden, a man defeated by his own sick libido. The woman is not beautiful except in her painted death. If Sickert himself briefly became a murder suspect, it is because we all feel the link between the criminal and artistic impulses. Both reduce a woman to inert object.'

351 characters.

Suddenly feeling immensely pleased with himself and absolutely determined that one way or another he would go and see the show, *his* show, Morris opened Parkes's website. He clicked on the contact page and mailed him half a dozen captions. 'Dear Mr Parkes,' he wrote. 'Professor Zolla informed me that you will be writing the captions for the show *Painting Death*. Since the idea for the show was mine and I was originally to have written the captions myself, I thought you might appreciate seeing those I had already prepared. If you should wish to use them, or just cherry-pick a phrase here or there, be my guest. With admiration and best regards, your fellow Veronese and countryman, Morris Arthur Duckworth.'

Fairer than that, Morris thought, one could not get, and he decided that the thing to do with the Massacre of the Innocents was to compare it with all those American school killings. Obviously killing children en masse was an archetypal fantasy. Not something I've ever been guilty of, he reflected, and had just begun to write when a reply pinged back from Parkes.

'Dear Morris (if I may),

'How nice to hear from you. Needless to say, I have followed your career with interest over the years and was concerned to see that you have recently run into trouble with the law again. It would be a sad day for the English community in Verona if you were ever to be found guilty as charged. As for your captions, I shall certainly bear them in mind, though I think the comparison between killer and artist in the Sickert is a little strained. True the woman is dead and painted, but not killed by pen or paintbrush. Anyway, many thanks for these. Your friend Zolla has given me an impossible deadline, so they may come in handy. If there's anything I can do in return, let me know. And *buona fortuna*!'

Come in handy! Morris had always loathed correspondents who presumptuously if-I-mayed your first name, then wouldn't even sign their own. He replied: 'Many thanks for this swift response, Mr Parkes. The paintbrush may not kill, but it certainly embalms. Could you do something for me in return? Find out who really killed Doctor Volpi!'

That same afternoon Morris's lawyer Carla Cogni came by with two policemen in attendance. Meaty in a tight skirt, the forty-five-year-old was insanely busy with her hands, writing notes, lighting cigarettes, sending text messages, lifting and dropping two pairs of glasses strung round her neck depending on what she needed to be looking at from hard shiny eyes.

'The good news,' she quickly told him, 'is that we have an early date for the trial. 10 July.'

The 10th! That was just twenty-four hours after the opening of *Painting Death*. Morris couldn't quite see why this surprising celerity was so positive. He was beginning to enjoy house arrest.

'The forensic evidence is good too,' she told him, flicking through papers and playing with a pen. 'I won't bore you with the technicalities of blood coagulation and bruising, but it seems the corpse was already undressed when stabbed and already on the chair. It will be clear that your confession was made up.'

'That part of it,' Morris rejoined.

'Obviously, we'll be expecting your wife to testify that you were sitting together on the sofa the Saturday evening. And hopefully the children and the maid. I presume there won't be any problem with that? Family testimony doesn't count for much, but if we don't get it, it could be damaging.'

Carla looked at her client blindly through her reading glasses which made her shiny eyes rather grotesque, Morris thought. The truth was he had begun to feel that all this was irrelevant. If he didn't do as he was asked by the cardinal and Co., he would be found guilty. And if he did, there would no longer be any need to defend himself. The charges would evaporate. As they had for his son.

'Antonella has chucked me out of the house,' he reminded her.

'A marital tiff is hardly a reason for her to perjure herself,' the lawyer smiled. 'In the end it's hardly in her interest to have the father of her children found guilty of murder.'

'She's refusing to see me,' Morris insisted. 'I don't know what she will testify. And I honestly can't remember if I saw the children or the maid that evening.'

'But since the truth is that you *were* at home with her, she is bound to say that, under oath. Isn't she?'

'I presume so,' Morris agreed, then added: 'Carla, look, I feel terribly depressed. It all seems so hopeless. The truth is, I've been framed. They've stitched me up. Nobody who knows me would ever imagine I could do this kind of thing.'

Carla laughed. 'That's exactly what we'll be saying in court. And they'll believe us. You don't go to all the effort to kill someone in these strange circumstances unless you're sending an elaborate message to your enemies. This kind of killing has nothing to do with a personal disagreement about curating an art show. It's to do with Freemasonry, or organised crime or both. Someone somewhere will have understood it as a coded communication.'

'We have no evidence of that.'

'It's not our job to have evidence,' Carla told him. 'It's theirs. We just show that you're an individual Englishman who has never had anything to do with all that Italian skulduggery.' Carla chuckled: 'On the evidence side, though, we do now know that Volpi left a job in Reggio Calabria because he was accused of molesting a young male member of staff, and another in Bari because two artworks under his care disappeared. He was dismissed from the University in Cagliari for selling exams, and from the civic museum in Crotone for taking a cut when handing out the contract for the museum's alarm system.'

'And so?'

'And so he *still* found a job running Castelvecchio. What does that tell you?'

Morris stared at her. 'That they have a lousy selection procedure.'

The lawyer laughed heartily. 'We also know that he spent his last holiday with Zolla, sharing the same suite in a hotel in Benghazi.'

'Benghazi!'

'Yes.'

'But why would anyone go on holiday in Benghazi?'

'Morris, that's hardly a question we need to answer. The point is that we can now prove beyond reasonable doubt that there was an intimate relationship which had clearly soured, if Zolla was sitting on the floor in Volpi's office crying. The younger man felt humiliated. He had a motive to kill.'

Morris shook his head. 'Carla, I'm in your hands,' he said. 'I've told you all I know. For the rest I give up.'

The lawyer gathered her papers, got to her feet. 'We will get your name cleared, Signor Duckworth,' she assured him. 'Believe me, you will walk free.'

Towards seven that evening, as he was eating a risotto with radicchio rosso, listening to the evening news on the radio and glancing through photos of VIPs in their swimwear on *Corriere della Sera*'s home page, a slip of paper was pushed under the door.

'Please come after midnight to the sixth floor, where your presence is required.'

CHAPTER TWENTY

MORRIS WAITED FOR SAMIRA to knock and told her she would have to spend some time alone. He had been called *upstairs*. He was late. The girl became thoughtful.

'Remember, Morris. If it's really what you want, I'm with you,' she said. 'I'll give any help you need.'

Morris felt moved. Climbing the stairs, he remembered his recurrent Holofernes dream. Would Samira betray him as Antonella had? His wife had cut the jugular, now he was putting his mistress in a position to sever his head. Not a picture he ever wanted to see.

Mariella opened the door in baby-blue pyjamas, braless, her hair loose.

'You're late, Dottor Duckworth.'

'The invitation said *after* midnight.' It was quarter past one. Morris pretended the embarrassment of the man growing older. 'I fell asleep for a while.'

In a cloud of smoke in the sitting room, two men were playing cards.

'*Buona sera,*' said the mayor.

Morris did not show so much as a flicker of surprise. Recent events had taught him that much. The room was as he remembered it, the low lighting, the lines of well-dusted photos, and the gloomily polished furniture. You always felt Mass was about to be intoned in these well-to-do Veronese homes.

'Do fix Dottor Duckworth a drink,' said a gravelly, ecclesiastical voice. In his red dressing gown, Cardinal Rusconi was studying the cards in his hand. 'Forgive us, will you, if we finish our little game,' he said without looking up.

'Forgiven,' Morris conceded, pulling up a chair. The mayor grinned at the new arrival more frankly. In jeans and v-neck tee shirt, his square jaw unshaven, he might have been a worker on one of Morris's building sites. The man's shoes, in particular, were the slip-on moccasin kind that Morris felt sent all the wrong signals. When he tasted Jack Daniels, he said at once to Mariella, '*Chiedo scusa*, but I really would prefer a Scotch.'

'Of course,' she said.

Morris had no idea what game the two men were playing; they were bent over a low glass table, slapping down cards and picking up from a stack, occasionally muttering the name of the card as they revealed its face. It was childish. Settling in a deep armchair, he asked coolly, 'One thing I'd very much like to know, Your Eminence, is how Don Lorenzo ended up with such a bad leg. I'd always meant to ask him and I always forgot.'

The mayor threw Morris a quizzical look from eyes closer set than eyes should ever be. But the cardinal had begun to chuckle.

'How funny you should ask, Dottor Duckworth. It was so many years ago. But hard to forget. We were at the funeral of a famous local personage – my bishop days, this was. Don Lorenzo was one of the coffin bearers. Holding the back right corner. I remember because I was walking directly behind him. Anyway, he tripped, or rather, as he privately complained to me later, *was* tripped, and the coffin crashed down on his leg. We were at the top of the steps coming out of San Zeno and I remember feeling we were rather lucky the thing didn't split open and send the body tumbling down into the piazza. It was only sometime later that we realised how badly poor Lorenzo had been hurt. He was in plaster for months.'

The cardinal continued to play as he spoke, chuckling all the time, his cigar, as ever, smouldering at the corner of his mouth. Having reflected for a moment on the discrepancies with the version he had heard some months earlier, Morris asked: 'And who was the rather famous personage, pray?'

The cardinal hesitated. 'A very wonderful man.'

Morris waited.

'A mayor.'

'Of Verona?' the present mayor enquired.

'Of Bussolengo,' the cardinal replied, laying down his penultimate card. 'A rather flamboyant fellow. Not without his faults, alas, but nothing the Almighty hasn't forgiven, I'm sure.'

'You haven't told us his name.'

'D'Alessio, a most charismatic character if ever there was one. Gigi D'Alessio.'

'The judge's father, then?' Morris quickly enquired.

'His uncle.'

'The D'Alessio family owns half the property between Bussolengo and Lake Garda,' the mayor said respectfully. 'But I'm sure Morris knows this. You don't mind my calling you Morris, do you? Please do call me Roberto.'

'To tell the truth the cardinal was calling me Morris last time I was here.'

'So I was,' Rusconi remembered.

'As I recall,' Morris observed, 'the main property owner in that area is Malesani.'

'That's the grandfather's wife, I believe. There was some convenience in keeping the property in her name. But the actual owners are the D'Alessios.'

'And why would anyone want to trip a poor priest and mourner, at such a moment?'

The cardinal laid down his last card, raising a silent smile of triumph to the mayor who shook his head ruefully. The churchman then sat up and turned to Morris, a more businesslike tone creeping into his voice: 'It was a long and complicated affair, Morris. I was never sure I understood it, and I certainly don't think we have time to go into it now. We mustn't rob our mayor of too much of his beauty sleep.'

'D'Alessio was Signora Trevisan's, my defunct mother-in-law's lover,' Morris guessed confidently. 'I presume that Signor Trevisan's friend Don Lorenzo had tried to intervene. What I don't understand is who at the funeral would have wanted to trip Don Lorenzo for this act of mediation.'

'*Santo cielo*,' the cardinal sighed deeply. 'I'm very much afraid that you are, how do you English say, barking about the wrong bush, Morris. The fact is that the good Don, perhaps not so absolutely good as some in the town believed, for we all have our small faults and foibles' – he winked here and half frowned too at Morris, as if to intimate that the mayor was not to be brought in on any other sensitive information regarding the dead priest – 'the good Don had become rather, er, intimate with D'Alessio's wife; it was even rumoured that it was this, yes, intimacy, that had driven the mayor, this flamboyant mayor, very much in love with his own charisma, a very vain man, to his early grave. It would have been the nephew, that is our present judge D'Alessio, bearing the back left corner of the coffin, as I recall, who would have been in a position to trip Don Lorenzo, if that is indeed what happened, feeling as he no doubt did that the priest had no business to be at the funeral of a man he had cuckolded, never mind carrying his coffin. Dear D'Alessio was very attached to his uncle for reasons that escape me. Perhaps you could ask him. In any event, my own opinion on these matters is that a man's dealings with a woman need never come between the fraternal instincts of true male friendship. Isn't that true, *cara*?' He turned again to Mariella and smiled unctuously. She was sitting apart, on a straight-backed chair at the dinner table, knitting what looked like a very small sweater, and received his occasional attentions with quick pursings of puckered lips.

'So there you are.'

Morris found himself staring at the cardinal's soft, beringed fingers holding the turd-like cigar whose smoke wrapped up every conversation in a stench of stale sophistication. Once again, he thought, Italy was making an utter fool of him.

'I wonder, though,' the cardinal went on, 'why you are so fascinated by the events of thirty and more years ago.'

'I believe,' Morris said matter-of-factly, brushing imagined crumbs from his knees, 'that my son owes his red hair to the D'Alessio family.'

'*Davvero!*' The cardinal twisted his mouth in theatrical reflection. 'How interesting. And you set about establishing this by asking me about Don Lorenzo's ankle?'

'The two facts are connected, I believe.'

'You know a great deal, Morris.'

'Never enough, it would seem.'

'But again, I'm not quite clear in my mind why you would raise this issue *at this moment*.'

Morris hesitated: 'Because I fear, Your Eminence, that I may not have many further occasions for tapping your considerable knowledge.'

'*Per favore!* Quite the contrary,' the cardinal assured him. 'When we have overcome this little legal hiccup of yours, I'm sure we will have plenty of time for discussing all sorts of things. And if I am to call you Morris, you really must call me Paolo.'

'Let's come closer to home, then, Paolo,' Morris said abruptly. 'Why was Professor Zolla weeping in Volpi's office that morning?'

'Ah, there's a question!' The churchman stood up and went to the sideboard to refresh his glass. 'It was a most distasteful incident.'

But the mayor was looking at his watch.

'Paolo, perhaps we'd better . . .'

'Of course,' the cardinal conceded. 'We can discuss this later, Morris. However, the reason we are met here this evening is because the good mayor has a proposal to put to you.'

The Northern League man turned to Morris, rubbed his square hands and set his jaw.

'Morris, we would like you and Fratelli Trevisan Enterprises to be responsible for guiding the project to build a road tunnel under the Torricelli. No doubt you are familiar with the plan: the tunnel will link the east and west of the city passing under the hills to the north of the river, thus removing at a single stroke all the traffic congestion that has been holding back our urban development for so long. One of the reasons for making you an honorary citizen, in fact, was to prepare your public profile for this offer. I'll be frank: we feel that your company, owning as it does considerable chunks of the property above the route of the tunnel, will be well placed to head off some of the middle-class opposition to the project. The excavations, for example, will pass under the old Trevisan estates in Quinzano, and the fact that you are not concerned about this and actually involved in the tunnel's construction will reassure the other landowners.'

The mayor paused.

'We expect to be opening the project to official tender in the next few weeks and assigning the contract early autumn. Needless to say, this will be the largest public works in Verona since Mussolini had the river embankments built in the twenties. It is a huge opportunity, hence not a decision we have taken lightly. Having watched the way you have worked, Morris, over the last thirty years, we believe that more than any local entrepreneur, you have the expertise and psychological stamina to see it through. We have been deeply impressed by your combination of efficiency, long-term strategy and absolute discretion, not to mention your immense charitable involvement in everything Veronese.'

Morris could not believe it. If only this offer had come three months ago! It was an extraordinary gesture of faith in his regard. He sighed heavily, turning to look in frank amazement from one man to the other.

'*Caro, carissimo* Roberto,' he eventually said. 'I am honoured, deeply honoured. But I must remind you, gentlemen, that I am presently under arrest for murder. Am I not? My trial starts on 10 July. How can I tender for a major public project in these circumstances? I would have to start talks at once to put together a consortium of companies with the appropriate experience. I should also say that since my wife has asked for the annulment of our marriage I am not even sure what my legal position in Fratelli Trevisan really is any more.'

When the mayor's face broke into a grin Morris was struck by the thought that the corners of his huge mouth were indeed further apart than the outer corners of his eyes.

'What did I tell you?' he said to the cardinal.

'And I said you were right.'

The mayor smiled at Morris. 'Paolo and I had a little bet together on your reaction to the offer, knowing what a correct kind of man you are. We were not wrong.'

'That may be so,' Morris began, 'but—'

The mayor had held up his hand. 'Morris, my friend, as for your legal troubles, the cardinal has assured me that you two have an agreement that will lead to their rapid resolution. So let's hear nothing more of the matter. Concerning the consortium, we are already putting that together. Don't worry. We have excellent engineers in mind. Your job will be to head the team. If we give that privilege to a Veronese, there will be endless infighting and envy.'

Morris stared. 'If it's merely a question of using Fratelli Trevisan,' he said, 'my son Mauro is presently at the helm and—'

'Ha!' The mayor laughed heartily. 'You son is an excellent Hellas fan, Morris; but I'm afraid he does not have the maturity for a project of this magnitude.'

The cardinal coughed. 'If I may, Morris: regarding your position in the company and so on, I think you will soon be hearing some good news from your dear Antonella. I have personally spent many hours in prayer and Bible-reading with her, pointing out that you two have been living together happily for more than twenty years, which would hardly be the case if you were some sort of monster. In any event, she is now persuaded that the, er, wild charges against you, past and present, are mere nonsense.'

'I'm very grateful,' Morris said humbly, appreciating that the cardinal was warning him that the other man knew nothing of this aspect of the situation.

Looking at his watch again, the mayor jumped to his feet. 'Talking about wives, mine will be getting suspicious!' He smiled at Mariella. 'Thank you so much for your hospitality, Mari. Our cardinal is such a lucky man!' A moment later the city's first citizen was gone, leaving Cardinal Rusconi, who hadn't risen from his seat, smiling complacently at Morris from over his drink.

'Are you pleased?' the churchman asked.

'I don't know what to say,' Morris said.

'My purpose in bringing the mayor here this evening,' the cardinal went on, 'was to reassure you that we are keeping our side of the bargain. You can trust us. We are willing to put you right at the heart of Veronese society, back in your palazzo in Via Oberdan, where you belong, back beside your wonderful wife who has been so sadly and needlessly upset. All you have to do in return, Morris' – at this point the cardinal reached deep into his dressing gown – 'is use this.'

He pulled a small handgun from a pocket and laid it down on the glass coffee table beside the drinks and packs of cards. From his other pocket he removed a thick cylinder about six inches long. He placed this on the table beside the weapon.

'I believe the combination amounts to the most silent handgun on the market.'

Morris waited a few moments before asking: 'And who am I to point it at?'

The cardinal squeezed the very tip of his nose. 'Morris, the last time we met you said you were very eager to see the art show that you had been involved in promoting, *Painting Death*.'

Morris waited.

'The opening is on 9 July, am I right?'

Morris did not comment.

'At the show, and I must say this is a rather genial idea of Professor Zolla's, there will be a dark room where visitors can simulate involvement in murders. They can touch period weapons, they can interact with holograms. They can watch video reconstructions of famous assassinations, pretending to be the participants.'

Morris did not waste time informing the cardinal that this had actually been his idea.

'On the opening day, you will be in that dark room with this, er, *instrument*.' He waved a hand over the gun. 'We will get you into the building unseen the morning of the opening. You will have plenty of time to visit and enjoy the show. Immediately before the ceremony begins, and only then, we will indicate to you who will be the, er, object of your attention. After Zolla's opening speech, there will be a guided visit to the show. You will wait till your target enters the dark room, you then do your duty, which will only take a moment, and walk quickly out of the show. The confusion in that room will be such that you will not be apprehended. We will return you unseen to your home in Via Oberdan where your wife will welcome you back and all will be as it was before this nightmare began. At the opening of the trial on the following day, evidence will emerge suggesting that the man you killed in the museum was Volpi's murderer. There will be excellent reasons for believing this and the charges against you will be dropped. Is all that clear?'

As mud ever can be, Morris thought. He sighed deeply. 'Now please tell me,' he said, 'why Zolla was sitting on the floor in Volpi's office that morning.'

CHAPTER TWENTY-ONE

STANDING BEFORE *Cain and Abel*, Morris wept. How well Titian understood killing: on one side innocence and unpreparedness, on the other sudden, ruthless, crushing violence. Morris saw now, examining the master's brushwork in the hazy light of a summer's dawn, how the painting's odd perspective beautifully reinforced this ugly truth: the low angle, almost from under the tumbling Abel, foreshortened the towering Cain into a whirlwind of clubbing fury, fusing killer with stormy sky and victim with stony ground. Murder crashed down on the dark earth from the darker heavens, irresistible and inexplicable as a thunderbolt.

How could one not be impressed! How could the tears not flow, particularly for a man like Morris, who had lived through these experiences? As you entered the exhibition, emerging from a little passageway of modern screens offering far too much by the way of introductory text – acknowledgements, curator, sponsors, themes, technicalities – the great painting was suddenly there, not hanging on the wall to one side, but right in your face, almost too close, mounted on its own stand, a visual blow to match the blow Cain struck. Morris was delighted. If he wept, it was as much for joy as horror, gratitude as repentance. They had even kept his caption, word for perfect word. This was too good to be true. Except of course that it was attributed to Tim Parkes. This is my destiny, Morris muttered. A talented also-ran. But the game wasn't quite over yet.

How had Zolla arranged the other exhibits? Had crude chronology carried the day? All alone in the museum, Morris left Titian and headed into the first room: here to the left three more Cain and Abels hung on a black background while to the right three David and Goliaths stood out against a creamy white. *Killings Abhorred by God,* read a banner over the black, *Killings Approved by God,* ran another crowning the white.

Not bad, Morris thought, not bad at all! He appreciated this polarity. Even his own poor murders, he reflected, could easily be divided into the abhorrent and the admirable. To kill the pure young Massimina had been utterly unforgiveable; but when it came to extinguishing Forbes, he had been as much an instrument of God's wrath as the young David with his sling.

And the murder he was supposed to carry out today?

Today Morris did not even know whom he would be killing, nor in what cause.

Mariella had woken him at five. Morris had his smartest black suit and Tonbridge School tie laid out ready on the sofa. Somehow it seemed appropriate to dress exactly as he had for the ceremony that had conferred upon him his honorary citizenship.

Together they went down the stairs to the underground garage. Morris covered himself with a blanket on the back seat of Mariella's Punto until they were beyond the CCTV camera that watched the entrance to the block.

'Seems crazy going to work this early,' she remarked when he threw off the blanket and sat up. The streets were empty and the traffic lights flashing yellow. The dawn had barely greyed the sky, but Morris was wide awake. It was to be the defining day of his life, what was left of it.

'You weren't there the night it all happened,' he remarked, offhand.

'Women are hardly invited,' Mariella observed.

Morris faked a yawn. 'As Zolla's secretary, though, you would have been involved in the arrangements, I suppose.'

'Actually, no.' A wry expression curled her lips. Eventually she said: 'I'm afraid you'll have to get coffee at the machine at the office, Dottor Duckworth. It wouldn't do for you to be seen in a café.'

'In any event, I just wondered if you had seen the video.'

She hesitated. 'You mean, what Professor Zolla filmed on his mobile?'

Morris waited. What else could he have meant?

'Yes I have.'

'And what, pray, was your impression?'

Mariella hesitated. 'Mostly boring. I mean the whole initiation process.' She laughed. 'You'll think me naive, Dottor Duckworth, or perhaps presumptuous, but I've always felt that these solemn male associations are rather childish. The silly symbols, the nudity. I'm amazed they take themselves seriously.'

Extraordinary, Morris thought, how you asked people for facts and they were immediately eager to establish some sort of moral and intellectual superiority.

'You looked like a fish out of water, to be honest.' She half laughed.

'Really?'

'I mean, it was obvious they'd pulled you in at the last minute. You just look bemused, dazed even.'

'And why do you think they did that?'

Mariella frowned. 'Surely you know that better than I ever could.'

'I'm just eager to hear what you thought.'

'Well, I know one of the director's Arab contacts felt you might help with building a mosque for them. Apparently they have some property up on the Torricelli.'

Above the prospected tunnel, Morris thought.

'Then I had the impression Don Lorenzo wanted you and Volpi to be reconciled. What a lovely old man he was. Actually, I half wondered whether it wasn't your wife who had told him to arrange that, since of course she has a lot of contacts with the confraternity members.'

'That's true,' Morris acknowledged.

Mariella hesitated. 'But I also think the director was punishing Professor Zolla in some way. Giving you prominence.'

'Ah.'

Morris felt as if an icy clump of ignorance was slowly thawing. But too slowly.

'One thing I would love to know,' he hazarded, 'is what actually happened that morning when I found Zolla in a heap on the floor of Volpi's office.'

A deep sigh lifted the lady's blouse.

'Dottor Duckworth, wouldn't it be wiser of you to concentrate on your task today? If all goes well, in forty-eight hours you'll be a free man.'

'Far from concentrating, I need a little distraction. Why don't you tell me? What can it possibly matter?'

Unexpectedly, she started to speak: 'Dottor Duckworth, over the last few years, our museum director had become, well, embarrassing. I'm sure you'd understood that. Paolo, Cardinal Rusconi, had gone to talk to him. During their meeting, Angelo let something slip about certain interests of theirs, I believe in the Middle East. It was the breaking point for Paolo. Volpi was furious, called Zolla an imbecile, said he should never have raised him from the gutter.'

This was a completely different version from the one Morris had heard from Cardinal Rusconi.

'So it wasn't to do with their fighting over the same younger man?'

Mariella actually laughed. 'I wouldn't know anything about that.'

Morris didn't believe a word of it.

'And the murder?' He reckoned he had five minutes to get something definite out of her.

The Punto was stuck behind an empty bus.

'It all happened so quickly. Then of course Professor Zolla dropped his phone, so there's only the audio at the actual moment.'

'Screaming?'

'Exactly. More Angelo than the director. He had one of his fits of hysterics. You could hear the others clearing out.'

'You didn't actually see the knife go in.'

'Thank heavens, no.'

'Or my fainting.'

'No. Did you?'

'I think I did, yes.'

After a moment, Morris asked, 'And did you feel I was in any way . . . justified?'

'How so?'

'I mean, with Volpi provoking me and so on.'

Mariella glanced in the rear-view mirror and their eyes met.

'I'm sorry, but I couldn't see how you were provoked at all. One moment you were kneeling in front of him – it's such a stupid ceremony – the next you pulled the knife from nowhere. Then the picture went.'

Morris's mouth had gone dry. As she described it, he saw it all, but without remembering.

'So why do you think I did it?'

Mariella hesitated. 'You really want my opinion?'

'I do, yes.'

She breathed deeply. 'Because you're mad, Dottor Duckworth.'

The woman drew the car to a halt. They were still about a hundred metres before the museum. 'There are no TV cameras here,' she explained. 'Don't walk to the main entrance. Go through the park where they're doing building work on the Arch. There is a gap in the fence that will bring you to the service doors. The code on the touch pad is 83381. 83381. You have the instructions for deactivating the alarm?'

'Yes.'

The woman smiled. 'Enjoy the show, Dottor Duckworth. I know it means a lot to you.'

So it did, so it did. Though Caravaggio's David, Morris reflected now, was definitely gay, or at least an object of homosexual desire; that bare shoulder and the pretty nipple of his adolescent torso, the way the decapitating sword was held so that its tip seemed to disappear into the boy's own suggestively swelling crotch. Parkes had missed a chance here, Morris felt, to talk about the scandalous homoeroticism in so much Renaissance art. Not to mention the linkage of all that eroticism with moments of violence and killing. Donatello's David was another; the younger sexier person always seemed to be in complacent possession of an old and grizzled head.

For a few moments, enjoying the wonderful painting and the extraordinary privilege of being here alone, Morris tried to make some sense of homosexuality and its constant closeness to art and religion. He could not. He remembered Tarik that evening in San Zeno. Why had it been so exciting, even revelatory? And how could the boy pass straight from that extraordinary intimacy to Zolla and Volpi and no doubt a host of other filthy, insignificant men who just gave him cash? Was that what had inspired his fury against the fat man? Three nights ago Morris had finally contacted his daughter on a mobile phone in San Diego.

'Papà. *Che bello!*'

She had seemed genuinely enthusiastic, as if wondering why it had taken her father so long to be in touch. He asked if she was well. As if by prior agreement, no mention was made of his arrest.

'Sorry if I sounded a bit odd when you called that night,' he said.

'No, you were sweet!' she protested. 'I was expecting you'd be grumpy, waking you up as well to give you difficult news like that. But I thought it was better than having you worry.'

'I can't remember,' he tried, 'whether I actually told you what happened that evening.'

'You were so happy,' she laughed. 'You said something about joining an important club and making great art.'

Morris didn't know what to think.

'You really don't mind my being here?' she asked. 'With a girlfriend?'

'I'm just glad it isn't Stan,' Morris had told her.

Full daylight was streaming through the castle's barred windows now. Morris had been told he could stay in the exhibition till just before eight, then must retire to the basement until they called him up to give him the name and the gun. Leaving Cain and David, Abel and Goliath behind, he moved into a room where the killers were all women. Excellent! No sooner, it seemed, had Morris been removed from the scene than Professor Zolla had felt free to adopt all his ideas. Here Judith hacked at Holofernes' neck, Jahel placed her giant nail against Sisera's sleeping temples, Bonnaud's Salome sat in naked splendour on her silky bedspread with the Baptist's severed head gazing on in admiration.

The thing to have commented here, Morris thought, reading an uninspired caption that merely summarised the Salome story, was surely the dish. Why had the dancing girl asked for the prophet's head *on a dish*? All the artists had picked up on this, from Andrea del Sarto right down to Frey-Mook. Gold dishes, silver dishes, dishes of dark blue glass. Parkes had completely failed to comment. It must have to do, Morris realised, with a desire to shift attention from the act itself, the ugly hacking at the neck, to the notion of an aesthetic presentation; the head became a sculpture, a work of art framed, haloed even, by a shiny dish, at which point the unpleasant narrative behind the killing disappeared. As with a well-basted beast on a gleaming platter, butchery became beauty. Who could disapprove?

Morris was just congratulating himself on these incisive reflections when he remembered Samira's account of his phone conversation with Don Lorenzo just a couple of hours before Volpi's death. Why had they invited him that evening? And why had the meeting so rapidly culminated in Volpi's murder? Was it the cocaine? And today? What if he were to lose his memory definitively this time? He was too old to kill, he lacked the psychological strength. That had been evident in the church with Stan. Morris shook his head. Volpi *must* have provoked him. When had he ever killed anyone unprovoked and unthreatened?

He stood staring at Titian's version where the sad modesty of Salome's girlish face and the serenity of the Baptist's quietly closed eyes seemed to make the ugly event at once beautiful and inevitable, *desirable* even. And at last a new thought occurred to him. An almost convincing explanation. Might it not be that the lurid scene-setting that night in the old museum, the great throne, the robed man's naked obesity, all in all the amazing similarity with the biblical woodcut of the Eglon and Ehud drama, had simply invited Morris to, as it were, *complete the picture*. He had seen the tableau, found himself in it rather, and in his delirious state, had felt *compelled* to strike. Instead of sublimating his murderous instincts, art had guided his hand.

And the elaborate nature of the execution had nothing to do with coded messages between mafias. It was painting.

Was that possible?

Morris left Salome and walked through into a room of martyrs. San Bartolomeo had cleaned up nicely. His flayed muscles gleamed like . . . well, like fresh paint, as if it was the artist's scarlet brush that had peeled away the pale skin. Masaccio and Caravaggio crucified San Peter upside down. Vasari stoned St Steven. Mantegna shot San Sebastian full of arrows. They loved it, Morris realised. He couldn't be bothered to read the captions now. The works were overpowering. The old masters loved painting death and violence. Supposedly evoking piety and pathos, they revelled in brutality. And we love looking at it, Morris thought. We always have. In a way we've all killed a million times, in our heads. What did it really matter who actually pushed the knife into Volpi or why? These things happen. Art *requires* them.

In the next room painters of all schools and centuries had a go at slaughtering the Innocents. This was my idea! Morris thought, shocked by its gruesome impact. These originals were so much more powerful than any copies. Giotto's heap of dead white babies simply glowed. Pietro Testa's murderous sword shone as it pierced an infant navel. Morris shook his head. What if some nutcase visited the exhibition then went straight off to a nursery school to hack a few bambini to bits? A private art room was one thing, but here all this awful negative energy was to be made available to a huge international audience. There would be those less sound of mind than Morris who would not be able to handle it.

Why on earth did I want this, he wondered?

Disorientated, Morris looked at his watch. 7.45. To his left now was the space they had set aside for Interactivity. Another idea he had rejoiced in. A series of booths invited you to contemplate mocked-up murder scenes – Julius Caesar, Thomas à Becket – to finger sharp weapons and watch archive footage of famous assassinations, Kennedy and Luther King. Would it make people feel sick of violence, Morris wondered, or would it thrill them? Might someone decide they hadn't lived till they had killed?

All of a sudden he wanted no more of it. Leaving half of the show unexplored, he turned, hurried back the way he had come and opened the door leading down to the storerooms where he must wait till they called him. Why did I agree to this, he wondered? So I can return to a meaningless life with a woman I don't really love, a woman who doesn't love me? So I can occupy an honoured place in a dishonourable world, accumulate a wealth I can't really enjoy, because I am not free and never have been from the moment I first killed? For nigh on thirty years, Morris told himself, stepping carefully down the steep stone stairs into the storeroom, I have lived on sufferance, closely monitored by a Catholic Church that collected my conscience money and waited for the day when my 'special skills' could be turned to advantage. Don Lorenzo was my *minder*, Morris realised.

What if, far from planning a reconciliation, Don Lorenzo had encouraged Morris to stick Volpi? Or Zolla for that matter? That would be another way of explaining the absence of provocation, as reported by Mariella. What if Tarik during his disgraceful embraces with Zolla had informed the man that Morris was so high on dope and coke he would commit any crime they cared to ask of him? Just put a knife in his hand and set the scene.

'The outcome might even be described as an answer to prayer,' the cardinal had said. 'Volpi had overstepped himself.' 'Something about a painting he wanted someone to paint,' Samira had said. The King Eglon tableau? If only Morris could get access to that famous video footage.

Down in the basement, everything was uncannily similar to the scene he had explored some months before; there were the same canvases and sculptures under wraps, the same ancient metal cabinets, locked and unlocked, the same harsh, ugly light from fluorescent tubes. Morris walked through the damp dusty air, lifting a piece of plastic sheeting here, a filthy cloth drape there. There was no sign that the place had been thoroughly searched. Even the medieval daggers were still heaped in their cupboards. Again Morris took one in his hands, careful this time not to touch the point. The Trecento arms industry, he thought. Suddenly he laughed, thinking of his thuggish son attacking a policeman with a plastic stick weighing eighty grams. How droll!

The door to the passageway that he had discovered that fateful morning was closed. But not locked. Morris went through. There were no police seals to prevent entry to the scene of the crime. Could it even be that the police themselves were only going through the motions? They had decided (been told?) Morris was the killer and that was that. Tomorrow they would be told he wasn't. After Morris had dispatched the appointed culprit. There was nothing more convenient than finding dead men guilty of old crimes.

He found a light and turned it on. The various pieces of lush furniture – thrones and chaises longues – had been covered with dust sheets. The blood had been scrubbed from the stone floor. The rugs had been rolled against the far wall. Fat Volpi had met his death here. Morris still found it hard to believe he had been responsible. One moment you were kneeling in front of him. An initiation ceremony. The next you pulled the knife. Said

Mariella. You were so happy to have joined the club, Papà! To have made great art. Massimina. Had he had to take his clothes off, Morris wondered? Or just to bare his back for a few slaps of the scourge. When had he stashed the dagger in his belt? Or had Don Lorenzo given it to him? Or Zolla? After all that coke, I would happily have killed him, Morris realised. Probably it was a huge pleasure. A relief too, after the failure with Stan, to know he could still raise a dagger. Old age hadn't blunted him.

Too bad he couldn't recall it to savour the moment again.

For some time Morris walked this way and that around the huge chair on which Volpi had sat. Naked. Dead. Perhaps he was about to find some telltale clue. Some object would gleam on the floor. He would recognise it and memory would flood back. He would remember everything. He would know what he had done and why and consequently what to do next.

How stupid! Even if he had been entirely compos mentis throughout, Morris realised, even if his mind had retained every tiny detail, or recovered it all now, he still wouldn't *understand*. In the end, what had happened that mysterious night was no more than emblematic of a debilitating ignorance that had haunted this English expat for decades. Morris had never understood who he was or who he had spent his life with. Certainly he had never understood Italy.

'But I don't *want* to understand!' Suddenly he shouted the words out loud in defiance and frustration. 'I don't want to understand. I want *out*!'

With the thought came a wave of emotion. Morris began to cry. He wanted out; out of his marriage, his family, his work, his *life*. Out of Italy. Out of a culture that had transformed him into an ugly and helpless killer. He did not want to make a fortune digging a tunnel under the Torricelli, or building mosques on property that had lost its value. He did not want to fall forever into their provincial Catholic mesh.

'I WANT OUT!'

Control yourself, Morris muttered. Get a grip!

'Dottor Duckworth.' A voice called quietly from above. It was Mariella. Morris recrossed the storeroom and climbed the stairs.

'Before you open the package, please put the gloves on.'

They were in Volpi's office. Morris had been here now for more than an hour. Mariella had brought him two cups of coffee, an excellent brioche from a *pasticceria* in Via Roma. It was oddly as if he were the one shortly to be executed, enjoying a final meal, not the executioner at all. But Morris had always thought the roles interchangeable. He had wandered round the room and tried to recall exactly how it had looked that morning he had brought San Bartolomeo to the storeroom then come up to the offices on the off-chance. Everything had been in disorder, but in a rather inconsequential way, it occurred to him now. If you were really looking for something there was hardly any need to push over chairs and scatter papers on the floor. Would Volpi really have left a porn video running on his PC? Surely not. Zolla had put it there, to discredit the man. Killing him wasn't enough. His reputation had to be ruined. So that the guilty parties could feel less guilty.

Idly, Morris turned on the computer but it demanded a password. He stood up and walked round the room again, looking at the old panels and posters against the walls. An advertisement for a show on De Chirico. What an oddball he had been: Roman temples, armchairs, tailors' dummies. And here was the panel he had seen behind Zolla when the man had sunk to the floor that morning: 'Devotees of the Bianchi made their pilgrimages barefoot, slept on straw, abstained from meat-eating, and scourged themselves while calling for mercy and peace.' It must be a caption for some quattrocento altar panel. Volpi had come north, Morris mused, infiltrated the local religio-political-Masonic confraternity, then begun to use his knowledge on behalf of old friends in Naples, or Benghazi even. The mayor's Arab delegations. But this sounded like any of a million conspiracy-obsessed articles crowding the pages of supposedly serious organs of investigative journalism.

More likely he just enjoyed bossing his younger lover about.

Talk of the Devil. With no warning, the door opened and the cardinal and Zolla came in.

'My dear Morris, my good man,' the cardinal cried. 'I knew you wouldn't let us down.'

White-faced in blue pinstripe, carrying a large padded envelope under his arm, Zolla looked distraught. The art history professor placed the package on the desk and with barely a glance at Morris trod stiffly across the room to the window.

'*Buon giorno,* Angelo,' Morris said. Nothing cheered him more than another's uneasiness.

Zolla kept his back to them. He was looking out at the river. The cardinal, resplendent in red, but with a rather vulgar gold chain round his neck, narrowed his eyes and grimaced, as if to confirm for Morris their shared superiority to the younger man.

'Before you open the package,' the ecclesiast warned, 'remember you need gloves. There's a pair in the first drawer on the left.'

The cardinal's voice carried a calm authority. Morris opened the drawer and found a pair of white cotton gloves. Surprisingly, the scourge Volpi had once showed him, the same black leather stick with lashes that he had also seen at the scene of the crime, was now back in the drawer along with an assortment of staplers, scissors and pens. Shouldn't this be a police exhibit?

The cardinal was watching him carefully, squinting as he lit a cigar. Morris pulled on the gloves and found them way too big. The fingertips hung empty like the tips of so many condoms. For some reason Zolla had shaved his moustache. He looked naked.

'Sit down, Morris, take your time, open the envelope, study the details,' the cardinal said.

Morris sat. But Volpi's swivel chair was huge. He seemed to be falling backwards into something deep and soft. Opening the envelope, he said:

'By the way, Angelo, I love the way you've laid out the show. Really, congratulations.'

Zolla didn't turn. Through the fine wool of his suit, his back radiated an unhappy tension.

'It was great to see some of my ideas still in there. Thanks for that.'

Zolla breathed deeply. He had too much gel on his hair.

'Particularly the captions.'

'The captions are all the work of the author Tim Parkes,' the show's curator said sharply.

'I emailed Parkes some of my own attempts,' Morris said. 'The opening *Cain and Abel* one, for example. He was most appreciative.'

Rusconi interrupted: 'Gentlemen, I know we still have half an hour but Morris needs to look at these papers now. He has a job to do.'

The cardinal lifted the skirts of his cassock and sat on the chair across the desk. Watching his English assassin, he seemed to be mouthing silent words around the damp stub of the cigar. Saying a rosary, Morris wondered? He reached a hand into the envelope, which was unsealed, and pulled out first the gun, then three sheets of paper. The gun was already complete with silencer. It had a very ordinary, kitchen-utensil feel to it. Not at all nervous now, Morris laid the weapon on the desk, then unfolded the sheets of paper. The first was a printed programme for the day's events, beginning with a presentation of *Painting Death* to the press and 'friends of the museum'. Doors open at 10.00. Curator's address, 10.30. Drinks and guided visit to the show, 11.00 till 12.00. Followed by lunch.

'Prepared a good speech, Angelo?' Morris asked coolly. 'Mariella was telling me you will be having yourself videoed.'

Suddenly Zolla turned. 'Why do we have to deal with this monster?' he demanded. His face was white. From his breathing it would have seemed he had just run up five flights of stairs. 'He's already made one holy mess for us. How can we possibly trust him?'

The cardinal cleared his throat and raised a thick eyebrow, but said nothing.

'Holy mess, holy Mass,' Morris said lightly. 'By the way, that was my caption Parkes used for Gentileschi's Holofernes. The "Dressed to Decapitate" one. Did you like it?' Turning to the second piece of paper he found his own schedule.

'10.25 take up position in the Interactive Room. 11.05 slide back the safety catch on the gun. *Circa* 11.15. Your target will be one of the first to enter the room. He will be in conversation with the cardinal who will guide him to the hologram of John Lennon entering the Dakota building on Central Park West. As soon as you have positively recognised your target, step towards him through the hologram, push the gun into his heart and shoot four times. There are four bullets in the gun. Please use all of them.'

Fascinating, Morris thought, the use of 'please'.

'Lennon was shot in the back,' he observed. It was taking some effort not to rush to the third paper and see who this target was.

'Please follow instructions and shoot at the heart,' the cardinal said matter-of-factly. 'Your man will think you are part of the show. After the first shot I will hold him to stop him from falling and you will fire the other three in quick succession.'

Morris shook his head. 'Is there any particular prayer I should say, around 11.10 maybe? The Lord is my shepherd? Now let thy servant depart in peace?'

The cardinal smoked and smiled. 'You could profitably ask the Lord to guide your hand, Morris. This is not a decision we have taken casually. You can consider yourself an emissary.'

'Stop!' Zolla yelled. 'Stop all this nonsense. I'm not having it in my museum!'

The cardinal sighed. His rugged features were unruffled.

'Cold feet?' Morris enquired, looking up at Zolla. He unfolded the last piece of paper and found himself looking at four photographs of a middle-aged Arab man, thickset and solemn. That was a relief. He had been anxious that his target might be someone he knew, someone who would recognise him as he pulled the trigger.

'Or would you prefer to pull the trigger yourself?'

Zolla was beside himself. 'I insist that this madness be called off.' He had begun to walk up and down the room in a strangely jerky kind of way.

Rusconi smoked and observed the younger man intently.

'It will ruin the show. It will damage the town's reputation. It will be a catastrophe.'

'It will save our skin,' the cardinal said coolly. 'It will link the two murders as something quite extraneous to our confraternity.'

Morris watched. He wouldn't even try to understand, he decided.

'I AM NOT GOING TO ALLOW THIS TO HAPPEN,' Zolla yelled. 'This is *my* museum now. This is *my* show. This is *my* day. There must be other ways.'

The cardinal checked his watch. It was fourteen minutes past ten. Morris looked at the Arab man in the photographs. He had an oddly oval head, chubby cheeks, very smooth skin, and small black eyes behind severe glasses. In all four of the pictures he was wearing a thin green tie. A man in the first phase of maturity, Morris thought, mid to late forties, intelligent, committed, perhaps passionate. The assassin began to feel a liking for his target.

Zolla tried to reason, but he was breathing hard. 'We are not the secret services. So why are we doing their work for them?'

The cardinal smiled. 'You know the answer to that all too well, Angelo. Now that Giuseppe is no longer with us there is no reason why our victim would not use all he knows to—'

'You are not going to do this to me,' Zolla shrieked. 'And above all you are not going to ask Duckworth to do it. He's a madman. And a bungler with it. A murderer who collapses and has to be walked home, for Christ's sake. We'll all be in gaol.'

Zolla was trembling. Morris was fascinated at the way all this stuff was finally coming out.

'Explain to the cardinal, Angelo,' he said quietly, 'about putting that knife in my hand before the ceremony.'

'I beg your pardon?'

'Explain to him that your little fuck Tarik, the Arab boy, had told you I was high. I would do anything.'

Zolla simply stared.

'I saw you two leave his apartment in San Zeno together earlier in the evening. For one of your little sessions.'

'That's a lie!' Zolla shouted.

The cardinal was intrigued.

'You wanted Volpi dead. He was humiliating you every day. He didn't want you sharing Tarik. And you knew the cardinal wanted him dead too. You put the knife in my hand, because someone had told you I'd murdered in the past. I was coked to the eyeballs, Angelo. But I remember perfectly.'

'This man is talking slanderous nonsense,' Zolla snorted. But his hand on the desk was trembling.

'We'll do the show together, you said. You and me, without Beppe getting in the way.'

'This is complete fabrication!'

The cardinal's voice cut in calmly and evenly. 'Angelo, there's no time for this little squabble now. As for today's business, I am satisfied that what we are doing is right and that this is the propitious moment to do it. Afterwards five witnesses will describe the killer as a young Arab man. The murder will appear to be part of a feud between the moderates and the jihadists.'

The cardinal paused and puffed. He looked down at his cigar and then up at Zolla, who had the trembling lips of a panicking adolescent.

'Let's be clear too about your situation, Angelo. You owe your career to Volpi's infatuation. You are implicated in various unpleasant activities he was involved in. Now you owe this to us, and to the city of Verona, which needs neither mosques nor gun money.'

Zolla clenched his fists. 'I have my publications like any other professor. All in respectable journals.'

'Funded and edited by Volpi,' the cardinal chuckled.

There was silence. The minutes were ticking by. The gun was

sitting on the desktop. Morris looked at the safety catch and reflected that it resembled nothing more than the sliding switch on an electric train he had owned as a child.

'Do it,' a voice said.

Morris started.

'I said do it, Morrees.'

She was back!

With flaunted sangfroid, Morris asked Zolla: 'What exactly are you planning to say in your opening speech, Angelo?'

Standing while the other two were sitting, the art historian seemed displaced and vulnerable.

'Do it,' the girl repeated.

'Actually, if it's any consolation to you, Angelo,' Morris said smilingly, 'I can't think of better publicity for this particular show than a murder on the first day. The media will be thrilled.'

Suddenly, Morris felt extremely confident.

Zolla turned to the cardinal. 'He behaved crazily last time, why should he do any different now?'

'*Coraggio!*' Mimi was laughing softly. Morris felt as though heat were rising from the floor through the soles of his feet. Thighs and buttocks were glowing.

'As I understand it,' the cardinal said calmly, 'by the time Duckworth was contacted that unfortunate Saturday evening he was drunk and possibly drugged. Today he is sober and prepared, and if he does not do the job as asked he will spend the rest of his life in gaol for murder.'

'Do it,' the girl repeated. First she didn't speak for weeks, now she was interrupting him when he needed to think.

'I do kill better when I'm compos mentis,' Morris agreed cheerfully. 'Though come to think of it, I would very much like to see this famous video you have of my Eglon tableau.'

Both men seemed taken aback.

'As the good cardinal says, I was in quite a state that evening. It would be good to see how it looked.'

'You're disgusting,' Zolla told him.

'Afterwards,' the cardinal said. 'Professor Zolla will show you the video at the first possible opportunity.'

'They'll never show it to you,' Mimi shouted. 'They're setting you up again.'

Morris felt extremely lucid and extremely excited.

'Just tell me exactly who this guy is I'm to kill. So I feel I have a reason for pulling the trigger.'

The cardinal frowned, looked at his cigar and stubbed it out in an ashtray on the desktop.

'Time to go,' he said. 'You will just have to trust me, Morris.'

'I'm not going to kill unless you tell me.'

'He's officially a Libyan diplomat,' Zolla said abruptly. 'But actually supplying all kinds of unpleasant people with dangerous things.'

'With Volpi's help, I suppose?'

Evidently irritated that Zolla had given this information, the cardinal shook his head. 'It's not quite that simple, Morris. Please do not try to understand just now. I assure you that within the week your name will be cleared and you will be back with your beloved wife, who by the way is here this morning for the opening of the show.'

'She hates you!' Mimi whispered.

Again the cardinal looked at his watch. 'Angelo, you'll have to get moving now. People will be waiting. And please pull yourself together. For your own sake. Weren't you going to have the video relayed to your mother? You wouldn't want to let her down. Morris?' The cardinal turned to look at the Englishman. 'Keep the papers in your pockets, please. They mustn't be found lying around. You will have time to read the instructions again while waiting. As soon as you have carried out your task, you leave through the emergency door in the Interactive Room behind the Martin Luther King exhibit. Mariella will be waiting to escort you out. Check the route carefully.'

The churchman got to his feet and shook out the skirts of his cassock. 'I will take you there now.'

'Now,' Mimi whispered.

Morris picked up the gun in his gloved hand, got to his feet and walked round the desk. Only Zolla seemed unable to get moving. He had pulled two sheets of paper from his pocket and was trying to read, his lips moving with the words. Morris approached him while the cardinal was already heading for the door.

'All prepared for the big speech?'

Zolla couldn't answer.

'It must be exciting to think your mamma will be watching you open a major international show.'

The art expert was trembling.

'You will mention my sponsorship at least?'

Morris moved up close.

Zolla began to stutter. *'Id-d-diota! B-buffone!'*

'Now, Morrees!'

'Ing-glese di merda.' Zolla's face twisted in a panicky sneer. *'Inc-capace!'*

That did it. Lowering his left hand to release the catch on the side of the gun, Morris raised his right, pressed the barrel into Zolla's chest and pulled the trigger.

'Sei splendido!'

The noise was no more than a sharp thud. Zolla did not even cry out. Before he had clattered to the floor, Morris was rushing across the room toward the red bulk of the cardinal, waving the gun before him. No fainting this time. At last, he had surprised them!

Shocked, the big clergyman raised his hands to his face, as if skin and bone could offer any protection.

'Per l'amore di Dio!' he protested.

It occurred to Morris then, in the hallucinatory intensity of the moment, that he might now, if he so wished, as in a movie, force the cardinal to tell him all kinds of interesting things: about what really went on in the Museo di Castelvecchio, about the real nature of the *confraternità,* about the real identity of the Arab man in the photograph, about what really happened the night Volpi died. And so on. All this the cardinal could have been forced to disclose with the barrel of a gun in his gut. Especially a hot gun.

'Don't,' Mimi said.

Morris Duckworth hesitated.

'Don't waste time. Morrees. Don't make this mistake.'

She was right.

'Turn round, Paolo, *per favore*,' Morris said, 'and lead me to where I have to do my job.' He smiled reassuringly. '*You* can give the opening speech. I'm sure you'll do it better than our professor would have. Let's go now.'

Slowly the cardinal dropped his hands. His face, even his nose, had suddenly drained white, but there was the faintest smile on his lips now, a smile of intense recognition, as of a man confirmed at last in the opinion that he has met someone truly special: Morris Arthur Duckworth. It was a moment to be painted, Morris thought, if ever there was one.

'As you will,' the churchman stammered. 'I'm sure we'll, er, fix this, somehow. Yes. The important thing is Al Zuwaid.'

That name!

The cardinal turned to open the door. As he did so, Morris raised the gun so that it pointed upward from the bottom of the skull under the right ear and shot. The red pillar of righteousness crashed. Morris hurried back across the room, pointed the gun into one of Zolla's eyes and fired again. This really was so much easier than bludgeoning people with candlesticks. The mature man's weapon. If he'd had a gun that day, Stan wouldn't have had a chance. Then back again to the cardinal. One bullet would have to do here. Morris crouched, found the man's right hand, opened it and slipped in the gun. Uncannily the fingers closed around the butt of their own accord.

'Just like when you were young,' Mimi breathed.

'*Signori e signore*, welcome to *Painting Death*!'

Three minutes later, climbing on the dais of the conference

room and stepping up to the microphone, Morris was not even short of breath. How long did he have? Not long.

'As Professor Zolla will shortly be explaining to you, this is by far the most ambitious art exhibition that this wonderful museum has ever offered to a loyal citizenry, and probably the most innovative in all of Italy this year. If not Europe. Hence it is with immense pride, as one of the show's sponsors, through the Duckworth Foundation, and perhaps its warmest advocate, that I stand before you now to, how can I put it, *signori e signore*, let's say to *prepare* you for what you are about to see. Because this show is not for the squeamish or faint-hearted. It is dynamite.'

Even as he spoke then, looking boldly into the crowd – and the room was packed with journalists, art historians and local dignitaries – even as he spoke Morris became aware of a fine spray of red dots on his left sleeve resting on the lectern.

'Don't worry,' Mimi murmured. 'Just keep going.'

'Some of you, I'm sure, will have wondered whether it might not be rather morbid to offer the public no less than one hundred masterful depictions of murder and violent death. Believe me, the first time I actually saw the show in its entirety I was overwhelmed, stunned.'

Suddenly an eye in the first row caught his. Mariella. If some of the others present looked surprised to see Morris on the podium, her expression was one of alarm. She seemed ready to jump to her feet and rush out. On the other hand she had the distinguished head of Florence's Strozzi museum, James Bradburne, to her left and the equally distinguished Uffizi art historian, Cristina Acidini, to her right. Both of them were listening to Morris with great attention. Meantime, at the back of the room, half a dozen TV cameras were recording every word for news bulletins around the world, not to mention the video for Zolla's mother; from the floor beneath the dais came the flashes of the newspaper photographers. A sense of occasion tends to intimidate, Morris knew; no one wishes to do something rash and appear ridiculous on camera. In a charming gesture of friendliness, Morris smiled into the woman's eyes, as if to say, everything under control, *cara*.

'Which it is, Morrees. It is. Except . . .'

'However, before we wonder about the wisdom of this decision, let's remember some of the great names who have given us those depictions.'

Morris paused and puffed up his chest. The slight pressure of the Tonbridge School tie around his neck was strangely thrilling.

'Giotto, Botticelli, Bellini' – Zolla would have needed notes to remember the names – 'Masaccio, Caravaggio, Goya, Poussin, Titian' – the art historian was a nobody – 'Tiepolo, Gentileschi, Giorgione' – utterly without charisma – 'Rubens, Stuck, Klimt, Delacroix' – Morris beamed – 'and many *many* others.'

Talk about *idiota* now, Mr Sole Curator. Talk about *buffone* now, Mr Dead Man!

Glancing down for a moment, Morris noticed that there was actually a rather large splash of red on the toe of his left shoe. He felt elated. And to think that he had blown away that mountain of ecclesiastical presumption too, pulling the very trigger the pompous fool had put into his hand.

'I'm so happy for you,' Mimi frothed. 'Only that . . .'

'*Signore e signori*, why did these great minds feel the need to paint scenes that bring together two of the unhappiest aspects of human life, our mortality and our cruelty? Why did they want to show that? Why lavish their ineffable creative skills on Cain clubbing Abel to death, on Judith hacking through Holofernes' neck, on the soldiers flaying San Bartolomeo, on Othello strangling Desdemona? Was it just because these stories are in the Bible, or at the centre of our cultural heritage? Was that all it was?'

It was strange. Morris hadn't prepared this speech in any way. Yet everything was coming out with the greatest ease and fluency. Perhaps it was because Mimi was back. As he spoke he even had time to scan the crowd. There was no sign, he saw, of his designated victim, Al Zuwaid. Samira's father? Her uncle? He had got wind. She had warned him. But Antonella was there in the second row, with Mauro on her right and, yes, Stan on her left. Stan Albertini! For Christ's sake. The meddling Californian was back *again*. He had heard that their marriage was over no doubt. He was trying to step into Morris Duckworth's affluent shoes and take over the Trevisan fortune. For a moment Morris's eyes met Antonella's. Her round pale face was absolutely inscrutable.

'. . . only it would be very nice, Morrees,' Mimi whispered, 'to have our older sister join us.'

He mustn't let himself be distracted.

'She hates you, Morrees. She betrayed you.'

'*Signore e signori*, we live in a country which is famous for its mysteries, for its conspiracies, for its occulting of power. One thinks of Aldo Moro, of Ustica, of Piazza Fontana. So many unexplained deaths. And we live in an age that does everything to hide our mortality behind hospital screens, to disguise the ugly reality of our prejudices in the sham of political correctness. Such hypocrisies are not new. So as you walk through the show, and I will detain you no longer . . .'

As he said this Morris smiled at the mayor, in the front row beside Bradburne, recalling that moment, less than a year ago, when the Northern League man had been in such a hurry to meet the Arab delegation (could Al Zuwaid have been among them? Why hadn't Samira told him who her father was?). He too, the mayor that is, seemed puzzled to have Morris at the microphone, but clearly appreciated his public-speaking skills. Bradburne, who was wearing a rather ridiculous, but also rather marvellous mauve silk waistcoat, seemed hugely impressed. Then Morris realised that the pudgy presumptuous face behind him, with its holier-than-thou simper, the man with the bald spot and the turkey neck must be Parkes. Thirty years in Verona and they met at last! I'll show the bastard who's the real artist, Morris thought.

'You!' Mimi assured him. 'Only you could bring three sisters together in heaven. Do it, Morrees!'

'So as you walk through the show, *signore e signori*, with all its rich and varied representations of fratricide and matricide, of stabbing and stoning and beheading, may I invite you to reflect on this: what our artists are showing us is the stark reality of the fact, the baseline fact of *violence*; violence beyond any explanation or mystification, beyond any motive and technique or fancy detective-story narrative of the variety that usually occupies our minds and distracts us from the awfulness of what has actually, physically happened. To the artist it hardly matters *how* or *why* each death occurs, the motives, the conspiracies, the techniques. Rather a terrible brutality is made briefly beautiful, *seeable*, in order that we may be reminded of what, in essence, we all are: *savages*.'

At this point a cry was raised. *'Aiuto, aiuto, o aiuto. Sono morti.'*

Someone was running along the corridor.

'Aiuto! Chiamate la polizia. Sono morti ammazzati!'

The door was thrown open. Morris recognised one of the young women who worked alongside Mariella. She held on to the door handle as if she might faint. People were getting to their feet, turning to the door.

'Anto,' Mimi told him. 'Do it now! Quick.'

So this was what she had come back for, Morris thought. Not to help him, but to fetch her sister.

'She knows, Morrees. She knows about you. She's got to go.'

'But I don't have the gun.'

In the crush Antonella was moving arm in arm with Stan towards the exit.

'When did you ever need a gun, Morrees?'

'She's the mother of my children, Mimi.'

'She betrayed you with Don Lorenzo, Morris. She betrayed you with Stan.'

What nonsense. Morris shook his head. He felt oddly queasy, faint even.

'Morrees, you must—'

'No!'

Struggling to get a grip on rising nausea, Morris put aside the microphone and headed the opposite way from the crowd, across the dais, down along the front wall, through the corridor of screens that led to the entrance to the show. He mustn't faint this time. If I faint I'm dead. Nodding to a uniformed attendant, he strode quickly past the introductory panels, past Cain and Abel, David and Goliath, Judith and Holofernes, Jael and Sisera, past Salome and John the Baptist – my glorious predecessors, he fleetingly thought, he felt better now, artists, killers and victims all – past St Steven, San Sebastian, San Bartolomeo – Morris too was a martyr, past St Peter crucified and Santa Chiara with her eyes poked out. But now Morris stopped a moment spying a canvas he wasn't familiar with, a bearded man with a top knot poking out of a great black cauldron under which a bonfire had been lit. 'Bhai Dayala Ji being boiled alive,' the caption read, 'by the orders of Mughul Emperor Aurangzeb in November 1675.' Morris shook his head. What was Zolla thinking of?

'What are *you* thinking of?' Mimi was petulant. 'I'm so disappointed.'

Morris stood staring at the awful painting. Boiling in his pot Dayala Ji wore a top knot and a heavily bearded smile.

'There's still time,' she insisted.

'Enough, Mimi,' Morris muttered. 'I'm my own man. I do what I want.'

If all went to plan, Samira would be waiting. His mind was clearing now.

'Go to your whore and you'll never hear from me again.'

'That's fine by me,' Morris told her sharply.

Now he heard footsteps. Damn. Morris turned and resumed his previous pace, walking swiftly past Medea and Achilles and Perseus, past Sickert's sad assassins and the waxy nudity of their pathetic victims. The footsteps were gaining on him.

'Rot in hell,' Mimi was calling.

Oddly, this was exactly what Morris wanted to hear. He was through with her.

Closing the show as it had opened, with a grand canvas in the centre of the thoroughfare, was Delacroix's *Sardanapalus*. An excellent decision. Morris stopped and waited. He had guessed who his pursuer was. He might as well enjoy one long look at this magnificent painting, in the original flesh. The richness of its colour, the extraordinary reconciliation of chaos and violence with form and beauty, was breathtaking. So much finer than Forbes's copy.

'Mariella,' he said as the footsteps approached. He didn't turn. 'A great picture, no?'

'What in God's name is going on?' her voice quavered.

'You're a wonderful woman,' Morris told her. 'You deserved better than that pious old fraud.'

'What did you do?' she shrieked.

Morris's ear picked up the sound of sirens. Still without turning, he said: 'It will be in your interest, Mariella, to agree that the cardinal was depressed and must have shot first Zolla, then himself. Out of guilt for their murdering Volpi. Think about it.'

He walked round the painting and made for the exit.

'If you get into that car, it's all over with me,' Mimi told him.

Morris didn't bother to reply. Outside, on Via Cavour, Samira's Cinquecento was on the double yellow line. The sirens were coming from behind them. Morris opened the door with deliberate calm. There was no need to say anything. She pulled away. He watched her profile as she shifted gear, intent and practical, the lips puckering around the tip of the tongue. She had put her hair up. The neck was long and the chin firm. What a beautiful young woman she was. How mad of her to accept the challenge of going on the run with Morris. And how long could it last? Twenty-four hours? Forty-eight? What chances did they have? In a Cinquecento! Yet this madness had seemed so much better than a contract killer's return to the suffocating marital propriety of Via Oberdan. This moment of wild freedom was what his whole life had pointed to, Morris thought. He wouldn't let his woman down this time.

'I love you, Samira,' he breathed. 'I can't believe you're doing this for me.'

She smiled, turned, smiled more warmly, and drove on through San Zeno, then the circular road. Near the stadium she turned off.

'What's up?'

She stopped just before the stadium car park. Immediately in front of them was a large black luxury sedan. Again she smiled.

'We're changing cars, Mo.'

Morris was alert, not alarmed, but ready to be so.

'And the bags?'

'Already in there.' She motioned with her head to the larger car, a Mercedes of some kind. The windows were dark. Morris noticed an unusual licence plate. A blue Arab scrawl.

'Quick now.'

'But . . .' Morris hesitated.

Samira hurried forward and opened the back left door of the larger vehicle. Why the back? Wasn't she driving? Morris had no alternative but to follow. As he opened the back door on the other side he saw two men in the front. For a second he thought of fleeing, but he had to trust the girl. Looking over his shoulder from the driving wheel, Tarik said: 'Welcome to Libya, Morris. Next stop, Tripoli. You have just done our country an immense service.'

Even though he hadn't seen the face yet, Morris realised that the older man up front must be his designated victim, Al Zuwaid. He turned to look at Samira. She raised a plucked eyebrow and opened her arms, 'New family, Morris,' she smiled. 'New country, new lady, new life.'

Some weeks later, lounging beside a swimming pool with a gin and tonic in his right hand and a copy of *L'Étranger* in his left, it occurred to Morris that he had never asked anyone about that call from Volpi the same night the man was killed. Perhaps everything they had told him, he thought, had been a pack of lies. Putting the book aside to let his fingers trail on the stomach of the beautiful woman beside him, his eyes dazzled by the Libyan sun dancing on the palace pool, Morris frowned and puzzled and speculated, until finally it occurred to him that he really had left Italy at last. He had left it behind, that country of conspiracies, and his old double life with it. Mimi too. The ghost was gone. His scarred face relaxed in a slow smile and at that very moment the surface of the bright water broke and a lithe figure climbed out. Square-shouldered and stark naked, Tarik was grinning at him. Morris Duckworth closed his own blue eyes in placid assent. A mellow old age lay before him.